DEMON DEFEAT

PART ONE

Also by
M.J. Haag

Fairy Tale Retellings
(ALL IN THE SAME WORLD)

BEASTLY TALES

Depravity

Deceit

Devastation

TALES OF CINDER

Disowned (prequel) *

Defiant

Disdain

Damnation

RESURRECTION CHRONICLES
(hottie demons!)

Demon Ember	*Demon Night*	*Demon Fall*
Demon Flames	*Demon Dawn*	*Demon Kept* *
Demon Ash	*Demon Disgrace*	*Demon Blind* *
Demon Escape	*Demon Design* *	*Demon Defeat - 1*
Demon Deception	*Demon Discord* *	*Demon Defeat - 2*

* novella

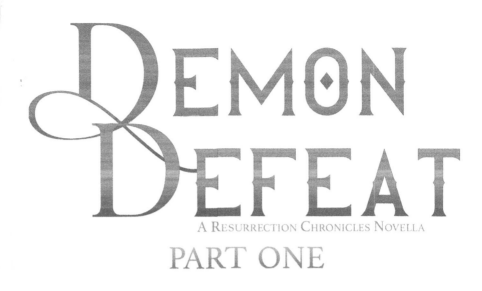

DEMON DEFEAT

A RESURRECTION CHRONICLES NOVELLA

PART ONE

M.J. HAAG

Shattered Glass
— PUBLISHING —

RESURRECTION WORLD TIMELINE

WEEK 1

| 1 | 2 | 3 | 4 | 5 | 6 | 7 | 8 | 9 | 10 | 11 | 12 | 13 | 14 | 15 | 16 | 17 | 18 | 19 | 20 | 21 |

DEMON EMBER

DEMON FLAMES

DEMON ASH

DEMON ESCAPE

DEMON DECEPTION

DEMON NIGHT

DEMON DAWN

DEMON DISGRACE

DEMON DESIGN

DEMON DISCORD

DEMON FALL

DEMON KEPT

DEMON BLND

DEMON DEFEAT PART 1

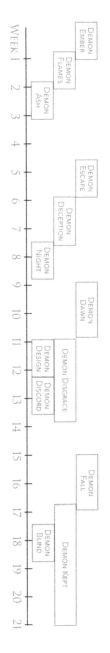

PROLOGUE

MOLEV, BEFORE THE EARTHQUAKES...

I STARED at the source's pulsing blue light and felt the familiar surge of conflicted emotions. How many times had I returned to the source to recharge my crystal? So many I couldn't count them. The wonder and joy I'd felt had long ago faded, but not the memory of that very first moment waking in these caves. How the source crystal had surrendered pieces of itself to us so we could navigate our dark world.

With a weary sigh, I sat on a stone near the source and ran my finger over the dim crystal on my wrist. We'd learned time near the source's energy would recharge our crystals. It became part of our routine to return here often. No one had questioned whether the crystals we wore had another purpose. Not until Olem.

My thoughts turned to my brother. Gone now for endless resting periods. Yet, the ache of his loss sat just as heavily in my chest as when I first heard the news.

A distant howl echoed not far from the source cave. Likely the hound that had followed me here.

"I'm tired," I said softly. "And angry. I can't sleep at night because I am so filled with anger. I am angry at Olem for leaving us, and I cannot forgive Merdon and Thallirin.

"I see a hopelessness spreading through my brothers. With each resurrection, we lose more of ourselves. How much longer until they think as I do and wonder if they should stop wearing their crystals as well?"

I rested my arms on my knees and bowed my head.

"I resent the responsibility I feel toward my remaining brothers. If not for that, I would have already joined Olem."

Another howl rang out.

"Please let the suffering of this endless existence end. I do not know how much longer I can endure."

The light surged brightly, and I looked up at the source.

A sense of comfort washed through me, and I sighed. It was always like this with the crystal. When I spoke to it, it gave me what I needed to carry on. But I could no longer bear the burden.

"Drav is strong. He hasn't lost as much hope as some of my other brothers. He will be a good leader."

The crystal surged again even brighter, and I felt a faint rumbling in the stone beneath me.

"I am grateful for your protection and patience, but it is time."

My fingers went to the leather cords tying the crystal on my wrist.

The tremors became more pronounced, and the crystal's light grew blinding. Shielding my eyes, I stood and stumbled down the path as a chorus of howls rang through the caves.

CHAPTER ONE

FIVE WEEKS POST-EARTHQUAKES...

"JESUS FUCKING CHRIST."

Patrick wasn't an eloquent man, but his mumbled cussing summed up our current circumstances pretty well.

"Andie, do you see the size of that?" Cody asked from beside me.

It was hard to miss. The hand-shaped dent around the tank's gun was as big as my head, and the thing that had crushed that metal had been even bigger. Grey-skinned and built like a Viking bodybuilder, the creature had moved with the speed and fluid grace of an apex predator.

And he'd watched me like I was his prey too.

"We need to move," Patrick said.

I tore my gaze from the wrecked tank gun and glanced at the rest of my team. The ten of us hadn't stood a chance against the creature, which is why I hadn't resisted and was still conscious. Unlike Roni. I went to check her pulse, but as soon as I touched her, she flipped to her feet and kicked out at me. Only quick reflexes on my part and disorientation on hers saved me from a concussion.

"Easy, Roni," I said, holding up my hands. "They're gone."

Her hard brown gaze swept the area, and she swiped a hand over her shaved brown hair as she noted the five prone men on the ground. Our men. When she looked outside the fence, I followed her gaze to the mounds of beheaded bodies staining the snow red. Not a single one of those deaths was due to us.

How many of those grey creatures had it taken to wipe out that many undead? Maybe two dozen? Even outnumbered four to one, those creatures had jumped the fence without hesitation. While that group had decimated the undead within minutes, another two dozen had stayed with the woman. A human woman who had called them friends but had looked at that larger one often for direction.

"You going to help or what?" Patrick called as he and Cody hoisted Tommy to the top of the tank.

Roni arched a brow at me.

"We need to move," I said. "You try waking the others, and I'll check the guns."

She went to help Roland lift Kevin, and I started collecting the discarded weapons. Our supplies weren't limitless. We needed each firearm and every bullet. But that lady's "friends" had bent the barrel of every single gun aimed at them.

The weight of the sidearm in my cargo pocket reassured me that we weren't completely defenseless. Between what we'd found in the tank and what we had in our convoy, we'd be fine until we could secure more. I hoped.

Tommy and Jackson came to easily enough and sat up top with Roni and me. We held onto Kevin and Steve while Evan and the rest stowed away inside. The rumble of the tank starting made me internally cringe, and I scanned the nearby houses for movement.

Sound attracted the infected, the undead. So did light.

In the five weeks since the earthquakes released the plague, so much had changed. The dead no longer stayed dead, and the bitten became undead. There were more undead than survivors roaming the United States, and based on the last communication from overseas, it was the same everywhere else. Except for Madagascar and a few other island regions. They were the only true sanctuaries now.

At times, it didn't feel real that I'd been serving coffee and living peacefully only five weeks ago. The crash course training a large group of us had received at Fort Irwin felt like a dream. Everything did.

At any minute, I'd wake up and realize I was late for work. And all the death I'd witnessed wouldn't be real. That those creatures with the grey skin, pointed ears, and yellow-green eyes hadn't been real.

"What in the hell do you think they are?" Roni asked quietly as if reading my mind.

"I wish I knew."

"They took the woman with them."

It wasn't a statement or a question but something in between.

"Yeah. She was looking for her baby. I hope she finds it alive," I said, thinking back to the harsh truth Patrick had dished out to her. Babies didn't live long. They made too much noise. What did that say about our future as a race if we couldn't keep the remaining kids alive? They were our only hope and why my ass was on top of the tank.

"You're worried about a baby after seeing those things?" Tommy asked.

An undead shambled out from between the buildings and ran toward the fence separating us.

"Looks like they didn't get them all," Roni said.

"We'd be better off on foot," Kevin said.

"Hell no. You saw how they jumped the fence," Tommy said, no longer talking about the thing on the other side of the fence but about the grey creatures who'd knocked him unconscious.

"We did," Roni agreed calmly. "And we saw how easily they wrecked our weapons and what they did to the undead. How is it that you managed to knock some of them out and steal their supply truck?"

He gave us all a hard look.

"You don't think I'm asking myself the same question? Shit's getting smarter out here. Smart enough to play possum. Obviously, I was tricked. So what? I won't fall for it next time."

"You're lucky there still *is* a next time," Roni said, shaking her head and tracking the undead keeping pace with us.

I did the same and wondered if we would ever know why the fence had been placed here.

At our last stop, a forward operating base just south of Wichita, we'd found a secured control gate and empty facilities. Everything left behind indicated two squads had been sent to Parsons. We'd found trucks with fencing, the tank, and some other armored vehicles, but no personnel. Only their abandoned weapons and a lot of blood.

Whatever they'd been trying to do, they'd obviously failed. Honestly, after everything I'd seen and done over the last three weeks, I'd thought our mission would be a failure too.

The source of the plague, vicious monstrosities that looked like dogs, attacked any living thing. Nothing could stop them. Not bullets. Not explosives. Nothing. And nothing survived...

unless coming back as one of the undead counted as surviving. Thankfully, however, the dogs only moved at night.

Unfortunately, they were only one piece of the apocalyptic puzzle. The grey creatures were the other piece. Footage showed two of them leaving the ground zero crater in the States, preceding hundreds of those dogs.

We didn't know why they'd come or what they'd wanted, other than the obvious—our deaths. And we hadn't had time to ask. The world had fallen apart fast.

The dogs had started the sickness, and the undead humans continued to spread it like wildfire.

One week post-earthquakes, we'd bombed our evacuated cities in an attempt to control the spread of the infection. The bombs had sent the dogs running back to the ground zero crater in Irving, Texas. However, a week later, satellite images had shown a mass exodus of those grey creatures leaving it. Once again, the dogs had followed. The grey creatures had continued north, and the dogs had spread out, searching for humans.

As my thoughts circled, I watched another undead join the first and scanned the surrounding buildings for signs of traps.

If we had any hope of saving what was left of humanity, we needed answers, and we needed them fast. Our mission was to locate the grey creatures and figure out how they and their pet dogs could be stopped. However, after the way the grey creatures had crushed our weapons, stopping them from doing anything seemed laughable.

The impossibility of our task didn't change anyone's determination to see our mission through, though. We'd volunteered for a reason, and I knew each member of this team would give their life to find the key to stopping the infection. We all had people we wanted to save.

Rather than thinking of Zion, I focused on what I'd witnessed.

Those grey-skinned creatures had all been huge, easily surpassing Jackson's impressive six-foot-four-inch height. And they weren't only tall. They had strength, speed, intelligence...

I recalled the look in the big one's eyes and shook my head to dislodge the image.

There had been way too much intelligence there.

Why would creatures that smart want us dead? Was it a superiority thing?

If so, what was up with the woman with them? Why save one of us only to kill the rest? It didn't make sense.

Not that she had acted saved. Sure, she'd called them friends and claimed they were helping her find her baby, but what was up with all the looks she'd been giving them? It reminded me of a kid looking at their mom for permission.

A captive maybe? The only reason to take a prisoner would be for information or bait. I wasn't sure what information she could possibly have that they'd want. Then again, no one had any clue what they wanted, so maybe she did.

More likely, though, she'd been bait.

We'd seen some of the undead do the same thing with a small dog a few days ago. The animal had been barking like crazy inside the open bay door of a warehouse. If the lack of undead drawn to the noise hadn't been a clue, the rope tied around its waist would have been.

Since Patrick hadn't ordered us to stop, I'd kept my foot on the gas and my eyes on the road. Kevin had watched the warehouse, though, and given me a play-by-play. Once the last vehicle drove past, a rotting corpse missing half its arm had appeared in the opening and stared after our convoy.

So were the grey creatures hoping that we'd follow the woman? It didn't make much sense when they had been steps away from us and had knocked out half the team. Why not just take us?

None of it made any sense.

I thought of the bigger grey again. The one who had crushed the tank's weapon. The same one who'd watched me with an intense focus that made my hands shake. Not that I'd let it show. Patrick had been clear before we'd set up our own trap. Stay in character. Pretend we were the ones who created the fence channel if someone showed up, and above all, don't panic. Ever. People made stupid mistakes and died when their fear got the better of them, and we'd lost too many people in the last three weeks to lose more.

However, Patrick had been thinking we would likely run into raiders when he'd given that order, not the greys. I wondered what he was thinking now. Would we continue to Whiteman, the place the woman had mentioned? Or would we find backup first after seeing what we were up against?

My thoughts continued to whirl, and the number of undead slowly increased as we traveled the length of the fence channel.

It took forty minutes to reach the trucks. My ass felt bruised by the time the tank's engine cut and I could climb down.

The five-person team assigned to watch the opening quickly eliminated the dozen undead we'd attracted, and the rest of us packed up anything useful the Wichita platoon had left behind. We moved quietly and efficiently, and once we had everything, I headed toward the Humvee.

"What about the rest?" Tommy asked, gesturing at the three trucks stocked with fencing supplies.

The MRAP and Humvee we'd used to get here would fit the fourteen of us. We didn't have any need for more transportation when the rest of our crew waited with the bulk of ours a few miles outside of town. But Tommy wasn't asking because of that.

No one wanted to leave anything behind that might be used against us.

"We have company," Tamra said from her position on top a truck.

I followed the direction of her gaze and saw six of the grey creatures running our way. The hodgepodge mix of human clothes they wore barely fit them. Cotton t-shirts that stretched impossibly thin couldn't do much to keep them warm. They didn't seem to mind, though. I watched the ridges in the big one's chest move as he approached. Cotton molded to his top half, and leather hugged the bottom.

Dear Lord, his thighs…

"What do you want me to do?" Tamra asked softly.

"Do not fire your weapon, female," the big one called, his voice filled with warning.

"Hold fire," Patrick said.

The grey creatures came to a stop almost fifty feet away. My palms started to sweat even as I kept my breathing steady.

The big one's gaze swept over us.

"Came back to steal more from us?" Patrick asked with attitude.

"We need three of your trucks. Those." He pointed at the three we would have left behind.

"Why?" Patrick asked. "Building a fence?"

"No. You can keep what's within them. We only want the trucks."

"Is this a negotiation?" Patrick asked.

"Where's the woman?" The question was out of my mouth before I could stop myself. The big one's gaze shifted my way, pinning me with its weight.

"Safe."

"Did you find the baby?"

He blinked at me. That was it. Yet, it was enough. I wanted to curse myself for giving away that I cared about the woman they'd taken. Caring was a sign of weakness in this new world. Caring got you killed.

And I'd been good about not caring. About the people we'd already lost. About the undead we killed every day. About exhaustion and hunger. But when it came to kids, it was a lot harder.

"Take the trucks," Patrick said. "We keep the supplies."

He kept his same pissy tone, but I knew what he was doing. Trying to save my ass. At least, he was smart enough to stay in role while doing it.

The big one glanced at Patrick and nodded. But while the five other grey creatures went to toss the supplies from the backs of the trucks, the big one gave me a long, considering look and slowly closed the distance between us.

My sweeping gaze made up for my complete stillness as he approached. He had scars. A lot of them. His face. His neck. His arms. He had a neat length of stitches on his forearm. The injury looked fairly fresh.

Blood spattered his shirt and his pants, but his hands and arms were clean. He kept his hands loose at his sides, but he didn't come across as relaxed. Tension radiated from him. It was in the set of his shoulders and the way he held himself.

His black hair was pulled back from his face in a series of braids that hung down his back. And he didn't look away from my face. Not once.

I tried to see everything without staring at anything. Details mattered. Details could save lives.

He stopped within arm's reach of me. His, not mine.

"The woman's name is Cassie," he said, his voice a low rumble. "We found her baby."

He didn't say anything else, and I could feel the question bubbling up. I knew I shouldn't. It was probably some kind of test. But I had to know.

"Alive?"

"Yes. Alive."

Relief rushed through me. A baby. Alive.

"How?" I asked before I could stop myself.

"Another female hid with the baby. Both were without food for two days."

He tilted his head and studied me. "Will you survive without the trucks?"

The question surprised me.

"As well as we would with them," I said with an indifferent shrug.

His gaze finally lifted from mine and swept over the rest of my group.

"The infected are growing smarter," he said, speaking only to me. "Be careful."

He gave me another long look then motioned to his friends. Three hopped into the cabs, and two joined him as they skirted around the fence and started running back in the direction they'd come.

"Move, Andie," Patrick said as the rumble of the truck engines faded.

I hustled to the Humvee and got behind the wheel. Kevin claimed the passenger seat, and Patrick climbed into the back, which shouldn't have surprised me.

The Mine Resistant Ambush Protected vehicle, known as the MRAP, led the way out of town, plowing through any undead who came running at the sound.

"Did you believe a word of that?" Patrick asked when we reached the first set of fields.

His doubt sent a shard of guilt through me. I hadn't even

thought to question whether the big one had been telling the truth. The blood covering the creature could have been the woman's blood for all I knew.

"I don't know," I admitted. "I can't see why he would need to lie about any of it. There's no reason to lull us when they obviously hold all the cards. You saw how quickly they disarmed us the first time. They took our weapons but not our lives. And why spare us just to send the dogs after us later? Or all those undead that had been outside the fence? They've had plenty of opportunity to end us and haven't."

"Knowledge," Patrick said. "The woman said Whiteman. That's where we were headed."

"Were?" Kevin asked, paying attention to our conversation even as he scanned for undead.

"I don't like that the woman gave us the location," Patrick said. "It feels like a trap."

"You think she was warning us?" I asked.

"Maybe."

Patrick wasn't an oversharer by any means, but he sure liked picking through everyone else's thoughts.

"What's the plan then?" I maneuvered around a car without slowing.

"We head back to the Wichita FOB and send a message to Irwin that we made contact. We need more men."

We fell silent after that. I wasn't sure what type of help Patrick thought we would get. Sure, I'd seen the impressive fleet of vehicles and aircraft at Fort Irwin, but I'd also seen how many had been put to use.

Despite the natural barrier the Rockies provided, personnel were still needed at the watchtowers to guard roads and passes. It took a lot of people to secure the west coast from the spreading sickness. And then there were the ongoing air evacuations for qualified civilians to the island sanctuaries.

And supply missions. And training programs. Everyone and everything was already being used for something. Why else would a barista be driving a Humvee?

Three weeks ago, we'd left with a forty-four-person volunteer-based platoon for a reason. While our mission was important, the people in charge hadn't been willing to sacrifice much-needed personnel.

"Tree line to the left," I said, spotting movement.

"What's the road look like ahead?" Kevin asked through the walkie.

"There's a line of cars positioned across it," Roland said. "We're going through."

The MRAP sped up. I kept my pace steady, letting myself fall just a bit behind.

"Hope they filled the washer reservoir," I said under my breath.

The MRAP hit the cars with a thundering bang, punching the first set of vehicles to the side and pushing the second one a distance before knocking it free.

The undead hiding within the cars couldn't spill out and watched us pass with their cloudy eyes.

"Tom hit it better this time," I said. "No wiper fluid needed. Tell him, 'Good job.'"

"A lot of undead in the tree line," Roland said over the walkie before Kevin could say anything. "It's going to get messy."

I groaned and caught up to the MRAP.

"Andie's on your tail," Kevin said.

The next three minutes were an absolute splat fest.

"I really hope the weather warms enough for rain," I said, using the wipers.

"Don't count on it," Kevin said with a chuckle.

We reached the four remaining members of our team thirty

minutes later. They sheltered beside a building in the center of a field. Two were on the roof as lookouts, and two were on top the trucks. We'd learned quickly not to leave the trucks unattended.

Mateo's voice came over the walkie.

"Land, sea, or sky?"

"Unground," came Roland's coded reply. "Any problems?"

"A few. We handled them quietly."

We bumped along through the field and came to a stop beside the other vehicles, immediately cutting our engines. Idling drew too much attention.

"We move in five," Patrick said, getting out.

Kevin relayed the message while I stretched my legs outside and looked up at the partly cloudy sky.

The sun was well past its zenith. We had another two hours of light before we'd need to hunker down for the night. Hopefully, that'd be at the FOB, which Roni affectionately called, "fucking oasis, bitch." Each of those forward operating bases truly was an oasis and much better than holing up in the MRAPs and Stryker overnight.

Tamra climbed down the rope ladder with Mateo and joined the others. We divided the supplies and split our numbers between the six remaining vehicles. Our convoy had been bigger when we'd started out, but as our numbers thinned, we'd left unneeded vehicles behind at the FOBs we passed along the way.

The two MRAPs carried our "nightlights." The telescoping poles with LED spotlights tipped to the ground kept us safe from the dogs at night. Didn't do a damn thing to keep away the undead, though. However, without the lights taking up space, the MRAP provided a decent amount of room for a few hours of sleep.

The Stryker was our security blanket. It moved debris off

the road just as well as the MRAPs but came with the added bonus of the forward-looking infrared cameras, also known as FLIR. It allowed us to spot undead and dogs at a distance. The two Humvees carried our backup MRE rations, which remanded mostly untouched. And the fueler kept us from having to search for fuel. So far, anyway.

The two newly acquired electric cars were purely to help with scouting since they ran quieter than the Humvees.

I typically drove an MRAP when we were all together. My aim with a weapon was passable, but I made up for my lack of firearm skills behind the wheel.

We were on the road again within Patrick's allotted time, heading west on every imaginable backroad known to man south of Parsons and Wichita. Patrick was in the lead MRAP with Tom, reading the maps and avoiding any roads we'd used on the way in. I brought up the rear with Kevin in the passenger seat and Katie watching out the back.

"Did he give any reason why we're backtracking?" Katie asked.

"Yeah," Kevin said. "We located the source. There were at least fifty of them. Faster than we suspected. Wrecked my weapon before my finger even twitched on the trigger. We need more men to complete the mission."

I could feel his glance.

"Or women," he added. "They seemed to have a thing for women."

"What do you mean?" she asked.

"I wouldn't call my stupidity a thing," I said. "I should have kept my mouth shut."

"I don't think so. You got him talking. And the way he looked at you…" Kevin shook his head. "It looked like that big guy wanted to take you instead of a truck."

CHAPTER TWO

"WHAT ARE YOU TALKING ABOUT?" KATIE ASKED AS I RECALLED the grey who'd spoken to me.

Yes, I'd noticed the intensity in his gaze, but it hadn't struck me as sexual interest. Just intensity.

"We followed the fence a few minutes to about the center point of Parsons, maybe," I said. "Patrick used a bullhorn he found and started acting the part of a raider just to see what was out there. For a while, all we saw were undead. Then a handful of those grey-skinned creatures showed up. One was carrying a woman. She claimed they were friendly and helping her find her baby."

Katie interrupted me, her tone laced with doubt. "A baby? Seriously?"

I nodded. "That's what the lady said. Tom, who was supposed to be watching the other end of the fence, suddenly pulled up with a truck. Claimed he found it. The woman called him on his BS and said it was theirs. Patrick tried to flex."

"And most of us ended up with a concussion," Kevin said. "Except for pretty Andie here. You had a gun, didn't you?"

"Before you say I was spared because I'm a woman, I'd like to point out that Roni was on the ground with you."

"There's very little physical difference between me and Roni," Kevin said dryly.

Katie snorted. "I'm going to tell her you said that."

"She'd probably high-five me."

"Anyway," I continued, "I think I was spared because I wasn't dumb enough to point my weapon at anyone, which is probably why the lady invited me to join them. I declined. They left. We left. But when we met up with the team at the other end of the fence, six of those grey guys showed up again and demanded three trucks. The ones the Wichita unit left behind.

"Patrick was in the middle of negotiating when I opened my mouth and asked if they'd found the baby. I shouldn't have shown I cared."

"I disagree," Kevin said. "As you already pointed out, if those creatures—whatever they are—wanted us dead, they would have killed us already. All you did was claim the biggest guy's attention for a minute. And I'm guessing, since that group found us easily enough, we probably already had their attention."

"Is it smart to return to the FOB then?" Katie asked. "What if they're tracking us?"

"That's why you're watching our tail," Kevin said.

"That didn't help us before," I said. "I was on top the tank, watching the entire time. We didn't have a tail. I know we didn't. And yet, they found us."

"So you think we're making a mistake?" he asked.

I shrugged.

"Hard to say. It's not like we're risking anyone else's lives by going back. The FOB was empty. I think Patrick's move makes sense. We located the creatures and made contact. We need to report it."

"Reporting that should count for something, right?" Katie asked.

She knew finding them wouldn't count for a damn thing.

The command at Irwin had been clear. Our one-way ticket to a sanctuary would only be redeemable when we found a way to *stop* the attacks. All of them. The greys. The dogs. The undead. Until then, we were stuck out here, chasing breadcrumbs and hoping not to die before we had the answers.

"If there were more men sitting around at Irwin, don't you think they would have sent someone to check on the FOB?" Katie asked after a while. "I mean, Irwin would have noticed the lack of contact by now, wouldn't they?"

"Maybe, maybe not," Kevin said.

With communications down, each FOB depended on long-range radio to pass messages on alternating frequencies. The coded check-ins were set at predetermined intervals. It would take time for word to get back to Irwin.

"Based on what we found, I don't think they've been missing long enough for any message to reach Irwin," I said.

"Maybe we'll get lucky and a message did reach them and a platoon is already on their way to reclaim the base," Katie said hopefully.

"When are we ever that lucky?" Kevin asked, pivoting in his seat and killing her optimism.

"Eyes to the side, Kevin," I said, watching the road, the Humvee ahead of me, and my side. "Maybe we'll get lucky. Maybe not. Whatever is going to happen will happen. Guessing and hoping won't change that, but it might distract us and get us killed. Let's focus."

We were about thirty minutes out from the base when Patrick's voice rang over the walkie.

"There's a pileup. Roland, get the Stryker up here. Tell us what you see, and break it up."

The MRAP and Humvee ahead of the Stryker veered to the right to make room. Roland accelerated past them.

"Undead in the cars, the ditches, and the tree lines," Steve said. "Over a hundred."

"You heard him," Patrick said. "Brace for a bloodbath. No gunners up top unless we have to stop."

I couldn't count the number of times we'd already gone through this exercise. Each time was just a little different.

The first week had been smooth sailing without a single trap. Back then, the undead just sort of shuffled along. The second week, they'd sped up to longer distance running, which hadn't been fun. Then they'd started hiding. Under cars. Behind trees. By week three, they were moving stuff into the road to slow us down so they could jump out at us. That's how we lost the first five of our platoon.

Now, we didn't stop unless we had to.

I could hear the Stryker's collision when it reached the barrier. The walkie stayed quiet, and I kept my foot light on the gas but ready to brake hard. The tanker didn't brake, though. A moment later, I saw the cars on the shoulder. Three high.

undead tumbled out of the doors and trunks. Broken or missing limbs didn't matter. They surged forward, a mess of ripped and bloody clothing that ran at the convoy.

Roni ran over a man with the electric car, and I winced. For the car, not the undead.

A few found their way under my tires, not that I noticed much. The MRAP plowed over them like they weren't even there. Sure left the undercarriage a gooey mess, though.

Within seconds, we passed through the main blockade with relative ease.

"They stopped running and are just standing in the middle of the road, staring after us," Katie said. "It's creepy."

"I saw one do that at the puppy warehouse," Kevin said. "Creepy as fuck."

"Can we not call it the puppy warehouse?" I asked.

Kevin laughed and got on the walkie.

"They aren't chasing us. Katie said they're staring. Anything on the FLIR?"

"The ones in the tree line aren't moving," Roland said.

Kevin and I watched the approaching tree line. Nothing moved as we passed it.

"That one was so messy we're still leaving a trail on the road. Ugh. I want a shower," Katie said. "A hot one."

Watching the red run down my passenger window, I couldn't agree with her more. It didn't matter that I wasn't dirty. I still felt that way.

"Let me know if you want help washing your back," Kevin said, his voice filled with humor.

Katie snorted.

"Having you stare is bad enough. I don't need you to add hands."

I almost grinned at their banter. Guarded, co-ed showers didn't bother Roni or me, but Tamra and Katie were shier. Their ingrained modesty cried louder than their common sense. The way I saw it, we were safer with people watching our backs. Who cared if they glanced our way as long as they were watching the door too?

Hell, I looked when it was my turn to guard. Curiosity got me every time.

"Something's not right," Katie said. "The trail is getting bigger."

"What do you mean?" I asked.

"It's getting wider. Not drips but a smear."

I looked at the road in front of us. The vehicles in front of us showed signs of ick, but there wasn't any blood on the road.

"Maybe something got caught up under us," I said with a glance at Kevin.

"If it did, it'll shake free eventually," he said.

We went a few more miles before Katie made a sound.

"What's left of the leg we were dragging just fell off. I'm skipping dinner tonight."

"Mmm. Beef stew from an MRE. That sounds good."

Katie made a pretend-gagging noise before swearing.

"There's got to be more under there. We're still leaving a trail."

Kevin got on the walkie.

"We're dragging something and leaving a trail on the road. A leg already fell off. Should we stop?"

Stopping without cover was dangerous. We'd learned that quickly. The sound of the engines drew the undead. Yet leaving a trail could be just as dangerous now that the grey creatures had already found us once. If they were tailing us, we were going to make their job really easy.

"Leave it for now," Patrick said. "We'll reevaluate at the next intersection."

Before we reached it, another leg tumbled out onto the road, and the path of red doubled in size. Patrick called a stop and sweep, telling Cody and Mateo to check our undercarriage.

"Engines idle. Make it fast," Patrick said.

As soon as the Humvee in front of us came to a stop, Cody and Mateo jumped out. They swept wide and low, reaching our back axle.

"Cody, get clear," I heard Mateo say.

Cody jogged toward the front of the MRAP, and two shots rang out. Mateo nodded to me as he and Cody ran back to the Humvee.

"Handled," Cody said over the walkie.

The convoy started forward.

"There were two undead holding onto the axle plates between the two back axles," he continued. "One was dragging itself. The other was just propped up in there. Neither of them let go when they saw us."

Kevin swore under his breath. We all knew what that meant. The undead had leveled up their game again. They'd been purposely leaving that blood trail. It explained why the others had stopped chasing us.

"I liked it better when they could only run for short bursts and didn't see you if you held real still," Katie said.

"Same," I agreed.

"Good work, everyone," Patrick said. "Keep watching for new tricks."

Kevin made a disgusted sound. "How many more tricks does he think they can come up with?"

I didn't want to know the answer to that question.

The sun sank lower in the sky, and we had to work our way around two towns and through three more traps. Thankfully, the undead at those traps weren't as clever as the previous one.

I was ready for a shower, food, and bed—in that order—when we finally reached the FOB. It didn't matter that the sun hadn't yet set. I'd pulled guard duty before we'd left and wanted sleep. A lot of it. Unfortunately, our way back into the FOB was slowed down by a few undead at the gate. All of them were in uniform. They sprinted toward the convoy when they heard us, moving just like newly turned undead.

"Do you think they walked from Parsons, or did we miss them on our initial sweep?" I asked.

"Don't know; don't care," Kevin said.

A series of shots rang out, and the undead fell to the ground.

"Bet it was Sid," Kevin said.

"Probably," I agreed. Sid was the most accurate shot in our group.

I eased forward, following the rest of the vehicles in, and nodded to Sid at the gate.

"Home sweet home," Katie said. "How long do you think we'll stay? We didn't even get three meals in at the FOB before this one before we had to move."

"We're not on vacation, Katie," Kevin said as I parked.

"Ease up," I said. "We know we're not."

"Yeah, well, we're all tired, and whining about it won't fix anything."

He got out, and I glanced back at Katie.

"He's right," she said. "I was whining. And reminding him of the things he's missing too doesn't help his mood."

"Nope. Sure doesn't."

She gave me a tired smile then hopped out to help Sid with the bodies. Cody and Ted were already dragging two inside. Leaving them to the clean-up, I joined Roni and Tom's team. We worked together to sweep through the buildings, searching for any undead we might have missed.

We found Patrick with the radio while Roland and Sean watched the door.

"Everything's clear," Roni said.

"Move the vehicles inside. Prep the lights. Keep 'em dark unless we need them. Eat and clean up while it's still light out. You know the drill."

The drill. We were going to treat this like a night in the

field. And that didn't bother me one bit. I felt safer knowing more of us would be guarding than sleeping. But there was still that part of me that missed the old world. It hadn't been without its violence, but I'd been able to sleep through the night back then and wished I could travel back in time to better appreciate those solid, eight-hour nights.

Using my time wisely, I joined Roni in the shower then ate a cold MRE before bunking down inside the MRAP. The half-inch thick foam mat that we'd found along the way helped make the floor bearable. It was still uncomfortable as hell, especially when I knew there was a bunkhouse with actual beds and mattresses. But I slept better inside the armored vehicle.

When Roni woke me for my shift, I sat up with a groan and rubbed my shoulder.

"You're upper deck. Send Cody down. And thanks for warming my spot, princess," she said with a grin.

"Make sure you return the favor tomorrow night." I got up and tossed her my blanket—also known as a woobie by Roni and the few other military-minded people in our squad.

Before this, I'd known nothing military-related. The number of terms I'd picked up over the last few weeks boggled my mind, but I understood that what I knew still barely scratched the surface. Thankfully, Patrick was less concerned about saluting and correct terminology and more interested in skills and survival.

As a mashup of mostly civilians, we'd been selected because we had all shown some kind of beneficial aptitude. My steady nerves and adept driving skills under pressure had won me a spot in the Platoon. And it was a win...even if it was also a guaranteed death sentence.

I stretched outside the MRAP and checked the time. Six fitful hours wasn't bad these days, but it meant we still had a long time until dawn. Leaving the building, I found the ladder and climbed to the roof. Cody saw me, nodded, and carefully rose to a crouch. He handed off his walkie and binoculars when I reached his position.

"Been quiet," he said softly. He moved to the ladder and disappeared over the edge.

The stars and moon lit the night enough that I could see my breath cloud as I settled onto my belly. A cold wind blew over the roof, and I knew it would be a long night.

I listened and watched, using the thermal binoculars only occasionally to save the batteries.

Slowly, the sky lightened and the stars disappeared. Predawn signaled the end of the night's guard duty. I gathered everything up and went to the ladder. Katie and Roland were already headed toward the mobile lighting we'd set up in case one of those dogs had gotten close. They dismantled it quickly, and I hurried to the mess hall, hoping someone had made something hot. I found coffee and eggs. Mateo showed up as I was guzzling coffee in between wolfed-down bites of eggs.

"We leave in five," he said.

"Any word from Irwin?" I asked.

He shook his head. "The message was relayed yesterday morning that this FOB hadn't responded to the check-in. Patrick thinks we'd missed them by a day."

Selfishly, I was glad. If we'd been with them, our fate probably would have been the same.

"So we're not waiting for backup?" I asked.

"Wichita isn't the only FOB to go dark. We're headed south toward Vance Air Force Base. I think Patrick is hoping to pick up more bodies there."

"How far away is that?"

"Two hours without any problems. But don't count on no

problems. We need to cross the Arkansas River. The fastest way is through Arkansas city."

"Please tell me Patrick isn't taking us that way."

Mateo shot me a quick grin.

"No, he's smarter than that. We're hooking up with North Silverdale off 141st Rd and winding our way south along the river. We'll attract some attention, but we should be able to cross East River Road in better shape than going through the city."

Patrick was smart. He avoided as many cities and towns as he could now, but that meant long backroad drives. Two hours could easily translate to all day in the MRAP.

I finished my meal, used the facilities, then got behind the wheel. We closed up as we left the FOB and bumped over the tracks made through the field.

Roland, my navigator for the day, lifted his binoculars and looked out his window. Swearing, he clicked over the walkie.

"You see that?" he asked. "One field over. There are at least seven bodies there."

"Active?" Patrick asked.

"Nothing's moving," Roland answered.

"Keep an eye on it. No stopping unless we need to thin the numbers we attract."

The walkie went quiet after that, and I glanced at Roland. He was frowning.

"What aren't you saying?" I asked.

The glance he gave me churned the eggs in my stomach.

"The angle's not right to see clearly, but I think one of them is missing its head. The shadow's wrong. Or I'm wrong."

I tapped the wheel and thought for a minute.

"You need to tell Patrick. We need to know."

He got on the walkie again. Patrick ordered Roni and Cody in the Humvee to check it out.

They drove off while we continued on. The Humvee swung close, then turned sharply and headed back.

"All headless. No signs of anything else."

Patrick didn't say anything to that, but we all knew what it meant. One or more of those greys had tracked us.

We drove for several minutes before Patrick's voice broke the silence.

"Little town of Silverdale coming up. Stay sharp."

I looked back at Katie, who watched out the rear windows. We weren't the end of the line, but after yesterday's undead stunt, Patrick wanted more eyes on our trail.

"Get ready to hang on," I warned her.

"Yes, Mom."

I focused on the road.

The engines didn't draw undead but an actual person. The man waved with both arms from an open, top-story window of his house.

"Cut the engines. Stand ready," Patrick said over the walkie.

This wasn't the first living person we'd encountered. It could be a trap for supplies, or it could be an honest person looking for a ride to somewhere safe. Only time would tell which.

Roland left his seat to help Katie open the top of the MRAP. He watched the house while Katie took the other side.

In the silence, I could hear everything.

"Howdy, friend," Patrick called, getting out of his vehicle.

"Thank God you showed up," the man said. "We need help. Can you get us out of here? Please tell me the whole world ain't like this."

While I listened, I watched. Body language said a lot about a person. The man hanging out the window broadcast his desperation in every twitch and facial feature. If it was a trap, the guy was playing up his part pretty well.

"We've got some room. How many are with you?" Patrick asked.

"There's six of us," he said. "We boarded up the bottom half of the house. Give us a minute. Please don't leave. We're coming out."

When a pregnant woman waddled out with a toddler on her hip fifteen minutes later, I knew it wasn't a trap. The man helped an older woman with a walker, and another man and a teen boy followed.

Patrick hustled everyone toward the two electric cars. He didn't waste time with introductions. Just shoved them in and hurried to his own vehicle.

We started up again as an undead came shambling down the road.

"Roni and Tom, radio off for five."

"Copy," they both said.

After a count of ten, Patrick came back on. "I think these people are exactly what they seem, but watch our tail. Once we cross the river, we're stopping."

I glanced at my mirror to check the road behind us. The undead trailed after Steve and Jackson's MRAP. Beyond that, nothing moved in the sleepy village of Silverdale.

As I looked forward, I thought I saw something move in one of the buildings across the street. When I glanced at it, though, everything was still.

A feeling teased my mind, regardless. Like we were being watched.

CHAPTER THREE

WITH A CLEAR VIEW OF THE BRIDGE, WE CIRCLED THE VEHICLES ON the west side of the river. Roland, Jackson, and Steve kept watch on the east side. Katie and Tamra took their positions on top the trucks to watch our side. The rest of us stretched and listened to the people we'd rescued.

Off the beaten path, the town hadn't fallen with the rest of the world. They'd watched the news until everything had gone dark but had been smart enough to hole up. Eventually, one of the neighbors had left for supplies and had shown up a few days later, on foot and very undead. Then another tried. And another. Each one found their way home again, but not alive. The two men had taken care of all of the undead.

If we hadn't have come along when we did, the remaining survivors would have tried striking out on their own because they were out of food. Without needing to be told, I went to the MRAP and grabbed some MREs for them.

"Where are we headed?" the man finally asked.

"An air force base not too far from here. Hopefully, they'll be able to evacuate you." Patrick glanced at the men and the boy. "They might ask a few of you to stay and help."

The men got real quiet for a moment.

"It's that bad out there?" one asked.

"It is," Patrick said.

Their excitement over being rescued faded. I looked at the little girl who reminded me so much of my niece, Nova. Her sad gaze met mine, and I winked at her.

"There's dessert in that bag you're holding," I said. "If you're lucky, it's M&M'S."

The girl looked at the bag she clutched and then at me.

"Should we open it?" I asked.

She nodded and handed it to me. I glanced at the woman.

"Why not give your back a break and have her sit in the car and eat?"

We moved away from the men as they continued to discuss what we'd likely find at the base. Patrick wouldn't sugarcoat anything, and the kid didn't need any more of a reality check. I showed the mother and daughter how to open the bags and all the "goodies" in an MRE. Then I stood guard as they both took care of business on the far side of the car.

"How long have you been doing this?" the mom asked as she cleaned her daughter's hands.

"Three weeks on the road so far."

"Is there any hope?" she asked, her hand rubbing over her belly.

"There's always hope," I said with a wink at the little girl. She smiled back and took a bite of her ravioli. "That hope might look a little different than you're used to, though."

The mother nodded and started to eat her meal.

After thirty minutes of nothing from the lookouts, Patrick signaled that we should pack up. The girl waved at me before getting into her car, and the mom smiled her thanks. If only they knew the real reason we'd stopped hadn't been to feed them.

I started the MRAP and glanced at Roland as he got in.

"Maybe the greys just followed us to see what we were doing," he said.

"Maybe," I agreed, hoping he was right.

It took hours to work our way along the back roads, but not because of the greys.

To avoid the city of Enid, situated just north of Vance Air Force Base, we had to circle south on the back roads. We did our best to avoid towns, but we still attracted unwanted attention when we got close. Stopping to remove the buildup of undead trailing us was necessary but time-consuming. Messy too. Same with the roadblocks the undead persistently attempted.

And after each one, we would need to wait for the pregnant woman to finish throwing up. I felt bad for her.

By late afternoon, the base beckoned in the distance. The sight of the closed southern gate and fortified fence was a welcomed relief. However, I couldn't see any visible guards when we neared.

"Not again," Roland muttered.

"What? What do you see?" Katie asked.

"An unguarded gate. What do you see?" I asked.

"Ted winking and blowing kisses at me," she said dryly.

Roland chuckled.

"He needs to pay attention," I said.

"He has been," Katie said. "Mostly. William smacked him once. That was pretty funny. Any guards yet?"

"Nothing yet."

The words were barely out of my mouth when a voice cut over the walkie.

"Stop where you are, and state your business."

"This is Sergeant Patrick Bromwell. We picked up six civilians in Silverdale who need evacuation."

33

The gate swung open, and we drove through. Inside, several guns were pointed at us.

"Stay in your vehicles," one man ordered. Several others did a thorough sweep of every vehicle.

"Follow that Humvee," the same man said when they finished.

A vehicle parked to the side roared to life and started down the road. We drove farther into the base and stopped outside of a hotel. We left the civilians there and continued on. I couldn't say I minded when we braked in front of some military housing and were told to clean up and rest while Patrick met with Vance's commanding officer.

The private, hot shower was nice. The real bed was even better, though. I fell into a light sleep without hesitation.

Yelling woke me.

I bolted upright and stared at the hallway. Someone ran past. Another person stopped in the opening.

"Get up, Andie. They have a breach."

I scrambled out of the bed. "What kind? Dog or undead?"

"Undead, I think."

I scrambled into my gear, cursing myself for not sleeping with it on like when we were in the field. The riot gear prevented bites but made for a miserable night's sleep. A minute behind Roni, I rushed toward the exit and took position just inside the door.

"Ready?" she asked.

At my nod, she opened the door to darkness.

Distant pops rang out. Roni signaled forward, and I followed, watching our backs. We crossed the parking lot, spotting another pair moving like we were. Undead didn't move with stealth. They either ran or shambled. But they didn't crouch and move from cover to cover. So it was easy enough to identify our own…if we could see them.

If I got shot by friendly fire after surviving the last three weeks of madness, I was going to be furious.

We worked our way toward the gunfire, and I saw the horde of undead piled up near a section of lit fence. They were climbing over each other, reaching the top, and toppling over inside. Most of them were shot before they even reached the ground. But that was only creating a pile-up of bodies on both sides.

"It's a body bridge," Roni said.

I looked at the number still outside the fence.

"Where did they come from?" I asked. "Enid?"

"I hope not."

A roar filled the night, and for a heartbeat, everything froze. The gunfire paused, and the undead turned to look back at the darkness behind them. The back half of the horde started running into the dark.

Roni swore under her breath and brought up her weapon.

"Hit the ones away from the fence," she said.

For the next ten minutes, we did our best to thin the remaining number of undead. When the last one fell, my ears rang from the barrage of gunfire. Roni and I rushed forward, along with a dozen other men, to remove the buildup of bodies. Any without a headshot got one. We weren't taking chances.

When the inside was clear, a group left to dispose of the remains. We stayed by the fence, waiting for the truck to reappear on the other side. We covered them while they worked.

The smell of rot filled my nose. I didn't gag, and I didn't breathe through my mouth. Tasting that rot was worse than smelling it. They worked fast, removing every last corpse. A few undead wandered their way in from the dark, but Roni and I—mostly Roni—ensured they didn't get close.

We retreated, finding a less visible spot from which to watch the fence once they left. Neither of us looked away from the dark.

Something was out there.

Something that roared and called the undead to it.

Something I hoped I would never have to face because that sound had rattled my bones and shaken me to the core.

Hours later, the sky started to lighten, and someone came to relieve us.

"There's a mess hall that way," he said with a nod. "Hot coffee and hot food."

We nodded our thanks and headed in the direction he'd indicated.

Patrick found us in the mess hall fifteen minutes later.

"They lost ten men last night," he said without preamble. "Undead got 'em. I heard you were both at the breach."

"We got there when the bodies were already piled halfway up the fence."

He nodded and leaned closer. "And what did you hear?" he asked softly.

"Something I've never heard before," Roni said.

"Same," I added.

"Take a car and circle the base. Bring Cody and Roland with you. You know what you're looking for."

A sick feeling settled into my stomach at his implication. The greys were terrifying enough without an animalistic roar.

Hoping Patrick was wrong, I stood and followed Roni out of the mess hall.

We found Cody and Roland easily enough and left the base with little fuss. Twenty minutes later, we spotted a pile of headless bodies tucked away behind a line of trees on the other side of the field.

"Jesus. How many are there?" Cody asked.

"Don't know; don't care," Roni said. "Turn us around, Andie."

I executed a slow one-eighty, careful of the unseen bumps and ruts in the snow-dusted field. The last thing I wanted to do was to get stuck. No one spoke as we headed back toward the gate.

Patrick was waiting for us just inside.

"One or more followed us," Roland reported quietly as we walked away from the vehicle. "There were at least two dozen headless bodies out there. Left them in a pile like last time."

Patrick swore under his breath and looked at the fence. I knew he wasn't really seeing it, though. He was thinking. Weighing his options. His gaze settled back on us.

"Vance has lost too many men to hold it through another night. Air pickup is coming later this afternoon. The resources here are being reallocated but not to us.

"Our mission hasn't changed. We need to know what those things want. Having some of them follow us makes our job easier. Head back out. Try to track them down and attract their attention."

"And when we have it?" Cody asked.

"They talked to us once. Get them talking again." He looked at me. "The big one was willing to tell you about the baby. They might be interested in the pregnant woman we picked up."

"You want us to tell them we found a pregnant woman?" I asked, not sure I was hearing right. "And what if they want her to join them? Her husband might have something to say about that, I think."

"We just need to get them talking. About anything. Find out what they're interested in. Then we have a bargaining chip and a means for potential negotiations. It doesn't mean we hand anything or anyone over. Remember, we're trying to get information. What do they want? What is it going to take to stop the attacks?" Patrick gave each of us a hard look. "We're all putting our lives on the line to end this. I don't want to lose any more than necessary. But if another sacrifice is what it takes to save millions, who here wouldn't step up? Don't think for a moment that woman wouldn't do the same to save the child she already gave birth to if that's what it takes."

That cold, sick feeling settled into my middle again. I hated that Patrick was right. I'd seen firsthand the heartbreak a parent had to face by choosing one child's life over another. I thought of Zion again. No one had forced me to volunteer. I'd done it without hesitation for a chance to save him. Any sacrifice that mother made or didn't make would be her own choice, too.

"Take a Humvee this time. You want the attention. Good luck," Patrick said.

He walked away from us with purpose, flagging down someone in uniform.

From the corner of my eye, I caught Roni's scrutiny.

"You all right?" she asked.

"Are any of us okay with what's going on?" I asked as we changed direction. "How I feel or don't feel doesn't change what needs to be done."

"Amen to that," Cody said under his breath.

The four of us got into a Humvee and headed back out, returning to the same body pile as before. Roland checked the snow for any indication of how many of the greys we were possibly dealing with, but there were too many tracks to tell. In face, I couldn't spot any single set of tracks leading away into the trees.

The thing that killed them had either flown or returned to the fence using the trampled path of the undead. But we hadn't seen it last night, only heard it.

Staring at the bodies, I tried to wrap my head around this thing's motives. The greys controlled the dogs. The dogs attacked us humans. We turned undead, and the greys killed us by ripping off our heads.

Why create something only to kill it? It didn't make sense to me. Was it a hunting thing? Like a game farmer breeding program?

Pushing aside the thought that I might be future prey, I focused on what a hunter might do. While I wasn't one, I'd dated a guy who had been. He'd talked about baiting and blinds and trails. Hunters followed game or lured them in while staying hidden, waiting for the perfect shot.

Was that what last night had been? His yell had drawn the undead from the fence. Had he been waiting in this tree line to pick them off? I frowned, remembering how they'd dealt with the undead at the tank. They hadn't hidden then. They'd simply jumped into the fray, and heads had started flying.

I scanned down the line of trees, trying to make sense of the situation. Nothing was adding up for me. Where had the undead come from if they hadn't been baited in? If they'd been from Enid, they would have attacked farther north. The piece of fence they'd attacked was on the southeast side of the base.

I looked south and saw railroad tracks and railcars. The undead could have come from there, possibly.

"We should check those," I said with a nod. "Maybe the undead came from there."

"Why do we care where they came from?" Cody asked. "They aren't what we're looking for."

"When I lose something, I retrace my steps," I said, gesturing at the trodden path leading from the trees to the fence. Then, I gave Roland a shrug. "Maybe I'm not the only one who likes backtracking."

"Exactly what I was about to suggest," Roland said with a nod.

We returned to the Humvee and followed the path back to the fence. From there, we could see the individual tracks leading to the rails boarding a stone quarry.

At the first set, we found another small pile of bodies between the cars, heads stacked on top.

"Good call, Andie. Looks like this is the right spot." Roni clapped me on the shoulder as I cut the engine.

"You two stay with the Humvee," Roland said. "We'll work our way up the tracks."

"All yours," Roni said.

We got out with them and stood guard as they advanced down the line of railcars. They moved quietly and quickly, scanning above, below, and in between the metal cars. I thought of the undead we'd passed who'd hidden in the warehouse and wondered if some might be hiding in the cars. Or maybe a grey.

Roland and Cody seemed to have the same thought. When they reached one that wasn't locked from the outside, they slid the door open. The low rumble of the rollers drifted our way. I scanned the other cars and the field around us. Nothing moved except for the four of us.

Yet, tension coiled inside of me. I told myself the greys hadn't killed anyone the last time and that it wouldn't make any sense to kill anyone now, but it didn't help. What if some of them were in one of these cars? What if the pile of bodies was the bait to lure us in? Every question fed that ball of worry inside of me.

Cody and Roland's forms slowly shrank with their distance. The grass blew in the cold breeze, and shadows cast by clouds danced over the patchy snow.

Growing up in California, I was used to noise and warmth. I missed both more than I would have ever thought possible. Especially sound. There were no birds chirping or dogs barking. No planes flying overhead and traffic whizzing by. In the absence, a person could hear the wind as it rushed past an ear and teased dormant vegetation. That was it. Silence reigned.

A soft thump nearby had me whirling toward the railcars. My gun was up before I even registered the long braids of black hair that framed a vaguely familiar face.

As he slowly straightened from a crouch, I recognized his impressive size. He was the one who'd told me they'd found the baby. The really big one with the penetrating gaze, who was, even now, watching me with the intensity of a predator.

I'd witnessed his impressive speed before and knew he could remove the gun from my hand before I could blink. Yet, he didn't lunge at us or make any other sudden moves, for that matter. He seemed to be waiting for us to make the next move.

Taking a calculated risk, I quickly lowered my weapon. Was it my imagination, or had his lips moved just a little at the corners?

He inclined his head at me then glanced at Roni. She still had her weapon trained on him.

"Roni," I said softly. "Ease up."

She held steady for a moment before lowering her firearm halfway. I knew that was as much of a compromise as she would give and glanced at the creature to see if it was enough. Since he was watching me again, I figured it was.

"Why did you follow us?" I asked, going for direct but keeping my tone friendly.

"To learn more about you."

His yellow-green gaze swept over my face. It was as

41

intense as before, but this time, I watched for signs of any interest in me like Kevin had mentioned. I didn't see it.

His group already had a woman with them, so I knew he had at least some knowledge of humans. Before I could ask what specifically he wanted to learn, Roni snorted.

"I bet. Why send the undead after us, then?" she demanded.

His stoic expression didn't change as his gaze shifted to her.

"Undead? You mean the stupid humans? The undead?"

"Yes. Those." Impatience laced her tone.

He tilted his head and studied her for a moment, and I started to worry she might be pushing things too far.

"Are you a female?" His low tone didn't convey any emotion, but something about the slow way he asked his question made me think he was surprised.

"Does it matter if I am?" she countered.

He blinked at her. Not a general blink that we all were doing this whole time but a slow intentional one that a person might do when confronted with a bad smell or a punch to the nose. Only without the wince that usually went with it.

Roni caught it, and her gaze narrowed.

"Yes, she's female," I said quickly.

"You were there at the fence in Parsons," he said, still scrutinizing her.

"We both were," I said, reclaiming his attention.

"You were spared. She was hurt," he said.

Again, I couldn't quite tell his emotion behind those comments or decipher his meaning. Was it a good thing I wasn't hurt and she was? I wanted to ask but didn't want to damage an already fragile start to communicating with him.

"She's tougher than most of the men," I said. "And fine

now, but we'd both prefer if you didn't knock us unconscious."

His gaze shifted to her again. "I will not harm you."

"Then, why are you here? What do you want?" Roni asked.

"Want?" His gaze shifted to me then back to her. He crossed his arms, making his biceps bulge under the meager confines of his once-white cotton shirt. "Explain what you mean."

Anger radiated off of Roni. "I mean, why are you—"

I set my hand on Roni's arm, and she immediately stopped and took a calming breath. We both wanted the same answers, and she knew that. Just as we both knew she was a hothead, and that wasn't what this situation needed.

The creature's eyes shifted to me.

"My name's Andie," I said, trying another approach. "What's your name?"

"Molev. Do you lead the others, Andie?" he asked, his voice a deep rumble.

Lead the others? Is that what he wanted? To learn who our leader was?

Ignoring his question, I tried to find the answer to a more important one.

"I'm glad you're talking to us, Molev. We'd like to learn more about you, too. Are you alone, or did some of the others come with you?"

A sudden, distant shot rang out. I partially crouched and brought up my weapon as I glanced in that direction. From the corner of my eye, I saw Roni do the same.

Down the way, I saw two figures moving near the railcars.

"All clear," came Cody's voice over the walkie. "One undead, but no sign of any greys."

I glanced at Molev, but he wasn't there. He wasn't anywhere that I could see.

43

"Where'd he go?" I asked, looking at Roni.

She shook her head and continued to scan the railcars. I searched in and around our Humvee.

Molev was gone, and I didn't like how quickly and silently he'd left.

"Roni?" Cody asked again.

"Here," she said. "We're coming for you."

I hurried to the driver's seat and took off as soon as Roni was in. Attention split between the field in front of us and the railcars behind us, I almost missed the movement in my mirror.

"Top of the railcar," I said.

"I see him," Roni said.

Molev's bulk stood outlined against the cloudy sky. Impossibly broad shoulders turned toward us, he observed our retreat then disappeared off the other side.

CHAPTER FOUR

"THE FUCKERS ARE TOYING WITH US," RONI SAID.

"Fuckers? You think there's more than just the one then?"

"Why else would he show himself like that and disappear right after you asked? They're going to isolate us and pick us off, one at a time."

"Does that make sense, though? You saw how quickly they took us out last time. If there were a group of them, wouldn't they have just attacked?"

"Not if they don't want us to know how many there are. That one waited to show up until Roland and Cody were almost out of sight. That shows premeditative intelligence. They're in this for the long game."

"And we need to figure out what that long game is," I said more to myself than Roni.

While she'd made valid points, I couldn't help but think of another angle. We'd left Irwin with the orders to do whatever it took to discover the greys' plans and to figure out what it would take to stop them. What if that was why he'd left his group? What if he was the scout learning whatever he could about us? Discovering how many of us were left and what it would take to kill the rest?

That thought was just as scary as Roni's.

Cody and Roland had already moved a healthy distance from the railcars when I stopped for them.

"What happened?" Cody asked as soon as he got in.

"We definitely have a tail," Roni said. "He said he wants to learn more about us and asked who our leader was. He disappeared when we heard your gunfire."

Circling toward the gate, I checked the mirrors again and wondered what the creature's next move would be. So far, he'd hung back to observe, following at enough of a distance that we hadn't spotted him. But for how long? After decimating our numbers for five weeks, his kind had to have already figured out our weaknesses.

I thought over the two scenarios. Either there were more of them and they were preparing to spring a trap, or he was a lone scout learning more. Which was it? Was there another angle we hadn't yet considered? If only Cody and Roland hadn't fired that shot. What else could we have learned?

Patrick was just inside the gate, waiting for us when we returned.

"There were two piles," Roland said once we'd moved away from everyone else. "The one in the trees to the east and another by the railcars to the south." He looked at Roni and me.

"One of those greys showed up after Cody and Roland had almost reached the end of the railcar line," Roni said.

"It was the same one that had taken our trucks and told me about the baby," I said.

All four looked at me.

"Are you sure?" Patrick asked.

I glanced at Roni, looking for her to back me up, and she shrugged.

"They all looked the same to me."

"Seriously? He was bigger and had much longer hair than the other five with him. And he had braids with three orangish beads on one side and two orange and a brown one in the middle. A line of over a dozen stitches up his forearm. Scars on his neck right over his Adam's apple."

Cody smirked at me.

"You were really paying attention."

"She always pays attention," Patrick said. "What else did you see, Andie?"

"He's different. Closed off. We have body language and facial cues that give away what we're feeling. He either doesn't or is working not to show them. The first option just makes him harder to read and the second makes him... suspicious."

I'd almost gone with terrifying but didn't want to acknowledge how uncomfortable he made me feel.

Cody chuckled. "You're not going to let me forget that, are you?"

Early on, Cody had a problem with me due to my lack of reaction to almost anything. He understood me better now. They all did. I'd already come to terms with my inevitable death. Why waste the precious time I had left with useless emotions? It didn't mean I didn't feel; I simply chose not to react to how I felt.

Ignoring Cody, I continued talking to Patrick.

"His eye contact is the most telling," I said. "It's direct, and I don't know how to explain it, but it's like he's waiting for something. And he's one hundred percent focused on whatever it is he's waiting for. Intensely focused."

"Do you believe he's an immediate danger to this base?"

M.J. HAAG

"I might be good at reading people, Patrick, but he's something completely different. I can't—"

"You can. When you look at him, do you feel threatened?"

"Yes, but not. We've seen what the greys can do and know he's a danger. The immediacy of it is up to him. It feels like he's waiting for something. Watching to see what we'll do."

Patrick looked at Roni.

"What about you?"

She shook her head slightly.

"Andie lowered her weapon, and I followed her lead. As soon as it was down, he started talking. He's absolutely watching us. I can't decide if he's waiting to be reactive or waiting for the perfect moment."

Patrick glanced at the other two.

"I'm willing to risk myself and everyone else who signed up for this," Roland said. "But not the people here. If there's even a chance he's a threat, I say we immediately deal with it."

"I'd rather strike first and ask questions later," Cody said. "Less dead people on our side that way."

Patrick was quiet for a long moment.

"Gather the team, and meet at housing in ten."

We all split, going our separate ways. I headed for the mess and found Steve, William, and Kevin there.

"Meeting at housing in five. Spread the word, and hustle up," I said. They didn't groan at the news but hurriedly ditched their trays and rushed away. I snagged an apple, something I hadn't seen in weeks, and bit into it as I headed to the housing.

Roni was at the door to the building and directed me to the room where we were gathering. Most everyone was already there when I entered. Patrick waited for the last person then nodded to close the door.

"After the attack last night, Vance doesn't have the

personnel to stay operational. The survivors we brought in were the first ones they've seen in five days." His gaze swept over us. "Vance's request for another full platoon was denied, and they are pulling out this afternoon.

"Things are getting bad out there. We know that. We've seen bases understaffed or fallen, like Wichita."

He paused for a moment and rubbed a hand over his hair, the move conveying his frustration and exhaustion. The same things we all felt.

"We have a confirmed sighting of at least one grey to the south," he said finally. "There may be more. We can wait to see what it will do and potentially risk more lives, or we can head out now and try to make contact. Again. This isn't a democracy. I'm not asking for a vote. I'm asking for your thoughts on both options, though."

He looked at Evan first and slowly worked his way around the room. Patrick's ability to listen was one of his best personality traits. After hearing everyone's thoughts, he stood.

"I'd like to give you the rest you deserve, but time hasn't been our friend since the beginning. We roll out in twenty."

WE SEARCHED the railcars and found them all empty. The pile of bodies was still there, but the undead that Roland had shot now rested on top—proof that the grey had lingered after we'd left.

We divided into two groups. Eight of us drove the vehicles around to the stone yard's entrance while the rest went on foot. I doubted they'd find the grey hiding in the piles of stone but knew there were probably buildings or other equipment he could be using.

Cutting the engines by the main building, we divided our

numbers again. Two stayed inside the vehicles. Two on top to guard. And four of us went to the main building.

Roland motioned that he'd go in first. Evan, Derek, and I nodded. Hanging back, I watched the area around us and glanced up at William on the MRAP. He caught my gaze and nodded that it was all clear before I went inside the building last. It wasn't large, but it also wasn't lit.

It took us less than five minutes to verify it was clear and head back outside. William signaled everything was still fine, so we paired off. Roland and Derek went around the building, and Evan and I headed to the equipment parked nearby.

I didn't know what kind of machines they were, but they were huge with wide buckets attached to the front. We circled the first one, working together to check above and below. Evan kept his eyes on what lay in front of us, and I watched behind, keeping a safe distance between us to avoid accidents yet close enough not to be separated.

Or so I thought.

The moment we were no longer within sight of the guards, I heard a soft thud behind me. I whirled around but didn't automatically bring up my weapon, knowing Evan was just beyond the grey, who crouched between us.

With his gaze fixed on me, the grey slowly straightened. The sudden report of gunfire made me wince and duck. For a stunned moment, I couldn't believe Evan had fired.

The grey's expression twisted with anger as he stared at me cowering at his feet. He roared, turned, and cuffed Evan upside the head so hard that he flew sideways. His skull cracked against the equipment, and he crumpled to the ground.

My gaze shifted from my unconscious partner to the grey.

He wasn't looking at Evan but staring at me. His shoulders moved with his deep breath.

"Are you hurt?" he asked.

I shook my head and cautiously straightened, glancing at Evan, who wasn't yet moving.

Focus on the objective, Andie, I told myself. *Make contact. Get him talking. Think of Zion.*

"I'm not hurt," I said. "Molev, right?"

"Yes."

"Are you hurt?"

He blinked at me.

"You remind me of Mya," he said.

"Who's Mya?"

"A friend."

"Is she like you?" I asked, my gaze sweeping over his pointed ears.

"She is a human female."

"The one looking for her baby?"

"No."

He wasn't really giving me much in the way of information.

I opened my mouth to try another question when I heard a thwomp-thwomp from behind him.

His gaze held mine as his knees buckled. I could have sworn I saw the corners of his mouth curve again as they hit the ground. Stunned, I watched him topple face-first into the snow-dusted packed gravel.

Behind the grey, Roland stood with the riot shotgun. He kept it aimed at Molev.

"I didn't think it would work until I saw how much he was bleeding," he said.

I looked down at Molev, noting the two bean bags Roland had fired at close range and the weeping hole in Molev's back. Evan's shot.

Holy shit.

Moving quickly, I hurried to Evan while Roland covered Molev.

"Evan's breathing, but not responding," I said. "Head's bleeding."

I tugged his walkie free and used it.

"We have the grey to the west of the main entrance near the big earth movers. Evan's down and needs medical. The grey is down and needs medical too."

"Copy," Patrick returned.

Steve and Cody showed up first and helped carefully move Evan back to the MRAP. I stayed with Roland until more men showed up to help move the grey.

Six of them grunted under his weight, and one swore under his breath.

"What in the hell does he eat? Rocks?"

Roland smirked. "Think that's why he was in a quarry?"

A few of them chuckled as they carried him toward the other MRAP.

"Take Evan to the base," Patrick said to Tom and Cody.

"What about that one?" Tom asked.

We looked at the grey resting haphazardly on his stomach in my MRAP. His wound no longer bled, but that didn't mean he was fine. I'd been around guns enough to know that no exit wound meant the bullet was still inside.

"It's safer to keep him on this side of the fence until we know what we're dealing with. Any sign of more?" Patrick asked, looking at me.

"No. Just him so far."

He nodded and looked at the team.

"Finish sweeping the area while we wait for Tom and Cody. Andie, Roni, and Roland, stay with me."

Everyone hustled to their assigned duties.

"Roni, you're playing operation," Patrick said, tossing her a kit. "Andie and I will try to keep him still. Roland, stand ready."

I climbed into the back of the MRAP with Patrick and Roni and settled on my knees near the grey's stitched arm. Carefully trapping the limb between my legs, I studied the sutures. They weren't random or messy but placed with precision.

"I think they have more than one human with them," I said as Roni opened the kit. "He mentioned someone named Mya and said it wasn't the woman who was looking for the baby."

"What else did he say?" Patrick asked.

"Not much."

"Why Evan and not you?" Roni asked, removing a pair of really long tweezer-looking things.

"He dropped between me and Evan. I didn't lift my weapon. Evan took the shot, probably because Molev was facing me."

"Molev?" Patrick asked.

"He told us his name last time," Roni said.

"So he attacked Evan after he shot him?" Patrick asked.

"It was less of an attack and more of a backhand," I said. "Evan's head hit the truck, and it was immediate lights out."

Patrick made a non-committal sound.

"He didn't attack me once Evan was out, so I tried talking to him. He answered every question I asked but didn't ask any questions of his own."

"Which is weird for someone who said he was following us to learn more," Roni said as she eased the instrument into the hole in his back.

He didn't twitch, but I still winced on his behalf as she carefully dug around for the bullet. My fingers moved on his arm, comforting him even though he was out cold.

"Every encounter has been reactive," I said. "He watches and waits to see what we'll do before responding."

"You think Evan shouldn't have fired," Patrick said.

"Evan did what he thought was best. And because of him, we might now have a real opportunity to talk to Molev."

Patrick nodded. "I agree. We need to tread carefully, though. This one's shown his strength and his restraint. We want to encourage the latter while protecting ourselves from the former."

"Got it," Roni said, pulling the bullet free. More blood welled out, and she pressed a wad of gauze to it.

"He's going to be thirsty when he comes to. Let's start our goodwill campaign by ensuring he has something to drink and eat," Patrick said, easing off Molev's other arm.

I tried to do the same, but Molev's fingers caught on the cuff of my pants.

"Stay here with Roni," Patrick said. "I'll be right back."

He jumped out the back while I tried to gently untangle the large, grey fingers from my pants. They kept curling.

I glanced at Molev's face, which was turned toward me. Some part of me thought I'd find the corners of his mouth curving because it sure felt like he was messing with me. But his breathing was even, and his expression relaxed.

"Problem?" Roni asked.

"His fingers are caught in my pants."

She barked out a laugh.

"Cody's going to love hearing that."

I rolled my eyes at her and hooked my fingers around his, removing them all at the same time. But then they curled around mine. Considering his strength, it could have been worse. He could have crushed my fingers. Instead, his grip was firm but not painful.

Patiently, I untangled myself one finger at a time.

"He's like flypaper," Roni said, watching me.

"I should have just knelt on his arm like Patrick did."

"Why didn't you?"

I nodded to the row of stitches. "I don't think that's fully healed yet and didn't want to bust it open."

"Smart thinking. The gunshot is bad enough. Not sure taking out the bullet and giving him something to eat and drink will make things even."

"Would it make things even for you?" I asked.

"Nope. Hopefully, Patrick has a better olive branch than food and water up his sleeve."

He didn't. He returned with a massive set of chains and a heavy-duty padlock along with the promised food and water.

Did I feel bad watching Patrick and Roland chain the grey's arms behind his back? Not really. I'd seen what he could do and felt better knowing he couldn't easily grab anyone's head once he was awake. Because I was pretty sure he wouldn't be happy once he came to. I wouldn't be either.

While he rested in the MRAP with the door open and Roland on guard, we waited for the others to finish their sweep of the stone yard. Patrick was quiet, watching the grey and looking off in the direction of the base.

It didn't take too long for Cody and Tom to return. They reported that they'd safely delivered Evan, who needed more attention than the medic in Vance could provide.

"What about him?" Cody asked with a nod at Molev.

"Bullet's out, and he already stopped bleeding," Roni said.

"What's our next move?" Tom asked.

We all looked at Patrick.

"We move out and keep it random. If there are more of them, hopefully, they follow us. If not, we're still relocating a possible threat to Vance until they can evacuate."

"Incoming," William called from his roost. "Everyone's accounted for."

"But this is what we need, right?" Tom asked. "We're heading back to Irwin?"

"No. We assess, report, and wait for orders," Patrick replied.

Fifteen minutes later, we were driving south. My MRAP was in the middle of the convoy. Roland rode in back with the grey, and Kevin sat next to me. We made good time, putting some decent miles between us and Vance before the first roadblock.

The Stryker cleared it easily enough, so we didn't need to stop. The undead only threw themselves at our vehicles with more determination. The splatter effect was impressively disgusting, and my wipers ran continuously for the next mile. Bits of goo dried to the edges of the windshield just out of reach of the blades.

"I think we have another clinger," Jackson said over the walkie. "Last vehicle again."

"We don't see a trail," Brandon said. "Scratch that. It just started."

"We're stopping fast," Patrick said a second before brake lights went on ahead of me.

Kevin turned in his seat, watching the grey as I stopped.

We couldn't hear anything over the idling of the engine, but I saw Jackson's door open. A second later, a smattering of gunfire rang out. I checked the mirror and saw Jackson on the pavement and Steve standing there with his weapon still up. He only stayed like that for a second before pivoting and making his way to the final MRAP.

Three more shots echoed. Then he jogged to the Humvee, stepping over Jackson, and got in behind the wheel.

His voice came over the radio.

"We need to do a full sweep. There was a small one under our Humvee. It got Jackson."

A small one. We didn't call them kids. We tried not to see them or acknowledge what was happening to the future of humanity. I thought of Zion and felt a stab of desperation.

"We need to move," Brandon said. "A horde of undead from the roadblock is catching up."

Kevin swore.

"We'll be fine," I said. Evan the undead that moved faster didn't have the speed to keep up with our vehicles.

"Not that," he answered quietly.

I glanced at him and followed his gaze to the back where the grey was slowly sitting up.

Molev's gaze locked with mine.

From the corner of my eye, I saw Kevin lifting his weapon.

"Take my seat, Kevin," I said, already moving in front of the barrel to climb into the back.

Molev growled softly as he fully sat up, and I hoped it was due to pain rather than aggression as I continued toward him. The MRAP shifted underneath me as Kevin moved us forward.

"Sorry about the accommodations," I said. "And your back. We removed the bullet and stopped the bleeding. How are you feeling?"

He glanced from me to Roland, who had a bead on Molev.

"Take it easy, Roland," I said, unwilling to let him ruin this opportunity.

He lowered his weapon, and I grabbed one of the water bottles.

"Thirsty?" I twisted off the cap without waiting for an answer and held the bottle out.

Molev leaned forward, indicating he was willing to drink, and I scooted closer to lift the bottle to his lips. When he drained it and leaned back, he didn't mention the chains wrapping his wrists, so neither did I.

"Hungry?" I asked.

"No, Andie," he said, using my name for the first time. "Thank you."

"If you get hungry, we have a few options for you," I said, gesturing at the MRE packages. "They're not great, but they're not bad either."

He didn't even look at them but steadily watched me.

"You said you wanted to know more about us," I said. "Maybe we could use this as an opportunity to get to know each other. Would that interest you?"

This time, the slight lift in the corner of his mouth stayed for a full beat before disappearing.

"I would like that," he said. "How old are you, Andie?"

"Twenty-six. How old are you?"

"I don't know. Mya thinks thousands of years have passed since we last walked in the sun."

I wanted to crow and cheer at that bit of actual information. At least, I did until it sunk in.

"Thousands?"

He nodded.

"How many human survivors are there?" he asked.

The question wasn't unexpected.

"Do you mean in this group or in the world?" I asked.

"The world."

I found his answer telling. His lack of interest in our immediate group and in Vance made sense if his kind was after global conquest.

"I don't know the exact number, but I can tell you it's dropping rapidly every day. If the undead aren't called off soon, there won't be any of us left. Is that what you want?"

He blinked at me. Then looked at Kevin.

"What is that device called?"

I glanced at Kevin and saw he'd been broadcasting the

conversation to the others. He released the button now that he'd been noticed.

"It's a radio," I said. "It allows us to communicate between vehicles without having to get out."

"Do radios come in many sizes?"

"Yeah, I guess. Why?"

The intensity of his unblinking gaze made me wonder if I was asking too many questions. Hiding my discomfort, I waited. After an increasing silence, he rewarded my patience.

"Thank you for your honesty, Andie. Matt's radio is much larger."

So he'd already known that radios came in different sizes and had only asked that to test me? I wished there was a way for me to test the truth of everything he was telling me.

"Who's Matt?" I asked.

"A leader like Patrick."

"Is Matt your leader?"

The corner of Molev's mouth lifted briefly again.

"He is the leader of Whiteman. He commands the human survivors there."

"Whiteman military base?" Roland asked.

We all knew about Whiteman. It was the base that had gone quiet a few weeks ago, right after a report of dog attacks and nearby greys. That report had given us the beacon we'd needed when we'd left Fort Irwin. It was also the place the woman with the greys had mentioned.

"How many survivors are there?" I asked.

"Five hundred and eighty-three."

It filled me with hope and dread that there were so many. Were the greys collecting humans? If so, why? I wanted to ask but didn't want this "conversation" to feel any more like the interrogation it was.

"You've answered so many of my questions," I said instead. "Do you have any to ask me?"

"What do you miss from before the earthquakes?"

I wasn't prepared for that question and said nothing for a long moment.

"I miss a lot. But today, I realized how much I've missed sound. Birds singing. An airplane flying overhead. Music. The world is so quiet now."

"The engines are loud."

"They are," I agreed.

"Do you have a family?" he asked.

"Yes, and some of them are still alive."

His gaze shifted to my hands, which were resting on my thighs.

"No husband?"

"Nope. Never connected with anyone I would want to spend the rest of my life with."

"Any children?"

I wasn't sure how I felt about his focused questions. Was he trying to profile me in some way, or was he trying to build a rapport like I was?

"No. No kids. What about you? Do you have a wife and kids waiting for you back home?"

"No."

"What do you miss from back home?" Roland asked.

Molev held my gaze briefly before turning to look at Roland.

"Both our worlds changed with the earthquake. While there is much I miss, this world offers more than ours ever could."

"Is that why you're here? We have resources you need?" I asked.

Molev's gaze pinned me. "Yes."

CHAPTER FIVE

By the time we stopped, my ass was completely numb from sitting on the cold, vibrating floor of the MRAP. I could have taken Kevin's seat since, after answering the resource question, Molev had closed his eyes and reclined his head. But even though I'd respected the universal "Shut up; I'm tired" sign, I hadn't believed for a moment that he slept. Which was why I hadn't moved from my spot on the floor.

Now, as the engine died, I studied him.

Molev opened his eyes and lifted his head from the folded seat behind him. His immediate alertness confirmed what I'd suspected. He hadn't been sleeping at all.

Once again, his penetrating gaze unerringly found me.

"How are you feeling?" I asked. "Would you like another drink?"

"Please."

I stood to retrieve a water bottle.

Neither Kevin nor Roland made any move to exit the vehicle. It had been radio silence since Kevin broadcasted the start of my conversation with Molev, and I wondered what Patrick's next move would be.

Cracking open the seal on the bottle, I edged closer to Molev. He leaned forward willingly enough, and I helped him drink while he studied me.

While he'd pretended to sleep, I'd openly stared at his ears and grey skin. He looked so alien when his eyes were open with their vertical pupils narrowed on me. But with them closed? He'd seemed almost human. Very different, of course, but still human.

As soon as he drained the bottle, I retreated and sat on the floor again.

"What resources are you interested in?" I asked, picking up our conversation where we'd left off.

I was no spokesperson for the entire human race, but since he seemed willing enough to speak to me, I'd try to find anything useful that might help those in a position to bargain.

Molev considered me for a moment.

"The same as any survivor," he said. "The resources that will help create a peaceful, safe community where those I love can live purposeful lives."

He glanced at the back of the MRAP a second before the door opened.

I found myself staring at the wrong end of at least four firearms. Patrick stood just behind Sid, Sean, William, and Ted.

"How was the ride?" Patrick asked amiably.

"If you wish to keep your weapons intact, lower them," Molev said, his voice resonating with warning.

"Your threat is exactly why the weapons are here. The man you hit might not ever wake up again."

The corner of Molev's mouth turned down ever so slightly. Was he upset that he'd hurt Evan or disappointed Evan was still alive?

"Would you like to stretch your legs for a bit?" Patrick asked.

The four men moved back a few steps, leaving enough room around the door for someone to step out. Molev rose smoothly and fast, his crouching bulk blocking my view of the door as he exited. The gauze on his back only had a little bit of bleed-through on it. Less than I would have anticipated since the bullet hole hadn't been closed.

He stepped down and rose to his full, impressive height before glancing around him.

"Please, follow me," Patrick said, using his asshole-commander voice before walking away.

Molev hesitated for a moment then shadowed Patrick.

I waited until they were out of sight before exiting and shaking out my legs. Kevin came to stand beside me, and we watched Patrick and six others enter a barn with Molev.

"Tell me it feels like we have a sleeping cat by its tail," Kevin said.

"It does," I said. "I hope Patrick can find out what he wants. I'm ready to go home."

"Amen to that," Kevin said.

Patrick left the barn and jogged toward Roni, who was closest to him. They spoke for a minute. Then he pivoted and returned to the barn.

"Hunker down," Roni called.

We pitched in and unpacked what we'd need to stay the night at the secluded homestead. It had solar, which meant working showers, hot food, and heat. Real beds were a bonus. But none of that meant safety.

Mateo, Brandon, and Steve cleared the house, removing an undead from inside. Those of us who'd been up since the attack got first dibs on the shower. Once I was clean and fed, I claimed one of the three beds and crashed hard, fully dressed.

A hand on my shoulder brought me out of what felt like a

light doze. With a gasp, I shoved out before I even opened my eyes.

"Easy, Andie," Patrick said. "You're safe."

Heart pounding, I waited for the adrenaline spike to catch up to me and glanced at the window to orient myself. The sun had set, so I'd managed a few hours.

"Who am I taking over for?" I asked.

"Me," Patrick said. "The grey hasn't said a word other than, 'I need to piss' since he's been in the barn. Roland said that he was chatty with you. Mentioned he wanted resources. I'd like you to try to talk to him again."

"Okay." I stood and rolled my shoulders.

"Can I have five to use the bathroom first?"

Patrick nodded. "Meet me by the door."

He was pacing near the kitchen when I joined him.

"What else do you want to know other than the resources?" I asked.

"How many of them are there? Where did they come from? We know they emerged from the crater in Irving, but how did they get there? What do they want, and will they stop killing us when they get it? Assuming what they want isn't our annihilation," he added.

"And if I get all those answers, then what?"

"Then we end this."

He made it sound so definitively easy, but I knew better. It would be anything but easy even if we managed to get the answers. Like he'd said, the greys could want anything, even our deaths.

Arms still chained behind him, Molev sat against a support beam in the barn. A light was pointed right at him, which should have blinded him to just about everything else in the room. It didn't. His watering gaze immediately locked on me the moment I stepped inside the space.

Patrick closed the door behind us, his footfalls heavy on the cement as we approached.

Cody and Brandon stood between us and Molev, and I could see movement on the other side of the light. They had their guns ready but not pointed at him. At least, not until he shifted a little. Weapons flew into ready position.

We'd traveled in the MRAP for hours with only Roland standing watch. Maybe the extra eyes were why he wouldn't talk. And probably the light that was making his eyes water.

I veered around Cody and Brandon and adjusted the light, so it aimed at the floor several feet in front of Molev. Sitting in the pool of light, I looked at Patrick.

"Can we get some water and something to eat for both of us? And I think we only need one guard. The light wasn't visible from outside, and our voices shouldn't carry," I said as if they were here to protect Molev, not protect us from him.

Patrick nodded and motioned for everyone except Brandon to follow him out.

I waited until they were gone to look at Molev.

"You haven't slept since you were shot. You drank water, but I'm guessing you didn't eat anything. Does that mean you don't need sleep or food or that you're more like human men than we realize and are being stubborn for the sake of being stubborn?"

The corner of his mouth twitched.

"Stubborn then," I said.

I glanced at Brandon, who was watching us from the other side of the light.

"Can you go get something for him to sleep on? Maybe some blankets and a pillow from the house?"

"I don't think I should leave you alone."

"I think I can manage on my own for a few minutes. Please."

Brandon glanced at the door then at me, swore under his breath, and left.

When I faced Molev, he was watching me intently. I stared right back. The door closed behind Brandon. Molev didn't move an inch.

"That's what I thought," I said.

"What do you think?" he asked, the low rumble of his voice washing over me.

"You're not interested in trying to leave. Why?"

That corner of his mouth twitched again.

"Maybe I like it here."

"I doubt that. Your eyes are still watering from the light."

"Thank you for moving it."

"You're welcome. Why don't you tell me what questions they already asked you and which ones you won't answer so we don't waste any more of your time?"

"You think they are wasting my time?" he asked.

"Aren't they?" I returned.

He tipped his head and studied me for a moment.

"You're not like the others."

"How so?"

"You're fearless. You sit close to me. You speak frankly to me. You don't wave your weapon around in an attempt to intimidate me."

"Ah. You're mistaking my actions for courage I don't have. I'm sitting this close because distance doesn't matter. I've seen how fast you can move. Which is also why I'm not bothering with a weapon. I'd rather not have you wreck any more of them. And I'm only speaking some of what's on my mind, not all of it, to see how you'll react. A person's actions say a lot about them."

"And what are my actions saying about me?"

"I'm not exactly sure, which is why I'm willingly sitting here, talking to you."

"What do you mean?"

"Well, if I thought any of your actions so far were threatening, I wouldn't be here. I don't understand why you've knocked out the members of my team more than once, but I do know you've held back when you could have done more damage. So, I have to ask: What do you want with us? Why are you here? Because we both know you're sitting there by choice." I gestured to the emptiness around us. "No one's here to stop you from leaving."

"Why are you here, Andie?" Molev said.

"I already told you. To figure you out. To find out what you want from us. And by us, I mean humanity as a whole. Where did your people come from? Why are they attacking us?"

"We do not attack. We defend."

I let that statement hang between us for a moment as I thought about it. We had been the ones to shoot at them first at the tank. And Evan had shot at Molev before Molev had turned around.

"Okay. *You* haven't attacked us yet, but you've been attacked by us twice. So I'm even more confused why you'd want to stick around."

Another mouth-corner twitch.

"There are reasons," he said. "But I would like to keep those reasons to myself for now."

While I appreciated that we were speaking openly, it frustrated me that he was holding anything back.

"What about attacking humans in general?" I asked. "Why send the dogs after us? Why spread the disease that is causing people to turn undead?"

"Mya calls them infected."

"Infected then. Why allow the dogs to spread the infection?"

"We never meant to release the hounds. The earthquake did that."

"I saw the footage. Two of your kind led the dogs to the surface."

"Two of my kind were chased to the surface by the hounds. And they are now responsible for hunting the hounds and destroying them."

I let that settle in my mind as I watched him. If the hounds weren't theirs, it did clear things up a little.

"How many hounds are there, and how many have the two hunting them destroyed?"

"Many and not enough. The hounds hide during the day and hunt in pairs or packs at night. And they are not easily killed. A bullet. A knife. An arrow to the heart. Those are all useless. To kill—"

He stopped speaking and looked at the door.

A second later, it opened. Patrick and Brandon walked in.

Brandon had a pile of blankets in his arms along with a pillow. Patrick carried two MREs and two bottles of water. He radiated tension and disapproval.

"Molev was just telling me that the hounds chased two of his kind to the surface. They weren't led here like the video made it seem. He was also about to tell me how they could be killed."

I turned to Molev.

"The hounds aren't like anything we've ever seen before. Glowing red eyes, long legs, dark. One of them decimated a whole Company and a ton of people before running off like it wasn't carrying its weight in metal inside of it."

Molev shifted his attention from the men to me, and I waited for him to decide if he wanted to keep talking. I'd repeated some of what he'd said to pacify Patrick so he would let me continue and so Molev would understand that I would be relaying everything he said.

"They die when their heart is removed and crushed to black dust."

"That's disappointing," I said. "How many people died to figure that out?"

I couldn't imagine getting close enough to one of those things to dig out its heart.

"None," Molev said. "But a few were injured."

"Your kind can go toe-to-toe with the hounds?" I asked, just to be sure I was understanding.

"Explain what you mean," Molev said.

"I mean you can fight them and only get hurt. Not dead?"

"Yes. We aren't as fragile as humans." His gaze swept over me when he said it, but it didn't feel like a dismissive glance. More like one measuring exactly how fragile I was.

Rather than sit there under his scrutiny, I stood and collected the blankets from Brandon.

Molev watched me spread them out next to him and waited for me to approach with another bottle of water. He drank it down and didn't refuse the food I offered next. I glanced at Patrick, and he gave a minute shake of his head, answering my unspoken question to release Molev.

Feeling awkward but hiding it as I did with everything else I felt, I sat knee to knee with Molev and looked at the packs in my lap.

"All right. Our options tonight are beef in barbecue or beef tacos. Any preference?"

"You choose," he said.

I opened one at random. He asked a few questions about the flameless ration heater and the drinks but otherwise watched me closely. When I had the first taco made, I held it up to him. He looked down at the folded, filled tortilla for so long that I knew I was showing him something completely new to him.

"Like this," I said, turning the taco to me and taking a small bite.

The corner of his mouth moved again, and I was starting to get the feeling that half of what I did or said amused him. That rubbed me the wrong way. I was stuck in the bum-fuck nowhere of the central Midwest, fighting to survive and get the answers we needed to help our loved ones survive, and he was entertained by me?

Hell no.

I lowered my hand as I chewed instead of offering it to him again.

"Either you understand exactly what's happening and are indifferent to it, or you're clueless. Which one is it?" I asked.

The flicker of humor I could have sworn I'd seen vanished.

"Explain."

"I'm here because people are dying. Our world is dying. You have the ability to stop it, or you have answers that will enable us to stop it. Either way, our fate…the fate of our world rests in your hands, and you're sitting there, entertained by my efforts to learn what your role might be in saving us. And frankly, it's making me angry."

He took a slow, deep breath.

"I apologize, Andie. Finish your meal, and I will continue answering your questions."

"It's not my meal. It's yours. I was just showing you how to eat it because you were looking like you've never seen a taco before."

"I haven't."

He leaned forward, a show of willingness. I didn't

understand him, but when I'd let my frustration show, he hadn't reacted in kind. That meant something.

Lifting the food, I almost yipped in surprise when he moved forward quickly and took a bite so large his lips brushed my fingertips. My heart gave a stuttering beat at the shock of it.

He leaned back and chewed, the intensity of his gaze bringing to mind Kevin's words from several days ago. What had he said? That this one had looked at me like he'd wanted to take me instead of the trucks? Was he trying to hit on me, or was this another test? Did he think seducing me would lead to some kind of world secrets? If so, he was going to be disappointed on two fronts. I didn't seduce well. Men found me standoffish because I didn't wear my emotions on my face. And I didn't have a single helpful bit of knowledge for him.

I waited for him to swallow and offered the remains of the taco.

"Please don't bite my fingers," I said when he leaned forward.

His lips twitched. This time, it didn't offend me. His reaction was probably the same one any other guy would give. While he chewed that mouthful, I put together more food for him. Bite by bite, he consumed the entirety of the MRE. When I opened the next one and tried feeding that one to him, he shook his head.

"You eat, and I'll talk."

"Okay. How many of your kind are there?" I asked before taking a bite.

"Not enough to protect the remaining humans without help," he said.

"You want to help us?" Patrick asked. "Why?"

"I will keep that to myself for now."

"Why not tell us?" I asked before Patrick could get pissy about it.

"We don't yet trust each other," Molev said. "When we do, we will be able to speak freely and listen openly."

I paused mid-chew, a little awed by his understanding of the situation.

"Is that what this is then?" I asked after I swallowed. "A trust exercise?"

That corner of his lip curved again.

"Something like that."

"Okay. If you can't tell us how many of you there are or why you want to help us, can you tell us where you came from? We know you came from underground after the earthquake, but from where?"

He launched into a too-crazy-to-believe tale that involved fey, magic, and curses. It was a lot to take in, but every time I looked at his ears, I knew I couldn't doubt everything he said. After all, all stories had grains of truth in them, didn't they?

"Fey. So you've lived and died thousands of times in those caves?" I asked.

"Yes."

"You're immortal then?"

"No. Here, we can die."

"But like the dogs, not easily, I'm betting."

He dipped his head in a slight nod of agreement.

"We've taken up enough of your time," Patrick said, speaking for the first time in a while. "Get some rest. We'll talk again in the morning."

Hearing the words for the command they were, I rose smoothly.

"Good night, Molev. Sleep well," I said.

He remained sitting when I walked away but moved to lay down when I looked back.

Patrick waited until we were seated in the kitchen to say anything.

"I don't always understand how you think, Andie, and your intuition has rarely been wrong. But why did you risk yourself and the mission by sending Brandon out?"

"Too many things aren't adding up. I don't even know where to start.

"Every time a gun's been pointed at him, he hasn't responded well. Yet, he was sitting in the circle of light, eyes watering, surrounded by armed guards, like he didn't have a care in the world. No tension. Maybe a little annoyance.

"I think he's just sitting in there, waiting to see what we'll do next. Why else say nothing to you for hours? By sending everyone away, he had the perfect opportunity to run, chained or not. Yet, he didn't. That proves he's staying here by choice."

"Do you think he wants to help us like he said?"

"I don't know. He said some crazy stuff out there. It's a little hard to believe fey are real even when I'm staring at his pointed ears and unique eyes.

"But there was something that made complete sense to me. We don't trust each other. Trust needs to be earned. We're never going to earn his trust by keeping him in chains, which means, at some point, we're going to need to trust him enough not to murder us when the whim strikes."

Patrick made a non-committal noise and stared at the table for a drawn-out minute.

"Time isn't our friend," he said eventually.

"No, it isn't," I agreed.

"Any ideas on how to earn trust fast?"

"That would take a leap of faith from one of us."

"You want me to remove the chains."

"I want you to ask yourself if those chains are even doing anything to restrain a guy who crushed what is essentially a mini-cannon with his bare hands. I think everything he's doing is a test to see if we're worthy of his trust."

Patrick swore under his breath and stood.

"Take over for Mateo on the roof," he said before walking out the door.

Tiredly, I stood and followed, missing the good old days when nighttime was for sleeping and not keeping watch.

From the new vantage point of the roof, I saw Patrick leave the barn a while later. No one else emerged from the barn as the night progressed, though. If Molev were free, wouldn't he want to move around to test the limits of his freedom? I would. Did that then mean that Patrick had left him chained?

As the sun rose, I watched Roni head to the barn with two more MREs. The image of Molev mouthing her fingers as he'd done to mine popped into my head, and I felt a thread of concern. Roni wasn't the patient type. I shook my head, dislodging the thought. They'd be fine. Molev was smart. He had to know she'd punch him in the face for trying that.

Sid came to replace me, and I paused to stretch out when I reached the ground. My gaze kept drifting to the barn.

Too curious to stay away, I went to check on things. We all had a vested interest in the outcome of this mission, and if Molev was still in chains, I would try to find another way to build his trust in us. We needed him and the information he had.

Inside the barn, Roni and Ted lingered near the door, watching Molev from a respectable distance and not interacting with him at all. They glanced at me, but I paid them little attention, focusing instead on Molev and the fact that he wasn't chained.

He looked up from his intent study of the two MRE bags he held.

"Good morning," I said, already closing the distance between us.

"Good morning, Andie," he said. "Is one of these yours?"

"Uh, I don't think so," I said, glancing back at Roni.

She shrugged. "He's a big guy. I didn't think one would be filling."

Molev looked down at the packages again, his gaze flicking between descriptions printed on the fronts of both.

"Having a hard time deciding?" I asked.

"I cannot read your language." He held out both bags. "What do they say?"

I looked up into his eyes, understanding he was returning the trust Patrick had given him, and offered a smile in return.

"Cement floor dining isn't the right setting for," I glanced down at the bags, "beef ravioli or lemon pepper tuna. How would you like to eat at the table with me?"

When I lifted my gaze again, I caught the corner of his mouth moving.

"I would like that very much."

CHAPTER SIX

TOM AND KEVIN WERE ALREADY AT THE TABLE WHEN WE ENTERED the dining room.

"Molev, this is Tom and Kevin," I said, indicating each one. "They're two of the remaining members of our squad."

"Hello." Molev's tone didn't exactly convey welcome, but it wasn't filled with warning either.

"Mind if we join you?" I asked the pair.

Tom warily nodded and Kevin moved down a seat so that Molev and I could sit next to each other. It wasn't what I'd planned, but once he'd moved, I didn't have a choice but to cozy up to the grey behemoth. The chair creaked under his weight as he carefully sat.

"How many of those have you broken?" I asked.

"Many," he said.

"How much do you weigh?" Kevin asked.

Molev blinked at him. Although there weren't any facial expressions to go with it, that blink felt like he'd just judged Kevin an idiot. He sort of was, but I didn't like that Molev was judging him for a normal question.

"It took six people to lift you into the back of the MRAP

when you were shot, and you sat gently with the experience of a man who's broken his fair share of chairs. I think it was a valid question," I said, opening the first MRE.

Molev looked at me and tilted his head, studying me for a heartbeat.

"I have upset you again. How?"

"The way you looked at him just now inferred that you thought his question was stupid."

Molev grunted. I wasn't sure how to interrupt a grunt.

"If I misunderstood the situation," I said, "please educate me. We need to learn how to communicate if we want to work together."

"We're working together?" Tom asked Kevin under his breath.

"I do not know the answer to the question," Molev said.

"Okay. So I made the wrong assumption. I apologize."

Molev's gaze flicked over my face before he looked down at the food I'd spread out.

"Which one looks better?" I asked.

"Do you enjoy the red sauce?" he asked instead of choosing.

"As far as tomato sauces go, it's not bad. The desserts in both of these are better than the main meals, in my opinion, but I have a bit of a sweet tooth."

He blinked at me.

"You have a tooth that is sweet?"

"No, I mean I like sweets. Both of these meals have M&Ms. The tuna MRE is the one with peanut butter M&Ms and pound cake. This one has plain M&Ms but has a dessert bar that is probably one of my favorites."

"I think he knows more about her now than we do," Kevin said to Tom.

"What are M&Ms?" Molev asked.

"Oh you poor thing," I said with a slight smile to show I was teasing. I ripped open the peanut butter bag and handed him one. "Give it a try."

He popped it into his mouth and chewed thoughtfully.

"It is good," he said.

I slid the whole meal toward him and guided him through how to warm everything and put it together.

Tom and Kevin stayed at the table long after they were done eating to watch. Gradually, they joined the conversation and gave advice about which MREs were good and which ones to avoid. We all learned that Molev didn't care for anything with tomato in it and wasn't as into sweets as we were. Or vegetables. The way he talked about Spam had me inwardly grinning. The guy really liked his meat.

When we finished in the kitchen, I showed Molev to the bathroom, and he surprised me by asking if he could have a clean shirt to change into after his shower. It shouldn't have surprised me, though. His once-white t-shirt was covered in infected blood and a lot of his own on the back.

"Let me see what I can find, and I'll leave it outside the door for you."

"Thank you, Andie."

I asked Kevin and Tom to keep an eye on him and went to search the house for something he could use. Since the beds were occupied and I didn't want to wake anyone, it took me a while to find a shirt I thought would work.

When I finally returned to the main bathroom, I found it empty with the bloody shirt in the garbage. The dining room was empty too. Not sure where else to look, I went outside and headed for the barn. I found Molev there, arm wrestling with scrawny Tom. It wasn't an even match by a long shot. Tom tried to wrestle Molev's arm to the table by using both arms and all his body weight while Molev sat there smirking at Tom's brilliantly red face.

"Come on, Tom," Kevin said. "Use your legs and your core to push away from the floor. You're strong. You know you are."

He was, but not compared to Molev.

Molev's grey skin gleamed, and the spotlight highlighted every ridge. His pectorals jumped as he shifted position and glanced at me. I had a hard time looking away from that scar-riddled chest. Scars shouldn't have been that sexy. The grey skin either, for that matter.

Finally jerking my gaze up, I met his and held up the shirt.

"Whenever you're ready," I said.

Roni reached out and shoved my arm down. "If you love me, you'll leave him alone," she said softly. "I haven't seen this level of amazing in a very long time."

I wasn't sure if she meant the epic struggle or the muscle display. Both were nice to watch and far better than the endless monotony of travel, fighting the infected, and guard duty.

"I'm next," Roni called out when Tom finally gave up.

Molev gave her a look that was slightly different from his normal blank slate. He actually frowned a little.

"I do not wish to see you hurt again," he said.

"Please," Roni scoffed. "I could bench Tom."

"Whatever," Tom panted. "I used to weigh more."

Roni sat across from Molev and placed her elbow on the plank. Molev slowly lifted his arm. They clasped hands, and Roni grinned at him.

"I've seen what you can do and know you're holding back for us. But how much?" She barely finished speaking before slamming his hand to the surface of the plank.

"That's what I thought. Do it again," she demanded, releasing him and lifting her hand again.

They did that several more times, each match becoming increasingly harder until she was finally struggling like Tom had. Kevin chuckled, watching her, but Tom had already left.

"Son of a bitch," Roni panted. "Kevin, get in here and help me."

Kevin waited for Molev's nod before adding his weight to Roni's effort. I watched them struggle with growing amusement.

"Andie, get your ass over here," Roni said.

"I doubt it'll do any good." Yet, I moved closer and set the shirt for Molev on the plank. He watched me closely as I circled and went to join Kevin.

"No," Molev said. "If he loses his grip, he will hurt you. Go on the other side or help Roni."

"The hell!" Roni said, red face. "Is my effort that pathetic to you?"

Amused by her indignation, I took the other side of Kevin. Instead of standing opposite Molev, though, I planted myself next to him. As I leaned in and placed my hands on theirs, the light scent of soap smell filled my nose. It was much more pleasant than Roni's body odor and reminded me that I should sneak another shower before Patrick decided we needed to move again.

I'd only barely begun to push on their hands when Katie's voice crackled over Kevin's radio.

"Small group of undead to the south. They're standing at the edge of the trees just watching."

We all immediately let go. Roni and Kevin were faster in rushing toward the door. I got tangled in Molev's feet and would have tripped if not for the massive arm that banded around my waist. Annoyed, since I wasn't at all the clumsy type, I looked up at him.

"My apologies. Stay here." He picked me up and plopped

me down on the seat he'd vacated. A second later, he was by the door, turning Roni around. "Stay with Andie."

She frowned at me, and before either of us could register what was happening, he pulled Kevin through the door and shut it tight.

"Did the women folk just get put in their places?" she asked me.

"For his sake, I hope not. But *if* that's what this was, please keep in mind that we probably have completely different social structures. He didn't want to arm wrestle you, but when you insisted, he gave a little. You need to give a little in return."

"I was ready to give plenty until he pulled this caveman bullshit," she said with a scowl as I joined her.

I didn't pretend to mistake her meaning.

"He's been unchained for less than twelve hours, and we barely know anything about him. Maybe thoughts of having sex should wait a few weeks, don't you think?"

She shrugged. "I haven't been laid in so long Tom's starting to look good to me."

"I'm going to tell Patrick to put Tom in child protective custody to save you from yourself."

She flashed a grin at me.

"That boy wouldn't know what hit him. It'd be the best five minutes of his life and the most disappointing of mine."

We both smiled slightly then sobered.

"I'm going to check," she said.

I backed up a few steps, my hand resting on my sidearm. If the infected were at the edge of the field, they wouldn't have reached the barn yet.

She opened the door and frowned at the sight of Kevin's back.

"What in the hell are you doing?" Roni demanded.

He glanced back at us, grinning. "Mostly listening to Roni talk about—"

She hit him with enough force that he grunted. She could have hit him a lot harder, though.

"Where's the grey?" she asked.

"Molev," I said. "We're trying to build trust, not alienate him more."

"Fine. Where's Molev?"

Kevin glanced at the roof of the house and reached for his radio.

"Update?" he asked.

"He just removed the last head. I think he was bitten, though."

"Fuck," Roni breathed, conveying all the emotion in that one word that I felt.

"He's jogging back," the radio said. "Get ready."

We knew the drill. Any bitten person turned undead within about fifteen minutes. And once they turned, they would go after whoever was closest. The only good news was that most newly turned people were uncoordinated and slow. Would that be enough for us to kill Molev before he killed us, though? What if his version of slow was our version of normal?

Internally cringing, I ran around the side of the barn with the others and got into position. More of the team came running from the house. Obviously, we were all having the same thoughts. Stopping an infected grey wasn't going to be easy.

Molev's jog slowed when Roland, Sid, and Kevin brought up their guns.

"Were you bitten?" I yelled.

Molev stopped advancing altogether.

"Do you have a watch that works, Andie?" he called back, surprising me.

"Yeah."

"Start the timer, and you will know if I have been bitten or not."

I looked down at my watch and noted the hands.

"I can see a mark on his shoulder, Andie," Sid said. "There's no point in a timer. We should kill him now."

Patrick joined our group and brought up his own weapon with a scope on it.

"Turn around slowly so we can see your back," Patrick yelled.

Molev turned as instructed, and Sid swore.

"There are two bites on his front and at least six on his back," Patrick said. "We can't take the risk."

"Wait. Why would he—"

Two rapid shots rang out, signaling the start of a barrage I couldn't count. My ears rang, and I watched Molev burst into action, running and veering quickly until he disappeared into the distant trees.

Patrick swore long and hard before yelling that we were moving out immediately.

While everyone scrambled, I glanced down at my watch then at the tree line, my thoughts whirling. If he'd been bitten so many times, why would he tell me to start a timer? Why had he turned around instead of just running? He probably didn't know we could see him from that distance, but still... he'd been coming toward us. We would have seen the bites when he'd gotten closer.

"Andie!" Roni yelled, breaking through my thoughts.

Just before I turned, I saw movement in the trees. I couldn't see what it was, but I had a feeling Molev hadn't left and was watching us.

I took a seat in one of the Humvees this time and started up the engine. Katie got in next to me.

"Well, this has been an interesting morning," she said. "Heard you got to arm wrestle the grey before everyone tried to kill him. Was it fun?"

"Honestly, it kind of was." For a minute, I'd actually forgotten my death was just around the corner and had remembered what it was like to live.

"Good. We need more fun and less running for our lives. Do you think he's going to catch up to us and murder us all in our sleep?"

"I don't know."

We left the farm behind.

The first roadblock slowed us down a little as we headed south. It was three cars deep, and more than Patrick wanted Sean to try to punch through with the Stryker.

"We're going around," he said over the radio a second before they veered right into the ditch. Thankfully it wasn't a deep one, and there was enough room between the end car and the trees.

I could see the infected calling out as it passed them and took a steadying breath as the infected started to pour from the cars.

"They're going to swarm us," Katie said.

"They are," I agreed, keeping right on the fueler's tail.

It smoothly left the road like it was made to do, and I watched the infected topple under its large tires. I hoped it would keep most of the infected off of us, but that wasn't how it worked.

They just kept coming. From everywhere.

Running over a person in the larger vehicles wasn't a big deal. In the Humvee, though? I had to fight the wheel a little more. Goo spattered the windshield, but I couldn't let go to clean it.

It wasn't any better on the other side of the ditch. Our

slower speed had enabled them to gather in a larger herd. Some managed to crawl on top of the Humvee's hood instead of falling under the tires. I could barely see the tanker through the bodies and the blood. An infected on the hood grabbed the wiper when I finally used it and bent it back. Then it smeared its hand over the windshield in front of me, completely obliterating my view.

"Tell Brandon I'm driving blind," I said, dropping my speed by two miles.

Katie got on the radio and warned everyone.

"There's another roadblock ahead," Patrick said. "Keep your speeds steady at twenty-five miles per hour. Sean's going to break through this one."

"Katie, I need to see," I said calmly.

The Stryker would push cars to the side but never perfectly straight. I was using my side mirror to keep myself fairly centered on the road.

In that small view, I saw a flash of grey. I opened my mouth to tell Katie so she could warn the others, but before I could, Derek came on the radio.

"The grey found us."

In the two beats of silence, as we waited for Patrick's command, Molev appeared beside my window.

"I will remove them. Hold steady," he called.

"Wait, what does he mean?" Katie asked at the same time he flipped himself up onto the hood. He used the momentum and his leg to knock two of the infected off, then his hand swiped over the glass, clearing a strip for me to see.

In the next second, he was gone.

I hit the gas, closing the gap I'd created between me and the fueler. Ahead, we heard the Stryker hit the roadblock. More infected closed in around us as we navigated through the opening. Only this time, I could see and sped up with the rest of the convoy.

A few minutes later, the infected who'd tried to chase us fell out of sight.

"We have a few clingers again," Mateo said.

"We keep going," Patrick answered.

The infected fell off bit by bit, and the trail eventually ended. But Patrick didn't call a stop for another few hours. During that time, he got better at picking roads that weren't filled with traps.

"No one exits their vehicles. I'm not losing anyone else to stupid mistakes. I want someone out of the top of that last MRAP to cover Katie and Andie. They will exit one at a time and do a sweep."

"Got it," Brandon said.

A second later, the top of the MRAP opened, and Mateo popped out.

"Ready," Brandon said.

"I hate this part," Katie said, reaching for the handle.

The latch released, and the door opened an inch. She extended her leg, leaning forward to get out with her weapon ready.

"Wait!" Brandon said.

A shot rang out as a hand closed over Katie's ankle.

Her panicked cry filled the cab, and I grabbed her by the shoulders, trying to pull her back inside. A low moan echoed up from underneath us, and I leaned forward enough to see the infected's hand around her ankle and a hint of its head emerging from the undercarriage.

I pulled harder as she kicked and tried to dislodge its hold.

Another shot rang out. Then another. Suddenly, she flew back into me.

"It let go," she panted. "I think he got it.

"Did it bite you?" I asked, glancing at my watch.

"No. My boot wasn't even fully out the door. If it did bite me, it didn't break through the leather."

"Get in the back," I said.

While she moved to the rear, I aimed my firearm at the open door and waited.

"No movement," Brandon said after a while. "Was Katie bitten?"

"No. I'm fine. Well, not fine. Can I give my two weeks now?" Katie said.

Brandon laughed into the radio.

"Not worth the loss of your pension."

I leaned forward, grabbed the door, and slammed it closed.

"Tell him I'm trying my side," I said.

Once she did, I opened my door and watched below as I extended a leg. No hand thrust out to grab it.

"Stay here," I said to Katie.

"But Patrick—"

"The timer's running," I said, cutting her off.

"Oh."

I felt bad for saying it, but we couldn't just take her word that she hadn't been bitten. Leaving her in the Humvee, I started my sweep under Mateo's watchful eye.

"You're clear," I said to Brandon.

He got out and helped me sweep the rest. We found three more infected hidden in places they shouldn't have been able to hide.

"How the fuck do they do that?" Brandon said under his breath after shooting one and pulling it out from its place near an axle.

"Look at its leg." There were friction and heat marks there. "They can't feel pain, and I bet they don't feel exhaustion either. That means they'd hang on forever."

The last vehicle to check was my own again. Brandon and I shared a look as we approached. Katie slowly turned her head.

"Still alive," she called when she saw us. "Can I get out now?"

Exhaling in relief, I opened the door for her, and Brandon signaled that everything was clear.

Katie gave me a weak smile. "That was a close one. Let's hope that doesn't happen again."

Since it felt like the last three weeks were filled with close calls, I doubted her wish would come true.

"Are we going to talk about the grey?" Brandon asked when Patrick joined us.

"He wasn't infected, and his appearance had been well after the fifteen-minute mark," I said. "I think he knew he wouldn't turn. That's why he suggested I watch the time."

"Wait, that means he's immune, right?" Katie asked.

"Immune or the source. Either way, we need to find him or one of his friends," Patrick said.

"Since he was already following us, I'm betting we won't need to look too hard," Mateo said.

Patrick's speculative glance swept over me as he nodded. "We'll find somewhere to hole up for a while. Let's move, people!"

It was a good thing I didn't mind driving since I spent the majority of my waking hours behind the wheel now. But part of me still longed for that time when some of my day had been spent socializing.

"You just sighed. You never sigh. What's going on?" Katie asked.

"Sorry. Slipped into the past for a second there. I think I'm running low on real sleep."

"Yeah, I heard yours was cut short so you could talk to the grey."

"Molev," I said. "If he's not infected with whatever makes people undead, we need to treat him like a person and gain his trust so he'll help us."

Molev was the key to our future, whether we wanted him to be or not.

"And it was sleep I didn't mind losing. He's interesting to talk to. He said he's a fey, like the elves from our stories, and has lived thousands of years in caves beneath the surface. They were cursed there, apparently."

His eyes and the way he watched me with patient intensity filled my mind for a moment. No matter how much I didn't want to see it, I was starting to believe that Kevin might have been right. And considering the look Patrick gave me, he was obviously seeing it now too.

I wasn't sure I wanted to be the key to Molev's cooperation.

CHAPTER SEVEN

"Do you think he'll be able to trust us after everyone shot at him?"

"He might not want to, but we need to find a way to ensure he does. He didn't turn. We need him."

Out of the corner of my eye, I saw her shake her head.

"What's that for?" I asked.

"What do you think they'll do to him when they find out he's immune? I wouldn't want to be him. He'll either be dissected or spend the rest of his life as a lab rat."

"Maybe once upon a time in our history, but I don't think we can afford to do something like that anymore."

She snorted. "And everyone thinks I'm the naïve one."

"Hear me out," I said. "We know how strong and fast he is, right? And we know there's at least fifty more like him. Yet, only one followed us. Why? Because they didn't need to send more. Just like he knew he wouldn't turn, he knows he can wipe us out in a heartbeat. There aren't enough people left to handle a group of greys if they find out we're experimenting on one of their kind."

"And if they take him to one of the island locations where his kind can't reach him?"

"They wouldn't. Why risk spreading this problem to the only safe havens we have? No, if they wanted to experiment on him, they would do it in a location that wasn't being used for survivors. And you see how fast some of these secured bases are falling. There's nowhere safe to take him. It's smarter to collaborate. They'll ask nicely for blood samples and hope that he'll give them willingly."

"We're a species known for taking what we want when we want it. When has humanity ever gone the peaceful route in times of conflict?"

Inwardly, I cringed because she was right. Humans seemed to thrive on war and conflict. I just didn't think a war against the greys was one we could win. Hopefully, what was left of our government would agree.

The Stryker turned down a long drive that ended with another farmhouse and barn. No shortage of those in the Midwest. Finding a place with power was a little hit and miss on a failing grid, though.

We circled the vehicles then divided into three groups. Two lookouts would stay on top the MRAPs to guard our means of escape. Seven would clear inside and around the house. Eight would check inside and around the barn.

"Stay sharp," Patrick ordered.

I nodded to Derek, my partner for clearing around the barn. We moved together, working our way around the structure and outlying equipment counterclockwise. When we reached a grain bin, we found a headless undead on the ground.

"We know you're not infected, Molev," I said, scanning for him. "If you're nearby, let us know, and we'll lower our weapons. Otherwise, we're going to keep searching for more infected."

"I am here," Molev said.

Lowering my weapon, I looked around for him. He'd sounded close. When I saw Derek still had his rifle to his shoulder.

"Do you want to be the next one knocked out by him?" I asked.

He reluctantly lowered it, and Molev dropped from the barn roof, to the grain bin's roof, then to the ground in front of me.

"Impressive," I said. "Sorry about shooting at you again. We didn't know you wouldn't turn."

"But now you do."

"We do," I agreed, understanding his warning well enough. "Are you immune to their bites?"

He rolled his shoulders in the semblance of a shrug.

"They bite. I heal."

"Wish it worked that way for us. No human has ever survived a bite."

Molev grunted and looked toward the house.

"They are done clearing the infected."

"How do you know?" I asked.

A second later, the radio crackled. "The house is clear."

"I heard them," Molev said in the following silence.

"You can hear them from here?" Derek asked in disbelief.

"Yes. And I can hear the humans in the barn need help."

Derek made a frustrated sound and hurried forward.

Molev set his hand on my shoulder when I would have followed.

"We will go together," he said.

I ran. He kept pace. When we reached the barn, I could

hear the infected moans and soft cursing. Two shots rang out. Gripping my handgun, I crept inside with Molev beside me.

"We are here," he said. "Do not shoot."

"Shh," I said softly, scanning our dim surroundings. Did he honestly not know noise drew infected? Or did he somehow know those two shots were the last of them?

I'd barely had that thought when an infected came sprinting at me from behind a tractor. I aimed and exhaled, a second from pulling the trigger.

"Turn around, Andie," Molev ordered as he darted forward to meet the infected.

Lowering my weapon, I spun around as he ordered, already understanding what he meant to do. The way he removed heads was messy, and I was close enough to be in the splash zone.

However, as I turned, I saw another infected coming from the other direction. Behind it, Kevin lay on the ground.

A shot rang out before I even realized I'd aimed again. This close, I managed a clean headshot and dropped the infected just as Kevin started to move. I thought of Zion and pulled the trigger. It wasn't a clean shot. Kevin got to his feet. I exhaled and aimed again.

Hands gripped my waist, and my feet left the ground. My stomach lurched as I shot upward.

Molev's firm hold kept me upright as we landed in a hay loft. A cloud of dust billowed around us. Below, I heard an infected call out and leaned to the side to look down. Molev's hands slid to my hips, anchoring me.

I watched several infected run for the door. Kevin shambled slowly behind them. Shots rang out in the barn, and I watched the rest of the team surge after them, stepping right over my weapon, which laid on the barn floor below.

More shots rang out in the yard, likely from Katie and Sid on top of the MRAPs.

"We need to help them," I said, looking back at Molev.

His gaze locked with mine for a second before he knocked my feet out from under me and caught me in his arms. He jumped from the loft, and my stomach did another flip as we dropped. As soon as his feet hit the ground, he was off running.

I squinted against the sudden daylight. It didn't stop me from seeing the body in the dirt as he sprinted past the barn team and toward the vehicles and infected in front of us. Before he reached them, he jumped. We sailed through the air and lightly landed next to Katie on the MRAP.

She looked up at us with big eyes.

"You are safe," he said to her.

"Uh, okay."

I turned to look at the remaining infected. They stood between the barn and the vehicles, not exactly pinned down but experiencing gunfire from two sides.

Sid fired again, dropping another one.

"Stay low!" Brandon called from the barn.

"We need to get down," I said.

Molev grunted. Instead of getting low or jumping down, he turned around and shifted his hold, so I was shielded by his large torso.

"That's not helpful," I said just as the gunfire quieted.

I peeked over his shoulder to see the remaining two infected running for the trees. Sid fired again, and one dropped. He missed on the next shot, though.

He looked at Molev.

"A little help here," he said.

Molev glanced at me and was just setting me down when the door to the house banged open.

"Report," Patrick barked, falling into the military version of himself.

"Several undead just came out of the barn. Kevin was one of them. We brought down four, but the fifth escaped," Sid said.

Patrick looked at Molev.

"Why didn't you kill them?"

"He did," I said. "You'll find a headless body inside the barn."

Patrick stared at Molev for a long minute.

"We've seen what you can do. How fast you can move. You left neat little piles for us to find. Death shrines to show us how easy it is for you to kill them. Or maybe us? Is that why you didn't just wipe out all of the undead in there? Is everything you said about helping us a lie?"

"No."

"Then prove it. If you want us to believe you're not with them, go find and behead that one you let escape."

I stared at Patrick, unable to believe what he'd just said. When Molev slowly crossed his arms and looked down at him as well, I knew we were in trouble.

"I am not your weapon, and I am not the only one who needs to prove himself an ally. Walk with care, Patrick."

Patrick's gaze narrowed, but not in an angry way. More like he was weighing his options and deciding on his response. I hoped Patrick would get it through his head that Molev wasn't the type to respond well to threats and wouldn't try to strong-arm him again.

Molev didn't give Patrick time to speak. He jumped down from the vehicle and strode toward the barn. A few seconds later, the first body flew out. The head followed. The barn team moved away from the opening.

"We walked into a nest or something," Brandon said. "Ten

to twelve undead were just clustered together in the back corner, standing there, waiting for us to find them. As soon as William spotted them, they swarmed. William was bitten. I managed two kills before the rest scattered. It was like a game of hide-and-seek after that until Molev started talking. Two went for him. We didn't have a clear shot to assist until he and Andie jumped out of the way."

Brandon looked up at me as another body flew out of the barn. "It was an impressive jump."

"No more impressive than a guy tossing two-hundred-pound men at least twenty feet," I said, nodding toward the growing pile of bodies.

"All that has nothing on his hearing," Derek said, moving away from the throw zone. "He heard you cleared the house before you radioed it, and he heard there was trouble in the barn."

"And what did he do when he heard there was trouble?" Patrick asked.

"Nothing other than telling us about it," Derek said.

"Not true," I said. "He did come with us."

"No, he came with you," Derek said.

It felt like everyone turned to look at me.

"Try being nicer," I said.

Patrick rubbed a hand over his head. "We need to know if he's really with us, Andie."

Without acknowledging his unspoken command, I climbed off the top of the truck and entered the barn, careful to stay to the side so I wouldn't get hit by flying dead people.

This time, I let my eyes adjust. Molev was carrying another body toward me. His gaze swept me from head to toe like I was being judged or maybe scanned for a weapon. Then he dismissed me completely when he threw the body out.

He backtracked and sat on the ground, leaning back

against a support beam just like he had in the last barn. Only this time, he leaned his head back and closed his eyes.

He was definitely dismissing me.

Even if Patrick couldn't see that we'd just lost footing with him, I could. I wanted to swear. Instead, I joined him on the floor. Our shoulders brushed when I leaned back against the beam.

"You're strong, fast, and apparently have super hearing," I said. "Even with all of that, I wouldn't want to be you."

From the corner of my eye, I saw him turn his head to look at me.

"Why not?"

"You're either hated or feared for being different. No one trusts you. You're alone right now with no friends. No one you can count on." I met his gaze. "It makes people wonder why you're here and not back with your friends where you wouldn't be getting shot at."

He grunted and faced forward.

"I think there's something in it for you. When a person is desperate enough, they will suffer through anything to get what they want," I said, thinking of Zion.

"Patrick is right," Molev said after a lengthy silence. "I left those bodies so you would notice. Humans fear us, and I needed to give you a reason not to fear me."

"A pile of headless bodies isn't exactly a friendship gift. You can see how it could also be viewed as aggressive and threatening, right?"

"I *am* desperate for something, Andie. And I will suffer through anything to get it. What do I need to do to prove I am worthy of your trust?"

"Trust isn't won with a single act but a bunch of them. We were on our way to gaining the group's trust by sharing a meal and arm wrestling. We need to get back to that."

He leaned his head against the post and closed his eyes again.

"Why does gaining trust take many actions when losing it takes one? I have been shot at by every male out there for no other reason than the fact that I exist. How many chances should I give these humans, Andie? Why am I the one to earn their trust, but they feel no need to earn mine?"

He sounded so damn tired. Just like I'd felt when I'd watched my brother make the hardest choice of his life. It shouldn't be the way it was, but there was no rule that said life had to play out fair. It just played.

"You're right. Trust works both ways. I can't control how others act, but I can control how I behave. What can I do to earn your trust?"

"You've never shot at me, Andie. You already have a portion of it."

"I want all of it."

He looked at me again.

"Why?"

"So you'll help me stop what's happening. If everything you said is true, stopping what's happening is what you want too, and I think we'll need to work together to make that happen."

He grunted but didn't close his eyes or look away. I took that as a promising sign.

"Why don't you come inside with me and get cleaned up again? I'll see if I can find you a shirt you actually get to wear this time after we look at those bites, and maybe you can find a spot to get a little sleep. You look like you need it."

He stood smoothly, but I wasn't as quick to rise. He wasn't the only one needing some well-earned sleep. Unfortunately, I didn't imagine I'd get it. Not in a defenseless house in the middle of nowhere.

We left the barn, and I saw Steve and Sean working together to drag the bodies out of the yard. Sid and Katie were now on the roof instead of the vehicles. And Cody was lugging a ladder toward the side of the barn.

I only felt a little guilty when I went inside. We all had our different roles to play, and it looked like I was the current best fit for being a liaison.

Ted and Roland were in the kitchen, making a hot meal out of whatever they had found in the cupboards, while Patrick sat at the kitchen island with a stack of maps spread out in front of him. All three looked at us when we entered.

"The wiper on my vehicle was bent. Can one of you take a look at it? Molev and I showering then sleeping," I said.

"Together?" Ted asked with a stunned look.

Roland glanced at Molev. "If he's ever bitten, you won't need to remove his head. It's already up his ass."

Ignoring them, I continued through the room, looking for the bathroom.

I heard the water running before I reached it.

"Sounds like someone's beat you to the shower. If you want to stay here to save your place in line, I'll go look for a shirt."

He tipped his head at me, which I took for a nod, and carefully leaned back against the wall to avoid pressure on one of his bites that was either still bleeding or had reopened when he'd been cleaning up bodies.

"It won't take whoever is in there long," I promised, already moving away.

It only took me two minutes to find a hoodie that would fit him. However, as I jogged down the stairs, it occurred to me that I'd never seen him wear anything warmer than a short-sleeved shirt. Was that because he didn't need to or because he couldn't find anything to fit him?

When I found him again, he was staring down at Roni, who chose that moment to open the towel she wore.

"See? All woman."

Molev's gaze swept down her torso and lingered between her legs.

"If you change your mind and want a fuck that will rock your world, come find me."

"Not the kind of relationship building we're looking for, Roni," I said, trying to gauge Molev's reaction.

She closed the towel and winked at me as she walked down the hall.

Instead of staring after her, Molev looked at me with a very odd expression on his face.

"You okay?" I asked. "You look a little shell-shocked."

"Explain."

"I meant you look a little stunned by what just happened."

"I am. No female has openly shown her body to me like that. Until now."

I gave him a small smile. "We lost four of our team in less than two days. Everyone has different ways of processing their grief and the fear that they'll be next. I think sex—feeling something good—is Roni's way of coping with the bad. She wasn't trying to offend you."

"I wasn't offended."

I was about to tell him Roni would be glad to know that when he stepped closer to me.

"Are you grieving? Did you care for any of those males?"

The intensity of the question caught me off guard, and I looked down at the hoodie I held while trying to decide how honest I should be with him.

"After three weeks together, they should feel like my family. But I've worked really hard not to let that happen."

"Why?"

"When we set out with forty-four people, we all understood we would die. Most of us, including myself, only hoped that someone would live long enough to see our task through."

I met his intense gaze.

"What task?"

"Ultimately, to find a way to stop the infection from spreading. The people in command thought our best chance of that was making contact with your kind." I handed him the hoodie. "Go shower. We can talk more once you're clean."

Instead of taking the clothing, he glanced at his bloody hands.

"Right," I said. "I'll hang onto this until you're done."

He disappeared into the bathroom, and while I waited, what I'd said replayed in my head. He probably thought I was cold and heartless like the rest of the crew had believed in the beginning. Maybe I should have dialed back my honesty a little when explaining I wasn't grieving. Yet, I hadn't wanted him to think I was a broken mess he couldn't count on. Anyone like that was already dead. The few of us who were left were here because we knew how to keep it together. For the most part.

I tipped my head back against the wall and let myself relax for a minute. Exhaustion dragged at me. The balance between getting enough sleep to function effectively while still maintaining a rotation was tricky. We'd all done a decent job of saying when we'd reached a wall, and no one had died due to sleep deprivation-related mistakes. Yet. Which was probably why Patrick hadn't protested when I'd said I planned to shower and sleep.

When the shower turned off, I straightened and tried not to yawn. The door opened. Steam billowed out around a barely covered Molev.

Water dripped down the impressive expanse of his shoulders, rolling down his scarred pectorals to skip and jump down his insanely defined abs. The ridge of the towel at his waist ate the drops I'd been following.

In a different life, it might have been a mouthwatering view. Then again, I might have screamed and run for my life because of the skin, ears, and eyes. It was hard to say.

I looked down at his legs. He dripped water from the knees down too. But it was clear water. None of the bites were still bleeding.

"Um, I only found a top. Do you need pants too?" I asked as I stared at his bare feet.

"No. I will clean mine once the blood dries," he said.

My gaze shifted to the bundle of leather he held.

"Okay. Grab any bed. No one will care if you sleep in the buff—I mean, naked."

He grunted and stepped out of the way so I could have my turn at the shower.

Five minutes later, I emerged clean and wrapped in a towel. Roni was in the hall. She wore a white t-shirt that kissed her lower butt cheeks and a pair of men's white briefs. She handed the same items to me.

"Some clean clothes if you want. Patrick said we'll be here for a while, so I was going to wash what I have. Want me to wash yours too?"

I hesitated.

"Riot gear goes over anything," she said.

Sighing, I exchanged dirty for clean.

"Thanks."

"You got it. Now go help Molev pick somewhere to sleep. He's being weird about picking a bed."

The way she grinned made me wonder if she'd tried inserting herself in a bed with him.

I found him in the hallway, glancing into the two bedrooms. A king-sized bed waited in one room. Tom and Mateo were already passed out on it, sleeping back-to-back.

The other room had two twin beds.

"The smaller beds will hold you," I said softly.

He grunted but didn't make any move to claim a bed. Not sure why he was hesitating and too tired to care, I entered the room. With my towel in place, I slipped on the briefs, which were laughably loose, and then the shirt. Once I knew I was covered, I tugged the towel free and used it to dry my shoulder-length hair. I could feel Molev watching me as I tossed that to the floor and pulled back the covers.

"Still didn't make up your mind?" Roni asked, entering the room.

I glanced over my shoulder at Molev. He moved closer to me and my bed as Roni slid under the covers of the other one and patted the space in front of her.

"Offer is still open."

His gaze remained locked on me. Though his expression gave nothing away, I felt pretty confident he was silently begging me to share my bed.

"You can bunk with me," I said. "No sex, and you sleep against the wall."

I got into the bed, staying near the edge. Roni and I didn't have to wait long to see what he'd do. Holding his towel in place, he carefully eased himself behind me.

Roni grinned and winked at me before closing her eyes.

Molev moved slightly behind me, and his exhales gently tickled my cheek. I closed my eyes, feeling oddly comforted by him lying behind me.

"Incoming!"

Katie's yell startled me from the cusp of sleep. Disoriented, I bolted upright.

The bed behind me shifted, and a weight knocked me back down. As I stared at the tight, grey ass blocking my view of the doorway, my brain was still trying to figure out what was going on. Especially when Katie stepped into the room, took one look at Molev, and screamed.

She bolted the wrong way and face-planted into the half-opened door.

"Oh my God," Roni breathed.

I glanced her way and saw she was sitting up and staring wide-eyed at Molev.

Katie rubbed her head and took off down the hall.

"That can't be real," Roni said, drawing my attention again.

I glanced at Molev as his hands covered his front.

"I will remove the infected," he said, striding out of the room as I sat up again.

Roni flopped back onto the mattress, her face flushed.

"What in the hell just happened?" I asked.

"Incoming undead. We're supposed to get up. But from the looks of things, Molev was already up." She lifted her arm, made a fist, and gestured from elbow to knuckles. "About this size. I'm going to need a minute to process."

CHAPTER EIGHT

"WE DON'T HAVE A MINUTE," I SAID, THROWING BACK THE covers.

The cold air on my legs had me calling myself seven kinds of stupid. We both hurried down the hall and ignored Ted's wolf whistle as we started putting on our gear by the door.

"How many?" Roni asked.

"About a dozen," Ted said. "They're lingering at the edge of the trees again. Patrick thinks they'll attack all at once."

"Where did Molev go?" I asked.

"You mean the crazy, naked grey that just stormed out the door?"

I hurried outside in time to see Patrick disappear at a run around the opposite side of the barn. Roni and I both sprinted toward the vehicles where Katie was already climbing on top the MRAP.

"He wants us ready for retreat," Katie said when she saw us.

I started for the Humvee when Patrick's voice came over her radio.

"Stand down. The situation has been handled."

A dozen infected handled in two minutes?

Turning around, I jogged to the other side of the barn. Bodies littered the light dusting of snow near the tree line. Molev bent and picked up something from the ground. Then he turned and ran toward us. Naked.

I wasn't Katie or Tamra. But I wasn't Roni either to openly gawk. So I looked at the snow when he neared.

"No survivors." The wet sound that followed drew my attention up, and I saw the head tumble in the air. Patrick sidestepped the head Molev had tossed to him as Molev walked away from us all.

Patrick looked at me.

"Stay with him," he said.

I didn't immediately move. Instead, I glanced at the head on the ground. "If we want him to trust us, we need to treat him like an equal."

"He's far from being our equal," Patrick said.

"He killed them all faster than I can take a shit," Sean said.

"If he can still treat us like we're his equals, despite our inferiorities, why can't we do the same?" I asked.

"Understood," Patrick said. "Help him move past this. We won't be able to count on him if he's holding a grudge."

"He needs sleep."

"We'll give him as much as we can," Patrick said.

Shivering, I jogged back toward the house. The sudden heat stung my legs, but I didn't start stripping off my gear like Roni was already doing.

"Did you see him?" I asked.

"He was hard to miss."

"Where'd he go?" I asked.

"Shower."

I nodded and went down the hall. The shower turned off just as I reached up to knock on the door.

"Are you all right?" I called through the door. "No new bites?"

The door opened. Once more wrapped in a towel, Molev looked at me.

"A few. But I washed them with soap."

"Do you want any bandages or anything?"

"No. You look tired. You should go back to bed."

I nodded. "That was the plan. I just wanted to check on you first."

"Can I sleep by the wall again?" he asked as I turned to walk away.

"Yep. That space is all yours."

He followed me to the bedroom and took his place while I stripped off my gear and set it on the floor near the bed. Standing there in the t-shirt and underwear, I hesitated to turn in. Roni walked in while I was standing there.

"If you want to switch," she said. "I'm willing."

"No, I'm debating staying up to change over the laundry. I wasn't a fan of running outside without pants or being told I might need to leave them behind."

"Ted said he'd switch them for us," she said, going to her bed.

She turned on her side, facing Molev, and gave him a slow smile. He blinked at her and glanced at me.

Shaking my head slightly, I took my spot beside him, shielding him from Roni's suggestive stare.

"Go to sleep, Roni," I said, closing my eyes.

Heat radiated from Molev, which my still-freezing arms and legs appreciated. Sharing a bunk wasn't new or something I minded. The extra heat was always nice.

That was my last thought before I went under.

The scent of food pulled me from a deep sleep. My jaw

popped as I yawned and stretched then sat up in the dimly lit room.

Katie lay on the bed across from me, Roni's arm draped over her waist. A bruise was forming on her forehead, and I winced on her behalf.

I glanced at my watch. It confirmed that it didn't just feel like I'd slept for hours; I actually had. Nine of them. Real, dead-to-the-world sleep. Twisting around, I checked the empty space behind me. The bedding was cool to the touch, which meant Molev had been gone for a while.

Ignoring my growling stomach, I went to the laundry room and dressed in my clean clothes. When I emerged, basking in the scent of detergent rather than old sweat, I headed for the kitchen next for some food.

I found Derek at the table, his head bobbing as he tried to play solitaire.

"Go get some sleep," I said. "I'll take over for you."

"Thanks. Patrick is keeping watch with Molev and Ted. I'm just supposed to make sure things stay quiet in here so everyone sleeps as long as they can."

"I'm on it."

He left to find a bed, and I helped myself to the stew that was simmering on the stove. I managed a bowl of it and a few games before Roni came down.

"What year is it?" she asked.

"You slept almost ten hours. Katie still sleeping?"

"Yeah. Where's the eye candy?"

"According to Derek, Molev's keeping watch outside with Patrick and Ted. If you're going out there, maybe see if he wants to come in. I don't think he slept much."

"Oh, he slept plenty. He was still snuggled up behind you when Katie crawled in with me a few hours ago. Wish we could have traded partners."

Based on Molev's reactions to Roni so far, I didn't think he'd be okay with trading.

Roni ate quickly and went out to relieve Ted, who came in and went to bed without eating anything. A few more hours passed before the remaining crew woke and made their way to the kitchen. The sky was just starting to lighten.

"Did Patrick tell anyone what our next move will be?" Katie asked.

We all looked at each other, which obviously meant no one had an answer. Sid nudged Mateo when he finished eating, and the pair went out to relieve Molev and Patrick.

Molev's eyes found mine as soon as he entered the kitchen. He didn't say anything. Just took the chair beside me that Sid had vacated.

"What are today's orders?" Katie asked before Patrick, who looked dead on his feet, could leave.

"Hunker down," he said before looking at me. "Keep watch."

I knew he didn't mean outside but Molev.

"If we don't do something soon, I'm going to snap," Roni said, shifting her position on the roof beside me. "What the fuck is Patrick waiting for?"

I didn't have any answer for her. I wasn't sure I fully understood what Patrick was doing.

On the surface, it seemed like Patrick had given us the last four days to rest up and recover from losing Evan, Jackson, William, and Kevin. We slept, we ate, and we kept watch. Mostly on Molev.

"He just threw another body onto the pile," Roni said,

watching through her binoculars. "Why doesn't he just leave them in the woods?"

"Ask him when he comes in," I said.

Every morning, Molev ate with us. Then he left to patrol the surrounding woods. He'd done it since that first day. The moment Patrick slept, Molev had told me he would be back and left without another word. It was Sid on the roof who'd spotted the growing pile of bodies. Patrick had flipped out that we'd let Molev out of our sights. As if we had any chance of keeping up with him.

But the big grey man had returned at dinner and answered Patrick's questions about his day. He'd left to keep the woods clear so we could sleep more peacefully at night. That was it. Patrick hadn't believed him and had tried to go out with him the second day. He hadn't been able to keep up.

I rolled my shoulder, cracking my neck.

"Go take a break and bug Patrick," Roni said. "I've got this until someone else comes up. With him out there, nothing else is moving."

I headed down the ladder and found Patrick at the kitchen table where he was studying the map.

"What kind of body count are you waiting for?" I asked. "He's up to thirty so far. If it weren't this cold, we'd smell it already."

Patrick leaned back in his chair and gestured for me to take a seat.

"Have you gotten anything more out of him?" he asked.

"Like what?"

"Anything that would prove what he's saying is true. That he wants to help us."

"You're waiting for him to say something to validate what he's already said? You can hear how illogical that sounds, right?"

"Has he slipped up? Has he contradicted himself?"

"We've barely talked," I said.

"He's slept next to you three nights in a row."

"He takes the space next to me when I'm already sleeping and is gone before I wake up. There's no pillow talk if that's what you're hoping for. I see him at dinner like everyone else. Then he stays up, watching movies with whoever isn't on guard duty. Rinse and repeat, Patrick. What's going on?"

He leaned forward and laced his fingers together on the surface of the table.

"He was bitten and didn't turn, Andie. We need to know that he's actually on our side before we take him back to Irwin for a cure."

My conversation with Katie came back.

"He needs to be on our side and willing to come with us," I said.

"Of course," Patrick said too quickly. He even added a wave as if that gesture magically erased all of my concerns. It didn't.

"Spread the word," he said. "We head west in the morning."

My chest tightened at the thought of going home.

I nodded and left the kitchen, going back outside. When I reached the barn, I glanced back at the house and saw Mateo on the roof with Roni. I lifted my hand to let them know everything was fine then walked around the side of the barn toward the growing body pile.

It didn't matter that I was armed. Crossing that field in the open was a stupid thing to do, and I hadn't come this far only to die. Which was why I needed to test my theory before we left this place.

Several hundred feet still separated me from the infected pile when Molev jogged out of the trees.

"Hey, Molev. Looks like you're going for a record."

He stopped in front of me and said nothing.

"Can we talk?"

"We are talking."

I smiled slightly. He was very literal.

"There's a place on the west coast that has access to a lot of scientists and other smart people who want to stop this sickness from spreading and save whoever is left. Patrick wants to go there with you. They're going to want to take samples of your blood to study it and see if they can find a way to come up with a cure or a vaccine against whatever is killing us."

He looked off toward the buildings.

"Mya warned us that humans would either fear us or try to use us."

"Mya sounds pretty smart."

"She is."

"Then you already know you're going to get a lot of both— fear and manipulation—if you head west with us."

He pinned me with his gaze. "Do you fear me?"

"There's not much I fear lately. Fear tends to get people killed."

He grunted.

"Should I go?" he asked.

"That's something only you can decide."

"Do you want me to go with you?"

I gave a dry laugh. "I feel like you're testing how selfless I am. I won't pass that test, Molev. Yes, I want you to go with and endure rounds of testing and face the very real possibility that some idiot might try to restrain you just so I can save my nephew.

"See? Not very selfless, am I?"

He studied me for a moment. "If you were selfish, you

would have said you wanted to save yourself. I will go and help you save your nephew."

When he would have turned, I held out a hand to stop him.

"Thank you. When we get there, I'll try to help you identify the people who are likely to screw you over."

"Explain."

"People who would trick you into believing one thing while doing something you're not going to like."

He grunted, which I wasn't sure how to take. He was still hard to read.

"We'll leave tomorrow morning," I said. "See you at dinner?"

He nodded then stayed where he was as I started back. It felt like he was the parent watching to make sure their kid got on the bus safely. When I reached the barn, I turned and waved. He lifted his hand in return and then disappeared into the trees.

Staring at the body pile, I hoped I'd made the right choice in telling him the truth about what might wait for him at Irwin. Patrick was right to think that Molev might be a risk. But in my mind, the risk didn't outweigh the potential salvation.

The day passed quietly into evening, and when Molev returned for dinner, he had a new bite on his arm. Roni offered to clean it for him and take out the stitches that seemed overdue for removal.

He looked at me for a long moment before agreeing.

"I think he was hoping you'd offer to protect him," Katie said with a grin.

Each and every night, Roni invited Molev into her bed. He would turn her down, and she'd just grin, wink, and say she'd check again later like it was all a big game to her. I suspected it probably was. Just like I was pretty sure those invitations were why Molev waited until she was sleeping before lying down and closing his eyes.

"I'd be terrified of getting head from her too," Ted said. "I wouldn't be able to tell if I'd get the growl or bite. I'd rather be with someone who's not all teeth and claws." He gave Katie a playful look and blew her a kiss.

She flushed and turned away from him. The group chuckled. I said nothing. After all the time we'd spent together, I knew that Katie liked Ted. Timing and circumstance were the only things keeping her from taking him up on his offers.

I wondered if that was the same for Roni and Molev.

"Andie, make sure Roni stays on task," Patrick said with a nod down the hall. "Group meeting when they're done."

I left the kitchen and found Roni and Molev in the bathroom. She was kneeling between his legs as he sat on the closed toilet seat. The towel around his waist wouldn't have done much to stop her advances if she hadn't been focused on picking out the stitches.

"I'm glad you at least said yes to this," Roni said to him. "They were already growing in."

He grunted and looked up at me. His eyes appeared more green than yellow in this light. And not nearly as scary as they once had been.

"Patrick wants everyone to meet in the kitchen as soon as you're done," I said, shifting my attention to Roni.

"Hell yeah," she said, understanding what a group meeting meant. "Took him long enough."

She looked up at Molev and nudged his knee to get his attention.

"Our time might be severely limited now. Keep that in mind next time I ask."

He grunted, and I fought not to smile at Roni's disappointed expression.

Sighing, she went back to picking out the remaining stitches. Once the last one pulled free, she set the scissors aside and slipped her hand under his towel along his inner thigh.

He jolted back, and she grinned.

"For both our sakes, I really hope you're coming before we leave."

She rose quickly and sauntered away as he slowly stood.

"Are many women like her?" he asked, staring at the empty hallway.

"I can honestly say I've never witnessed a woman openly grabbing a man like that. So, I don't think there are many like her. Are you okay? Want me to tell her that she's gone too far?"

His gaze met mine, and he blinked at me.

"Can I sleep near you again tonight?" he asked instead of answering.

I couldn't stop my amused grin. "Sure. I'll keep you safe."

"Thank you."

Giving him privacy to get dressed, I returned to the kitchen. Since the space was already filling, I leaned against the wall near the hallway and watched the rest of my team.

Ted teased Katie. Tom added his commentary to whatever conversation was going on. Derek laughed and nudged Mateo. Any other observer would likely say they acted like family. And they did, in a way. But they also held themselves back from each other. Not to the degree that I held myself back but enough. And they were smart for doing it.

I looked at Steve and noted his momentary vacant stare until he caught himself and laughed with Tom. When my gaze shifted to Sid's, I saw he'd been watching Steve, too. He looked at me and nodded slightly before observing the others in the group. He'd had to pull the trigger on more than his share of turned teammates, and I could see the toll it took on him. The toll it took on us all.

Patrick set a radio on the table—so the guards on the roof could hear too—and glanced at me. I checked the hallway, saw Molev striding my way, and nodded to Patrick.

The moment Molev stood beside me, Patrick turned on the radio. His gaze swept the room as he started to speak.

"Four weeks ago, we left our families and friends on a seemingly impossible mission: Find a solution to the sickness killing humanity."

Patrick's gaze landed on Molev. "When we set out, looking for the creatures who unleashed this hell on us, we thought you were the enemy. Will you return to our leaders with us and tell them what you told us? Will you help save what's left of us?"

Patrick was more straightforward than I thought he'd be with Molev, and it relieved me a little.

Molev glanced at me.

"I will share what I know with your leaders."

"Thank you," Patrick said. "Then we leave at first light."

"Please tell me we're going back to Vance for an airlift," Tom said.

"We go back the same way we arrived. Any other questions? No? Good," he said without pause. "Rest up. Tomorrow, we go home."

He stood and left the kitchen, and the rest of the team broke apart.

Roni winked at Molev and motioned with her head that he should follow.

"Perhaps there is another you can find worthy of your companionship," Molev said in response.

"No one that would measure up to you. But don't worry. I'm not giving up hope. It took us three weeks to reach you. It'll take us at least three weeks to return. We'll have time to change your mind."

She strolled away, and Molev stared after her.

I watched him, trying to read what he might be thinking. He caught me staring when he turned back to me.

"Have you ever offered yourself to a male?" he asked.

"Not like that. Roni's very open."

He grunted and started for the door. "I will return."

Once he went outside, I searched for Patrick, who was looking at the maps with Sean.

"Where's our friend?" Patrick asked.

"He went outside. Roni hit on him again."

"Tell her to ease up. We don't want her scaring him off."

"I don't think that's going to happen. If I were to guess, their females obviously don't behave like Roni. He didn't seem offended. Just confused. Like he's still trying to figure us out. I imagine there are a lot of things we do that he finds confusing. For example, not calling for a ride out of here like Tom said."

"Does Molev fully trust us?" Patrick asked.

"I doubt it. I wouldn't if I were him."

"Then it's understandable that I still have reservations. I won't hand-deliver him to what remains of our people until I'm sure of his intentions. Would you?"

I tried imagining Molev meeting Zion. My four-year-old nephew would be terrified. So would Rachel, my sister-in-law. But how I thought Molev would act was more important. I didn't think he'd go on a killing spree or call in the dogs. Yet, I wasn't entirely sure of what he would do.

"Your hesitation is my answer," Patrick said. "We'll use the time it'll take us to reach our destination wisely. Get to know him and give him a better chance to get to know us."

I didn't like the answer but understood it. We'd lost so many of our number to get to where we were and the odds weren't good for everyone who remained. Yet, I wouldn't risk anyone else's life back home to save my own. That was the exact opposite reason I'd signed up for this mission.

With a nod of acknowledgment, I left the room and went outside to watch the moon rise from the roof with Sid. Since Molev started sleeping next to me, I hadn't had to pull a night shift. I didn't feel too guilty about it. Due to his daily patrols, there wasn't a lot of action at night, so guard duty was lighter than usual. Plus, Molev didn't sleep the whole night and always took over for whoever was on top the barn.

But I missed the night sky. With so little light pollution now, it glowed with those millions of distant suns, and nothing was prettier.

Sid nodded to me when I appeared at the top of the ladder. Neither of us spoke for several minutes after I sat next to him. While he studied our surroundings with his night vision binoculars, I soaked in the view of the stars.

"He went into the barn and hasn't come back out," Sid said softly. Then he glanced at me. "Ted and Katie went in there first."

I tore my gaze from the sky to consider the barn. Hadn't I just told Patrick that Molev was still trying to figure us out? Katie and Ted probably weren't the best case study for a normal relationship.

Resigned, I went to the ladder and descended.

It wasn't hard to find Molev. I simply followed the sound of Katie and Ted going at it like screech monkeys.

Molev leaned against some big piece of machinery, arms crossed and openly watching Ted's hips thrusting like mad as Katie dug her heels into his thighs. They were so oblivious that they didn't even notice him. But I knew Katie well enough to know she wouldn't like it.

So I tapped his arm to gain his attention then motioned for him to follow me. I stopped just outside the barn doors.

"I understand that you don't know all the rules we follow in our culture, but watching people have sex isn't okay for most people. Don't ever tell Katie you saw her doing that."

He grunted.

"Can I ask why you were watching?"

"I listened to a book that described sex. I wanted to know if it was telling the truth."

I stared at him for a very long moment, digesting what that meant.

"Molev, you said you lived thousands of years."

"I have."

"Are you saying you've never had sex?"

He glanced back through the barn door. The feel of his hand pressing against my lower back only startled me for a second before he moved me away from the entrance and toward the house.

"They are finished," he said softly.

"Does that mean you're not going to answer my question?"

He glanced at me from the corner of his eye.

"I have not had sex."

CHAPTER NINE

I SHOULDN'T CARE ABOUT HIS SEX LIFE. IT HAD NO IMPACT ON THE future of the world. Yet, didn't every member of this team have a responsibility to bond with him in some way? Or was I just trying to justify my reasons for asking all the questions I was dying to let loose?

Mentally saying screw it, I stopped in front of the door and faced him.

"Is that why you keep saying no to Roni?" I asked.

"No."

He didn't say anything more. I knew that meant he didn't want to talk about her and his continued rejection of her advances. Did that mean I couldn't ask more about his lack of sex life, though?

My gaze swept over his face as I tried to figure out why he had spent thousands of years single. He wasn't ugly. Unusual, yes, but not ugly. His square jaw hinted at a bit of stubbornness, and that wide, generous mouth rarely smiled. Yet, I'd glimpsed potential flashes of humor and his patience. His temper, too.

But I didn't think that was the problem. He'd seemed upset

by the fact Roni had been knocked out during our initial meeting. No, there had to be something else.

"Are you attracted to men?" I asked.

He blinked at me.

"It's fine if you are. I'm not judging."

"I am not attracted to males."

"Okay. I give up then. Why haven't any of your women given you a chance?"

He looked away from me, not at the barn or off in the distance but at the ground a distance from us.

"You don't trust me with the answer," I said, guessing at his reaction.

His gaze shifted back to me, and I suspected I was right.

"Listen, whatever the reason is, it doesn't matter as much as the fact that you still don't trust us. When you're ready, I'll be here to listen."

"We have no women," he said when I moved to go inside.

I stared at him as pieces clicked into place. How he wasn't sure what to make of Roni's advances. The way he'd hesitated to claim a bed. The way he sometimes watched me.

"Is that why so many of you were willing to help the woman find her baby? And what about Mya? Did she need help too?"

He dipped his head. "Drav was tracking two of our kind when he found her. He kept her safe. When the bombs started to fall, she returned to our caves and taught us your language."

"You didn't speak our language until then?"

"No."

The questions started piling up in my head, and I was still trying to decide what to focus on when Katie and Ted emerged from the barn, walking hand in hand.

Molev reached for the door, but I caught his hand.

"I don't want to go inside yet. I still have so many questions."

"You need sleep," he said.

"I do, but not yet."

He glanced from my hand holding his to Katie and Ted. I looked at them, too, and caught a flicker of shock in Katie's gaze before she released Ted's hand and smiled at us.

"It's a little chilly outside tonight. Perfect for watching the stars but not keeping the hands warm. G'night." She slipped inside, leaving Ted behind.

"Well, that stings a little," Ted said, shoving his hands into his pockets.

"Try not to take it too personally," I said. "We live in a world where you lose the ones you love the fastest. She's just trying to protect herself."

He nodded thoughtfully and went inside.

I finally released Molev's hand. "Can we talk some more, or do you want to go in?"

"I'll stay with you," he said.

We strolled away from the door as I let my thoughts circle back to our conversation before the interruption.

"Why didn't you want to tell me you have no women?" As soon as I asked it, that missing piece clicked into place. "Human women are the resource you mentioned. The one that you need. Am I right?"

He hesitated again before answering. "Yes. When we came here, we didn't know what females were. When Drav shared what he discovered, many of us didn't believe him and demanded proof. Many disagreed with Mya's place with our people." He glanced at me, and the corner of his mouth lifted slightly. "Mya did not approve of how we settled our disagreements. Since she came to us, she has helped us navigate the differences in our worlds and has shown us that we need to find a better way to live. Here, on the surface."

"This is better?" I asked.

"No. The hounds and the infected must be stopped. Only then will we all have a chance at a better life."

He looked up at Sid on the roof for a moment. "I would ask that you not share this information with the rest of your team yet. Just as Patrick intends to use the time it will take to return to your origin base to test my integrity, I intend to do the same. Very few of the interactions we have had with humans have gone well. We are mistrusted, threatened, and attacked when all we do is offer our help. And why? Because we are different. Because we were locked away under your earth and released at the same time as the hounds. Because two of our kind took the shots fired at them as a challenge and answered it in kind."

He exhaled heavily.

"There is much we need to change about this world if we both want to survive in it, Andie. Can I trust you to help me make those changes?"

"If you really are the person you seem to be, yes. You can." We continued toward the barn in silence and paused when we reached the doors. "If you're after women, why not take Roni up on her offer?"

"You have no male in your life. Why are you not offering to have sex with me?"

"I don't know you."

"Should choosing a partner be different for me?"

"I guess not. Although, I have to tell you that most human men are just after a quick hookup."

"Explain."

"A one-night stand. Where two people have sex once and never see each other again. I think that's what Roni's after, to be honest. The not seeing each other again thing would be a little hard to manage, though."

"I am not interested in one night. I want many nights to erase the memory of the thousands I spent alone."

"That woman who was with you. Cassie? Was she with one of you too?"

"Yes. She chose one while we were helping her find her son."

"Was that a condition of your help?"

"No. There are very few children left at Whiteman and none as small as what she described. We helped because we hoped to see the baby for ourselves."

The impact of having no females of their own hit home then. No women. No kids. No families.

"Will you tell me more about what your life was like before you came here?" I asked.

"Our lives? In the beginning, it was filled with survival, much like this. As time passed, I saw signs of darkness creeping into a few of my brothers. Some grew more distant. Restless. Others withdrew, choosing to live more isolated from each other.

"Their withdrawal ate at me, feeding my own hopelessness. In those caves, we had no true lives. No future. No hope. There is nothing there for us but an endless existence. Is it wrong to want more than that?"

He watched me steadily, waiting for my answer.

"No. It's not wrong to want more. But you understand that my government isn't going to just hand over women, though, right?"

He grunted again and looked off into the night.

"You need sleep," he said finally.

"And you don't?"

"I need less than you."

"I wouldn't share that bit of information either, or Patrick will have you pulling double guard shifts."

Molev nodded, and we started for the house. A movie already played inside, and Roni was on the couch with Katie and Ted. All three watched as Molev followed me down the hall.

I could only imagine how Katie had interpreted the hand-holding. Talking about us had probably deflected attention from her and Ted coming in so close together.

In the bedroom, I kicked off my boots and removed my jacket, adding both to my gear pile. Molev waited for me to settle in then took his place.

I should have fallen asleep quickly. I didn't, though. My mind went over what he'd revealed and what it might mean for our mission.

Patrick thought Molev might help us find a possible cure. Molev was willing to go along on the grounds of helping because he wanted women in return. Asking for women in exchange for a cure might be the very thing that would trigger the government to do what I'd said they wouldn't.

What would Molev do if the government tried to force his compliance without giving anything in return? I didn't want to find out.

He moved slightly behind me. A weight settled on my waist. His arm. He leaned closer and let out a long exhale.

"My fate is in your hands," he said softly.

He settled closer to me, his chest against my back, and his breathing evened out.

It took me a long while to do the same, and when I woke, he was gone, just like each of the previous mornings.

Roni sat on the bed across from me and extended a cup of coffee as soon as I opened my eyes.

"How was it?" she asked.

"How was what?" I took the cup and sat up.

"Sex with an alien, Andie. Please tell me you didn't let that ship sail. That mast was made for—"

"We slept. That's it," I said.

She groaned. "Andie. We're trying to build interspecies relations here. He's obviously interested in you."

I realized how all the time we'd spent together might seem to everyone else.

"Don't mistake growing trust for attraction, Roni. That's all that's going on. But if you want to build a different kind of relationship, go for it. Just maybe ease up on your game a little. He wants to get to know someone first before jumping in bed with them."

She grinned at me. "He's one of those?"

"I think they might all be," I said.

"I haven't had a shy guy in ages. This is going to be fun." She popped up from the bed and left me to sip my coffee and get dressed.

The sky was just starting to lighten when I walked into the kitchen and viewed the decimated remains of a home-cooked breakfast. I grabbed a pancake, rolling it up to eat it on the go, and headed out the door.

Some of the team was already quietly packing gear in the vehicles while the others kept watch.

I didn't see any sign of Molev until I looked up. He crouched on the barn, scanning the tree line on the other side.

Roni came out of the house behind me. "Patrick said that we're ditching the electric cars. He doesn't think there will be a need for scouting missions on the way back."

It made sense to leave them when there were only fifteen of us. Sixteen if we counted Molev. We needed at least two people per vehicle, one to drive and one to watch. It was safer than driving alone.

"Mind if I hitch a ride with you?" Roni asked with a grin.

"Not at all. But you know he might not choose my vehicle."

She snorted and followed me to one of the MRAPs. The back of it was already packed with rations and supplies, still leaving ample room for another passenger. In the yard, Patrick signaled for everyone to load up and waved for Molev to join him.

"He's a beast," Roni said, watching him jump from the roof. "Can you imagine his level of stamina in bed?"

"I heard the big muscley types get winded more easily," I said, only half joking.

Patrick spoke to Molev, and whatever Molev said in return had Patrick shaking his head.

"I can't argue with you there," Roni said, continuing our conversation. "But something tells me this one would be different."

"Was it the ears that gave him away?" I asked.

She snorted at my joke then groaned when Molev jogged toward the MRAP at the front of the line.

"He's hitching a ride with Roland?" She thumped the dash. "Dammit."

"We're moving out," Patrick said over the radio. "Don't run Molev over if he starts lagging."

Roni grabbed her radio as I started the engine.

"Repeat that," she said.

"You heard me. He's running alongside the convoy until he's tired," Patrick said.

Outside my window, I caught a glimpse of him walking alongside the fueler as it started out. Our vehicle brought up the rear.

"Maybe this isn't so bad," Roni said. "If he gets tired, we'll be the ones to pick him up.

However, Molev ruined her plans by running for hours.

When we did finally stop for a short break, he disappeared into the trees. She waited until the last second to get back in and tossed the MRE she'd wanted to offer him to the floor.

"Now he's just showing his sexy off," she said as she watched him start running again.

"Or he's just doing what he did when he followed us from Parsons to Vance," I said.

Even though I knew I was probably right, his stamina was impressive. As was the fact that he didn't seem to get winded at all while running endlessly. Not even a little.

When we hit our first roadblock, we all got a glimpse of what Molev could do. He jumped on top the Stryker before it punched its way through, then leap-frogged on the vehicles that followed, clearing off infected.

Roni and I heard him land on our cab. A leather boot kicked off the infected trying to climb up her side. A grey hand plucked the one off my windshield. And then we were through, cruising behind the others.

"I'll check for clingers," Roni said, crawling toward the back.

When she reached it, she chuckled.

"Looks like Molev is already on it. I don't need to be infected to want to bite some of that. Mmm."

"Easy, Roni," I said. "Maybe you should try playing hard to get for a while."

"Life's too short for that," she said, making her way back to her seat.

We drove 'til an hour before dusk. Patrick selected another house in the middle of nowhere with sight lines from all sides.

"Rig the lights just in case," he ordered as soon as we stopped. "I want a team of six sweeping the house. Tamra, Sid, Mateo, Roni—"

The crack of wood interrupted him, and everyone's

attention shifted to Molev as he disappeared inside the broken door. Patrick immediately looked at me.

"If he doesn't want to be a weapon, he should stop acting like one," he said.

"I don't think it was the tasks he objected to but being told when and how to do them," I said. "He seems to enjoy free will."

Patrick said something under his breath and focused on the four he'd called out.

"Sweep the house once he's clear," he said, his tone laced with annoyance.

I gathered up an armful of MREs and waited for the go-ahead to enter. When I did, the shower was already running, and Roni leaned against the wall just outside it.

"He already in there?" I asked.

"Sure is. He handled four infected. Waited until he took them out back to deal with them so nothing's dirty in here. Isn't that sweet?"

She didn't sound impressed. Like Patrick, she sounded annoyed, and I wasn't entirely sure why.

"You okay?" I asked.

She sighed and shook her head as if clearing it. "I'm fine. Frustrated. Tired. Hungry. It's making me moody."

I handed her one of the MREs. "Snack while you wait. I'll go look for clothes for him."

I was still searching one of the dressers when he found me. With only a towel wrapped around his waist, he slipped into the room and closed the door behind him.

Then he locked it.

Maybe that would have worried me if he didn't immediately head for the bed and lie on it.

"Was it the running that did you in or the running without eating or drinking?"

He grunted, and I tossed an MRE pack so it landed squarely on his chest.

"Eat, Molev. You're no good to anyone dead." I moved toward the door.

"Don't," he said.

I looked back at him. "Eat. Don't make me say it again. I'll be back in a minute with something to drink. Then you can sleep."

The corner of his mouth did that twitch thing that I hadn't seen in a while, and he didn't try stopping me from leaving a second time. When I saw Roland in the hallway, I told him to stand next to the door and not to let anyone in.

He didn't question me; he simply nodded and leaned against the wall.

When I returned, Roni was there, talking to him.

"Why can't anyone go in?" she asked.

"Because he's not in a people kind of mood right now. Get some sleep, and I'll try to talk him into less running tomorrow."

She didn't try to follow me inside.

When I entered, I found Molev sitting on the bed and working his way through his second MRE. I poured him a glass of water from the pitcher I'd brought and watched him drink it in a few gulps and set the empty glass aside.

I sat on the floor, watching him eat. He seemed distracted, not even noticing what he was eating.

"Just how far past done did you push yourself today?" I asked.

He finished his bite and focused on me.

"Do you trust Patrick?" he asked.

"I trust that we have the same goals."

"What goals are those?"

"To bring you to the leaders and the scientists so you can

help us find a solution for stopping the infection. Why are you asking?"

"If you trust that he means to return to those leaders, then you need to question his ability to read a map. He wasted too many hours driving south, only to drive north again. West to drive east. We've made very little progress from our original location. Fifteen miles at most."

"Patrick knows how to read a map. He keeps an eye on the roads ahead and reroutes us around any trouble and cities. Even the smaller towns give us trouble. Each day, there are more infected in the outlying areas. We were lucky to only hit one roadblock today."

Molev grunted and resumed eating.

"Ask him about tomorrow's route before we leave," I suggested. "He'll show you. It took us three weeks to reach Parsons. Granted, we stayed at a few bases for a full twenty-four hours so everyone could rest, and there were a few bases we helped along the way, too. But still, it took a lot longer than it would have before the quakes."

"What do you mean you helped bases?"

"Bases like Vance are struggling to maintain the number of personnel needed to operate. We ran across one that needed some extra support clearing out some infected so they could evacuate. We lost a four-man team there but saved twenty who probably would have eventually died."

Molev finished his second meal and poured himself some more water.

"How much sleep do you need every day?" I asked.

"You're concerned for me?"

"Yes, Molev. Please take better care of yourself. We need you."

He looked down at his hands for a moment then moved

over and lay down. Turning his head to watch me, he patted the empty space beside him.

"I told them to stay away. You'll be safe without me crowding your space."

"Words and a towel will not protect me from Roni's quick hands. You will."

I chuckled and got up to join him, lying on my back this time so I could look at him.

"I told her to ease up, but she liked what she saw that morning you flew out of bed naked."

"Liking the way someone looks does not entitle a person to their time or attention."

"You're absolutely right. Now, close your pretty eyes and get some sleep."

His mouth did that corner twitch again, and he closed his eyes.

"Thank you for caring, Andie. Not many would."

I felt a little tug in my middle at that, and I imagined the life—or rather *lives*—he had up until then. How lonely he had been. It was stupid of me to feel sorry for him. Stupid to care in any way. Yet, if I couldn't care about him, the person who could potentially save us all, who else should I care about?

Rolling toward him, I moved closer and closed my eyes. I wasn't sure he'd want any form of comfort from me, not that I was great at giving it. A hug for hurt feelings and a kiss near a scrape I could manage. But how did a person comfort someone who'd been alone his whole life? Someone who probably had no standards for appropriate social interaction.

Well, he knew enough to understand that Roni groping him under his towel hadn't been right.

While I was still debating what to do, the weight of his arm settled across my waist. I slipped my arm over his in return. He tensed, and I almost smiled.

"Relax, Molev. Your virtue is safe with me."

He exhaled heavily, and I wondered if he'd been afraid I would start acting like Roni.

It took him so long to fall asleep I started to doze myself until I heard his light snore. It was cute and made me smile. Then my stomach growled, reminding me I hadn't eaten dinner.

Molev's steady breathing paused, and his eyes opened the second I moved my hand.

"Sorry," I said softly. "Go back to sleep. I'm just going to get something to eat and be right back."

He grunted and closed his eyes again, removing his hand from my waist.

I got up and used an extra blanket to cover him before leaving the room. Patrick was in the kitchen, studying the maps when I entered. He didn't look up at me, so I went to the contents of the cupboards spread out on the counter and grabbed a pack of toaster pastries.

"He noticed you were looping around today. You might want to go over the route with him tomorrow, so he understands what you're doing."

"Why?" he asked without looking up.

"A show of collaboration to build trust."

Patrick sighed and sat back.

"Or opening ourselves for a potential ambush. He sleeps for a few hours then leaves until dawn. He says he's scouting for nearby infected, but what if he's not? What if he's meeting with others of his kind? He's already proven they can tail us without being spotted. Should I risk the lives of everyone on this team to test his trust with the location of our destination?"

His eyes were red. He had an empty cup of coffee next to him. His jacket was on the chair beside him.

"Did you eat or go straight for coffee and maps?" I asked.

He rubbed his hand over his hair, clearly frustrated.

"Just say what you need to say, Andie."

"I wasn't suggesting our destination but tomorrow's route just before we leave. Low risk since you change on the fly, based on what you see ahead. And you need to eat," I said, turning away to look at the food options.

"I'll eat after I'm done here."

I picked up a single-serve container of stew and popped it into the microwave. When I glanced at the dying light in the window, I saw he was already back to studying the maps. I didn't envy him for his job or the responsibility that came with it. Or the guilt. He'd changed a lot in the past weeks, and I could see the toll each death took on him.

The microwave beeped. He didn't look up. I went over to him and held out a spoon. When he looked up, I pulled the maps away from him and handed him the spoon.

"I'm going to tell you the same thing I told him. Take care of yourself. You're no good to us sleep-deprived or dead."

He didn't reclaim the maps when I turned my back on him to retrieve the stew from the microwave.

"Thank you, Andie," he said tiredly.

"Thank me by getting at least six hours of sleep tonight. There are enough of us to pull shifts so you can manage it."

Taking my pastry, I returned to the bedroom and quietly ate before slipping under the blanket next to Molev. His arm immediately looped around my waist and tugged me back against his chest.

His warmth enveloped me, and I fell asleep almost immediately.

CHAPTER TEN

THE SPACE BEHIND ME WAS EMPTY WHEN I WOKE TO THE WORST sound on the planet.

A howl.

I dove out of bed for my gear and was out the door before my eyes were fully open. Everyone else was scrambling too. Silent chaos ensued as we checked gear and weapons. We knew what a howl meant. We'd run into hounds before. And it was only dumb luck that those of us in the house were alive.

Two steps behind Roland, I rushed out the door and veered for the nearest light. One by one, they flooded the night with their brilliance.

I backed away from mine and gripped my weapon, scanning for eyes.

"Who's on the launcher?" Patrick demanded, coming out the door.

"On it," Steve and Sid called, each racing for an MRAP. Tamra hurried to join Sid, and Roni got in with Steve.

"Be ready!" Patrick scaled the ladder to the roof to coordinate our defense until sunrise.

I looked at my watch. Three a.m.

A calm certainty settled over me as the two engines started. We would never make it until dawn. The lights would draw in the infected, and there were too few of us left. They'd overwhelm one or more of us, and our lights would fall, one by one. The dog would come in and finish off anyone still alive.

"Molev's out there somewhere," Patrick called from above. "Try not to shoot him."

Another howl rang out, closer than before. One of the MRAP's lights blazed a path through the darkness beyond the floodlights while it backed up toward the house. The second one drove around to the other side. Both possible escape routes if things went bad quickly.

But more importantly, both were equipped with MK19s, rapid-fire grenade launchers. The only thing we'd found that could slow one of those dogs.

"Eyes!" someone yelled.

"Sid," I heard Patrick say. "We've got eyes on the hound southeast of your position."

A roar split the night. Even though I now knew it belonged to Molev, I still had that same feeling of not wanting to ever meet the creature that made that sound.

"Hold, Sid. It's circling. Steve, it's following the edge of the field, heading west. It's turned north. It's moving at—shit. Hold fire. Molev's running right at it."

Unable to see a thing beyond the lights, I side-stepped closer to Sean's position. It didn't do any good, but I couldn't think of anything beyond the fact that Molev was running at one of those dogs. Sure, he said he could kill them. But alone?

He'd also said he could die, and I'd seen what those hounds could do.

We needed Molev alive.

"Dammit," I said under my breath.

The dog broke out in vicious snarls that ebbed and swelled in volume.

"He's carrying the fucking thing toward us," Patrick yelled. "Steve! One hundred and ten yards due west of the house. Now."

"Patrick, no!" I yelled a beat before the bap-bap-bap of the launched grenades resonated in my chest.

I stared at the darkness in disbelieving horror.

"Move, Molev!" I screamed.

Explosions erupted. Light flared, momentarily blinding me. Had I just witnessed Patrick destroy our chance for a real future?

Zion's tear-streaked face rose up into my mind, feeding my anguish.

"No," I said brokenly.

Something ran at me from the darkness, too fast to see, until it caught me by the arms.

I blinked up at Molev's yellow-green eyes.

"I need the light to kill the hound." A howl rang out in time with his words.

"Okay."

He set his forehead to mine. A shot rang out at the same time he jolted. He snarled in my face and left as quickly as he arrived.

"Andie, are you all right?" Patrick called.

I looked up at the roof and saw his sidearm in his hand.

"He was trying to use the light to help kill it," I said. "Like he *told us* he could. He's going to try again. Stop fucking shooting at him, and let him try to save us."

Patrick held my gaze for a moment and shook his head as if he thought he was about to make the dumbest decision of his life.

"All right. Let's see what he can do."

Another storm of snarling broke out in the darkness. Patrick lifted the night vision to his eyes, pivoting slowly as he scanned for Molev.

"North-west," he called out. "Hold your fire."

The need to go there and ensure no one else shot at him had me stepping away from my assigned light. I took two steps before I realized what I was doing and looked back at Sean. He caught my gaze and nodded.

Taking that as permission, I left my spot and hurried to where Patrick was looking.

"Knife!" Molev yelled from the darkness.

Since I was right by the door, I darted inside, grabbed a knife from the butcher block, and rushed back out.

The yowling was louder, and I ran toward the sound.

Then I saw him. The beast struggled in Molev's straining and bulging arms. The saliva dripped from its fangs. Glowing, blood-red eyes darted toward me, and it thrashed harder to get free.

Molev shuffled forward three more steps, crossing into the dimmer edge of the light.

Smoke wisped up from the dog's black hide, and a terrifying whine-snarl ripped from its open jaws.

Molev pivoted so he faced the darkness and arched backward, using his body weight to flip the hound and drive its head into the ground. With one hand, he pinned the hound in the ring of light. It writhed under Molev's hold but was too dazed to slip free.

"Throw it to me," Molev said, holding out his free hand.

I didn't think. I just tossed the blade and hoped it wouldn't stab him. Molev caught the knife mid-flip and drove it into the hound's chest. Again. And again.

Wet noises filled my ears. Bones cracked. Chunks flew.

The dog's struggles grew more desperate. Even when a

large grey hand disappeared into that black chest cavity and came out holding a black stone that pulsed with a negative light, it clawed at him.

Molev's fist closed around the rock and squeezed. The heart exploded into dust that ran out of his fisted hand. The hound stilled even as its fur continued to smolder slowly.

Panting from the exertion of the fight, Molev looked up at me.

"Remember, they hunt in pairs or packs. Stay in the lights, Andie."

Twin red dots winked into existence behind him then disappeared. I opened my mouth to warn him. Before I could make a sound, Molev was yanked back into the darkness.

"There's another one! Does anyone have eyes on Molev?" Fear staked me as I listened for someone to say he was okay.

A yip and a roar came from the opposite side of the house. The scream that followed gave me my answer.

I wanted to run toward it, but common sense kicked in. Molev had proven he could kill them. With all the noise they were making, I needed to do my job and guard my assigned light. So I ran back to my position, scanning the darkness beyond the light for more glowing twin dots of red, and hoped we were only dealing with a pair, not a pack.

"Catch her." Molev's yell rose above the scuffle of sound from the other side of the house.

Another scream pierced the night. Patrick swore, and a scrabble of noise came from the roof above.

The burst of snarling that followed drowned out all other sound, making it impossible to hear distinct words when someone shouted. Then, Molev roared again. After a few more seconds of chaos, everything went silent.

Heart racing, I listened and waited for Patrick to say something. What I heard was the sound of someone crying. A woman. Either Katie or Tamra since I couldn't imagine Roni emitting those heartbroken sobs.

"Ted's gone," Patrick said. "Both dogs are down. Molev's hurt. Stay at your posts. With the lights and the sound, every undead within a mile of this place will be headed our way."

The next few hours passed in an exhausting blur. Molev patrolled just outside the pool of light, killing any infected that found their way to the farmhouse so we wouldn't need to fire any weapons and attract more.

Dawn gave me the first real glimpse of the damage the dogs had done to him. Long gashes scored his back. I couldn't believe he'd stayed on his feet for hours after receiving them.

"Go shower," I said when he would have continued circling the house.

He paused and glanced at me.

"I mean it. Go shower. I'll get the first aid kit." It contained a mess of stuff I didn't know how to use. And bandages, which I did know how to use. But I didn't think that would be enough. Some of those gashes were spread apart and hard to look at.

Hopefully, Roni could figure out how to give stitches as well as she could remove them.

Molev grunted and changed direction to head inside. His stride wasn't as purposeful as usual.

I glanced at Sean.

"Go," he said.

The shower was already running by the time I knocked on the bathroom door.

"Can I come in?" I asked.

"Yes."

I was expecting him to be behind the curtain. Instead, he stood in the small open space in front of the sink. With one hand braced on the counter, his other gripped the neck of his shirt behind his head. He tried pulling it up and over. Grunted and stopped.

"Here. Let me," I said.

"No."

The harsh command stopped me.

"I'm covered in infected blood. It's too dangerous."

I shook my head.

"If you haven't noticed, everything is too dangerous lately. And this wouldn't be my first time touching contaminated blood. If I start running away from it now, I'm as good as dead. So stop being a baby, and let me help you get this off so we can patch you up."

He turned his head to hold my gaze, and I arched a brow at him.

"I promise not to touch you inappropriately. Just let me help you, Molev."

He grunted.

I set the first aid kit on the sink and pulled out the scissors. He held still as I moved his long hair aside and cut his shirt free.

"Need help with the pants?" I asked.

"I can get them off without cutting them," he said.

"So can I."

He didn't fight me when I tugged the tie loose and worked the material down his thick thighs. I kept my head turned as I sank to my knees so he wouldn't feel embarrassed. The weight of his hand settled on my head. It almost felt like he was caressing my hair until he lifted his foot and stepped out of his pants. I understood then that he'd only been using me for balance.

When he turned away from me, I glanced at his backside again, surveying the damage. I hadn't meant to ogle when he was obviously in so much pain. Yet, that was exactly what happened. Even broken and bloody, he was beautiful to look at, defined like a bodybuilder, but without the overabundance of spray tan or veins.

He stepped into the shower and closed the curtain, blocking my view and breaking my trance.

I shook my head at myself, realizing how tired I was, and went to the sink to wash. Most of the blood on his shirt had been dry, so the water ran clear. When I turned off the tap, I noted the absence of washing sounds on the other side of the curtain.

Molev had to be even more tired than I was.

"You were gone when I heard the howl," I said. "How much sleep did you get last night?"

"Not much."

"No running to wherever we're headed today, okay? I want you sleeping in a vehicle if you can manage it."

He grunted.

"I'm going to get Roni to see if she knows how to close those gashes up."

I left the bathroom and found several of the others, including Patrick, waiting in the kitchen.

"His back is torn up," I said. "He needs stitches. A lot of them."

Roni shook her head. "I saw his back. I can sew him, but I think he needs someone who actually knows what they're doing."

"There's a FOB west of Woodward," Patrick said. "They should have a medic there."

Should. Woodward wasn't one of the bases we'd stopped at on the route to Parsons because of its closer proximity to the nearest town. The possibility of finding it overrun or simply abandoned like the one near Wichita was there.

"How long will it take us to reach it?" I asked.

Patrick looked down at his map.

"An hour or two if we risk the highway. Most of the day if we take a route that avoids drawing more attention than the FOB can handle when we arrive at their gates."

I considered the number of infected that could possibly tail us if we took the highway versus how badly Molev was injured.

Based on what I knew of him, the longer we took to get to the base, the greater the risk to him because he would insist on helping even if it made him bleed again. And he'd lost so much blood already. Taking the highway wasn't a guarantee that there would be more infected or roadblocks. We saw enough of those on the backroads too. But there was more risk. Cars still clogged the highways. We could push through most of them, but that meant noise and potential damage to our vehicles.

"We should have airlifted from Vance," Tom said tiredly.

Patrick's expression hardened. "This mission isn't without risks. You knew that when you signed up."

"Let's not sidetrack the discussion," I said.

"How bad is he?" Patrick asked.

"See for yourself," Roni said, nodding toward the opening to the kitchen.

Molev entered with only a towel wrapped around his waist. It was a lot smaller than the last one and barely covered his hips. Roni wasn't ogling him this time, though. She nudged Tom off his chair and turned it so Molev could sit.

"Don't lean back," she warned.

He sat with a slightly pained exhale and met Patrick's gaze.

"I cannot fight more hounds and win until I heal. You must reach the next base as quickly as possible if you do not want to lose more of your team."

Patrick studied Molev for a long minute then nodded.

"Roni, bandage him up as best as you can. We'll move out when you're done."

She used some glue sticks on the smaller gashes, closing what she could, and bandaged the rest.

"I've made a bed for him in Andie's ride," Katie said, coming into the kitchen. Her eyes were red and puffy from crying.

"Thank you, Katie," Molev said. He stood and set a hand on her shoulder. "Do not give up hope. This world still has much to offer you."

She gave him a wavery smile and nodded.

He released her and looked at me. "Is there anything I can wear until my leathers are dry?"

"I'll look," I said.

After finding some shorts, I grabbed his dirty clothes from the bathroom and rejoined him in the kitchen. He had an empty bowl in front of him, and Katie was refilling his glass of water. I didn't hand him the shorts but knelt at his feet.

"I can pull them up for you when you stand," I said. "Less stretching that way."

He grunted and let me help him dress. Once the towel was gone, Katie and I followed him out the door, watching the way he limped to the vehicle.

"Sit in back with him," I said to her when we reached the MRAP.

She nodded and helped him to the makeshift bed while I got in behind the wheel.

Patrick's voice crackled over the radio. "We don't stop unless we have to."

Engines started, and I glanced back at Molev, who already lay on his stomach. His grey skin looked paler.

"You still with me, Molev?" I called over the noise of the engine.

He lifted his head and looked me in the eyes.

"I will always be with you, Andie."

Those words startled me. While I knew he meant them in a saving-the-world kind of way, my mind questioned a different direction. A direction with meanings I didn't want to explore.

Facing forward again, I focused on following the Stryker.

Patrick took the most direct route to the highway, which led to our first roadblock of the day. Infected swarmed the vehicles, but we punched our way through and continued on. We encountered another trap avoiding Fairview but found Highway 412 relatively clear of traffic and easy to travel. Much better than some of the dirt roads we'd encountered.

A few infected sprinted out from the occasional buildings we passed, but they quickly fell behind. The highway was, overall, a faster way to travel. Then we started hitting patches with steep shoulders. All it would take was one roadblock we couldn't penetrate, and we'd be screwed. I tried not to let that thought take root.

We traveled in silence for another quarter of an hour before Patrick's voice came over the radio.

"How's our passenger?"

"Resting," Katie said behind me.

"The FOB is on the other side of Woodward. We'll need to go around to avoid attracting too many infected."

Shortly after that, we turned south off the highway until the first road west.

"Keep sharp. We're just south of Mooreland."

I wasn't sure how big the place was, but the road remained clear until we turned south again and came up to a plant on our left. A single pickup truck blocked the road. Before we reached it, I heard a pop.

"Was that a tire or gunfire?" Katie asked me.

"We're under fire," Patrick said on the radio.

The Stryker picked up speed. I did the same.

Something tumbled from the bed of the truck before the Stryker reached it. The man got to his feet and took aim again. I focused on the taillights in front of me. Nothing else mattered. Nothing else could matter.

Shots rang out, one after another, until I heard one ping off our vehicle.

"Molev, we're fine," I heard Katie say. "There's no need to get up."

"We're not stopping," I added. "Stay down."

"What is happening?" he asked.

"A roadblock. Humans this time. They're probably looking for supplies and trying to shoot out our tires. It won't work."

They'd likely lose their lives for nothing.

This was the part I hated most about the current state of the world. The ugly desperation was bringing out the worst in some people.

"Molev is bleeding again," Katie said. "And I think he passed out."

I thought she was telling me until Patrick's voice came over the radio. "We're almost there."

We picked up speed, continuing south for another few miles, then turned west again. Impatience pulled at me, and I found myself glancing back at Molev with more frequency. When Patrick turned us north fifteen minutes later, I knew we were almost there.

However, the sight of the tiny Woodward FOB didn't bring any sense of relief. There was no way it had a medic.

I glanced back at Molev again as we approached the gate and caught Katie's worried expression.

"He said he's tough," I told her.

She nodded.

"The dog lunged into the light and caught Ted. I wasn't thinking. I ran toward the edge of the light. Molev came out of nowhere and threw me on the roof. That's why he's so scratched up. The dog got him from behind when he was throwing me."

"It's not your fault, Katie. You know that."

"Knowing something and feeling something are two separate things."

"I'm sorry Ted's gone," I said.

"Me too. I liked him. A lot."

We let ourselves into the unmanned gate and drove down the length of pavement to a second fence. This one had guards that radioed us, asking for identification and the reason we were there. Patrick gave his usual identification then added, "We need a medic. Do you have one?"

"We do."

The guard directed us around to another secured building. I parked beside it and hopped out as several men came running out with a stretcher. Patrick jogged over and joined me at the back of the MRAP.

"Stay with him at all times, Andie," he said before he reached us. "No mistakes."

I understood what he wasn't saying. These were new people, and we'd messed up enough already when it came to Molev.

Patrick reached for the door, and I looked at the medic.

"It's a grey," I said. "And he's immune to the dogs and the infected. Save him, and you might be saving us all."

The men with the stretcher didn't hesitate once the door was open. They got in, took Katie's place, and worked together to get Molev onto the stretcher. I could see the strain when they lifted him out and walked toward the building.

I stuck with them, which was a good thing because Molev

groaned and lifted his head before they reached the door. When he saw the strange men, he growled.

"Molev," I said, moving closer to his head.

His gaze found mine, and the growling stopped.

"We're at the base. This is the medic. He'll be able to stitch you up."

Molev's gaze shifted to the closest man, and I could read the mistrust in his eyes before they shifted back to me.

"I'll be right here with you," I said. "I'm not going anywhere."

He grunted and rested his head on the stretcher once more, but he didn't close his eyes. They stayed fixed on me as we made our way inside and down a long hall to a makeshift operating room.

The medic moved quickly, prepping himself and the supplies he'd need.

"How long ago did this happen?" he asked.

"About six hours ago," I said. "Why?"

"It looks older," he said, examining Molev's back and arms.

"Can you still stitch him up?" I asked.

"I'll try. It looks like he's already been stitched once, so it should work. Do you know if he has any allergies to our medicines?"

"I don't know."

He frowned slightly. "I don't like the idea of doing this without anesthetic, but I'd rather not introduce anything that he might not tolerate. Does he trust you?"

"He is listening and can speak for himself," Molev said. "Yes, I trust Andie."

"Sorry. Usually, I'd use a local anesthetic to numb the area I need to work on. It's less painful for you and keeps you from moving. I don't know if it's safe for you, though. Were you given anything to numb the pain when you received your arm stitches?"

"No. I won't move," Molev said.

I could see the doubt on the medic's face.

"I've seen him do things no human could do. If he says he won't move, he won't move," I said.

"Okay." He turned away for a moment, and I went to stand near Molev's head.

"Do you want me to hold your hand or anything?" I asked softly.

Molev immediately shifted both arms up the table so that his hands rested by his head. His grip was warm and firm when his fingers wrapped around mine.

"Are you ready?" the medic asked.

CHAPTER ELEVEN

True to his word, Molev didn't flinch once while the medic stitched him. He did move, though. Just his thumbs. They swept over the backs of my hands in slow strokes, almost as if he was comforting *me*.

"That's the last one," the medic said, moving away from Molev and straightening his back. "You'll need to keep those covered for the first few days, and they'll need to come out in two weeks." He covered everything in a salve and placed bandages over it all.

While he worked, Molev continued trailing his thumbs over my skin. That stopped the second the medic taped the last bandage into place.

"If you're ready, we'll move you to a more comfortable room."

Molev shifted his legs over the side of the table and stood up.

"I was going to have them move you, but if you'd rather walk…"

"I would," Molev said.

Rather than walking out the door, he held his hand out to me.

If Molev were a human, I would have said it was a cover to hide his weakened state. But based on the mistrustful look he gave the medic as he showed us the way, I saw the gesture for what it was. A sign of his trust in me.

Molev didn't walk as slowly as he had getting into the MRAP that morning. But he sure wasn't jogging like he usually did. He kept his pace steady as we wound our way through the building to an empty room with two military-grade twin beds.

"Sorry it's not better," the medic said.

"It's fine," Molev said.

The door closed behind us, and Molev released my hand. I thought he'd collapse onto his bed. Instead, he pushed them together.

"Rest, Andie."

"I'm only lying down if you promise not to get up until I do."

He grunted.

"I'm not taking that for an answer this time. I want your word for two reasons. First, we're in a new place, and I don't trust them not to shoot at you. And second, you need some real sleep Molev. Please."

"I promise not to leave this room without you."

I'd take it.

Leaving my boots on, I got into bed and watched him ease himself onto the other mattress. His feet hung off the end as he settled onto his stomach. We watched each other for a long moment.

"You will lose many more people if Patrick doesn't request an air evacuation," he said finally.

"We know," I said.

"Did I not prove he can trust me with your lives?"

"You did. But he's not ready to trust you with the safety of the rest of humanity."

"Explain."

"He still suspects you're waiting to see where we're going so you can tell the rest of your people and kill us all."

Molev snorted and closed his eyes.

"I already know where he plans to take me. We head west to Fort Irwin."

"How do you know?" I asked.

"I've known since the beginning when I overheard your conversation."

"Before we knew you had good hearing," I said with sudden insight.

"Yes."

"I'll tell him you know."

"He needs to save the females," he said just before his breathing evened out.

Save the females.

With a growing understanding of what he would do to protect the resource he sought, I stared at Molev's gauze-covered back. He would do anything. Give anything. Even his life.

In that way, we were very alike. I'd already committed my life to seeing Zion reunited with my brother and niece in the safe zone. And I would do anything, even put my faith in Molev, to see that happen.

Exhaling heavily, I closed my eyes.

I couldn't be sure exactly how long I slept in the windowless room when I woke, and my first impulse was to check my watch. However, Molev's steady, slow breathing kept me from moving. I didn't want to wake him. Not yet. He needed as much sleep as he could get.

Eyes open in the dim light, I stared up at the ceiling and considered what might be happening outside our door. Patrick had likely sent word to command shortly after we'd arrived. It would take days for a response, most likely. Given his current attitude, he wouldn't contentedly settle in at this base to wait for one. He would want to push on as soon as Molev was awake.

What Molev said before falling asleep rolled through my mind. He wanted Patrick to get us an airlift out of here to save the four women left in the squad, including me. But it wasn't just our lives on the line if Patrick didn't get us a faster ticket home. It was all the women on the other side of the western barrier who were still waiting for their ticket to salvation, too.

There wasn't enough room on the islands for everyone. It was essential personnel plus one companion only. My brother's medical skills got him there, while my exceptional skill at frothing got me nothing but a front-row seat to watching my brother's family be torn apart.

I needed Molev on the other side of the barrier, working on a vaccine against infection so I'd get the ticket that I needed. It wasn't the plus companion option my brother had received, but it was still a way for Zion to join my brother.

With a vaccine, maybe the rest of us would have a fighting chance. I'd witnessed how Molev had killed a hound. It hadn't been easy. He'd almost died. But it *was* possible. If we didn't become infected, maybe some of us would live to see the other side of this hell.

"Are you hungry?" Molev asked.

I turned my head and found him watching me.

"You're supposed to be sleeping."

He grunted and moved slightly like he was testing how everything felt.

I sat up and checked my watch. Six hours had passed.

"If you want to get up and walk around a bit, we should be safe enough."

"Explain," he said, pushing himself up and carefully getting to his feet.

"Safe, as in we can leave this room and look for something to eat and drink without Patrick wanting us to roll out right away. Not this late in the afternoon. Not after last night. He'll give everyone tonight to rest up if he can."

Molev rolled his shoulders, and I watched his chest muscles ripple.

"How's it feeling?" I asked, getting to my feet.

"Tight."

"I've heard stitches can feel like that. Itchy will be next."

He grunted again.

"Ready?" I asked, heading toward the door.

I was surprised to see Roni and Roland standing guard in the hall.

Roni's gaze met mine then flicked to Molev. She looked tired. So did Roland.

"Have you been out here the whole time?" I asked.

"Just about," Roni answered.

"Why?" I asked.

"Keeping our eyes on the prize," she said.

"The base is smaller, and word spread about you," Roland said, looking over my shoulder at Molev. "People get curious. Patrick and the commander here just wanted to make sure you got the rest you needed."

I glanced back at Molev. His gaze flicked to me, his expression indecipherable. Was he second-guessing the reason for their presence too?

"Well, we're up now. If you two want to find your own bunks, go for it."

"Nah," Roni said. "We'll tag along with you two. I'm guessing latrine and mess, right?"

I nodded.

"Come on," she said, leading the way. Her typical swagger was missing, and her steps slowed at each hall intersection.

She was moving like she did when we checked a house for infected. But I knew that wasn't what she was doing. Not on base. She was watching out for our own. But why? We were all on the same side in this, weren't we? Get Molev to Irwin, and find a cure. Who wouldn't want that?

We made it to the latrine without incident.

"We're in here, Molev," Roland said, nodding toward the door marked for men.

Molev looked at me and held my gaze.

"Are your goals still aligned with mine, Andie?" he asked. His perception of the situation humbled me and made me feel a little sad for him.

"They are."

He grunted and disappeared into the bathroom. Roni didn't ask me what that was about as she followed me into ours, and I didn't ask her what was really going on. On a base like this, we usually didn't partner up to go to the bathroom. I chose not to worry about it, though. She or Patrick would tell me soon enough. Until then, my priority was getting Molev back on his feet. Metaphorically speaking, since he was already walking around.

Molev and Roland were waiting in the hall when we emerged.

"If we're lucky, there will be something hot and ready in the mess hall," I said. "If not, we can grab some MREs."

"Oh, I'll make sure he gets lucky tonight," Roni said with a smirk thrown over her shoulder.

I could smell the food before we turned the corner, and my stomach growled loudly.

"What is that?" I inhaled deeply, trying to pin the scent as my mouth watered. "It smells like backyard grilling."

"Close," Roni said. "Hamburgers and brats."

The cook behind the counter stared at Molev as we approached.

"I think you're going to like these," I said to Molev. "They should taste a bit like spam."

I made up a hot dog for myself, adding a bit of ketchup, then took a bite right there in line.

"It's good just like that," I said. "But you can skip the bun and condiments and just go straight for the meat."

"I've been trying," Roni said under her breath.

The cook frowned, showing his confusion as his gaze continued to bounce between us. Molev glanced at Roni before his gaze locked with mine again.

I took a tray and held it out to the cook. "Six dogs. Six brats. Two buns. Add some of those beans and a few hushpuppies."

Molev took his loaded tray and followed me to the table. Roland and Roni joined us with food of their own. As I'd guessed, Molev preferred the meat without the buns. He tried one hushpuppy and didn't touch the rest. But he downed the water Roni kept fetching for him.

"The medic wants to see you when you're done," she said when he finally declined her offer for more.

"Why?" he asked.

"To check the stitches." Her gaze flicked to me, though, and I knew there was more to it.

"We need to talk to Patrick first," I said. "Any idea where we might find him?"

"His bunk," Roni said. "He hit it three hours ago. Said to wake him after you've seen the medic."

"Okay. Medic it is then," I said.

The medic was sitting in his office, handwriting in a notebook when we arrived. He looked up at us and immediately set his pen aside.

"How are you feeling, Molev? Any dizziness? Nausea?"

"No."

I trailed behind as the medic led Molev to the exam room. He peeled back the bandages and gently probed the areas around the stitches with his gloved hands.

"You're healing remarkably well. Would you mind if I checked a few other things? Your pulse, blood pressure, listen to your heart and lungs?"

Molev glanced at me.

"Most humans have doctors do all of that once a year to establish the state of their general health," I said without him needing to ask for an explanation.

Molev looked at the medic. "You may check those things."

I watched the medic, noting the almost awed expression on his face as he went through the tests.

"Amazing," he said when he removed the stethoscope from his ears. "I hope I get another chance to take your vitals before you leave, Molev." His gaze slid to me. "When you speak to Sergeant Bromwell, let him know there are no signs of fever or infection and, based on his mobility, no reason Molev can't travel."

Curious about what Patrick planned, I took Molev there next with Roland and Roni in tow.

Patrick opened his door after the second knock.

"You look like hell," I said.

He motioned for us to enter and looked out at Roni and Roland. "Get Cody and Tamra to take over."

He closed the door on them and motioned Molev to the chair.

"Sit. Please. We have a lot to discuss."

"You have more need of the chair than I do," Molev said.

"Sitting probably won't feel good on the stitches," I added.

Either Patrick was too tired to notice Molev's slightly prickly response to take offense, or he didn't care because he took the chair with a sigh.

"Did the medic say you're ready for travel?" he asked.

"He did," Molev said.

"Good. Good. I'd prefer you ride inside a vehicle when we head out tomorrow but will let you be the judge of what you can and can't handle. I'd like us to work together, Molev. As equals.

"Andie let me know that you were questioning why we did so much backtracking. I'd like to go over tomorrow's route with you so you understand the dangers we've been avoiding and to see if you have any suggestions."

"I suggest an airlift out of here," Molev said, crossing his arms, which made every muscle he possessed flex in a power display.

Patrick wasn't impressed. Roni probably would have tried licking Molev if she'd witnessed it.

"Unfortunately, that's not an option. Humans work within a chain of command, and those at the top haven't cleared me to share our final destination with you."

"Cleared or not, Molev already knows. He's known since the day he was shot. He overheard us talking about it."

Patrick's gaze flicked between us, and I saw the doubt and suspicion there. So did Molev.

"When I lay bleeding in the back of the truck, another asked if you would return to Irwin, you said, 'No. We assess, report, and wait for orders.' While you assessed me, I assessed

163

all of you. How many times have human guns fired at me without provocation? How many times have I harmed a human without provocation?

"You say there is a chain of command that you follow. You, Sergeant Patrick Bromwell, mistrust every act of help and choose violence time and again. If you are a product of the chain you follow, your leaders will do the same. I have no interest in continuing to this Irwin to meet your smart people who will know how to use me to create a vaccine to save a human race that refuses to trust me."

Neither of their gazes wavered from the other's in the silence that followed. I let the silent pissing contest go for a few beats before speaking.

"So we have a choice, Patrick. We can either trust that Molev's here to help us, just like he's been saying, and airlift to Irwin, or we can watch our possible cure slip away."

"Do you know why I'm having a hard time trusting you? No one does something for nothing," Patrick said. "What do you get out of helping us?"

I looked at Molev, wondering if he would tell Patrick what he wanted. Molev's gaze flicked to mine, giving nothing of his thoughts away before he looked at Patrick.

"You are in no position to grant what I hope to receive. I will speak to those who are once we reach Irwin."

Patrick stood abruptly and went to the door.

"I would like to speak with Andie privately in the hall. Please wait here."

I turned to Molev. "You said you've lived a long time. Coming here had to be a huge change for you. I imagine it wasn't without some struggle."

Some of the tension disappeared from Molev's shoulders. "Yes."

"Patrick has spent most of his life in the military, barking orders and expecting to be obeyed. Believe it or not, he's mellowed a lot since being stuck with a group of clueless civilians. But he does take the time to listen to us all, even if it seems like he doesn't. A lot of this is new to all of us."

Molev uncrossed his arms and nodded.

Patrick didn't say anything as he opened the door for me or when he motioned for me to follow him down the hall. Only after we were closed in another room did he finally speak his mind.

"Do you think he'll leave?" Patrick asked.

"I don't think Molev has lied about anything yet. Why would he start now?"

"Do you feel safe with him?"

"Yes," I said without hesitation.

"Would you trust him around the people you love?"

"He's given me no reason not to."

"Hasn't he? He trailed us instead of making himself known. He pretended to be unconscious to gain classified information and withheld the extent of his abilities which jeopardized the lives of every person in this squad."

"Those are the same things we've done to assess situations. The electric cars for recon. The snipers on the roofs of the trucks. Pretending to be raiders. Why is it okay for us but not for him? He's killed countless infected, risked his life time and again, and almost lost it killing not one but two hounds. If that's not enough to gain your trust, he won't ever gain it.

"We've seen how the infected are changing. FOBs are going silent. What obstacles are another three weeks of travel going to bring? At the rate we're dying, will there be anyone left to actually get him to Irwin? He didn't turn, Patrick. If he doesn't hold the key to a vaccine, I don't know that anything will."

Patrick ran his hand over his head.

"If I make the wrong call, I will be remembered as the man who killed humanity."

"If humanity is dead, there won't be anyone to remember," I said.

Patrick huffed a breath. "And everyone thinks you have no sense of humor."

"What I have is an unyielding sense of obligation to my nephew. I want to see this through and get that ticket I was promised. Whatever it takes."

He nodded and opened the door. When we entered the hall, Cody and Tamra were standing outside Patrick's door.

"Stick with Molev and Andie," he said when we reached them. "Let me know if there are any problems."

They both glanced at me, questions in their gazes. But I didn't have any answers for them. I wasn't sure what Patrick was asking them to watch for. If Molev wanted to hurt us, he would have made his move by now. And if he was interested in going after our leaders, he'd wait until he met them. Either way, there wasn't any reason for Molev to change his behavior now.

"Andie, continue as you've been. Keep him close."

Then he opened the door to his room. Molev was standing right there, arms crossed, staring down at him.

"Go get some rest or food or whatever it is you need. I want my bed back and some shut-eye."

Molev moved a few inches to the side, his way of telling Patrick to go ahead. I could see Patrick didn't like it by the way he brushed past Molev.

Then the grey giant stepped out of Patrick's room and closed the door behind him, a complete dismissal of Patrick and his authority.

"Do your people have any kind of chain of command?" I asked him.

"They do."

And based on how Molev behaved with Patrick, I had a feeling Molev was probably near the top. But I didn't ask, preferring ignorance. I couldn't share or withhold what I didn't know.

"What do you need?" I asked. "More sleep? Food? Something to drink?"

"Sleep," Molev said.

We returned to our room, leaving Cody and Tamra in the hall.

Molev didn't move to the bed but watched me.

"Were you able to hear what Patrick and I discussed when we left?"

He nodded.

"I don't know which way Patrick will go, but I hope he chooses to trust you and orders the airlift out of here."

"And if he doesn't?"

"Then I guess you leave, and we'll head back to Parsons and hope another one of your people will be willing to help us."

He studied me for a long moment.

"Are you tired, Andie?"

"Over the last several weeks, I've learned to sleep when I can. So, tired or not, if you lie down, I'll join you."

He grunted and moved to lower himself to the bed. I was two seconds behind him.

"Will you tell me about your life before the earthquakes?" he asked, watching me.

"There's not a whole lot to tell. I wasn't interested in college after high school. So I got a job at a coffee shop for a while and saved enough to get to Europe. I worked in coffee shops there, exploring and saving money to get to the next place. People interested me. I liked learning new things and about different cultures. When my brother called and told me his wife was pregnant, I came back. I didn't want to miss my chance to be the cool aunt."

"Why did you never settle with a male and have children of your own?"

Since he'd already asked something similar, he either hadn't fully understood my previous answer or was asking something else.

"I've dated, but I never liked anyone enough to spend the rest of my life with them. They were fun to be with while they were interested and easy to say goodbye to when someone else caught their eye."

"I don't understand human males," he said, closing his eyes. "I would never lose interest in you."

"That's nice of you to say, but you don't know me. I've been called an emotional robot before. I tend not to open up to people."

His arm slipped over my waist.

"It sounds like they were never the right people."

"You might be right. Now get some sleep. Who knows how long we've got?"

I closed my eyes and took my own advice.

When I woke again, Molev's arm was still over my waist. This time, I checked my watch without guilt. Another four hours had passed.

"Are you hungry?" Molev asked.

"Not really. I think I want to get up and move around for a while though. How about you?"

He sat up with much more ease than the last time.

"How's everything feeling?"

"Good."

Yet when he turned his back to me, I saw a few spots on his white bandages that were dotted with blood.

"We might need to have the medic look at your stitches again. Looks like a few are bleeding."

"They will heal."

My gaze slid over the patchwork of scarring on his chest, and I realized how unimportant a few pulled stitches probably were to him.

"Ready to go for a walk then?" I asked.

He opened the door, drawing Cody and Tamra's attention.

"Anything happen while we were sleeping?" I asked.

"A few people came by and looked at your door, but that was it," Tamra said.

"Where are you going?" Cody asked.

"Just stretching our legs."

They fell in step behind us as we made our way to the latrine then the mess. Since it was the middle of the night, there wasn't much food out, but I did raid the leftovers and handed Molev a tin sheet filled with hotdogs.

The halls were quiet, which I didn't find comforting. Recalling our path earlier, I made our way to the exit and stepped outside. The night sky was lit with the stars that peeked through clouds. I paused and took a moment to just take it in.

Molev crumpled the tinfoil, adding sound to the silence.

I glanced his way to tell him what to do with his wrapper, but his gaze jumped from me to the distant fence. I couldn't see anything, but he slowly nudged me back toward the door.

"Wake Patrick," he said softly.

When he would have pushed me inside, I caught his arm.

"We stick together."

He glanced at the darkness again, then hurried inside. We ran down the halls, and Molev pulled ahead when we reached the hall that held Patrick's door. Molev didn't bother knocking but burst in.

"Patrick."

The boom of Molev's voice startled Patrick awake. He sat up, still fully dressed.

"There are three or more hounds to the north."

Cody and I swore, and Tamra paled. Patrick stood and started moving.

"Gear up," he barked.

"No," Molev said. "I cannot kill them. If we stay, you will all die."

CHAPTER TWELVE

"WE'VE DONE THIS BEFORE, MOLEV," PATRICK SAID. "WE AREN'T gearing up to kill them; we're guarding the lights. With the base personnel here, we can hold the base until dawn. We'll move out then."

Patrick nodded to Cody and Tamra and took off at a jog. The other two followed. I looked at Molev, knowing Patrick meant for me to stay with him.

Molev's gaze, which had been following Cody and Tamra, locked onto me.

"This is not a pair of hounds but a pack. They will circle the base and make much noise. This close to the city, many infected will come. If the infected were able to use their numbers to breach Vance's fence, why does Patrick think this one will hold?"

"Because it has to hold. Come on. I saw some pretty high roofs out there. Good vantage points if you can get up there without ripping any stitches."

He followed when I started walking.

I tried not to think about what he'd said. If I thought about all the things that could go wrong, I'd be letting fear in. And

171

fear broke focus, something I couldn't afford at the moment. I had to find a way to keep Molev from doing his roar thing and going after the hounds like my gut was telling me he would do if shit started going south.

When we'd almost reached the exterior exit, Molev side-stepped around me to open the door, filling the space with his bulk and blocking my view of the yard. He stayed there for two beats, then moved forward. Everything was quiet outside. No howls.

I stuck with him.

My hope was that he'd stay on the roof as a lookout. If everything went well, the lights would keep the hounds out, and our guns would keep the infected from piling up.

Molev turned suddenly, knocking my legs out from under me and catching me in one fluid motion. My gaze didn't go to his but swept the area around us, looking for whatever threat he'd seen that I hadn't. Before I could spot anything, he jumped. Not once but several times from one roof to the next, working his way to the highest building.

He stopped on the roof but didn't put me down. I finally looked up at him and caught his gaze.

"What was it?" I whispered.

"We stick together."

"Oh. Okay."

He set me down but kept an arm around my waist as he looked toward the south.

"Can you hear them?" I asked.

"No. They are silent now."

"Do you think they've passed us?"

He didn't answer.

We stayed on that roof for an hour before someone found us.

"Patrick wants to talk to you," Steve said. "Both of you."

"You can just pick me up," I said before Molev could knock my feet out from under me.

He grunted and swept me into his arms. We were off the roof a second later, and I mentally winced thinking about what that drop had to have felt like on his knees.

"After Patrick, we need to find the medic to check your stitches. Lifting me can't be good for them," I said.

Molev grunted and eased me to my feet.

We followed Steve inside, where Patrick was speaking with another man. They both turned toward us.

"What exactly did you hear?" the other man asked.

"Three or more hounds," Molev said.

"An hour," Patrick said. "And we haven't heard a single howl. What was the point of this? Did you want to see our response time? The number of personnel? What?"

"I wanted to warn you that I heard hounds."

The older man's expression hardened. "We're running low on sleep and patience. I don't give a damn if you're the next Christ or the devil incarnate. You pull this shit again, and I'll toss you out those gates so fast you'll—"

We all heard the howl even through the closed door.

"Order the airlift," Molev said.

"That takes time we don't have," the other man said before looking at Patrick. "You said he killed two?"

"He did."

"Good." The man's gaze swung to Molev. "Do it again."

"He barely survived what he did with two, and you're asking him to take on three or more?" I said before Molev could react. "If he, the one who can kill them, says run, we should run."

I could see in the other man's eyes that I'd crossed a line.

"Evacuation isn't an option," Patrick said. "Too many personnel."

"We only need to save one, Patrick," I said. "Our mission hasn't changed."

A smattering of gunfire echoed distantly, adding to the urgency of the moment, but the only reaction in the group was Molev's side glance at me.

Patrick finally looked at the other man. "Make it happen."

The muted sounds escalated the moment the door opened. The other man made it out two steps before something rushed him from the side and knocked him out of view.

My hand went to my sidearm, drawing it without thought.

Molev blocked me again when I tried to move forward.

"Behind me," he said.

"Head right outside the door," Patrick said from behind me. "The hangar is on the other side of the base. I'll find the pilot and meet you there."

"Stay close," Molev said a second before we were moving.

As soon as I cleared the door, I saw the infected the man was fighting. He moved his gun to the side of its head and pulled the trigger. Blood didn't spatter me because of Molev's quick reflexes.

Staring at Molev's broad back, I heard the man say, "Make this mean something," before there was another report. When Molev stepped aside, the bite mark on the man's face explained why he'd pulled the trigger on himself.

"Move," Patrick barked.

Molev swept me into his arms and looked down at me. "Turn your face."

Then he was running at an incredible speed. I heard infected call out in every direction. Some close. Some farther away. He didn't pause, but I could feel him veer as I pressed my face to his chest.

We reached the hangar a few moments later. Molev paused,

adjusting his hold on me, and opened the door. The metal structure did nothing to mute the chaos outside.

Molev placed me on my feet, his hand steadying me, as my eyes adjusted to the bright overhead lights. A woman stood near the helicopter, her firearm ready and pointed at us.

"We have orders to evacuate this man," I said, stepping in front of Molev. "He's immune to their bite and might hold the key to a vaccine. Sergeant Bromwell is trying to locate the pilot. Is that you?"

"No. Away from the door. Take cover by the tail. There's a back door, but it's already blocked."

A howl echoed nearby.

"This end of the base is darker," she said, her gaze never leaving the door.

We waited, listening to the yelling and the gunfire as it grew louder. Closer.

The soldier didn't flinch when the door opened with a bang. Roni, Katie, and Steve came in at a run, turned, and took a knee, weapons up and ready at the open door. I tried moving to see what or who they were waiting for, but Molev caught me around the waist and held me immobile.

"Move! Move! Move!" came from outside, but I didn't recognize the voice.

"Stay here," Molev said. Then he was gone out the door.

"Shit," Steve breathed. "Did you see that?"

Roland, Sid, and Brandon ran in with base personnel.

Those people went to the helicopter and started doing their thing as Brandon came over to me.

"Once we open the bay, we'll need to move fast. Half the lights are out, and the undead are going after the rest."

His voice rang in the abrupt silence.

We both looked at the door. Molev strode in, his arms and torso painted dark red. Patrick was two steps behind him.

"A squad is in position to hold the hangar. How soon until we're in the air?"

I looked back at the men who were moving something with wheels in front of the helicopter wheels.

"As soon as we tow it clear of the hangar," one of the men said.

"Get this door open and get it done," Patrick said.

Molev stopped beside me as a man ran over and used the controls to start opening the bay.

"Are you okay? I asked. "It looks like you have a few new bites."

"Yes."

"How are the stitches holding up?"

"Well enough," he said.

"I hope so."

The noise of the opening bay door carried through the building. I heard a few distant pops outside.

An infected darted under the growing gap. A shot to the head took it down. Another infected came running and was dropped just as quickly. They were going for the men operating the thing they meant to use to move the helicopter.

Molev saw the same thing I did.

"Stay here, Andie."

He left me with Brandon. When I saw he was going to go out the hangar door, though, I didn't stay put. I swore under my breath and jogged to the other side of the hangar, using the edge of the door as cover as I watched for infected from the other direction. Brandon joined me, taking a knee.

We shot what we saw as long as Molev was clear. He moved wickedly fast, beheading infected as he kept them away from the ground crew. As the helicopter emerged from the bay, we moved with it, shooting down the infected.

I saw Cody. He shambled forward the way a newly turned would. Someone shot him.

The sound of an engine starting didn't bring any relief. There were so many infected coming around the side of the building that I couldn't look away, never mind trying to get to the aircraft.

They came like a never-ending wave, rushing our position.

The blades started to whirl, that slow whoosh turning to a whomp-whomp-whomp that increased with each beat of my heart. The wind tugged at me.

Patrick yelled something.

I remained focused on the infected in front of me and hoped that the soldiers on the other side were doing the same.

Hands circled my waist, and I was lifted and turned in one smooth move. Molev shoved me into the aircraft and then was gone, sprinting into the mass of infected just outside our protective circle. Heart in my throat, I watched him behead the infected while the rest continued to fire. I thought I saw Molev jerk, but I couldn't be sure.

"Roni, get in!" he yelled.

She pivoted and leapt in beside me, taking a position near the door. As soon as she had, she yelled, "Cover them," and started shooting.

I did the same. Another soldier joined me, covering the others. Another joined us. Then another.

Everything was happening in seconds, yet nothing seemed to move fast enough. One of the soldiers fell to an infected on my side, and Molev roared on the other. The pilot yelled something I couldn't hear, and a moment later we jerked. The helicopter started to lift.

I held on and continued to shoot, ignoring the fear that we were leaving Molev behind.

The helicopter jolted, listing to one side before stabilizing.

I glanced over to see Molev squatting down with Tamra in his arms. He was pulling at her clothes, trying to take the riot gear off of her. She opened her eyes and set her palm on his cheek. Her lips moved, but I couldn't hear what she was saying.

He stopped trying to take her jacket off and cupped the back of her head to bring his forehead to hers. After a moment, he helped her sit up, facing out of the door. He looked at Patrick and for the first time, I could see the raw emotion in his eyes.

Anger.

So much anger.

When he stood and stepped back from Tamra, he held his hand out to me.

I understood what he wanted, but I didn't hand him my sidearm. I couldn't. Instead, I lifted my hand, ready to pull the trigger myself. Sid beat me to it.

Tamra toppled forward, falling from view as the helicopter raced forward through the night.

I settled in for the transport and focused on the moment rather than the last fifteen minutes. Molev sat next to me, his shoulder brushing against mine, and I met Sid's gaze. He looked tired as he gave me a single nod. I returned the gesture and gazed out at the darkness, not letting anything fill my mind.

No regret. No sorrow. I allowed nothing in.

When Sid and Roland began checking weapons, I forced myself to do the same, even though I knew the journey to Irwin would take hours.

Molev's hand slipped from his leg to lightly rest on my thigh. I glanced up at him and saw his head tipped back and his eyes closed. It was like we were back in the tank. He wasn't sleeping but shutting down and assessing. I wasn't so sure we humans were proving worthy of saving. How many times had he told Patrick to call for the airlift? How many times had he warned that we'd lose lives?

Without wanting to, I let my gaze sweep over the helicopter's occupants. Six of my squad remained, along with Patrick and seven of the base personnel. We'd lost so many tonight, and why? Because we couldn't trust what was new and different.

I tipped my head back and set my hand over Molev's. It wasn't comfort; it was camaraderie. Sacrifice for salvation. We were both in it so deep we'd drown in it. We knew it. Fighting it after embracing it would only change the focus from the sacrifice to the struggle.

So I maintained focus.

Zion and every other person on the planet were praying for a miracle. A miracle that was sitting beside me, hopefully.

Someone yelled something, and I opened my eyes to see the pilot motioning to Patrick, who was putting on a headset. They spoke for a moment, and then the helicopter veered to the left. Molev's hand tightened on my leg, and I realized this was probably his first time in the air. I patted his hand, and he turned his head to look at me in the dim light.

Our altitude dropped drastically.

His hand turned and clasped mine. I didn't mind since I wasn't a fan of the sudden fall, either.

The cabin began to brighten, and I realized we weren't crashing but landing. I looked at the base members as they got into position, weapons ready. My squad copied their moves. I stayed right where I was with Molev as we touched down.

The engine immediately shut down, and the doors opened. A bevy of activity around the nearby building had us all on high alert, but the people that came running our way moved with the fluidity of the living.

"How far in the ever-living fuck is your head up your ass?" the lead man demanded as he strode toward us. "You just painted a bullseye on this base with this night-flying stunt. Every infected in miles is now shambling their way here."

Patrick jumped out and faced him.

"Woodward has fallen. We have a person of interest we need to transport to Irwin ASAP. We need fuel, showers, and fresh fatigues if you have any."

"And a medic," I said.

Patrick nodded in acknowledgment without looking at me. The man's gaze swept over us, taking in our state before locking on Molev.

Then he gestured to Patrick to step away with them. They conversed softly for several moments before the man motioned to two of his soldiers.

"Fuel them up and get them what they need. I want them gone in thirty."

The majority of us went straight to the showers. Katie silently cried as she washed, and Roni and I shared a look. As soon as we finished, we found clean clothes waiting for us. Civilian clothes, which were fine with me. My riot gear fit over it just fine.

We headed out from the showers together, and I found Molev waiting for us, his hair dripping and bandages soaked but clean. Roland and Sid bookended him.

"He wouldn't see the medic without you," Sid said.

I didn't comment but motioned that we should follow the soldier waiting to lead us. The halls were crawling with personnel that looked dead on their feet.

"Skeleton crew?" I asked.

"Waiting for reinforcements. Put in the request eight days ago."

It was close to the same thing we'd heard in Woodward.

The medic looked pretty shocked to see Molev and wasn't as excited to care for him as the previous one. He removed the bandages. He said everything looked good, skipped the salve, and rewrapped what had been bandaged with new gauze.

We walked out onto their tarmac within the allotted time and saw Patrick still speaking with the commander there. When he saw us, he nodded and broke away.

"Our next stop is the Cochiti Lake FOB, west of Sante Fe. The bombs reduced the population of the undead significantly, and the base was active as of twelve hours ago. It's our next fuel point. Get in."

We were greeted the same way at the next FOB. Yelling for jeopardizing the base, quiet words with Patrick, then a refuel.

From Cochiti Lake, we headed west again to another FOB near the Grand Canyon. The sky was finally starting to lighten with the approaching dawn when we landed there. Fewer personnel occupied the base. All able-bodied individuals had been relocated to watch the mountain passes.

We refueled with less commotion and were airborne again as the sun crested the horizon.

It felt like a lifetime since I'd left the west coast. I guessed it truly was a lifetime, though, since that life was gone and never coming back.

Instead of dozing like the rest of my team, I vacantly gazed at the brilliantly lit sunrise and let myself think about my family. I'd left believing the mission was a death sentence. Yet, I was returning. I would be able to hug little Zion goodbye and be there with Rachel as she handed over her three-year-old son to the transport personnel. The ticket I'd earned would be bittersweet but worth it. Zion would be safe with his sister and my brother. And who knew, maybe Apollo would even have a hand in creating the vaccine.

Holding onto those hopeful thoughts, I watched the approach to our final destination.

Sid motioned to the window as the helicopter started to descend over the motor pool's now empty parking lots. The man next to Molev looked out then leaned over to shout in Molev's ear.

"Looks like a welcoming committee."

If he had super hearing, it had to have hurt since it had been loud enough for me to hear. But Molev didn't acknowledge it in any way.

How would I be feeling if I suddenly landed where a bunch of his kind was waiting for me?

Nervous maybe, but only because Molev hadn't given me any reason to doubt his intentions. However, we'd given him plenty. If I were in his place, I'd be terrified. Or maybe not. I'd witnessed how quickly he could move. And how he could take a bullet. My gaze flicked to the bandage on his shoulder then to Sid. He caught my eye and nodded. So did Roni, Roland, and the rest of the team.

When I looked at Patrick, he was watching Molev.

I hoped, for all our sakes, that he would prioritize Molev's safety and treatment so we didn't lose the chance we'd been given.

The engines wound down after we landed, and Roni and Sid joined the personnel from the base as they jumped out. When Molev would have exited, I held him back with a light touch on the arm.

Patrick jumped out and started forward. Only after he was halfway to the men waiting and the rest of our team was on the ground in a protective line did I motion that we were next.

Weapons weren't drawn on us, but they were out and ready as we emerged.

None of us moved as Patrick spoke to the general.

The engine quieted, but we weren't left in silence. An engine of some kind was running, drowning out the conversation the two were having.

"Can you hear what they're saying?" I asked softly.

"Patrick is telling him that I'm immune and have the strength and speed to kill the hellhounds. He says I've gained the trust of some of the team but not all. That I've saved lives but lost some, too, with my refusal to cooperate. He's suggesting I'm approached with diplomacy because it seems to have been an approach that worked well for you."

He glanced at me, and I thought I saw a slight twitch of his lips.

"I hope they listen," I said. "And for the record, I don't think your actions are the reason lives were lost."

He grunted, and I could see Steve give a slight nod too.

"He's also saying I have excellent hearing and am probably listening," Molev added. "That I am a flight risk but I would be difficult to detain without injury. The medic who assessed me couldn't be certain my physiology is compatible with human medicines."

Molev crossed his arms at that point and stared at the general who called out for a team. "Please escort our guest to his room."

Without asking them, Sid, Steve, Roland, Brandon, Roni, and Katie surrounded Molev as the team approached.

"This way, sir," the leader said, indicating a jeep in the distance.

Molev understood what we were doing and allowed us to escort him to the vehicle. However, the leader and two of the patrol got in, leaving only one space.

Molev's lips twitched again. He picked me up and placed me in the open seat then glanced at the rest, ending with Roni.

"How is your stamina?" he asked.

She choked on a laugh. "You're speaking my language. I've been dying to find out if I can keep up with you."

"An escort isn't necessary," the leader said to us. "We can take him from here."

"With respect," Sid said, "We've come too far and lost too many to take chances at this point. Lead the way, and we'll do our best to keep up."

Rather than argue, they started the engine and turned the vehicle toward the loop road that surrounded the base. They sped away, and I watched Molev and the rest rapidly fall back.

I smothered my grin, glad Molev saw it for the test it was. When their stunt to see how fast he could go failed, they slowed down and waited for the group to catch up.

After that, they turned left onto the loop and kept a moderate speed.

Sweat gathered on Steve's face, which Roni noticed. She smirked at him and pulled ahead a little. He swore and sped up. Molev let them pass him, and I saw him smile. It was small and brief but there.

Then Brandon and Roland got in on it. The jeep sped up to stay ahead of them.

Sid looked at Katie, and she shook her head.

We'd all had to pass a physical for our spots on the squad. Katie could run. It was a requirement that had saved her life several times. Her ability to quickly climb a ladder and her love of heights made her a perfect lookout. But we hadn't exactly been doing PT in the field, and after a few more minutes, I could see she was starting to lag.

Before I could catch Molev's eye, he pivoted, running backward to face her.

She rolled her eyes at him, and Sid laughed. Then she nodded.

In a blink, she was up in his arms, and he and Sid ran faster to catch up with the others.

"He do that often?" the leader asked.

"Protect us? Yes. He's the reason we're here," I said, facing forward. "And if the people in charge don't screw this up, he'll be the reason we're still here in another ten years."

"You believe he's immune then?"

"Look at his scars. He's been bitten more times than I can count. Does he look infected to you?"

CHAPTER THIRTEEN

A LOOK CROSSED THE MAN'S FACE. DOUBT MIXED WITH DISMISSAL and suspicion.

"Let me guess. You think he'll somehow start infecting all of us like the hounds because they came from the same place."

"We know nothing about him."

"You know nothing about him. He's been with us for over a week now. We've bunked with him. Shared meals with him. Fought beside him. We used the same shower. Don't let your fear of what might happen rob you of opportunities in the present. And he *is* giving us an opportunity. Don't ever doubt that. He knows we're looking for a way to end the plague and kill the hounds, and he's willingly here to help."

We passed the hospital, which was where I thought they were taking us, and turned left into the first housing area. I'd never been on this side of the base, but after what I'd seen in every town we'd checked, I was expecting cars abandoned in driveways and accumulating debris on the sidewalks. However, everything here was clean.

They pulled into the first driveway and parked.

"This is the assigned house," the man said, getting out.

I did the same as the others caught up. Roni was winded hard but grinning. Steve and Roland were about the same with Brandon a few yards behind. Sid stuck with Molev, who stopped at the end of the driveway and set Katie on her feet.

"Thanks," she said.

He nodded and came over to stand beside me as I looked at the house. Bars covered the windows, but when I looked, the rest of the homes had the same feature.

"Have there been problems here?" I asked the soldier beside me.

"Prepare for the worst and hope for the best, right?"

I nodded and followed them to the door.

"There are four bedrooms in this unit. The kitchen is fully stocked. Get some R and R while you can."

He opened the door and stepped back. Roland cut Molev off when he would have entered first.

"Not this time, my friend," he said.

Molev glanced at me, and I shrugged. Sid entered next, looking around the immediate area before motioning for us. The rest of us joined them, and Roni shut the door behind us. The heat was on, and the knives were still in the block on the counter.

"This is a good sign," I said. "They're treating you like a guest."

Roni went to the window.

"A guest that requires guards, though." She glanced at Molev. "So, is he being protected or monitored?"

"Probably both," I said.

Steve was already in the kitchen, rooting around in the fridge and freezer.

"They went all out. Pizza in the freezer and eggs, bacon, beer in the fridge." He groaned and pulled out a large bowl of cut fruit. "I never thought there would be a day I'd pass up pizza and beer for this."

He sat down with the bowl of fruit. Roni smacked the back of his head and took it away from him.

The familiarity and camaraderie touched a place inside me, but I pushed the feeling away.

Katie helped her dish out portions, and we all stood around in the kitchen as we ate the first fresh food in weeks. Molev seemed to enjoy the fruit well enough, but I couldn't imagine it would be enough for him.

"Sleep or bacon and eggs?" I asked.

His gaze locked with mine, and I noticed the way the sandy-colored flecks near the center of his mossy green eyes stood out in the early morning light. It surprised me to realize I thought he had really pretty eyes.

Pretty eyes. Amazing body. And a protective streak a mile long.

In another time and another place, it would have been an attractive combination.

"I wouldn't bother with sleep," Roni said, interrupting my thoughts. "Go with the food. Most likely, we'll hear a knock on the door within the hour."

"Nah," Steve said. "Patrick's probably being debriefed in private. The information will need to be shared with everyone above the general's pay grade. They'll need to decide on an approach and put together a medical team. We won't see them until next week."

Sid shook his head. "They don't have the time for that. FOBs are going dark."

"Patrick sent the message that we made contact days ago," Katie said. "And you can bet the bases we stopped at, especially the Grand Canyon FOB, have sent their own messages. How else did those guys out there know where to take us? They were told in advance. I'm betting a lot of preparations have already been made."

"And no one reacted to Molev's appearance. They were definitely forewarned," I said, agreeing with her.

"Breakfast it is," Brandon said.

While he started cracking eggs, I went to explore the house. Molev acted as my shadow until I reached the first bedroom room. With a hand on my shoulder, he stopped me from entering first and moved around me.

"There aren't any infected here," I said, a step behind him.

"Prepare for the worst and hope for the best," he quoted.

After we'd checked the house, we returned to the kitchen. Sid was out on the couch. Katie was in the bathroom. Roni was telling Brandon how to cook the bacon. And Steve and Roland were leaning back, taking it all in until Steve saw us.

"Which room did you pick?" he asked.

"Doesn't matter. They're all the same," I said. "Clean and undead free."

"I'll bunk with Katie," Roni said. She snatched a piece of bacon from the paper towel and yelled, "You okay with that?"

"Yeah," Katie called back through the bathroom door.

"Sid, you good being the little spoon?" Roland asked.

"Nope," Sid said, proving he slept light. "I'll take Brandon. He's pro-back-to-back."

"Looks like it's you and me, Steve," Roland said.

"Fine, but no complaining when I pull a *Planes, Trains, and Automobiles* move."

Sid snorted, and it felt real. More real than it had been in a long time. Yet, still only on the surface.

"Hope you're okay sharing with me," I said, looking at Molev.

He nodded once, taking in the group as much as I was.

When Katie emerged from the bathroom, her eyes were red. We all pretended not to notice.

After distributing the food he'd made, Brandon abandoned his position at the stove and told Sid to take clean up. They bantered while we quickly ate.

Roni and Katie finished first and went to claim a room. Sid started cleaning up. Feeling zero guilt, I left my dish next to the sink and took the first open bedroom with Molev.

"The humans I knew preferred sleeping at night," he said, watching me remove my gear.

"That's my preference too. But that's not how life's been working lately. So we rest up when we can. You should do the same."

He grunted and openly watched as I removed my pants. It didn't bother me. Some of the guys we'd been with along the way had watched me just as closely. And I'd openly studied Molev plenty of times.

I wondered if the time Roni had flashed him had been his first nude view of a woman. Then, I wondered what he thought of us in general. He was obviously protective. We were a resource he sought after all. That made me think of Tamra and the anger in his eyes when he'd understood she'd been bitten.

"What did Tamra say to you?" I asked. "At the end."

I pulled back the covers and got in. He looked at the door then joined me, rolling to his side.

"She said, 'Not everyone is worth saving. You're our future. Choose well.'" His gaze swept my face. "Patrick did not trust me, and she lost her life. I will not allow his suspicion to take more lives."

"What are you going to do about it?"

"Patrick said he would trust me if he understood my

motivation. I will tell your general what I want in return for my help."

I nodded slowly. "That might go a long way in reassuring him. But it might also cause some concern. Are you open to a suggestion?"

"Yes."

"Don't come out and say you want women."

"Explain."

"A lot of people would become reactive to that kind of statement like you're planning on taking women whether they want to be taken or not. And I don't think that's your intent."

He grunted.

"The woman you were with, Cassie, said you're at Whiteman, right? That's a military base. This is a military base. And every base between here and there has been understaffed or overrun. So, tell them you're looking for volunteers to help maintain base operations. Be specific in that you're looking for individuals without family ties and state you need to interview all the candidates to make sure they're a good fit with the humans already on the base. Tell them your end goal is to establish better relations between our two people. And when it comes time to selecting the volunteers, make sure you add a few men in to make it look good."

"Why do humans manipulate instead of speaking the truth?"

I thought about it for a moment.

"I think, for most people, by manipulating the outcome, there's less risk of not getting what they really want. If they come out and ask for what they want, there's a good chance they'll be told no."

"So I must manipulate in order to receive what I truly want? No. I will speak the truth and my terms. Manipulation will only feed the mistrust that's already grown. But I will take care with how I word my terms. Thank you, Andie."

He closed his eyes, an obvious signal that he was done talking. I did the same and slept a few hours until I got too hot. The heat from Molev's chest radiated against my face. I rolled onto my back and felt his hand slide from my waist to my stomach.

For a brief moment, I wondered if he was still worried that Roni would molest him in his sleep before I sank back into my own.

When I surfaced next, my face was melting into his pecs again. Just before I rolled away, I caught the scent of his own sweat. It wasn't unpleasant, but it did tell me he was just as hot as I was, and I forced my eyes open.

His were still closed.

Trying not to disturb him, I set the back of my hand against his forehead. He didn't feel too warm, so I didn't think he had a fever from an infection.

"I am well, Andie," he said without opening his eyes.

"You're sweating but still holding me close. I'm trying to figure out why," I said, being direct since he preferred it.

"If I hold you while you sleep, I know you are safe."

I couldn't speak for a moment. I often thought of Sid and all the people he'd had to kill, like Tamra, but I'd never considered that Molev might have had a similar role.

"Then hold away," I said. "When I sleep next to you, I feel safe too."

His arm lifted from my waist and smoothed down my arm like he was trying to comfort me. I should have been well past needing comfort, but damn if I didn't love it.

I lay there awake, letting him pet my arm as if I was a kid he was trying to get back to sleep after a nightmare. And I guessed that was pretty accurate. The last several weeks had been just that, and I didn't want to go back to it. I wanted to stay right where I was, with my eyes open, in this bed with Molev.

Tipping my head back, I looked up at him and found him watching me.

"Don't dwell on the bad things that have happened," I said. "They can't be undone. Instead, look forward to the good things you want to happen, and stay focused on what you can do to make those happen."

"What good things do you focus on?"

"Getting my nephew somewhere safe."

He grunted but didn't close his eyes.

"Did you sleep at all?" I asked, glancing at my watch. It was close to noon.

"Yes."

"Still tired?"

"No."

"Then let's get up and see if we've heard from anyone yet."

We were the first ones awake, but the others heard us moving around and joined us within twenty minutes.

"What are they waiting for?" Katie asked.

"Let's find out," Roland said, looking out the window.

We geared up and headed out the door. A jeep was still parked at the curb, but it didn't hold the same group that had delivered us. When they saw us emerge, they got out of the vehicle.

"What can we do for you?" one of them asked.

"Nothing," Roni said. "We're just stretching our legs."

The men didn't return to their vehicles, though. When we started along the housing sidewalk, they fell in behind us. They let us go until we wound our way out of the subdivision onto 5th street.

"We have orders to return you to your assigned housing," the man behind us said.

"And our orders are to do whatever is necessary to save what's left of the human population," Sid said without slowing.

"Please return to your assigned housing," the man repeated more firmly.

The rustle of noise behind us made my neck hair stand on end. I knew the sound of drawing a weapon.

Molev disappeared from my side. By the time I'd turned around, the men were gaping at their empty hands as Molev disappeared behind a nearby house.

"Give me your—" That's all the man managed before Molev returned.

"Shit," one of the others said, stepping back.

"I have seen too many humans die to waste more lives. If you wish to retrieve your weapons, they are that way. Undamaged this time. Do not draw them on these humans again."

"Should we tell him they were going to shoot him?" Katie stage-whispered.

Steve choked on a laugh.

"Pretty sure he knows," Roni said. "But I appreciate you thinking of us in the crossfire, big guy."

Molev grunted but didn't look away from the men as he crossed his arms.

"We're wasting time," I said to the soldiers. "He's here to work with the scientists to come up with a vaccine. If you're willing to escort us to whomever Molev needs to talk to, you're welcome to retrieve your weapons while we wait for you. If not, don't threaten our only chance to stop what's happening out there. We're following our orders just like you're following yours."

One of the soldiers frowned at me and glanced at Molev.

"You're wondering whose orders," I said, reading him easily.

"It crossed my mind."

"Molev doesn't give orders to us or anyone else that we've seen. But he does have boundaries. He doesn't like being shot at or told what to do. He's here, willing to help us, as long as we can respect those boundaries. So pointing a gun at him and telling him to go somewhere he doesn't want to go is counterintuitive if we really want to save what's left of the human race. And those were our orders. Find and secure a means to end the plague."

I gestured to Molev. "He's secured, and he's ready to start on the saving."

The soldier glanced at the guy with the radio and nodded toward the house. "Go check."

While that one jogged away, the first two stared at us.

"Are we waiting for an escort, or did you want to see him make balloon animals with your weapons?" Roland asked.

"They will escort us," Molev said. "the general will meet us at the hospital."

"Are you psychic or something?" one of the soldiers asked.

"What did they tell you about him?" I asked.

"It's classified."

I snorted. "I bet. Molev has really good hearing. It's not a secret."

When the soldier returned with their weapons and repeated what Molev had already announced, we started walking again, taking the next left.

By the time we reached the hospital, someone was waiting for us with more armed soldiers.

"Molev, please come with me. The rest of you are relieved of duty," he said.

Molev crossed his arms.

"There have been a few incidents," Roland said. "It would be better for everyone if we continued to escort him."

He didn't look happy but nodded. "Follow me."

Roni and Roland cut in front of us while the rest covered our backs. I took in everything from the number of personnel inside the hospital and what they were wearing to the number of turns it took us to reach our destination.

The barren room had a table, two chairs, and a mirror set into one wall. Based on the dust coating the floor below it and the unpainted edges, it was recently installed.

"Please have a seat," the man said. "the general will be right in."

He didn't try getting us to leave with him. He simply shut the door.

I glanced at Molev. He was taking in the room, looking at everything except the mirror. Was he noticing that there were no windows? No means of escape? I was, and it made me nervous. It felt like they were prepared to try to pin him down if this meeting didn't go as they planned. I had no doubt that Molev would be just fine. I'd witness the way he'd broken through a door. His speed, strength, and agility would get him out of there. But we would be losing our only hope with him.

For the sake of Zion and the rest of the world, I hoped the general would use diplomacy.

As the minutes ticked by, the others moved around the room. Steve took a chair and kicked his feet up on the table, shrugging at Katie's 'cut it out' look. Roni leaned against the back wall and grinned when Katie knocked his feet off the table. Sid pretended to stretch his back and roll his shoulders.

But none of us looked at the stupid mirror that was so damn obvious.

I faced the pointless piece of glass. "How many more

people do we need to lose before we stop playing games? We did our job. Now get in here and do yours."

Molev's hand pressed my lower back, guiding me around the table to where Roni and Katie stood. He glanced at Roni then stood in front of all three of us.

Roni didn't look upset like I thought she would. And the speculative look in her eyes as she studied his back seemed more thoughtful than hungry. Before I could try to figure out what she was thinking, the door opened.

"The guns can remain in the hallway for this discussion," Molev said.

Katie's gaze flicked from Molev to me.

Setting a hand on an unbandaged patch of skin, I stepped around him and looked at the general and his escort.

"He views your weapons as a threat."

"Yet you still have your weapons," the general said.

"We've learned not to point them at him."

He considered me for a long moment.

"Andromeda Wells?"

I nodded and felt Molev turn his head to look at me.

"Explain why you feel you need your weapons here," the general said.

"I've lost count of the number of places that have been overrun with the undead during our occupancy. The past five weeks have taught us to be armed at all times and to be very careful where we shoot."

"Sergeant Bromwell debriefed me regarding your squad's efforts to retrieve Molev." His gaze shifted to Molev. "I'm well aware of your preferences, and as Miss Wells stated, we exercise the same precautions on base as they did in the field."

"As Andie stated, they learned not to point their weapons at me. Your men have not. If you wish to negotiate for my help, I need a sign that you are willing to extend trust. The weapons stay in the hall. If there is a breach, there is no window in this room, and the humans with weapons can better protect you from the hall."

I kept a straight face but wanted to grin at Molev's sharp understanding of the situation.

"Is that what this is? A negotiation."

"How else would you like me to view this?" Molev asked. "A confrontation? An attempt to seize me? Take me hostage? If I do not respond well to your weapons, do you believe I will respond any better to your manipulations? I came to offer my help freely. However, Patrick told me that humans do not give something for nothing. So, I am here to negotiate a trade. But if you are as uninterested in my intent as Patrick was, I will leave."

If Patrick was on the other side of that glass, he had to be swearing up a storm.

Molev crossed his arms in the universal dude's-about-to-be-stubborn sign as the general considered him for a long minute. Just when I thought it would be a stalemate, the general nodded his head toward the door. The armed guards left.

"All right. What is it that you want, Molev?"

He glanced at me, his mossy green gaze sweeping my face.

"I want Andie."

It felt like the floor dropped out from under me for a moment. the general's gaze flicked to me, gauging my reaction, and I wasn't positive I was successfully keeping my shock from showing.

"If she agrees, I also want five hundred more willing females. In return, I will allow you to do your tests and create a vaccine from the samples you take of my blood. The women who volunteer to help improve relations between our people must be the first to receive the cure."

The general's expression gave nothing away as he looked at Molev. "You want women?"

"Yes."

But he didn't just want women. He wanted me. My hand dropped from his back, and I felt Katie's fingers slip into mine.

"I'll volunteer," Roni said, coming out from behind Molev.

"I wish I was a woman," Steve said. "I wouldn't mind being first in line for the vaccine."

The general gave them both a hard look, and I had a feeling that, if not for Molev's preferential treatment of us, they would have been dragged from the room and thrown into whatever the military's version of prison was.

"Why only women?" the general asked.

"Women are more willing to trust and less likely to use their weapons out of fear. However, Steve, Sid, Brandon, and Roland have proven themselves trustworthy. I will accept the four of them in place of four women if they are willing."

"Hell yes," Steve said under his breath this time.

The general glanced at me before answering. "I can't promise there will be five hundred female volunteers, but I will do my best to facilitate that. And any vaccine we create will need to run through trials to ensure it's safe for distribution. But the volunteers will be among the first people to receive it once it's approved."

Molev held out his hand, and the general shook it.

"Then let's get started. We have a team ready to collect samples and run tests." He gestured toward the door.

We fell in around Molev with me walking beside him until we reached a large glass window next to a glass door. Inside were all sorts of things. Weights. A treadmill. A tank with water. A chair with wires.

"No," I said before the general could open the door. "You can take his vitals and his blood, nothing else."

"Miss Wells, you're in no position to—"

"I'm in every position to stop you from making mistakes that will cost us—"

The general gestured while I was talking, and a hand closed around my arm.

All hell broke loose quickly. Molev twisted around, grabbed the throat of the soldier holding me, and lifted him off his feet with ease. The others drew their weapons. My group drew theirs.

A low rumble started in Molev's chest.

"Stand down," the general said.

The soldiers were a little too slow for Molev's liking. He threw the soldier he held at them, knocking them down along with Sid.

"I apologize, Sid," Molev said. "I thought he would keep his legs together."

Roni lost it. I'd never heard her laugh so hard in all the weeks we'd been together.

Ignoring her, I looked at the general.

"Molev gave Patrick chances to prove he was trustworthy time and again. And he made the wrong choice every time. This was *your* chance to prove you have good intentions, too. We, the exhausted and afraid remnants of humanity, can't afford more mistakes like this. We need Molev's help.

"Now take a sample of his blood, and get to work, or watch him walk out the door."

CHAPTER FOURTEEN

THE GENERAL REMAINED QUIET FOR A VERY LONG TIME.

"Very well, Miss Wells. How do you propose we collect our samples? Out here in the hallway?"

I met his condescending attitude with a slight shrug.

"Yes," Molev said. "Here in the hallway, not in your lab."

The general didn't try to fight it again.

While a woman in a lab coat took several vials of blood from Molev right there in the hallway, I studied the chair and the tank. I didn't know science, but I knew how to check the plug on an espresso machine. And a plug was a plug...and that chair had one. The wires connected to it could only have one purpose. The same with the tank that had a lid. It was open now, but I knew if Molev went in there, it wouldn't be. And why else have a huge hose at the bottom if not to fill the tank past where it was already filled?

More importantly, what had they been thinking? That he'd be okay with being electrocuted and drowned? And what would they have done if they'd killed him before finding a cure?

"How long will it take to find a vaccine?" I asked, looking at the woman.

"In simple terms, we need to analyze his blood and isolate the parts that make him immune," she said. "But it sounds easier than it is."

"The team will be working around the clock until we have what we need," the general said.

"How soon do we get our tickets out of here?" Sid asked.

"On behalf of the United States and the world, we thank you for your service and sacrifice to escort...Molev here. Due to your extended time in the field, you will need to undergo a period of observation and testing before we can—"

"My ticket isn't for me," I said.

"Mine either," Roland said.

Everyone nodded in agreement.

"I understand. I will send someone to your assigned housing to take down the names of the people you are sending in your place."

He looked at the guard Molev tossed. "Please see that they reach their assigned housing safely."

Then the general met my gaze again. "For Molev's safety, he should remain in the house. Let the guards outside know if you require anything."

Molev made a sound that wasn't quite a grunt or a snort but somewhere in between.

"Do not mistake my cooperation for compliance. I am not your prisoner. If you care for my safety and that of your people, warn them not to point their weapons at me."

The skin at the edge of the general's collar turned red. The flush slowly crept upward as Molev dismissed the man by turning his back on him.

I met Molev's gaze as he indicated I should lead the way. It didn't escape my notice that he was putting himself between me and the soldiers, and his first demand echoed in my mind again.

I want Andie.

We got a ride from the hospital. This time in a vehicle big enough to accommodate all of us. Even our escort.

No one said anything until we were back in the house.

"What the fuck was that?" Sid asked as soon as the door closed.

"What part?" I asked, removing my riot gear. "The part where they were observing us with a poorly hidden two-way mirror? Or the part where I saw they had the equivalent of an electric chair in the testing room?"

"My vote is the part where Molev asked for women," Roni said. "That one really has me curious."

Sid paused his angry pacing. "Yeah, I'm curious about that. But it was the general's attempt to put off our evac with 'observation and testing' that I'm questioning."

"Totally thought it was going to be the part where Molev knocked you down by throwing another person at you," Brandon said with a smirk.

Roni sniggered.

Steve strolled over to the window and moved the curtain to look out. "So you think we're not getting our tickets?" he asked with an angry note in his voice.

My gaze slid to Molev's, who was watching me closely.

"If they're fast with the vaccine, we might not need to worry about it," Katie said.

No one contradicted her. We all knew it wasn't simply a bite that killed a person. We'd seen how torn apart some of the undead were, and I was pretty sure most of it hadn't happened after infection.

"Okay. We'll take one day at a time like we always do," Sid said. "We give them today and see what happens. But we should talk about the way you threw the soldier."

All eyes turned to Molev, and he finally looked away from me.

"As impressive as that was, I would recommend against that in the future," Sid said. "Based on what was in that room, they want to test you. And that kind of display is just going to make them more curious about what you can do."

Katie glanced at me then Molev before shaking her head.

"I think we got lucky this time. But I don't think that will be the end of it. Patrick would have reported what we've all seen. The way you wrecked the tank and survived a hellhound attack?" she shook her head. "There are going to be a lot of people interested in just how strong you are and what kind of threat you pose. I'm betting their team isn't just working around the clock on a vaccine."

"Explain," Molev said.

"I think they're going to be picking apart your DNA. Imagine coming up with a drug that would boost strength, speed, and agility. Don't get me wrong. They'll be focused on a vaccine, too. But after seeing you, they're going to want to find a way to ensure you don't have the upper hand."

"Creating a super soldier drug might be a stretch," Roni said. "But I could see them trying to make a sedative or some other way to slow you down."

Molev crossed his arms and glanced at the window for a long moment.

"Thank you for trusting me with your thoughts," he said finally. "Will you join me when it's time to leave?"

They all nodded their agreement, and I waited until he looked at me.

"I have some questions about that. Would we be going to Whiteman? How secure is it? You saw the other bases. They're falling, one by one. How do you know your base is still whole?"

"I will keep you safe, Andie." He looked at the rest. "My brothers and I will keep you all safe."

"We appreciate that, but it doesn't answer my questions," I said. "Where would we be living? Tents? Homes? The undead population is increasing every day. And they keep learning new tricks. By dangling the promise of a vaccine, you're going to have a lot of people throwing their lives into your hands. Probably a lot of moms with kids since you didn't specify women without family attachments, and I just want to be sure you have this all planned out."

"Will you walk with me, Andie?" Molev asked instead of answering.

"Sure."

He looked at the others. "We will return."

The second we were out the door, he picked me up and took off at a run. He easily cleared the perimeter fence without slowing and kept going. The barren landscape blurred by us for several minutes before he stopped and looked down at me.

"Did we just run away?" I asked.

"There is no buzzing here. Before I left, Ryan explained things to me. Cameras. Listening devices. Human technology. He said that the people in charge shut down much of it because they feared we would find a way to listen to their plans. I believe that is what they are doing in our assigned house."

"Okay," I said, trying to ignore the sudden intensity of his gaze. "Thanks for explaining. Would you mind putting me down?"

He glanced around the sunlit landscape then placed me on my feet. The wind played with my hair, and the waning midday sun helped warm my face.

"The humans at Whiteman were filled with anger and hate. Mya saw that they wanted to treat us as slaves, not as equals. We left Whiteman and created a new home. A place where humans and fey could live together without prejudice.

"We built a wall around many homes, using vehicles left behind by the infected. You saw how easily only a few of my brothers killed many of the infected. It is safe."

His gaze scanned the area around us and returned to me. His silent study brought back the way he'd named me first, before his request for females. My thoughts hadn't veered toward the logical. I'd been thinking of how cozy we were at night. I'd thought it was for safety, but what if I'd been misreading things all along?

I needed to know.

Unlike Patrick, however, I knew how to ease into topics.

"You were smart to make vaccinating the volunteers part of the bargain you struck. I don't think you'll have a problem finding five hundred. But I need to know…what are you going to do with all of them? Is each woman going to be assigned to one of your men to help guide them like I helped you?"

"No. We will not assign anyone. The women may choose."

"Okay. And once they choose, what are they going to be doing?"

"Improving relations between our two people."

"That's a vague answer, and you know it. Say what you really mean." I crossed my arms and stared up at him, mimicking the stubborn stance he favored.

His lips twitched as he studied me. Then he reached out, slowly cupping the back of my head.

"You spoke to me and showed concern for another in my care. Because of that, I followed you. I watched to see if you were who I hoped you would be."

"And who is that?" I asked.

"Mine."

His fingers caressed the back of my head.

"I've witnessed your courage and resolution. You fear nothing, including me. When the others still mistrusted me, you showed kindness. When you thought I needed protection, you gave compassion and allowed me to hold you in my arms. I want you, Andie, but it is your choice."

But it wasn't. Not really. If I said no and Molev said he was okay with that, the general wouldn't take the rest of what Molev said seriously. Best case scenario, refusing Molev would put him at risk. Worst case, Molev would leave before we have a vaccine. I was fairly certain he wasn't the type of person to do that. However, I also had to acknowledge he wasn't any type of person I'd encountered before.

He withdrew his hand, jarring me from my thoughts.

"I apologize. I thought—"

"It's fine." I blew out a short breath. "What I mean is that I'll go with you, Molev. I understand what you want, and I'll go with you."

He studied me again in that way he did. Assessing. But what? I waited patiently.

"When you look at me, what do you see, Andie?"

I took a moment to consider him, knowing what he wanted. He wanted me to see him as more than a potential cure. More than a creature with the strength surpassed by men. More than a killer of the hounds.

He wanted me to see him as a man.

And I did. I couldn't not. But I wasn't ready to throw myself at him just because he was physically attractive.

"Do you know why I think I never connected with anyone?" I asked. "After a while, they always wanted me to be something I'm not. To slip into a role for them. Something they had in their heads but never came out and said. And it would happen slowly over time. Little things, like, 'oh, you want to go out again? Wouldn't you rather stay in?' or 'babe, why didn't you wash my clothes too?' or 'what's for dinner?' I absolutely hated that last one, by the way.

"So, when I look at you, I see a very attractive man with a lot of responsibility on his shoulders. The fate of the world, really. And he's looking for someone to fill a role, but he hasn't really come out and said what it would be yet. So, I'm trying not to feel any attraction. Instead, I'm assessing the situation."

His lips twitched again. "Will you tell me if I do something you don't like?"

"I will."

"Will you tell me if I do something you do like?"

That question surprised me a little. "Sure. I can do that too."

"Good." His hand cupped the back of my head again. "Your pulse jumps when I do this. Do you like it?"

"You can hear my heartbeat?"

"Faintly when we're alone. I can see it here, too," he said, tracing a finger down my throat.

He had to see what he was doing to me then.

"Yes. I like both things."

His pupils, which had been vertical slits in the light, expanded for a brief second.

"Do you like when I sleep beside you?"

"Yes."

The hold on the back of my head firmed, and a wave of heat swept through me.

"I don't want you to fit into my life, Andie, any more than I want to fit into yours. I want us to make our own lives together. Equals. Companions. Do you understand?"

I nodded.

His gaze dipped to my mouth, and he started to lean closer.

I hadn't thought about kissing Molev because I hadn't let myself. But now that I knew exactly what he wanted, I was curious what it would be like. I'd heard his savage cries and witnessed his brutal strength. Yet, he was so restrained.

Part of me feared what would happen when that tight control snapped.

A darker part of me wanted to see it happen....just not with me.

Before I could decide whether to lean in or turn away, he jerked back from me, his head whipping toward the direction of the base.

"Something is coming," he said.

He picked me up and started running toward the base, passing under a drone before he reached the perimeter.

He didn't even glance at it, but I did. A drone...a bugged house...guards outside the door...orders to stay put. The people in charge didn't trust Molev, and I didn't see how this would end well if that didn't change.

The soldiers in the jeep on the other side of the fence were smart enough not to draw their weapons at our approach. They were a bit more reactive when Molev cleared the barrier and their heads in one impressive jump.

He landed lightly on the pavement and continued running even as the soldier yelled at him to stop. I tried to look over Molev's shoulder, but he shifted me back into place, protectively shielded by his torso.

I looked up at him, seeing his actions through a new lens. He wasn't protecting me to prove himself in our eyes or because he was a good person. He was protecting me because I meant something to him.

Molev didn't put me down to open the door. He didn't juggle me around, either. He simply one-armed my weight and let us in.

"Welcome back. Do anything fun other than upset your watchdogs?" Roland asked from his place by the front window.

Tires squealed outside, and he looked out.

"You aren't exactly making friends, pulling these stunts, Molev," he commented.

"I can walk now," I said when Molev didn't put me down.

He glanced at me and the others before reluctantly releasing me.

"He's right," I said. "You aren't helping matters when you do that stuff. But, I understand they aren't exactly being friendly either."

I joined Katie on the couch and looked at the rest. "We went for a run outside the fence. We weren't gone for more than what? Seven or eight minutes? Five minutes in, they sent a drone after us. Molev's here willingly, yet he has guards and now a drone assigned to him. It makes me wonder what other monitoring might be going on in this pre-assigned house."

Sid swore under his breath.

"Well, I'm not sure about the rest of you, but I'm not going to be able to enjoy my intimate time with myself until I know for sure," Steve said, standing. "I'm starting with my room."

"Our room," Roland said. "And no touching yourself when you're in it."

"I guess I could touch you, but you have to promise to touch me back," Steve said with a smirk.

"Touch me and get a boot up your ass," Roland, moving to follow Steve.

"Keep your kink to yourselves," Brandon called.

"Kink and cameras go hand in hand," Roni said, turning over the toaster in the kitchen.

They spread out, looking for devices and giving Molev the

perfect cover he needed to find stuff without being overly obvious.

Before I could ask if he wanted to help me look, a shout came from the bedrooms.

"Son of a bitch. You were right," Steve shouted.

After that, we all looked and found something. Hints from Molev weren't necessary. We removed each device, bagged them up, and set them outside like trash.

"That's probably not going to go over well," I said after the door closed.

"I stopped caring when I shot Tamra," Sid said bluntly. "I know Molev warned Patrick to order an airlift."

"Mistakes were made," I said. "On all sides. We need to stop making them."

"Do you think removing the surveillance is a mistake?" Sid asked.

"No. But I think removing them will cause more mistrust." I looked at Molev. "They're obviously curious about you. They've heard what you can do from Patrick, but they haven't seen it for themselves. You need to find a way to start building trust on your terms like you did with us."

He crossed his arms in that stubborn way of his as his pensive gaze swept over us.

"Come with me." That's all he said before he turned and started for the door.

Roland shrugged and trailed after him. The rest of us hurried to do the same. When we left, the soldiers were right there, following us on foot. So was the drone.

Molev stuck to the path we'd taken earlier, and when we reached a table near the playground, he stopped and sat. The soldiers hung back as Molev put his elbow on the table and gestured to Roni. Her eyes lit with understanding.

"Hell yes," she said. She sat down opposite Molev but didn't take his hand. "Katie and Andie, get in here."

I moved around the table, standing by his shoulder, thinking I'd be able to use my body weight to push his arm over. When I wrapped my hands around his forearm, his gaze flicked to mine.

"If we do something that hurts, you'll tell us, right?" I asked.

The corners of his mouth twitched. "You won't hurt me."

"Challenge accepted," Roni said. "Go!"

Katie started pulling, Roni started muscling him, and I threw my weight against Molev's forearm. I tried not to pay attention to the feel of his warm skin under my hands and put my effort into moving him. Both were impossible, though. Pressed against him, my face was close to his, reminding me of our almost kiss.

I was still curious about what it would be like. More than that, I was interested in finding out. And that was a problem. I couldn't afford the distraction. Not now, when I was so close to getting Zion the ticket he needed.

Roni grunted and then started swearing under her breath as she strained harder.

"I give," I said, acknowledging what Roni never would. "We're not budging him."

When I released Molev, his leg brushed against mine. But he didn't look at me. Probably a good thing since the drone was still flying overhead.

Roni got up and gave the soldiers a pointed look. No one could antagonize with just a glance like she could.

"Man up and give it a try," she said.

The drone sank lower and drifted closer.

"Come. Your people wish to see my strength," Molev said. "I will take care not to harm you."

"No weapons and no dirty tricks," I warned. "He won't tolerate either. But if you want to see if you can beat him, step up."

One of the soldiers did. Molev toyed with him. I could see that hint of a smirk on his face as he gave the guy an inch, only to slam his hand down a second later.

"I'd suggest all three of you," I said when the guy swore.

They tried that, and then Roland, Brandon, and Steve got in on it.

Sid laughed and shook his head as they piled on top of each other, grunting and groaning.

"It was a solid effort," Molev said when they finally gave up. "Even my brothers struggle to beat me."

"How many of them does it take to win?" one of the soldiers asked.

"We arm wrestle one-on-one," Molev said, standing.

"Wait, we want to try again."

Molev shook his head. "Katie is hungry."

Everyone looked at Katie, and her face flushed scarlet. "Was my stomach that loud?"

"I didn't hear anything," one of the soldiers said.

Molev motioned for Katie to lead the way, and we all fell in around him.

The soldiers followed us back but lingered by the jeep as we went to the house. The bag with the devices was gone, and I wasn't the only one to suspect they'd been rehidden inside. However, another sweep through the house turned up nothing.

"I'll make lunch," I volunteered once we knew the house was clean.

Everyone migrated in that direction and watched me pull out what was needed for sandwiches.

"They want more than arm wrestling," Molev said as he removed plates from the cupboard.

"What do you mean?" Brandon asked.

"After the match ended, the voice in one's ear said to take me to the course and time me."

Roni snorted. "I mean, I'd love to see that myself."

"Same," Sid said. "But knowing how fast he can complete the course doesn't help them create a vaccine." He looked at Molev. "I don't think you should do it."

Molev picked up a piece of bread and started slathering it with peanut butter.

"You believe like Katie and Roni that they will use the knowledge they gain to find a way to hurt my kind?"

"With every move they make, it's looking more likely," Sid said. "The longer you stay here, the more they'll push."

"Then perhaps I shouldn't stay."

CHAPTER FIFTEEN

"IS THAT WHAT YOU WANT?" I ASKED, MY STOMACH DROPPING AT the thought of Molev leaving now. If he left, we would never see our tickets.

We needed him to stay. *I* needed him to stay. But no matter how desperately I wanted to save my nephew, staying had to be Molev's choice, not mine.

"I agree that their behavior is suspicious, but they have questions about you and are looking for answers. Running will make it look like you have something to hide. Instead of running, call them on their bullshit. Ask what your physical abilities have to do with the vaccine. Ask why they're treating you like a prisoner instead of a guest. Tell them your suspicions and see what happens. Most people back down when they're confronted."

"Most people," Roni said, taking the first completed sandwich. "Not the desperate ones, though."

"I say we hang around the house and see if they actually follow through with what they promised," Sid said. "And if not, we complain and start questioning things."

I didn't disagree with that approach, and based on Molev's

slow nod, neither did he. The others finished their sandwiches, one by one, and drifted to the living room to watch movies. Molev started cleaning up even though he'd helped with the prep. I pitched in.

When we finished, he caught my hand before I could drift to the living room and nodded in the direction of our bedroom.

Unsure why he wanted to speak privately, I followed him there. The thought that he might want to pick up where he'd left off outside the perimeter didn't cross my mind until he closed the door behind us. However, he didn't reach for me. Instead, he sat on the bed and rested his forearms on his knees in a very tired gesture.

"Everything okay?" I asked.

"Suggesting we leave scared you. Why?"

"We? You said 'I' out there, not we."

"You have all agreed to come with me when it is time to leave. When I leave, we all leave."

"Ah."

Lightning fast, he reached out and tugged me forward so I stood between his spread legs. He tipped his head only a little to look up at me.

"You have no need for fear. I will never abandon you, Andie."

His expression hinted that he wanted me to promise the same thing. But I couldn't. I'd meant what I'd said. I didn't know him well enough yet to understand what my place would be in his life. But more than that, I just wasn't sure of anything yet. I struggled to envision a future at all, never mind one with him.

"It wasn't the thought of you leaving without me," I said honestly. "It was the thought of you leaving before they give us what they promised us.

"My nephew is only three years old. The mountains are keeping most of the infected and the hounds to the east. But it's only a matter of time before they breach the barriers. I was promised a ticket to an island sanctuary, a place the infected and hounds can't reach. I'm afraid that if you leave, they won't give me that ticket, and my nephew will die here."

Molev reached up and trailed his fingers down my throat. As it had last time, the touch set my pulse racing. Even if I wasn't sure about any type of future for us, I had no doubts about my attraction to him.

I'd witnessed his power time and again. His savagery. Seeing it and feeling his hand on my skin sparked something inside of me, a fear-driven anticipation. I wanted to feel his hand resting at the base of my throat and know that, for me, he would be gentle. For me, he would be whatever I needed.

Struggling to focus on our conversation rather than my desire, I licked my lips and looked away from his intense gaze.

"I think Sid's right, and not only because I'm thinking of my nephew. By waiting to see if they follow through, we'll be able to gauge their intent with you."

His fingers stroked down my throat again.

"Your eyes say you hunger for me as I hunger for you even when your lips remain silent. You tempt me to break the rules, Andie." His fingers slid alongside my neck and dug into the hair at the base of my skull. They tightened on the strands, pulling slightly so my head tipped back. That subtle assertion of dominance sent flames of need licking through my body.

My lips parted.

He stood, towering over me as his gaze locked on my mouth. The raw hunger in his expression goaded me. I wanted that. I wanted him.

"But I am not a human man, Andie," he said, breaking into my thoughts. "I will not take what is not freely given."

"What are you saying?" I asked breathlessly.

"When you want my lips on yours, you will need to tell me. Do you understand?"

I couldn't nod. He was holding my hair too tight.

"Do you understand?" he repeated.

"Yes."

His gaze caressed my face. "Do you like this, Andie? Do you like when I hold you so you cannot move?"

I closed my eyes, debating the wisdom of how I should answer him. I decided on the truth.

"I do like this, but it makes me question my sanity."

"Explain," he commanded before I felt the fingers of his free hand stroking my skin.

"Considering your strength, I shouldn't be encouraging any form of dominance. Too much force could hurt me."

His gaze flicked from my face to my throat, and he frowned. His hold immediately began to loosen.

"Do you fear I will hurt you?"

I caught one of his braids and firmly applied pressure until he bent toward me. I could see the way his pupils dilated because of what I was doing.

"I'm exerting dominance. Are you afraid?"

His lips curled into a wickedly hungry smile.

"Andie, I fear very little. It excites me when you toy with me."

"Then you understand how I feel when you use just a little bit of force on me."

He groaned lightly. "Tell me your lips are mine. Tell me I can kiss you whenever…however…I wish."

I held his braid, realizing what I was doing. Playing with fire.

"Molev, I…can't."

He didn't get upset. He simply grabbed my hair the way I like and set his forehead to mine.

"You are right. Neither of us can afford to be distracted by your tempting lips. Not yet. But soon, Andie. Soon you will tell me you're mine."

He released me and stepped back.

"Go watch your movie with the others. I will join you soon." He closed himself in our bathroom.

Shaking from the adrenaline rush, I stood there for a moment and listened to the shower run. We liked toying with each other. Did he have any idea how badly I wanted to march into that bathroom and see how far I could push him? Exhaling slowly, I left him alone as he asked.

When he joined us, his hair was wet, his bandages were missing, and he was wearing a pair of athletic shorts that fit him like spandex. I looked at what he was packing. Roni had said it was the size of her forearm, and that wasn't much of an exaggeration.

Roni glanced at him and did a double-take. "Now you're just being a tease, Molev."

Roland looked at him and recoiled. "That's just not right."

"It looks like he's smuggling an overgrown zucchini, right?" Roni said, her unblinking stare at Molev's groin making him frown.

"Nope," Steve said, standing. "We are not looking at that for the next however many hours or days it takes to make a vaccine."

"Try weeks," Katie said. "Maybe even months." She was doing her own share of staring.

Steve threw open the door and strode outside.

"I really hope it's months," Roni said under her breath.

"I second that nope," Brandon said, vaulting over the couch and bolting out the door.

Molev looked at me.

"They'll find you some looser clothes," I said.

Molev grunted and took Brandon's place on the couch beside me. Roni smirked and wiggled her eyebrows. Katie looked like she was trying to do long division in her head.

"Shouldn't your stitches be covered?" I asked Molev, trying to shift their focus.

"They were starting to itch."

"Itching is a sign of healing," Katie said. "So that's good."

"How long were the stitches in your arm before I removed them?" Roni asked.

"Seven, maybe eight days," he answered.

"About the same for a human," she said. "But yours looked like they were in a week too long. We'll need to watch the stitches on your back. Maybe start wearing shirts around other people if you don't want anyone else to realize just how fast you heal."

I glanced at Molev and wondered if that was something they would be able to tell by his blood.

"What are you thinking?" he asked.

"That you're taking a lot of risk for very little reward."

"There is no reason to remain in this world if all the humans die," he said.

"Whoa," Katie said softly.

"Yeah. Why do we mean so much to you?" Roland asked.

Molev met his gaze. "We have no females of our own."

Roland made a choked sound and sat up a little straighter. "You serious right now?"

"Uh, so when you said all those female volunteers were going to help improve relations, you meant 'relations,'" Roland said, air-quoting the word.

"There are going to be a lot of happy women if all your

kind are built like you," Roni said with a significant glance at his clearly defined package.

"Will they be happy, though?" Katie asked. "I wouldn't be if I were forced into having relations with someone I didn't know. Someone I didn't care about."

"Nothing will be forced," I said quickly.

"Where's the guarantee?" she asked.

"It's here. It's us right now. He's giving *me* a choice."

"Damn, gurl," Roni drawled. "I knew you had it in you. Well, you will have it in you." She winked.

Katie shook her head, still looking troubled.

"Tell me about the course they wanted me to complete," Molev said, giving us the change in topic we needed.

"When things went to hell and they realized they needed more people in the field, they set up areas where they could test physical fitness," Roni said. "There are several courses. They started the civilians out on the easy ones, and if they passed the minimum thresholds for time, they moved up to the next course and the next."

"The final course is intense," Katie said. "And it's not timed."

"They just used it to weed through the people who had the guts to keep pushing even when we knew we would fail," Roni said, sharing a look with me and Katie.

The fact that Katie and I had kept going was the reason we'd even been considered for the squad.

"It's physically challenging," I said. "A lot of crawling under things, over things, running, jumping, climbing, balancing…and there's no stopping anywhere for a break."

"I would like to look at these courses," Molev said.

"Can't hurt to look," Sid said with a shrug.

"Maybe not the day it was suggested in someone's

earpiece, though," Roland said. "Unless you want them to know how sharp your hearing is."

An engine rumbled outside, and Roland got up to check the window.

"Another vehicle. Looks like a civilian driving it. She handed off a bag to the guards. Looks like Steve and Brandon made nice with the guards. They've got the bag and are laughing and chatting."

Steve and Brandon joined us a while later, tossing a paper bag to Molev.

"Something in there should fit you better," Sid said. "And if it doesn't, they said they'll find something else."

Molev left with the clothes.

"Next time they want him to do something physical, he should wear those shorts," Roni said, watching him leave. "It'll distract everyone."

"Roni, that itch you've got isn't going to scratch itself. You want help with that?" Steve said with a smirk.

"Hell no. There's more where he came from. I'm going to let this itch build."

"Poor unknown man won't know what hit him," Roland said with a shake of his head.

Once Molev returned in looser-fitting shorts and a shirt, we watched movies and waited. When dinnertime rolled around, no one needed to voice their doubts, and I tried not to think about what the delay might mean.

The light faded outside. Katie was the first one to start yawning and drift away. Steve and Brandon were next. Roni started another movie, and even though I was tired, I didn't leave. I wasn't ready yet for snuggle time next to Molev.

Sid gave up after another thirty minutes. Roland watched him go and looked at us.

"I know there are guards outside and a fence around the

perimeter and a whole damn mountain range keeping the infected out, but it still feels weird just going to bed without a lookout, you know?"

"Hit the rack," Roni said. "I'll stay up."

He smiled slightly, nodded, and left us.

Roni waited until the door closed then stopped the movie.

"Put on your big girl pants and take him to bed. Tomorrow will come early. It always does."

She left me alone with Molev.

"I hope one of your brothers likes aggressive women," I said, staring after her.

"Roni will find what she is looking for when we return." He moved his arm to rest on the back of the couch behind me, and I almost grinned. Did he know that was a human move? Probably not.

"Are you tired?" he asked.

"Yeah." I turned to him, sitting sideways on the couch. "It's not a good sign that they didn't send anyone today. It could mean they don't intend to keep their word. And if they can't keep their word with this, how can we trust anything they say, including your request for volunteers."

He cupped the back of my head and brought his forehead to mine. His eyes closed, and he took a slow calming breath. I did the same and realized how much I'd needed to take a moment and just breathe.

He held us together like that for several more breaths before he released me.

"You need sleep." He stood and held out his hand.

"I'm not ready for things to be different between us," I admitted.

"I know. Come."

I wasn't exactly sure if that meant nothing would change or if he was just acknowledging my reluctance.

With my hand in his, he led me to our bedroom. Like the night before, I stripped out of my pants and tossed my bra aside, choosing to sleep in my shirt and underwear.

Molev kept his shorts and shirt on as he got in beside me. He didn't leave space between us tonight but went straight for the cusp-of-sleep snuggles, pulling me close to his side and resting an arm over my middle.

"I understand nicknames," he said out of nowhere. "Mom is a nickname for Julie and a title of respect. It has meaning for her. Why are you called Andie? Does it have meaning?"

The question relaxed me, and I rolled toward him.

"Not really. It's just a shortened version of Andromeda. I liked it because it was gender-neutral. So when I was applying for jobs, they couldn't tell if I was a girl or boy."

"Why does that matter?"

"It's not supposed to, but it does. Men tended to get more preference in our society. They have more control."

Molev gave a slight laugh. "I hope they continue thinking that way."

"Why?"

"If they realize how important females are and how much they control the future of this world, your human men will never allow me to leave with five hundred of them."

"I suppose not," I said.

I closed my eyes and let myself relax more.

"I hope they send someone tomorrow," I said.

"If they don't, we will encourage them to make the right choices."

I grinned a little. "You sound like Rachel. I really need to see her."

His hand smoothed over my arm, and I let go of the rest of my worry, willingly sinking into sleep.

As Roni had predicted, morning came early. The hint of

dawn's light peeking around the curtains was enough to coax my eyes open. Molev's exhale teased the skin at the back of my neck while the arm around my waist firmly anchored my back against his front.

And I didn't hate any of it. The way his hand splayed over my stomach, just below my breasts, did things to me. If Molev and I were the only two people in the house...if I wasn't worried about my nephew...if I didn't think the military was scheming and watching, waiting for a chance to pounce, I would have rolled over and started something that likely would have ended with me mindlessly blissed out. Or, maybe not if he'd never been with a woman before.

"You're frowning," Molev said, his voice a low rumble. "You rarely frown. Are you angry?"

I twisted in his arms to look at him and found him wide awake and watching me.

"No. Curious. But realizing I can't do anything to ease my curiosity just yet. Did you sleep well?"

"Very well." Holding onto me, he rolled to his back, taking me with him but somehow managing to turn me in the process so we were face-to-face.

His hard chest wasn't the only thing pressing against me. I swallowed and stared vacantly at Molev's face as I visualized his size based on where his length was digging into me.

"What are you curious about?" he asked.

I focused on his mossy green eyes with those sand-colored flecks and struggled to remember why straddling his hips and having some fun was a bad idea.

"I'm usually pretty good at reading people and most situations, but I'm not thinking as clearly as I used to. And I don't think it's the exhaustion of the last couple of weeks catching up to me. I think it's because you're distracting me, Molev."

His lips twitched. "Good."

"No, not good. We need me to focus so you don't end up as a lab rat and my nephew doesn't end up as a chew toy. Please."

His fingers feathered over my cheek.

"Your observations and determination to lead remind me of Mya. But like Mya, you haven't yet realized you don't need to lead alone. I am not blind. I see the dangers you see and carefully choose who to trust. Now, place your trust in me as I have placed my trust in you."

"I do trust you. If I didn't, I wouldn't be lying on top of you."

"Mmm. Or perhaps, if you trusted me more, you would be lying on top of me without these."

He tugged at the waistband of my underwear.

My pulse leapt, and my gaze dipped to his mouth. The fingers on my cheek shifted around to the back of my head, curling in my hair and drawing me close. My lips parted.

I knew this wasn't smart, but my body was screaming *yes*.

The hand at my waist slid lower, smoothing down my ass and curling around a thigh. He tugged my legs apart until my knee touched the mattress.

"Do you like this, Andie?"

"I'm trying really hard not to," I said, struggling to think clearly.

"I want you to like it. Tell me you like it, and I'll show you what I want to do next."

That hand on my thigh drifted between my legs and feathered over the thin barrier keeping me from having the time of my life.

"Tell me you like it. Let me taste your lips. Let me—"

The finger teasing my slit stilled at the knock on our door. And for a split second, Molev's expression showed a level of rage I'd never witnessed. One that matched the roar I'd heard more than once.

I framed his face with my hands.

"Hey," I said softly. "This is why I was trying not to feel anything. Now isn't the time or the place for this. Okay?"

His expression calmed, and he released me. I slid off of him, my leg riding way more of his length than it should have, and I went to the door.

"Sup?" I asked Roni, who was grinning at me.

"Katie and I made breakfast. There's a new guard outside, and I'm itching to do something. Come eat, and let's go find out what progress has been made."

I closed the door as she left and saw Molev had already closed himself into the bathroom. Taking advantage of the privacy, I dressed again and made a mental note to ask for some different clothes if we were going to be here for a while.

The others were already in the kitchen when I joined them.

"Have a good night?" Roni asked.

I shook my head at her and helped myself to some eggs.

"So, what's the plan for today?" I asked.

"Sid and I are restless. We think we should tour the courses. We can show Molev what they're all about while he watches. If they're as excited to test him out as I think they are, they're going to try to get him to play too. That's when we'll have them by the short hairs and can start asking questions of our own."

"I don't know," I said. "They've been playing nice so far because we brought them what they asked for, and Molev's let them know he trusts us. How do you think they'll respond if we start stirring things up?"

"They won't," Molev said, coming up behind me. "They are still assessing our bonds and will try to separate each of you from the group to speak to you individually. Andie, if they know you desire safety for your nephew, they will use that as leverage to get what they want."

I paused eating to look at him in stunned silence. It made perfect sense. Why rush giving me what they promised when they could still use it against me?

"What do they want?" Katie asked.

"Everything," he said. "Humans always want everything."

We all stared at him as he helped himself to a portion of the eggs.

"I want to be offended," Steve said, "but I think you're right."

"If that's how you really think," I said, "do you truly trust any of us?"

His gaze swept over the group. "You are all willing to give your lives to a single purpose, a purpose I share. We must find a way to stop the infected and the hounds and save the people who remain. Nothing else matters. That is why I trust you."

Was that what his advance was this morning? To test my resolve?

I started eating my eggs again and decided it didn't matter if it was or wasn't because he was right. We shared a single purpose, and that was all that mattered.

"Okay," Roni said. "Then we finish up here and head to the courses."

We spent the morning there under the watchful eyes of our guards. Roni and Steve competed hard to see who had the fastest times. No one showed up. Not even the drone. We ate lunch back at the house and set out for the second course. Roland and Sid took over on that one. They didn't compete but horsed around and explained things to Molev.

The group's frustration mounted as the light faded. We were all quiet as we made our way back to the house. As soon as we entered, Molev's gaze swept the room.

"Someone was here," he said.

"How do you know?" Roland asked.

"No," Roni said. "We don't play question and answer until we sweep the house again."

Twenty minutes later, we tossed another bag out onto the lawn and shut the door.

I looked at Molev, and he nodded.

"What now?" Steve asked. "Are they just going to keep fucking with us, or are they going to get serious?"

"Don't forget you're dealing with two groups," Sid said. "I'm betting the scientists have been working non-stop. They're probably finding some neat things in Molev's blood that are raising questions. This is the military's way of trying to supply the answers without ruffling feathers."

"Well, they did a shit job," Steve said. "My feathers are ruffled. They should have just come out and asked."

"They won't belicve what I tell them," Molev said. "Their attention is focused on us. We only need to use the right bait to lure them out. Rest well tonight. Tomorrow will be challenging."

CHAPTER SIXTEEN

MOLEV WOULDN'T TELL US WHAT HE HAD PLANNED, AND THAT annoyed me enough that I didn't welcome cuddle time when I went to bed. It wasn't that I didn't trust Molev. I trusted him plenty. I didn't fully trust the people in charge, though. Not with Molev. They'd made too many mistakes already. Which is why I wanted to know what Molev had planned so I could help him avoid things that would lead them to making more mistakes.

However, despite my distance when I'd gone to bed, I woke up in little-spoon position again anyway.

"I'm still annoyed with you," I said as soon as I opened my eyes.

"I know."

"So then, you're purposely annoying me?"

"No," he said, smoothing his hand over my stomach. "I'm trying to prove you do not need to lead alone. That we can lead together."

"Not telling me what you have planned isn't leading together."

"No. But it will show that I am capable of understanding

how human minds work. You trust me to protect you but little else."

I turned in his arms and considered him for a moment as I thought back. I hadn't shown any confidence in him. Patrick gave an order, and I followed it because I trusted him to lead. When I'd been giving Molev suggestions, he'd followed them, showing that he trusted me to lead. But had I ever shown Molev that I would follow him the same way? Not really.

"You're right, and I'm sorry. I'll embrace the suspense and see what the day brings. I do trust you."

He rolled me onto his chest just like the previous morning.

"How much do you trust me?"

"Enough to know that we both understand this isn't going to lead to anything." I patted his chest and pushed myself up. "Get dressed. I think it's our turn to make breakfast."

Just before I moved away, I thought I saw him scowl, but when I glanced back as I tugged on my pants, his expression was as stoic as always.

"Don't take too long. If I do all the cooking, you do all the cleaning," I said as I left the room.

He joined me in the kitchen when I was still looking over the food options.

"We have enough eggs to make some pancakes, but I'm not sure they'll be your favorite." I checked the freezer and found two tubes of sausage. "Perfect. We're going to need to request more supplies soon."

We worked together to start breakfast, and as the smell of food filled the air, the others slowly trickled out of their rooms.

"Did you loosen his lips last night?" Roni asked as she sat at the table.

"No," I said. "With all the ears we've found around us, maybe it's better that he doesn't share what he has planned."

"Good point," Steve said before looking at Molev. "Then I

guess we'll wait for your orders." He held up his plate and grinned. "Four, please."

Molev stacked four pancakes on his plate without batting an eye then looked at Sid.

"Let the guards know we are returning to the second course after we eat. Request they restock the food while we are gone, and warn them that we will search for their devices each time we leave this house."

Sid got up and went to deliver the message. Molev had a plate waiting for him when he came back in.

"They're radioing for more food. I told them to add more meat this time."

"Thank you," Molev said.

Rather than making a plate for himself, since everyone was eating, he took a sausage patty and slathered it with peanut butter.

"I think I just threw up in my mouth," Katie said under her breath.

I'd known from watching Molev eat the MREs that he avoided all tomato-based foods but really enjoyed meat. He'd eaten most of the bread products, though. But this made me realize how little I knew about his preferences. In the field, we ate to live. Here, we had the luxury of eating what we liked. Sort of.

"How does that taste?" Roland asked, already reaching for the peanut butter.

"Different," Molev said. "Better than bread and jelly."

Roland shrugged when he tried his own. "Not as disturbing as I would have thought, and it's high in protein."

Molev ate three more slathered disks then surprised us all by making sandwiches. He tucked each one into a baggy, stacking them five high before starting on a new stack.

I wanted to ask what they were for and saw I wasn't the

only one. But we all kept quiet, knowing Molev had a plan, whatever it was. As soon as everyone finished, I started the clean-up, and Katie helped since Molev was still sandwich-making.

After packing a large paper bag with twenty sandwiches and enough water bottles for everyone, he motioned for the door.

"Time to go," he said.

"What are the chances all that food's for a nice relaxing picnic?" Steve asked.

Molev made a noise that sounded like a laugh as he led the way outside. The guards followed us as we jogged to the second course but hung back as Molev set the bag down and faced us.

"You've all agreed to return with me and understand what it's like out there. While your scientists work on a cure, we'll train. Tamra died because of a simple mistake. When we leave, there will be no mistakes. No more lives lost." His gaze swept over all of us. "Are you ready?"

"Hell yes," Roni said.

Molev's idea of training wasn't pushups and obstacle courses. He had us fighting hand-to-hand but with a twist.

"You win when you bite the other person," he said.

Katie made a panicked sound.

"Not hard," he added.

Molev paired us up and watched, giving us pointers as we fought. Wrestling around to avoid being bitten was the most physically taxing thing on the planet. Mostly because Roland, Steve, and Roni were competitive as hell. The water and sandwiches made sense when Molev finally called for a break.

I collapsed on the ground beside Katie.

"I'd rather do sit-ups until I barf," she panted.

"No, you wouldn't," I said, struggling to get enough air.

"We'll see if you still say that tomorrow," she said.

Molev handed us both a bottle of water and watched to make sure we started drinking before handing out the rest.

"It's hard," I agreed, "But what he's teaching us might save our lives."

We ate a sandwich each and rested for twenty minutes before he called us back. This time, he paired up with Sid to show us what he was seeing.

"If you bite me, I'm quitting Camp Molev," Sid said.

"I will not bite you. You will try to bite me, and I will show you how to avoid being bitten."

"Says the guy with all the bite scars," Roland said dryly.

Molev ignored him and waved Sid forward. Sid came at him like an infected would but stopped at the last second.

"No removing my head either," Sid said.

Molev snorted, which had us all grinning.

"I will be gentle," Molev said.

"I need a cold shower," Roni muttered.

Katie and Steve sniggered.

Sid leapt at Molev. Molev brought his arm up to block Sid then pushed him back. Not with Molev-type strength, though, just human. Sid stumbled back a few steps.

"I prevented a bite and created space between us. That space will allow you to draw your weapon, or if you call for help, it will allow someone else to kill the infected for you."

"Smart," Roni said, focused.

Molev turned, facing away from Sid.

"You've been working in pairs. One watches forward, and one watches behind. What happens when you lose your partner? How do you prevent a bite you cannot see?"

He went through several more examples, and when he finished, he reshuffled the pairs and had us go again. Steve had a solid sixty pounds on me and wasn't easy to push back, no matter how hard I tried. It didn't help that I was tired from the first session. Each time we broke apart and he came back at me, it was harder to fight him off.

Until I couldn't.

My strength quit on me, and Steve darted in. His teeth dug into my neck, and I grunted at the pain.

He was off of me a second later, dangling by the collar clenched in Molev's fist.

"I said no hard biting." The anger on Molev's face and the growl in his words had Steve nodding.

"It was an accident. I didn't expect her to stop trying."

Molev set Steve down and turned to me. The anger was still in his eyes when he grabbed my chin and turned my head to inspect my neck.

"The skin isn't broken. Why did you stop trying?" he demanded.

"It wasn't a conscious decision. My arm just gave out. We've been stuck in survival mode for weeks, Molev. Eat, sleep, and guard duty. Most of our days were spent in the trucks. This is the most exercise I've had since we left."

Molev exhaled heavily and looked at the others, who'd stopped practicing too.

"Am I asking too much of you?" The open concern in his question had Steve standing straighter and wiped some of the shock off Brandon's expression.

"You're asking us to survive," Roni said. "It's not something that's going to be easy, but it's something we all want to do."

Molev nodded and looked at me again.

"You will likely wear more of these marks, then," he said, trailing his fingers over the bite. Then he lowered his voice and added, "Get stronger faster, Andie. Please."

I nodded, and he stepped away.

"That's enough of this practice for now. When your strength is failing and the infected are near, you have two options. Run or climb high. Which do you prefer?"

"Run," I said immediately since my arms were too tired for climbing.

"Then we run."

That's when I noticed there were a few more soldiers by the jeep. They watched us all jog around the spread-out course. I wasn't sure how many laps we did, but I was winded by the time Molev finally stopped us for another break.

This one was longer, and I took a nap on the rope netting.

After that, we climbed until I thought my arms would fall off.

The end of the day didn't come soon enough. And I wasn't the only one thinking that way. Even Roni's gung-ho attitude had faded to mutters about sadism.

When the sun started to set, Molev finally called it quits. There were four jeeps parked by the original one now.

"Anyone want a lift?" one of the soldiers called.

We all made a beeline for the vehicles, except for Molev. He trailed behind at a leisurely jog.

"Will you be training again tomorrow?" the guard asked.

Roland groaned, and I looked back at Molev, who nodded at me.

"Yes. We'll be there. Why?" I asked.

"Think there's room for one or two more?"

"Yeah," I said without looking at Molev. I didn't need to. What he'd done was now glaringly obvious. Openly teaching us ways to survive showed his intent better than any words he could have spoken. He'd extended the olive branch, and at least a few of them were taking it. Tomorrow, there would probably be more.

"I'm going to die," Katie said beside me.

"No, you won't. You're going to get up, and you're going to keep fighting even when everything hurts. You'll wake up with a smile tomorrow because you know you're going to survive it."

"But will I?" she asked, closing her eyes.

Roland put his arm around her, giving her a comforting side hug, which she turned into a catnap. When the jeeps stopped in front of the house, we all groaned as we got out and shuffled toward the door.

Every one of us collapsed on the couch and chairs as soon as we were inside. Except for Molev. He went to the kitchen to start cooking.

"They restocked the food," he said. "We can do a sweep of the house after you rest."

THE NEXT DAY, five soldiers joined us. The day after, ten. They didn't talk much, but they paid attention and learned whatever Molev was willing to teach. The following day, some of the faces changed.

It went on like that for a week. Sleep, eat, train until I wanted to collapse, then eat, train some more, eat, and repeat. I was so exhausted by the end of each day I didn't always remember going to bed. And I was so sore that I could barely stand getting out of bed.

The core group of us started snapping at each other over little things. Molev didn't comment, letting us be as long as we were practicing. Until Roni tried punching Steve. Molev plucked her off by the back of her shirt and gave her a stern finger-wag accompanied by a "no hitting Steve when he wins" lecture.

Before she could come back with something appropriately

rage-filled and "Roni," another jeep pulled up. This one wasn't filled with soldiers looking for some extra training, though. The woman from the hospital was there with a medic kit.

"Hello, Molev," she said with a smile. "I'm here for another blood draw."

Molev looked at me. "Did you give your nephew's name to anyone?"

I shook my head, and he looked at Sid. "Did anyone talk to you like the general promised?"

"No, sir. They did not."

Molev faced the doctor. "These men and women kept their word and brought me here. I kept my word and allowed you to take my blood. Now it is time for the general to keep his word."

"Uh, I don't have anything to do with that. I'm just here for a new batch of samples."

"He's telling you no," Roni said. "But politely. We're all about polite these days." She side-eyed Steve.

"But you came here to help us," she said to Molev.

"I am helping," Molev said, crossing his arms. "I'm training anyone who is interested in how to fight the infected."

She glanced at the soldiers assigned to guard us this morning...the ones who were also practicing with us.

"I believe this is an issue for the general," one of them said. "Would you like to report it to him directly, or should I radio it in?"

She looked at her kit then at Molev. "I'll go speak to him."

"Thank you," Molev said.

It didn't take long for the general to show up. He didn't look too happy when he got out of the vehicle and marched over to Molev.

"I've been told you're no longer willing to cooperate," he said.

"How am I not cooperating?" Molev asked.

"You were brought here to provide the samples we need to create the vaccine and are no longer willing to provide those samples. That is not cooperating."

"I was brought here by these men and women, who were promised a ticket to sanctuary in return for their efforts. No one has contacted them for the names of their family like you promised."

"The deal was a ticket for a way to stop this plague. There's no cure yet, and there won't be one without more samples. If you're truly here to help us, you'll give us what we need and stop involving yourself in what isn't your concern."

"Your inability to keep your word is my concern. I agreed to work with your scientists after a mutually beneficial exchange of promises. These men and women brought you a way to stop the infection from spreading as you asked. Do not hold them to blame for your scientists' failures. Keep your word."

The general narrowed his eyes. "I will not give you what you want."

The way he said it poked at me, and I realized the general's refusal to keep his word had nothing to do with getting our tickets.

I huffed out a breath and sat.

"He thinks you're trying to get the location to where they're sending all the essential personnel. It's the backup plan for humanity. If everything goes to shit here and we all die, there are still pockets of humans the infected and hounds can't reach."

Molev crossed his arms and looked at the general's reddening face.

"Patrick thought the same thing about revealing this location. He delayed an airlift because of it. Tamra, Cody,

Tommy, Sean, Derek, Mateo. Humans, your humans, were lost because of fear and mistrust. Don't make the same mistakes."

Molev turned his back on the general. "Seven laps. The last one has to climb the tower twice."

Everyone took off at a sprint except for me.

I moved to stand next to Molev.

"We're out of here tomorrow morning," I said, knowing we couldn't give another inch. "Either we're heading east on our own or west in an airlift you arrange so we can say goodbye to the people we've selected to go in our places. The choice is yours."

"You might be willing to risk the lives of every man, woman, and child left on this continent, Miss Wells, but I'm not."

"Don't be blinded by your prejudice. Risking their lives is exactly what you're doing. And before you say Molev is by withholding his blood, think. Molev knows you're not just using it for a vaccine. He's been dealing with our prejudice and fear for weeks. Yet, he's still here. He's still trying to show you through his actions that he truly is helping us. What are your actions showing him?

"Don't make Patrick's mistakes."

The general left without a word, and after everyone finished their laps and climb, we returned to the house early.

Since the first day of training, we'd checked the house for devices each time we returned. We'd never found anything. That wasn't the case this time. They were everywhere, and we didn't stop until Molev called it.

"Sid, take these to our guards," Molev said.

He started making spaghetti for dinner while we waited for Sid to return.

"Andie has given the general two options," he said. "Either

he keeps his word in the morning, or we leave to join my people. The choice to join me is still yours."

"We're with you," Roni said.

The rest nodded. Katie a little hesitantly.

"Eat. Rest. We leave at first light."

Dinner was quiet. Normally, we'd all be so exhausted that we shuffled to our beds and dropped in fully dressed. Tonight, Roni found a pad of paper and started writing. We all hung back, wanting to do the same—write a letter to the people we were leaving behind. While I waited, I helped Molev clean up, something he'd been doing on his own for the past week.

"Who bit you today?" he asked.

"I didn't catch his name."

"He bit too hard. If you see him in the morning, tell me."

I stopped drying and laughed. "I will not. Steve's been letting me win because he's afraid to make you mad."

"I have not," Steve said. "You're getting better, and Molev is calling breaks before your arms give out."

"Notice how he didn't say he's not afraid of making you mad," Roni said, passing off the pad of paper. "I'll be right back."

She went out the front door, and Roland watched out the window.

When she returned, she was smiling. "They're willing to get our letters to where they need to go."

Katie found more pens, and they shared the paper. I claimed my piece as soon as I was done cleaning.

Rachel,
Things didn't go like I'd hoped, and it looks like the ticket might not happen. But they're working on a cure. While they do that, I'm going back out to see if there's another way to stop what's happening.

You, Zion, Nova, and Apollo are in my thoughts always.
Andie

I FOLDED it and wrote her name and camp number on the outside. Steve took mine out with everyone else's. Exhausted, despite the shortened training, I headed for our room and hit the shower. I focused on how much I would miss that convenience instead of what Rachel would feel when she got my letter.

By the time I finished, Molev was sitting on our bed, waiting for his turn.

"Better hurry before we run out of hot water," I said. "I'm pretty sure everyone's going to take one tonight, just in case we can't have one tomorrow."

I went to the dresser and grabbed some clean clothes, courtesy of whoever had stocked our fridge that first time. Keeping the towel in place, I pulled them on. When I turned, Molev was still there, watching me.

"What's going through your head?" I asked.

He held out his hand to me, and I went to him. His lips twitched as he looked down at my fingers.

"I've been waiting for this," he said. "The moment you would come to me without any hesitation."

"Pretty sure it's happened a few times already."

He shook his head and tugged me to stand between his legs.

"You think before you act. You question 'why' in your head. Not this time. This time you just...came."

He released my hand and wrapped his arms around me, pulling me forward until my knees hit the bed. He rested his forehead against my chest. It wasn't a pass but a moment of surrender. He needed something from me that I suspected no one had ever given him before. Comfort.

I reached forward and gently ran my fingers over his hair.

"Talk to me. What's wrong?"

"I wanted the vaccine. For you. For every female left."

"Careful," I teased. "Steve would be upset to hear you talk like that."

Molev harrumphed but continued to hold me.

"I'm sorry the general didn't keep his word," I said. "I know you don't like returning empty-handed."

He looked up at me.

"My hands are not empty, and my brothers will understand. Knowing that more humans still survive will give them hope. Many will want to come here to see for themselves."

"I'm not sure that will go over well."

Molev shrugged slightly.

"Hope carries us forward and blinds us to the reality that we are hated for no other reason than our existence."

"Not by everyone," I said, tracing a finger over a scar on his jaw. "Some people really like you. A lot."

His pupils expanded, and I smiled.

"Hurry up and shower. I might still be awake when you settle in to spoon me tonight."

He grunted but still didn't release me.

"What do you want, Molev?"

"You. Just you."

I framed his face with my hands, memorizing each scar-marked feature. Giving into an impulse, I leaned in and kissed his cheek. His arms tightened around my waist, but he released me willingly enough when I pulled back.

"You're a handsome man, Molev. But I'm not sure what I want beyond saving my nephew."

His gaze held mine as he stood. He didn't hide any of the hunger he had for me.

"I understand," he said.

I watched him close himself in the bathroom and wondered how long his understanding would last.

CHAPTER SEVENTEEN

I passed out before Molev returned and definitely didn't expect to wake on my own the next morning with him still spooning me. Over the past week, he typically woke me with a gentle shoulder shake and a softly rumbled, "It's time." But never while he was still in bed with me. Due to the extreme training he was putting us through, he woke first and made breakfast, allowing the rest of us to sleep until the last minute.

So I lay there for a second, without opening my eyes and acknowledging I was awake. Despite telling him I wasn't ready for a relationship, there were aspects of having one that I missed. Such as waking up with a partner on a lazy Saturday morning. Staying in bed and talking about nothing for hours. Moments of snuggling. Tender looks. But those things tended to only happen at the beginning of a relationship and faded over time. Which was probably why most of my relationships never lasted very long. I knew what I wanted, and as soon as I was the only one compromising, I was out.

In some ways, I felt bad that I wasn't willing to give Molev a real chance. He seemed willing to compromise, but what point was there in trying when I didn't even know what the next day would bring? Or the current one, for that matter. How could I commit to anything with everything so uncertain?

His fingers moved slightly against my stomach.

"No early morning wake-up today?" I asked quietly.

His hand moved over my stomach. A caress and a comfort.

"You are exhausted from the training, and today will be difficult. No matter what your leaders decide, you will be saying goodbye to your nephew. I wanted to spare you from that for a while longer."

I turned in his arms and stared at his compassionate gaze, stunned by how very much he understood. My trust in him grew.

"You're right. Either way, today's going to be hard," I said. "But whether we're leaving to see him off or to go to Whiteman, I'm not giving up on finding a way to end this. An island isn't a permanent solution; it's temporary safety. We need to stop this plague, or this hell we're in is never going to end. No human will ever be safe."

He nodded slowly.

"Mya told us that we have a responsibility to help kill the hounds since we were the ones who accidentally created them."

"What do you mean you created them?" I asked, stunned.

"I told you about our curse, but I didn't explain everything.

"Mya saw our history when she touched the primary crystal in our caves. It showed her a time long ago when my people first came to this land in search of a new home. My brothers and I found a possible location in the caves. The crystal's power was similar to the power we had in our homeland. It gave eternal life to the creatures that lived there. Whatever we hunted was resurrected, whole and healthy, to be hunted again. There would be no hunger if we lived in those caves. However, some of our people saw the dissimilarities as dangerous. We were locked away in the caves for pursuing the crystals and cursed by our own people so we would never know peace.

"We have no memory of the time before the caves and our exploration of them. It was taken with the curse. We hunted and explored with no understanding of where we were or how we got there.

"It took many months before we noticed the deer we hunted for food weren't coming back the same. When we did, it was already too late. The hounds hunted us in those caves for countless lifetimes. Only the sturdy rock wall surrounding our city kept them at bay and gave us any peace.

"It was a bleak and lonely existence I would not wish on anyone." His hand caressed my stomach again. "We will not stop until we kill every last hound."

"So the hounds were made in those caves because of the curse that locked you in there?"

"Yes."

"And there's magic in the crystal?" I still couldn't quite wrap my head around the magic aspect involved in his story. Yet, I'd seen the hounds with their glowing red eyes. I'd seen how they couldn't be killed and felt that unexplained darkness when Molev ripped the heart out of one of them.

"Yes. In the source crystal."

"Is the crystal still there?"

"Yes."

"If the crystal is how the curse and the hounds were created, what would happen if we destroyed it?"

He lifted his hand from my stomach and looked at the bracelet he wore. The coarse leather cords encased a chunk of raw crystal.

. HAAG

I ran a finger over the stone. It didn't feel like anything. Just stone.

"I do not know," Molev said. "It is a large crystal that extends from floor to ceiling. Five times taller than I stand."

A knock on our door interrupted our conversation.

"Get out here," Steve called. "There's news."

I scrambled out of bed and tugged on my pants as I hopped toward the door. Molev was slower to rise until I tripped. He moved lightning fast and caught me in his arms before I hit the floor.

"Take care, Andie."

"Yeah, got it," I said breathlessly, looking up at him.

"The news will still be there after you're dressed."

"Right." He steadied me and watched as I finished pulling on my pants before stepping away to open the door.

We joined the others in the living room where a uniformed soldier also waited.

"Okay, we're all here," Roni said. "What's the verdict?"

The guy smiled a little and pulled out a thin stack of folded papers from his pocket.

"You can deliver these in person. We leave in twenty to rendezvous at the evac site."

I took my letter to Rachel and felt so many things. Relief and devastation were the biggest. Zion would finally be safe, but I was dreading what would happen next. I'd been there when Apollo left with Nova. It hadn't been pretty. Zion hadn't understood why his dad and sister were leaving. And I could only imagine what my sweet little nephew would do when Rachel tried putting him on the transport without her.

The rest of the group was looking just as shell-shocked as I felt. Sid had his head bowed and was wiping at his eyes. Steve looked like he was going to throw up. Brandon was staring at nothing, just holding the letter. Roland's gaze met mine.

"My daughter's fifteen," he said. "I haven't seen her in six months."

Katie sniffled and hugged her knees to her chest.

"My brother's twenty-five," she said. "Three years older than me. I'm not even sure he knows I left. Special needs. Do you think your daughter would watch over him for me?"

The desperation in her voice triggered all the things I'd been holding back. Feeling every fracture in that wall I'd been holding in place, I turned on my heel and left the room. It took me ten minutes to pull myself together. Another five with a cold washcloth on my face before I was willing to walk out the door.

When I did, Molev was waiting for me.

He took my hand without speaking and led me out of the house to one of the waiting vehicles. A few of the others were already there. Once I was situated, he went back in. The rest came out with him.

It was a quiet drive around the base to the helicopter pad. The whir of the blades warming up made it all that much more real. The ride to the evac site didn't take too long, and I observed the chaos as we touched down.

Hundreds of people stood outside the evacuation area's fence, yelling and begging for a seat on the large carrier that was being loaded with supplies. Armed guards stood inside the fence, looking out, making sure no one tried to climb over the razor wire. I couldn't imagine facing that level of desperation day after day.

"Head there," the soldier yelled, pointing toward another building.

We jumped out and ran together. The yelling outside the fence slowly died as people caught sight of Molev until we only heard the engines of the vehicles moving supplies.

One of the soldiers guarding the door stepped aside and

opened it for us when we neared. His gaze never left Molev, and his partner kept his hands on his weapon. Whatever information they'd been given, it was clear they'd expected Molev and didn't trust him.

"He doesn't bite," I said. "The infected do."

The soldier didn't acknowledge me as I moved past him, so I didn't bother trying to say more.

More soldiers were inside the smaller building.

All armed. All facing the door.

Over half of them pointed their weapons at Molev as he entered with us.

"Molev, run!" I said when I realized what was happening.

That roar that I'd hoped never to hear again echoed behind me. The soldiers raced at us. One grabbed me. A burst of shots was fired outside while scuffling continued inside. When the soldier holding me turned to pull me away, I saw why.

The door was still open. Molev was gone. And the rest of the team was fighting.

Sid swore and head-butted the soldier trying to hold him back.

"Fucking idiots. What are you doing?" he yelled before he threw a punch and swore again. Roni was trying to bite hers.

"Stop!" I yelled without fighting my captor as he dragged me farther away from the door.

No one inside listened to me. Outside, though, there was another roar and more gunfire.

"Dammit, Molev, we're fine!" I yelled. "Just go!"

"Sid. Roni," I called. "If you don't stop fighting, he's going to think we need his help and risk himself to save your sorry asses. Is that what you want?"

They both stopped. Roni's nose was bleeding, and Sid had a black eye.

I shook my head at both of them and looked at the others

before I spotted the general emerging from a door down the hall.

"Call him back," the general said.

"Do you think he's a runaway pet?" I asked. "He doesn't come when I whistle."

"But he would return if he thought you were in trouble. You just said so yourself."

"What is wrong with you?" Roland said. "He was willing to cooperate. He already let you take blood samples as proof of that. He was training men how to better kill infected and stay alive. All you had to do was keep your word."

"Do you see what's happening out there?" the general demanded. "Do you see how many people are desperately waiting for their chance at salvation? A salvation that just ran off? While you're selfishly trying to save a handful of relatives, I'm trying to save everyone that's left."

"Bring them," he ordered, moving toward the door.

"This is not going to end well," Katie said, looking at me.

"I don't think so either," I said.

We were led outside a distance from the buildings. A vehicle waited, and when the soldier fetched the general a bullhorn, I wanted to groan.

Instead, I beat him to whatever announcement he wanted to make.

"We found the cure," I shouted to the now-silent crowd. "It's the grey."

"Shut her up," the general ordered.

The hand that covered my mouth didn't silence the truth.

"They're trying to kill him," Steve yelled before he and the others were silenced.

The previously quiet crowd started to murmur. The fence rattled, and their volume increased.

The general lifted his bullhorn.

"Back away from the fence, or we will open fire," he said. "Molev, you have three seconds to comply or—"

There was a thump on metal behind us. I couldn't turn to look and closed my eyes when I heard Molev's voice.

"Look at my arms," he called. "See the scars, and know I've been bitten and have survived."

"Descend from the roof and surrender yourself to our custody," the general said over Molev.

"Your leaders made promises in exchange for my help," Molev said, continuing to speak to the crowd. "Promises they have not kept."

"If you choose not to comply, you risk your life and the lives of everyone you care about," the general boomed through the speaker.

"If you wish for a cure and my help, have your leaders release those who have gained my trust, and keep their promises."

The general tossed the bullhorn to a soldier.

"Get a drone in the air. Now. Follow him."

I elbowed the person holding me, not to break free but to get him to ease up.

"And them?" another soldier asked.

"Take them back inside for questioning."

"WHERE DID HE GO?" the general asked yet again.

"How am I supposed to know? I'm not the one following him with a drone."

"Miss Wells, I don't believe you understand the gravity of the situation you find yourself in."

"The handcuffs, armed guards, and fat lip are a pretty good indication," I said. "But do you understand the gravity of your situation? You've fucked up as hard and as thoroughly as humanly possible. He was our chance to end this."

"He still is. But your current circumstance wasn't what I was referring to. You were so concerned about sending your nephew to join your brother and niece that you never considered that your brother and niece could just as easily return to join your nephew. We have plenty of people eager to take their places."

I let out a slow, tired breath.

"Do what you need to do. It doesn't matter. Bring them here. Leave them there. Our days are limited either way. That many people can't live on an island forever, and we both know it." I closed my eyes and stretched my neck. "All we can do now is hope our end is quick."

"Sergeant Bromwell claimed you were an asset to the squad. You were good at reading people. Do you think I'm bluffing, Miss Wells?"

I opened my eyes and looked at him.

"That's not the right question."

"Then what is?"

"Will it even matter that humans ever existed on this planet once we're gone?"

He stood abruptly and walked out of the room. It wasn't the first time he'd left, and I doubted it would be the last.

I looked at the soldiers he'd left to guard me. They kept their eyes straight ahead as if I wasn't there.

"If Molev comes back, don't try to shoot him. He's a little rough on weapons and low on patience with people who try to hurt him."

They didn't acknowledge me.

"He's got moves that you can't even see. But he showed us a few. Told us we're too reliant on our guns when killing the infected. Taught us how to survive hand-to-hand with the infected so we don't get bitten. I think losing half our team really got to him. He doesn't want any more humans to die."

"Then why did he run?" one of the soldiers asked.

"Because he's not willing to be a puppet to save us. I think we have enough of those, don't you?"

His gaze flicked to me.

"Shut up," another guard said. "Both of you."

"If a slap didn't get me talking, do you honestly think a scolding will quiet me?" I asked.

We all heard a thump outside the door, but they didn't move.

I frowned and shook my head.

"Seriously? There's a weird thump in the hallway and nothing."

"Our orders are to guard you."

When there was another sound—a rasp—I twisted in my chair to look at the door. The knob rattled. Only one thing tried opening a door like that.

I slowly got to my feet.

"Sit down," one of the soldiers said, clapping a hand on my shoulder.

A soft groan came from the door. Then the snap of breaking metal. The knob fell to the floor. Finally, the soldiers with me reacted.

Weapons drawn, they faced the door. After several moments of nothing happening, they got into position to check.

As soon as the soldier stepped into the hallway, he was gone. The remaining two looked at each other. I was pulled to my feet and shoved forward. I didn't fight them. I knew it wasn't an infected waiting out there but Molev. I'd guessed it when the knob had broken, but the pile of bodies with their heads still attached proved it.

The second I passed over the threshold, he materialized before me.

His gaze swept over my face, and his eyes narrowed when he saw my lip. Then he was around me, and the door shut between us. A gun went off. Several grunts followed. Then silence.

"Please tell me you didn't kill them," I said. "I need to know where the key is to these handcuffs."

The door opened. "I did not kill them."

"Good. We don't have a lot of time. Check their pockets. We need to find the key and get out of here."

"We have time," Molev said.

"We do?"

I glanced at the pile of unconscious people again and saw the general there.

"That's not going to go over well."

Molev grunted as he searched for the key. When he found it, I held out my hands.

"Where are the others?" I asked.

"Safe," he said as he unlocked me.

Once I was free, he captured my chin and tipped my head to get a better look at my lip.

"What happened?" he asked.

"Fear happened, and it's not going to stop happening until the infected and hounds are no longer a threat. We tried it their way. Maybe now we try it ours."

Molev's gaze searched mine for a long moment.

"Mya, the human that touched the crystal was bitten. She died but didn't become stupid when she woke up. She is the same as before."

I was stunned.

"She doesn't understand why she is immune, but she believes it was the crystal."

I immediately saw the problem.

"So if we destroy it," I said, "we would potentially also be destroying a cure. But we still have her. If she's immune, she could hold the key to a cure as well."

He shook his head. "I've seen how your leaders would treat her. Until I can trust them to care for her, I will not tell them."

"Then what do we do?"

"We keep trying here."

I glanced at the bodies. "I'm pretty sure they won't be in a listening mood when they come to."

"Then we help them listen."

"And how are we going to do that? Keep knocking them out each time they act like assholes?"

Molev shifted his hold on my chin to cup the back of my head.

"Or when they hurt you," he said.

He set his forehead on mine and did one of those deep breaths that people did when they were trying to keep their cool.

"They are lucky they still have their heads," he said softly.

I stared into his eyes and felt something stir inside of me. He surrounded me with his presence, gently wrapping me in his protection. No matter how much I tried not to overthink it, I saw in his gaze how much I meant to him, and it wormed into my head, testing my resolve to keep him at arm's length.

"A puffy lip is nothing compared to what will happen if we can't reason with them," I said. "Or if they get their hands on you. You should leave, Molev. If you die, we all die."

"What she said," Steve said, entering the hallway. "Some of them are starting to come to in here. Let us deal with this for now."

Molev's fingers twitched in my hair.

"I will be close," he said softly.

And then he was gone again.

"Come on," I said to Steve. "Help me unstack them. If they wake up in a slightly more dignified way, hopefully, they'll be less afraid."

"And how does that help us?"

"Fear leads to mistakes. I think they've already made enough of those, don't you?"

The rest of the team helped spread out the personnel, so they woke in groups. One of us with each group. I got the general by himself in the room I'd occupied. I found a fridge somewhere else in the building and grabbed a soda can to use as an ice pack for the lump on his head.

When he came to, he was just a confused man for a few minutes.

"What happened?" he asked.

"You have a lump on your head. How are you feeling? Nauseous? Headache?"

"Yeah, a little of all of it," he said.

"You might have a concussion. But I'm not a medic to say for sure." I handed him the soda can so he could hold it to his head or drink it if he wanted.

"Do you know your first name?" I asked.

"Yeah. Thomas. Tom."

I knew his brain was a little scrambled then.

"Tom, I'm Andie. Do you remember me?"

He focused on me for a long moment, and I could see exactly when the switch flicked in his brain. That open confusion disappeared, replaced by a slow boil of anger and calculation. His gaze swept the room, taking in the table and the chair he sat in. My chair.

"I see it's starting to come back," I said, straightening away from him. "The soldiers are across the hall. Steve's helping them. You might want to take another minute before you try standing, though."

"What happened?" he repeated, this time in his signature commanding tone.

"You were knocked out. But I think what happened is less important than why it happened."

"Enlighten me, Miss Wells."

"My friends call me Andie."

The silence lengthened as we stared at one another.

"I'll be back when you're ready to listen," I said.

His hand closed over my forearm with bruising force before I managed a step.

"You're not going anywhere."

"How many hits to the head do you think you can take?" I asked.

"Are you threatening me?"

"No, I'm actually trying to help you, but you're too blind to see that."

"And you've sold yourself to the enemy. For what? The promise of a cure that doesn't even exist yet? You're a traitor to your own people."

I shook my head slowly in disbelief.

"A traitor? I risked my life to find him. And did the same to bring him back. The only promise Molev ever gave me was that, if I was honest with him, he would come here and do whatever he could to help create a cure. He kept his word. But it's too far-fetched for you to believe that he's helping simply for the sake of helping because most humans don't do that. Oh, they say they do, but they don't. They help when there's something in it for them. When it's convenient. But here's a news flash. He's not human. Stop holding him to human standards. Just because humans can't keep their word doesn't mean that his kind are the same way. Now let go of me before he comes back in here and tries knocking some sense into you again."

I jerked my arm free. the general stood quickly to grab me again and stumbled a step. A second later, he was vomiting on the table.

"Oh, and Tom, let whomever you report to know that Molev is no longer interested in negotiating with you. If there's a woman in charge, he'll talk to her. He finds that women are inherently less confrontational and more open to listening."

I walked out the door.

"We're leaving," I called.

The group hurried out of their rooms.

"There are a lot of dazed and confused people in there," Roni said, walking beside me. "They're not going to stay that way for long."

"I know," I said.

"Where are we going then?" Sid asked.

"Back to the base," I said.

"What about Molev?" Katie asked.

"He's coming, too," I said.

As soon as we opened the door, I saw why no one had come in to check on what was going on inside the building. The crowd by the fence had doubled. The guards were no longer just standing there but actively had their guns pointed at the people who were yelling about a "cure" and shaking the fence.

We headed to the helicopter where the pilot and our escort were waiting.

"Miss Wells, we have orders to—"

"Don't," I said, cutting off the guard. "It's obvious this was all a setup. If we don't leave and things don't calm down, those people are going to break through that fence. More lives will be lost, and we can't afford that. So make the right choice, and get this thing in the air."

"We can't," he said. "If we go against orders, we'll—

"Help us, or go over there and help them," Roni said, indicating the fence. "Standing in our way isn't an option."

The pilot made up her mind first and moved to her seat. When the blades started moving overhead, I raised a brow at the guard. He stepped aside and indicated we should get in.

I turned back toward the buildings.

"Come on, Molev. Staying here isn't going to help anything."

A minute later, a grey blur came running at me. He swept me off my feet and into the helicopter. It lifted off the ground before he sat with me in his arms. His heavy exhale and the weight of his head settling over mine comforted me.

"Hopefully, they'll send someone else, and the next one will be better," I said.

Molev grunted underneath me.

CHAPTER EIGHTEEN

NO ONE WAS WAITING FOR US WHEN WE TOUCHED DOWN AT IRWIN, and I wasn't sure if that was a good thing or a bad thing. Neither the pilot nor the guard said anything to us as the rotors stilled.

"Now what?" Katie asked once we were all out.

"We return home, prepare food, and head to the training course," Molev said.

Brandon groaned, and Steve pretended to cry.

"Are you sure?" I asked.

"Being out in the open is better than being trapped in the house when the general returns."

We jogged back to the house and made some food before jogging to the course.

It only took thirty minutes before people noticed us training. In no time, we had our regulars there as Molev coached us through using different techniques.

The exercise, while physically draining, also stopped me from thinking of the trouble coming our way and kept me in the moment. I wasn't a fan of being bitten. Yet, one of the soldiers managed to get my hand.

"Fuck," I muttered as I jerked it back.

"No biting hard." The harsh reprimand came from directly behind me, and the soldier in front of me swallowed visibly.

"I don't know, Molev," I said, glancing back at him. "The harder the bite, the more determined I am not to be bitten again. It's a pretty good reminder of why I need to keep fighting even when my arms are shaking with strain."

He grunted, and his gaze locked with mine.

"And if you keep scaring everyone when they bite me, pretty soon, no one will want to partner with me."

"I will," he said.

"I'd rather have their teeth on me than yours. Don't think I haven't noticed all those points you're hiding behind those pretty lips."

He blinked at me.

I smirked.

He blinked again, and I wondered how much flirting he'd dealt with in his life.

"Would you like to take a break?" he asked.

"I think everyone would."

He called a break and passed out the food to everyone, not just our team. I bit into my sandwich and wondered what the general's next move would be.

Near dusk, we heard the aircraft. Training stopped as we all watched the sky for its approach.

"Rest well tonight," Molev called when he spotted it. "We will meet here again tomorrow."

Dismissed for the night, the soldiers who had joined us drifted away while those of us in the core team gathered.

"What's our next move?" Sid asked.

"We welcome whoever is arriving," Molev said.

It was a bold move after what happened at the evac site, but I understood why he needed to do it. He couldn't show any signs of weakness or backing down. If he did, they would keep pressing. So, we went with him. Sweaty and exhausted, we maintained a grueling pace and made it to the landing site just as the engines wound down. Katie bent at the waist and put her hands on her knees.

"Have I mentioned how much I hate cardio?" she panted.

"At least a dozen times," Brandon said, watching the craft with the rest of us.

The door opened, and a woman stepped out. She was wearing a business suit, which seemed so ridiculously out of place yet sent a clear message. This wasn't a person who was living in fear every day. This was someone from one of the sanctuaries.

"Based on her clothes, she's someone important," I said to Molev.

He grunted and remained beside us as the woman strode toward the military personnel waiting for her. I could see by the uniforms that they were officers but had no idea about their ranks. Thankfully, I didn't see the general among them.

Before the woman reached them, she noticed our group. Her steps faltered, and she started to go down. Molev disappeared and was at her side just before she would have hit the pavement. She stared up at him for a beat, nodded her head, and started talking.

I itched to join them but held myself in check. After all, he'd specifically asked for my trust during situations like this. So, I waited, and I watched.

When she stepped back, she held out her hand to Molev. He shook it and indicated the rest of us. She nodded, and he jogged back.

"She would like to speak with us and agreed to come to our assigned house, so we know it is not a trap," he said.

M.J. HAAG

"Good thinking," Sid said as I marveled at just how well Molev understood human thought.

"Please tell me we don't have to run all the way back there," Katie said.

Molev looked her over. "Would you like me to carry you?"

"God, yes."

"Damn it," Roni said. "Why didn't I think of that?"

She smirked at Molev, but it didn't have its previous hungry aggression.

Fortunately, no one needed to be carried. The woman sent two vehicles our way, and we got a lift to our house with her leading the way. She didn't bat an eye when Molev opened the door for her and let her enter first.

"Can we get you anything to drink or eat?" Roland asked.

"Water, please. It was a long flight," she said, moving to the couch.

I tried to place her accent and couldn't.

Roland went to the kitchen with Katie. She returned with the drink as he started pulling out food for dinner. Rude or not, I doubted he cared. We were all starving after that workout and dead on our feet. Which was why I sat next to the well-dressed woman on the couch and made introductions.

"I'm Andie. This is Katie, Sid, Brandon, Roni, Steve, and Roland in the kitchen there. And you've already met Molev."

"Pleasure to meet you all. I'm Waurlyn." She looked at Molev. "I've heard a lot about you, and I must admit it doesn't paint a pretty picture."

"Tell me what you've heard, and we will tell you if it's true," Molev said, crossing his arms.

"You're immune and came here under the pretense of cooperation but haven't cooperated."

Molev didn't say anything. He didn't have to. The rest of

268

the team reacted with muttered words and general expressions of anger.

"Let me guess. Tom's report?" I asked.

She nodded. "And Patrick's."

I appreciated that she'd used their first names.

"It's an unfair assessment," I said. "Imagine that Tom needed a kidney and you were his match. But he's not happy with the one kidney you're offering. Even though one is all he needs to save himself, he wants them both. What would you do?"

"Not give him both kidneys," she said.

"They had a room set up to test Molev's abilities. He's strong and fast. He can do things we can't. They're curious, and he gets that. But it doesn't mean he has to cooperate when they want to experiment on him. So he put his foot down on the first day here. He refused to go into the room with the electric chair and a drowning tank. But he did allow them to take blood samples. Since then, the house has been bugged numerous times. And when Molev called Tom out for not keeping his promise to us, the people who risked our lives to bring Molev here, Tom made the choice to try to capture Molev instead of talking."

"I see," she said. She looked at Molev. "Tell me what you want then."

"I want the original promise fulfilled, and I want fair treatment while I help your people find a cure."

She nodded. "I also heard you want women. Can you tell me about that?"

"Like Tom, I am thinking of the future. Where he would like to use my blood to find a way to kill all my people, I would like to find a way for our people to coexist. Women are calmer and not as quick to anger. However, the men in this house have proven themselves and are willing to join the number of women I requested. There are a few other soldiers who have been training with us that may also be suitable."

Molev uncrossed his arms. "Creating a cure is the first step, Waurlyn. Creating a world where children can thrive is the second. Patrick and Tom were too shortsighted to understand what conflict between our two people would do. Without peace, there is no future."

"I see." She looked around the room before her gaze settled on me. "Tom repeated what you said. Not only your request for someone new to negotiate with Molev but regarding not treating him like a human. While he may not have fully grasped the message, I do, and what I see in this room isn't desertion from your original mission but embracing the coexistence that Molev would like to create." She looked at Molev. "I read Patrick's report about the body piles and the aggression. And his side note stating all of the aggression was toward those who tried to harm you first. I won't make Patrick and Tom's mistakes. However, if you break your word or act with aggression without cause, our amicable relationship will end. Does that sound fair to you?"

"Yes," Molev said.

"Good. The scientists have exhausted their current supply of samples for running tests. Would you be willing to allow another draw?"

Molev nodded.

"Thank you. I will arrange for the doctor to come here tomorrow. But I would like you to consider allowing some physical tests as well. Yes, we are curious about you and would love to know your limits. But more importantly, we want to ensure the blood we're taking isn't having any ill effects."

"I will consider the request," Molev said.

She smiled and set her empty glass aside.

"Thank you for helping us, Molev. The risk that you've taken—that you all have taken—will not be forgotten. Your loved ones will be at the evac site tomorrow. If you would like to accompany me to see them off, I promise there will not be a repeat of today."

Molev's gaze found mine, and I knew we were both having doubts.

"Is that smart?" I asked Waurlyn. "After the exchange today, the crowd wasn't happy."

"Which is why I'm hoping to return with the man you said would be their cure. Perhaps the three of us could find the words to assure them that Molev's life is no longer in danger and that we're doing everything within our power to find a solution to what we all fear."

I studied her for a moment. Her expression and body language exuded sincerity, yet I couldn't help but feel we'd been cleverly maneuvered into a corner.

"You wish to test me," Molev said, seeing the same thing I was. "I will allow more samples. In return, you will give the promised tickets. In return, I will speak to your humans and calm them. Will it always be like this with humans? Will they always demand more than they are willing to give?"

Waurlyn gave a small laugh. "I hope not. I hope we'll change the world for the better."

She started for the door. "I will see you all in the morning."

After Steve walked her out, we all melted into our seats.

"Well, that was fun," Roni said.

"Hey, at least, we get another break from training," Katie said before she gave Molev an apologetic look. "Not that training is bad."

His mouth quirked a little. "It is bad. But being bitten by an infected would be worse. Eat, then rest. Tomorrow will come early."

While the others were quick to listen, I lingered over the pasta Roland had made...until Brandon said I had to wash my own plate and left me alone with Molev.

I looked at him.

"I think this one will keep her word, but she's going to push just as hard for more than you might be willing to give," I said.

He grunted and looked at my plate.

"Does it hurt your mouth to eat?" he asked.

"A little."

He reached out, probably intending to grab my chin again. I caught his hand before he could.

"Don't let your guard down. Not even when things start going well. Promise me."

He looked at the table and smiled.

"I fully trust you, Andie. When will you fully trust me?"

"When you stop putting yourself in danger to save every woman you meet," I said dryly. "Don't think I've been blind to what you've been doing. And you're lucky Roni hasn't hit you yet for your macho act."

His lips parted in a full-blown grin.

"Roni is biding her time. She knows I am not the one for her and is saving her fight for one of my brothers."

I cringed a little, already imagining Roni trying to coax another one of them into bed.

"I thought you liked your brothers."

"I do."

"Do you think they're going to appreciate being groped by Roni any more than you did?"

"Very much. Any of my brothers would welcome her attention and quickly accept her offer. The one she chooses will find ways to appease her fierce heart without allowing her to endanger herself."

"Uh, that sounds like someone might be getting his ass kicked. Roni isn't the sit-at-home and be-idle type."

"She will learn."

I snorted and shook my head.

"This is exactly what I was talking about. She's not going to want to be forced into a role any more than I do. And this way of thinking is why I'm warning you about Waurlyn. Yes, you're clever and see a lot, but when it comes to women, I think you don't see as clearly."

Molev sighed and turned his hand in mine, stroking my fingers.

"I think we have a misunderstanding. If Roni wishes to hunt infected, no one would stop her. However, each of my brothers would shield her from harm."

"Just like you've been doing for us," I said.

He exhaled heavily. "Just as I've tried doing."

"Don't blame yourself for what happened to Tamra. We knew the risks when we signed up for this mission. You didn't kill her. Neither did Sid."

Molev's gaze lifted from our joined hands to meet mine.

"Finish eating," he said. "You need rest."

"Maybe if you joined in, you would need more rest too."

"Maybe," he said, releasing my hand so I could do as he'd asked.

When I finished, he insisted on washing my plate and told me to get ready for bed. I was just settling under the covers when he came in and turned off the lights.

The bed dipped as he eased in behind me.

"I hope they find a cure soon," I said softly. "Each day that passes, we're losing more people. And it's hard not to feel guilty about that when we're sitting here doing nothing."

Molev's warm arm settled over my waist.

"We are all doing something. The scientists are working on

a cure, and we are helping the soldiers learn how to fight the infected that will be coming."

I twisted around to look at him.

"There are watchtowers and barricades through the mountain roads that are still open and walls where there was open land. I saw it myself when we left. The undead can't get in here."

"The infected return to the places they know best. After that, they wander, seeking humans."

"Why just humans?"

"That I do not know. But my brothers and I have witnessed it many times. The infected only attack us to get to the humans."

"Maybe they know we're weaker," I said.

He grunted and closed his eyes. "Sleep, Andie."

Internally shaking my head at his bossy ways but knowing he was right, I closed my eyes and cleared my mind. Tomorrow would be what it was, and worrying about what might be never changed what would be.

It felt like I'd barely closed my eyes when Molev was gently shaking my shoulder.

"I made pancakes," he said. "You should eat."

"Sausage too?" I asked, rubbing my face.

"No. We have none."

I sat up and looked at him. "What are you going to eat? I think we're out of peanut butter too."

His hair was still wet enough that it was dripping down his shirt. Something he still wore at all times to hide the fact he no longer had the stitches he'd been given.

"You know, if they want to know more about you, we should tell them you need more protein than they've been providing. At least, you'd get some direct benefit of that bit of information sharing."

"I second that," Roni said, walking by our door. "We need more meat in the house. Nice big juicy cuts of meat."

I shook my head. "She's not going to stop talking about meat now."

"I will speak to Waurlyn while you dress."

"She's here already?" I looked out the window at the early morning light as I threw back the covers.

"Yes. She and the doctor are waiting in the living room."

He watched me tug my pants up in a hurry, and his lips quirked.

"You should have woken me up right away." I ran my fingers through my hair and strode toward the door. Molev followed only a few steps behind me.

The rest of the group was eating and talking amongst themselves in the kitchen while Waurlyn and the doctor sat in silence in the living room.

"Morning," I said when they saw me. "None of us realized you'd be here this early."

"The vaccine research has already been stalled for more than twenty-four hours. We couldn't wait longer," Waurlyn said.

"They took so many vials last time. How is it gone already?" I asked.

"We're not only analyzing it but testing it. Each test destroys whatever we've used," the doctor said. "And it's not just a few people researching and testing. There are a lot of us working on this."

"Take your samples," Molev said, standing beside me.

The doctor stood and went to her case, unbothered by the fact Molev wouldn't be sitting for this blood draw either.

"We're running low on food," I said. "At least the stuff that he prefers to eat. His diet is more protein based. Can you have more sent over?"

"I will ensure it happens immediately," Waurlyn said. "Is there anything else you need?"

"Let the soldiers know they are welcome to train with us," Molev said, surprising me. "Not just the soldiers who were ordered to do so."

"Done," Waurlyn said. "If there's anything else, let me know."

"When are you leaving for the evac site?" I asked.

"In three hours. Would you like me to arrange transportation for any of you?"

"Yes," Sid said. "I want to go. I won't believe it's done unless I see it with my own eyes."

I wanted to go, too. Like Sid, I needed to see Zion get on that plane. But I didn't want to risk Molev either by taking him with me or by leaving him behind.

I glanced at Molev.

"Where you go, I go," he said as if reading my mind.

When I faced Waurlyn and found her watching me closely, I briefly wondered if that feeling of being scrutinized and judged was how I made people feel when I watched them.

"Yes, please arrange for transportation for all of us."

She nodded and stood as the doctor started packing up. As soon as they were gone, I dug into the breakfast Molev had prepared and groaned with the rest when Molev started making jelly sandwiches.

"Wouldn't it be better to take the morning off?" I asked.

"No," Molev said. "I don't know how long we have here, and we need to use every moment to prepare. No more needless death."

No one else groaned or tried to argue. We worked together and cleaned up.

"Well, this is interesting," Brandon said, walking out the door first.

The rest of us trailed out behind him and saw the vacant curb in front of our house.

"No guards." I looked at Molev. "It's a sign of trust."

Molev grunted in his noncommittal way.

"We'll see if our house is bugged again when we get back," Sid said.

We ran to the course, which Molev considered our warm-up, then immediately paired off. However, he changed up the game. Instead of trying to bite each other, we practiced how to get out of holds, and Sid showed us how to incapacitate without permanent damage. We all understood this wasn't for the infected but in case we were tricked again.

My gaze slid to Molev. He stood to the side, his observant gaze missing nothing as Katie struggled to turn Brandon away. I could see Molev's need to protect in the way he uncrossed his arms when Katie lost her footing and the way he nodded slightly when Brandon caught her.

Then Molev darted in and spun Brandon around while he was distracted.

"When you're helping your team, don't forget to watch your own back. You can't help anyone when you're dead," he said, straightening Brandon.

I realized how much Molev was like Patrick in the way he pushed us to be better. Both did it so we would survive.

When a few other soldiers showed up, we reverted to our biting. But Molev was more involved this round, sneaking around to grab someone's arm to distract them or pluck someone off their feet and redirect the other person to gang up in someone else's group. The core group rolled with it. The others faltered. Our training had leveled up in ways that started to show the soldiers there what it would be like beyond the barrier.

The rumble of several engines interrupted us.

"Never stop fighting," Molev barked. "Distractions cost lives."

Everyone jumped back into motion as the vehicles came to a stop at the edge of the course.

"Enough," Molev called. "We'll start again tomorrow. Expect a full day."

I internally cringed, but thoughts of the next day faded as I made my way to our rides. My somber expression was reflected in everyone else's. When I sat next to Katie, she took my hand.

"I need this time to be different," she said softly.

I looked at Waurlyn in the lead vehicle and hoped it would be.

We didn't talk once we were in the air, but we all watched our approach. The fence around the perimeter had been fortified on the inside with big blocks, which were probably the only reason the fence was still standing. The number of people outside of it had doubled since the previous day, and the crowd looked even angrier.

Waurlyn broke our silence as we began to set down.

"Your family will come out of the building to the right to load into the aircraft. Due to the size of the crowd, I'm afraid you won't have much time to say goodbye. We want to get them in the air before the people outside have a chance to breach the fence. They're unlikely to do that once the plane is in the air."

I nodded my understanding with the rest and looked toward the building. We'd barely set down when the doors opened. People spilled out, hurrying toward us. I saw Rachel with Zion in her arms and started running toward them the second my feet touched the ground.

"You did it," she said, opening one arm to wrap me in a hug with Zion in the middle.

"We don't have a lot of time. They're worried about the crowd. Get him on the plane, Rachel." I gave my nephew several quick kisses on his cheek. "Auntie Andie loves you to the moon and back, Zion. Never forget that."

I released her and hurried with them toward the plane.

"Zion, baby, you're going with Allison now, okay?" she said. Zion looked up at her then at the teen girl who was standing close. "She's going to take you to see Daddy."

Zion looked like he was two seconds from a complete meltdown. I yanked him from Rachel's arms and shoved him at the girl. He started to flail as Allison reached for him.

"Hold him tight," I said.

A soldier helped her into the plane with the wailing child. Rachel stood beside me, watching her son leave.

I saw another younger girl helping a boy that I assumed was Katie's brother.

Holding onto Rachel, I shuffled us back as the door closed. The sounds of the engines and the crowds weren't enough to drown out the first of her heart-wrenching sobs. She shook against me as guards herded us farther away while the plane started to taxi into position.

"We need to talk to them," Waurlyn shouted.

I glanced over my shoulder and saw she was speaking to Molev, not that he was listening. He was watching me and Rachel, an almost angry look in his eyes.

"Come on," I said to Rachel.

Towing her with me, I went to Molev.

"Waurlyn's right," I said. "Too many people will be hurt if the crowd gets inside."

His gaze flicked between Rachel and the plane before he nodded, spun around, and swept Waurlyn up into his arms. She gave a startled squawk that silenced when he ran and jumped to the top of our helicopter.

CHAPTER NINETEEN

"Do you want the truth?" Molev yelled, his voice carrying over the crowd.

Their volume fell a little.

"Do you want to know what's happening on the other side of those mountains?" he asked.

It got a little quieter yet.

"Do you want to know how to save your children and yourselves?"

The crowd's anger shifted. They no longer randomly yelled but actually responded with "yes" to his question.

"I am Molev," he called, setting Waurlyn down and holding her steady with one arm while holding out the other. "Look at my arm. See the scars. I've been bitten but did not die or turn stupid. Your leaders are studying my blood to find a cure. Yesterday, they did not want to keep a promise they made to these people." He indicated us. "In exchange for risking their lives to find me and convince me to return with them, they were promised a ticket to save a loved one. Just one. Many gave their lives to save yours.

"The infection is spreading on the other side of the

mountains. There are fewer healthy humans every day, and those who remain are not all good. They kill one another for food and safety. It is not a good world. We need to work together to make it better."

"Our scientists are working around the clock," Waurlyn said, her voice carrying further in the hush. "They know the cost of each minute that we don't have a cure in our hands and are running on very little sleep because of it."

"And what happens when there's a cure?" someone shouted. "It's not going to do any of us any good. It'll be just like the evacuation."

The crowd's volume started to rise.

"The islands are not the only safe havens available to you. My people have created more with the help of a few humans. It is a place where the infected avoid. I've asked for five hundred human volunteers to help with this effort to create more safe havens. The humans who volunteer will be among the first to receive the vaccine."

A different kind of murmur rose at that news. Rather than look at the crowd, though, I stared at the clever man speaking and wondered if Waurlyn was regretting asking for his help.

"Tomorrow, we will start taking names of anyone who wants to volunteer," Waurlyn said without hesitation. "You will be interviewed for suitability as a representative to build better relations between our two races. No specializations are required. Just an amiable personality."

A few people laughed at that, and some grumbled, but the angry mood had dissipated.

Waurlyn glanced at Molev, and he picked her up and jumped back down with her. She smoothed back her hair when she was on her own feet and looked at Molev.

"Not quite what I had in mind but effective," she said.

"Next time, maybe a little warning before you pick me up, though."

He nodded and came over to me and Rachel.

"Molev, this is my sister-in-law, Rachel. Rachel, this is Molev." I looked at her. "He's the reason Zion's on that plane." Her eyes were puffy and red from crying.

"Thank you," she said.

Molev shook his head. "Do not thank me for separating you from your child. What I witnessed..." Molev shook his head. "It should have never happened."

"There is limited space in the sanctuaries," Waurlyn said. "It's already overcrowded, and without the supplies we've been flying in, they would have run out of food a long while ago. If we could have fit more people, we would have. The scientists who came here to work on the cure are why we could send over more people now."

"I understand," Rachel said to her. "Molev, even though that was hard, I would rather say goodbye for now than goodbye forever. This way, there's a better chance I'll see him again someday."

"Volunteer to help my people," Molev said. "You will be safer there."

Waurlyn looked at Molev. "Whiteman is in the middle of what we consider a hot zone. Why do you think it's safer?"

"Because there are more of us to keep the humans safe."

Rachel looked at me. "Will you be going?"

"I will. We're waiting until the vaccine is ready, so there's time to decide."

"If there's a vaccine, why go?" she asked.

I stared at her, wondering how much to say. "It's bad out there, Rachel. These things don't just give you a single bite and run away."

She exhaled heavily. "Okay. Then, I'll go. There's nothing else here for me anyway."

I hugged her hard. "Stay safe until it's time to leave."

"I will."

I HAD a hard time focusing when we returned, and Molev knew it. His growl each time I was bitten grew in volume until he finally called a stop. The others drifted away as he stalked toward me.

"What's wrong?" he asked. "Are you too tired?"

"I am tired, but it's my head and what I said to Rachel. The vaccine won't be enough, but that's all people like Waurlyn seem to be focusing on."

He cupped the back of my head and set his forehead to mine.

In front of everyone.

"Damn," Roni said nearby. "Thought he was going in for a kiss."

Someone snorted.

"The vaccine is a start," Molev said softly, ignoring our audience. "My brothers are hunting the hounds, even now, decreasing their numbers. Do not give up. Not now, Andie. Keep fighting."

I pulled back and met his gaze.

"I'm not giving up."

"Then keep fighting."

I smiled slightly. "Yes, sir."

He grunted but didn't release me. Instead, he held my gaze, and I could see the hunger creep into his. My smile faded.

"Do it!" Roni yelled. "Slip her some tongue."

I twisted out of Molev's hold and gave her a dry look.

"You have way too much energy. Obviously, you're not trying hard enough either."

Molev paired us off again, and this time, it was Steve and me against Roni. She didn't bite me as much but not from lack of effort on her part.

By the time we headed back to the house, I was dead on my feet and too focused on how I'd survive the next day to worry about the future.

We continued our intense training, and one day blurred into the next in a familiar routine of fatigue and survival that reminded me of our time in the field. And I didn't mind it. It made our time waiting for news feel like we were actually doing something constructive.

On our fifth day, though, the routine was interrupted by the arrival of a truck full of soldiers in full gear.

Waurlyn was with them.

"Molev, the men and women you've been training are having more success when deployed. Would you be willing to train on a larger level?"

"I will welcome anyone who is willing to learn," he said.

After that, we had a full platoon with us every day. Some of them talked about the missions they ran to gather supplies from places on the other side of the mountain range. Thanks to them, we learned how things had changed in the three weeks since we'd been here. The undead were getting smarter with their traps and were working together in bigger groups to ambush squads.

"I swear that I can actually see some of them thinking now," one man said. "Creepy as fuck. And some of their eyes don't look as cloudy."

"The worst is when you see the new ones," another said. "They prove there are still people out there."

"How often do you leave for supplies?" Molev asked.

They exchanged a look.

"No need to answer," he said. "I will speak with Waurlyn."

We saw her that evening with the doctor.

"How are your supplies?" she asked. "Is there enough protein?"

The afternoon we'd returned from the evac, our fridge had been stocked with burgers, brats, and steak. And it was restocked every four days now.

"The supplies are good," Molev said. "Thank you. I would like to leave with your next supply run and see the changes I've been hearing for myself."

Waurlyn's friendly expression didn't waver, but she wasn't as smooth with her body language.

"That upset you," I said. "Why?"

"Molev is very important to our efforts. We're close to a vaccine and can't afford to lose him to a careless mistake until we have a vaccine that works."

"How close?" Roni asked.

"We've run three trials. The first two were failures. The last one was promising and fought the infection for three days before succumbing."

"Wait…when you say trials are you saying you're testing on humans?" Katie asked.

Waurlyn looked suitably sad when she nodded.

"Human volunteers who, like you, understand the risk in exchange for the reward. Each volunteer who dies moves a family member to a more secure location."

Roland swore under his breath and rubbed the back of his neck.

"If there was another way to ensure it worked, we would take it," she said. "Do you understand why I can't let you go?"

Molev's lips quirked a little.

"You misunderstand. I am not asking for your permission to leave but to join the people I am training."

She sighed.

"I can see why Tom had a hard time dealing with you. When you set your mind to something, there's very little compromise. Very well, I would rather you were with our people so they can keep you safe than if you head out on your own. The next squad leaves in two days. I will inform them of the change."

"I'm going too," I said.

"Same," Sid said.

"We're all going," Brandon said. "We stick together."

"Very well," she said.

Molev's training was even more relentless the next day. He hounded us to move faster, use more force, and try harder. When he finally called it a night, I wasn't the only one to sit down right where I stood.

"Tomorrow, we rest," he called. "No training."

I looked up at him outlined by the sunset.

"No training?" I asked.

He shook his head. "When we leave, I want you alert, not exhausted."

"Thank God," Steve said, lying on his back. "I'm sleeping until noon tomorrow."

Molev grunted and held out his hand for me to stand. I did so reluctantly.

"Once we stop moving, things will tighten up," Roni said. "Active rest tomorrow. No sleeping until noon."

I wasn't sure I still liked Roni, and something must have shown on my face because Molev chuckled.

"She is right," he said, wrapping his fingers around the back of my neck. "I didn't mean we should do nothing tomorrow."

Everyone groaned.

"Come. Let's go home and eat."

Molev grilled the burgers on the patio, and I sat on the lawn chair, watching him.

"Speak what's on your mind, Andie," he said after a while.

"Waurlyn's not wrong about the risk. So why are we going out there again?"

"The infected have been changing from the start and haven't stopped. They're growing more intelligent. Are they evolving back into humans like you?"

Stunned, I just stared at him for a moment.

"I hope not. Half of them are missing parts. They don't bleed anymore. They don't eat. They just bite. How can they be human when they clearly aren't alive?" I tapped my finger on the chair's armrest. "I think we need to tell Waurlyn what we know about how this started with the curse and the hunting."

"Mya said humans don't believe in magic."

"Most don't. I didn't. But I saw the hound's glowing eyes and felt the wrongness when you removed its heart. That was all it took to convince me. Well, that and you. No one thought fey were real either. It's kind of hard to say something doesn't exist when you're here."

He grunted and closed the lid on the empty grill.

"Do you trust Waurlyn?" he asked.

"I trust her like I trusted Patrick. Our goals are aligned. She understands better than Patrick did that your cooperation is important. The better question is—will the scientists be able to figure out how to stop the infected and the hounds without this information? I know a group of your kind can kill hundreds of infected with ease. I saw that for myself at the tank. But there are millions of people in the United States, and only what? Five hundred of you? If the infected are starting to work together to set bigger traps, at what point will it be too much for you to handle on your own? Once you die, we all die."

"Then I will speak with Waurlyn tomorrow."

"Okay."

Steve was already passed out when we came back in with the food. Roni splashed water on his face. It turned into a fight that Molev broke up with a single, stern, "Stop."

Roni grinned. Steve scowled. Katie shook her head while Sid hid his smile. They all did an amazing job of acting like everything was fine, but I saw the pain underneath. They'd all said goodbye to someone they may never see again.

"I saw some board games in the closet," I said. "Who's up for some burgers, beer, and fun?"

We stayed up later than we would have, playing games and sipping our beer. When Katie had everyone's play money and was laughing like a maniac, I grinned around a yawn.

Molev's hand settled on the back of my neck, squeezing it slightly. The affectionate and slightly possessive hold had me leaning into his side. It wasn't until he wrapped his arm around my shoulders that I realized what I'd done. It had been so natural. Instinctual. And snuggling up against him felt right.

Rather than fighting it or regretting it, I rested my head against his shoulder and watched the others horse around, trying to steal Katie's money.

"This was good," I said to him.

"When we get back, we'll do it again," he said.

I tipped my head to look at him. "Are you saying you're going to start giving us a day off every now and again?"

"Please say yes," Brandon said.

His words brought everyone else's attention to us. Roni and Katie both smirked at me. I rolled my eyes.

"One day of rest in every seven," Molev said.

"I'll take it," Roland said, standing. "G'Night, folks. Don't wake me up for breakfast."

After that, the group broke up, drifting off to bed until it was just Molev and me in the living room.

"Are you tired?" he asked.

"So tired I don't want to move."

In a blink, I was cradled in his arms as he walked to our bedroom.

"I would have walked," I said softly. "Eventually."

"This is better," he said.

I didn't ask him what he meant by that. With the way he was looking at me, it was pretty clear he liked carrying me.

"Thank you for everything you've done to help us. Making them keep their word. The donations. Putting up with the lies and manipulation. I know it isn't easy." I considered him for a minute. "But you were brilliant today, mentioning the volunteers to the crowd. There's no way for Waurlyn to go back on what she said. Not without causing more trouble."

"She will keep her word. To her, she is sacrificing a few to help the many by thinning the number of people who will be beating at the fence with their anger and fear. Patrick and the general were unwilling to sacrifice anyone."

I'd never thought of it that way. And when I did, I saw that Waurlyn might be even more dangerous than the general. Yet, I didn't doubt for a second that she would be honest with the volunteers, regarding the risks. Just like those in my original group and those who stepped up for the vaccine trials, there were people who were willing to risk anything to save the person they loved.

"I'm suitably impressed by your perception of her and the situation. You obviously don't need my help anymore." I had no intention of leaving him yet but wanted to see how he'd react to the possibility.

His expression hardened, and he released my legs slowly, letting my body slide against his.

"I need you, Andie."

I could feel exactly how he needed me, and with my hands on his shoulders, I debated wrapping my legs around his waist and testing that hunger. In the end, I played it safe and stepped away when my feet hit the ground.

"Then, don't mistake Patrick and Tom's stubbornness in giving an inch for compassion. They all want to save as many people as possible. Waurlyn is just using her eyes and willing to bend a little more."

"Explain."

"You've won the loyalty of the people in this house. You're training us and others to survive whatever we find when we finally have to go back out there. You ask for very little for yourself and ask for more for others. Because of all of that, she sees you as more than a vaccine. Just like we do.

"And I truly believe she wants to save as many people as possible. As you pointed out, there are too many people on this side of the mountain range. We're going to start running low on resources, and people will get more desperate when that happens. People will die. Sending some of them with you when we leave is a way to possibly save a few more from whatever fate overpopulation might bring here."

"It's also a way for them to send people to monitor my brothers and me and see how many of us there are."

"It is. Is that a chance you're willing to take?"

He brushed his fingers over my cheek. "When I left them, I thought I was willing to risk anything to give my brothers a chance at the joy I saw between Mya and Drav. But I see things are not so clear and understand that I risk destroying one brother's happiness to give it to others."

I understood that he was talking about Mya's immunity.

"Is that why you mentioned building more safe havens? So your brothers could come and go and no one would know how many of you there are?"

His lips quirked.

"What's funny?" I asked.

"You bring me joy. The way you think. Your trust in me. The way you look at me." He slid his fingers from my jaw to the back of my neck, holding me still to rest his forehead against mine. "I find it difficult to focus when I am with you. I want to hold you and listen to your thoughts." His fingers gripped my hair tighter. "I want to taste you, Andie. I want it more than I've wanted anything else in my existence."

My insides were liquefied by his admission and the intensity behind it. It would be so easy to tilt my head and give in to the curiosity and need I felt.

"I'm afraid that once you've had your taste, you won't let go," I whispered.

"I already won't let go, Andie. You're mine."

Gripping my hair, he gently forced my head back. My lips parted as I stared at the raw need in his expression.

He growled low and dipped his head, pausing only an inch away from my mouth.

"Stop me," he said softly.

"Stop you?" I gave a breathless laugh. "Can anything stop you?"

"You can."

"How?"

"Just say the word. I am yours, Andie, as much as you are mine."

He closed the distance between us and lightly brushed his lips against mine. I swallowed hard at the electric jolt that shot through me at the contact. The need to feel something good brought my hand to his cheek.

He made a tortured sound and captured my hand, pressing it more firmly against his skin. I knew kissing him would create more problems than I wanted to deal with. Emotional entanglements. Distractions neither of us could afford. But I wanted to know what it would be like to be kissed by someone like him. And not the gentle version of him either.

So, I opened my mouth and nipped his bottom lip.

He froze for a second then jerked back to look at me.

"Too much?" I asked.

"Not nearly enough."

His fingers dug into the back of my head as his mouth crashed against mine. I welcomed his aggression and dominance, holding back at the first exploratory sweep of his tongue. He growled low and cupped my ass with his other hand, lifting me higher and giving himself better access to my mouth. Wrapping my arms around his neck, I angled my head and started kissing him back.

He wasn't gentle or teasing. Every ounce of his hunger was poured into the bruising kiss, and I loved it. Need coursed through me. That itch that I loved to scratch with the right person grew more insistent. I knew I needed to stop this insanity, but at the same time, I didn't want it to end.

With Molev, there wouldn't be any give-and-take between two people. He would take and give what he wanted, and I would just need to hold on for dear life during the process. And as tempting as that prospect was, it also terrified me.

So, I turned my head, tearing my mouth from his as I gasped for air.

His lips drifted down my neck, nipping, licking, and kissing all at once and sending more of the wrong signals to my core.

"Molev, stop," I managed.

He did, but he didn't release me. I could feel his heavy gaze on my averted face as we both caught our breath.

"Did I hurt you?" he finally asked, his fingers gently caressing my scalp.

"No."

"Did you like it?"

I turned my head to meet his gaze. "I liked it—all of it—a lot."

"Then why did you tell me to stop?"

No censure laced the question, only open confusion.

"Saving what's left of the world has to come first."

He studied me for a long moment. "What I feel for you is the only reason what's left might be worth saving."

I swallowed hard again.

"I'm too tired to make smart decisions," I said. "Can we talk about this when we wake up?"

He exhaled heavily as he briefly set his forehead to mine then lowered me to the floor. On my own two feet again, I looked up at him.

"I'm not trying to tease you or lead you on."

"That is disappointing. But perhaps someday, you will try, and we'll both enjoy it."

My stomach flipped at the promise in his eyes.

"Go to sleep, Andie. I'll be back soon."

He left me alone in the room. Assuming he was just cleaning up, I got ready for bed and slipped under the covers without him.

The harsh pounding on our front door pulled me from what felt like a very truncated night's sleep. I threw back the covers and hurried to the hallway, meeting up with Brandon and Sid.

Sid reached the door first, so Brandon and I hung back.

Waurlyn stood in the opening, looking perfectly put

together even though it was still pitch-black outside. I looked at the clock. It was just past eleven. I hadn't even slept for more than thirty minutes.

Holding back my frown, I looked at her again.

"Did he tell any of you where he was going?" she asked, entering the house.

Behind her, I saw a flurry of activity. Guards jumping out of vehicles. A drone in the air, buzzing around.

"Who?" Brandon asked before looking at me. "Molev?"

I shrugged slightly. "When we all turned in, he said he would be back soon. I'm assuming he went for a run. He's been cooped up for a while. It would make sense."

Waurlyn studied me for a long moment.

"I'm walking a very fine line here, Andie. We all answer to someone, and the sooner Molev understands that, the safer he will be. He needs to tell me when he plans to leave."

"You think you're protecting him from higher up the food chain?" I shook my head. "I pity anyone who tries to use him like their personal asset. We're not keeping him safe; he's keeping us safe."

"The mountains and our men are doing that."

"For now, but not forever. Every person we lose is another undead."

"Exactly. Their numbers are growing, and our time is limited. We need him here."

"And he will be as long as we all remember he's his own person exercising the same free will you and I enjoy on a daily basis. Now, if you'll excuse me, I'm going back to bed."

"We need to work together, Andie," she said as I walked away.

"We are," I said. "Stop trying to control him, and he'll stick around. Smother him, and he'll run just like any other man in existence."

She didn't try to follow me or say anything else, so I crawled back into bed and closed my eyes for much longer because, the next time I surfaced, it was light outside, and Molev's arm was across my waist.

"You kicked the hornet's nest last night," I said, closing my eyes again.

"Explain."

"You upset Waurlyn by leaving without letting her know first. She thought you'd left for good."

His arm tightened around me, pulling me closer to his chest.

"Never," he said softly.

"I know that, but she doesn't. Where did you go?"

"Outside the perimeter. I wanted to test her trust."

I twisted to look back at him. "And?"

"She removed the guards and cameras from the house, but both are still there. Only more distant. The guards in the house across the street used their radios as soon as I left. A drone tried to follow me. When it couldn't, she came to speak to you."

He lifted his arms from around my waist and smoothed his hand over my arm.

"I apologize for not telling you, Andie, but I needed to know what she would do to you if I left."

"You needed to know if she was like the general," I said. "I understand. Was the test only for her, though?"

His lips twitched.

"That's what I thought. You better make me a really good breakfast, and not as an apology for testing me but for waking me up after I just fell asleep. You do that again, and I won't be responsible for my actions."

He chuckled. The sexy sound shot straight through me.

"Tell me your favorite breakfast, and I will make it for you."

"Lemon ricotta stuffed french toast with a blueberry glaze. And I'm not telling you how to make it. You get to run around bugging people like people bugged me last night. Good luck."

Internally grinning, I turned away from him and closed my eyes again.

"Tread carefully, Andie," he said close to my ear. "I love a challenge and always win."

CHAPTER TWENTY

THE SOFT MURMUR OF VOICES DRIFTING INTO MY BEDROOM SLOWLY woke me again. Stretching, I inhaled the scent of French toast and looked at my watch. It was just past ten. I hadn't managed almost twelve hours of sleep in forever. The last time had probably been due to a hangover.

Inhaling deeply, I got out of bed, too curious about what Molev had managed to find.

I found him in the kitchen with Katie, who was explaining the different ways to make stuffed French toast.

"Just spread it between two pieces of bread," Steve said. "That sounds like the fastest way to get it in my belly."

Katie grinned and shook her head. "You're like a vulture. If you're hungry, make your own breakfast. There's plenty in there."

"But that looks and sounds better than anything I can make," Steve said, leaning against the counter.

"Smells better than anything you've made, too," I said.

Molev's attention shifted from whatever he was stirring on the stove. His gaze raked up my bare legs before settling on my face. Ignoring the heat in that sweeping glance, I went to him and peeked at what was in the pot.

"Where did you find the blueberries?"

"I asked for them."

"And the ricotta?" I asked, looking at the bowl.

"Yes," he said.

"Who did you ask?"

Katie started to laugh. "Our neighbors. You should have seen it. When he asked me to go with him to ask for the ingredients, I wasn't sure what was going on. Especially when we walked across the street and he knocked on the door. I was still trying to figure out how to tell him the house was empty when he grabbed the doorknob and gave it a push. It didn't even look like a hard push.

"The lock busted right out of the frame. He walked right in and was all, 'Hello, tell Waurlyn that I need blueberries and ricotta cheese.' The living room was empty. There wasn't a person in sight. And I was like, 'Who are you talking to, Molev?' He said, 'The men in the other room.' A second later, a guy walked out, looked at the door, looked at Molev, looked at me, and just nodded and said he would let Waurlyn know right away.

"Thirty minutes later, we had our ingredients."

"I can't imagine that went over well," I commented.

"Nah, it was fine. Molev stayed at their place and showed them how to better block the door and fixed the busted lock."

"So no one yelled at you?" I asked.

"Not for that part," Katie said, still speaking on Molev's behalf. "Waurlyn delivered the ingredients herself and asked where Molev went last night. He told her he went for a run, and she asked him to stay inside the perimeter from now on. He said it was too small for a good run then picked her up and took off with her. She was pretty quiet when he brought her back."

I glanced at Molev. "What did you do?"

"I took her to the same spot I took you and told her that I was not interested in her smothering attention but that I had several brothers who would be. She asked me to return her to the base, and I did. Before she left, I told her that the food I requested was to make amends for her behavior last night. I asked her never to wake the people in my house again unless it was an emergency."

I stared at him, processing what he'd done. He'd acknowledged the presence of his hidden guards in a non-confrontational way, had proven this base couldn't contain him while also giving Waurlyn a taste of why it couldn't, and had shown his protectiveness over us without any serious flexing.

"You're a smart man, Molev," I said.

"If he was smart, he would have talked Katie into making breakfast instead of doing it himself."

I tore my gaze from Molev's so he wouldn't see how much it meant to me that he hadn't.

"Careful, Steve," I said. "He might drop yours on the floor."

Brandon snorted from his place on the couch. "Like that would stop any of us from eating it. This is gourmet-level food. Who knows the next time we'll eat something like this? What are a few stray chest hairs stuck to it going to matter?"

"Why is nothing sacred to you?" Steve said, turning to give Brandon a disgusted look.

Keeping my amusement to myself, I headed back to the bedroom to shower and change. By the time I reemerged, Steve and Katie were eating, and Brandon and Roni were nearby, salivating.

"This is so good," Katie said around a mouthful. "Seriously, Molev. When all of this is done, I'm planting some blueberry bushes and finding a cow so you can keep making this."

"What about the lemons?" Roni asked.

"There's got to be orchards still standing somewhere, right?" she said.

Molev handed over another two plates and added two more dipped sandwiches into the pan.

"So what are the plans for today, other than brunch?" I asked.

"More games," Molev said. "Katie can see if the guards next door want to play once she's done."

I couldn't decide if he was trying to cause trouble or prevent it with that kind of move.

"What about inviting Waurlyn too?" I asked just to see.

He blinked at me and slowly grinned.

"That is a good idea."

I wasn't completely convinced it was until we had a houseful of people a few hours later. We split into two large teams for charades, which started a little stilted but quickly became a laugh fest. Molev openly acknowledged his inability to read during his turn, so I helped him. Waurlyn watched everything closely but joined in and even laughed.

Molev cooked up what we had for burgers and brats for dinner, and we continued until Waurlyn said she had to go. The guards from next door were quick to leave then too.

Knowing that the evening was wrapping up and preferring not to face alone time with Molev, I tried to sneak away and get ready for bed without him.

"Let's go for a run," Roni said before I could escape. She waved her hand at Sid when he groaned. "Not you. Girls-only run. You in Katie?"

"I think I'd rather take kitchen cleanup," she said.

"Suit yourself. Come on, Andie."

The hard stare she gave me was enough to know that Roni had something on her mind that she didn't want to say in front of the others. Considering how outspoken she was, I nodded and said goodbye to my chance of escaping another quiet conversation with Molev. It wasn't that I didn't enjoy them. I did. Too much. Which was why avoiding seemed the best way to keep the distance we needed because, based on the long looks he'd been giving me all day, cozying up with me again was definitely on his mind.

"Why are you being such a baby?" Roni asked as we started an easy jog.

"About what?" I asked.

"Rocking his world. He's obviously interested, and you're interested, no matter how much you're trying to hide it."

I side-glanced at her.

"Is this where you volunteer to have a go if I don't step up? Because have at it. He's more than I can mentally or emotionally take on at the moment."

She snorted.

"I would love to climb that tree and play Tarzan with his vine, but it's not swinging my way. It's swinging yours. And who cares if you're not mentally or emotionally ready? Would anyone be ready for that level of impalement?"

"You're ridiculous," I said.

"You know I'm right. He only has eyes for you."

"Why are we talking about this?"

"Dick envy mostly," she said. "And because you're starting to make things weird."

I glanced at her again. "Too cozy?"

She snorted. "You really are something. You're too distant, Andie. We can all see how much he likes you. You don't tell him 'no,' but you're not telling him yes either. The rest of us have no idea what's going on with you, so we don't know how to react when he does stuff like making a special breakfast just because you asked him to."

"You say thank you. That's what I did."

She punched my arm. It was probably meant to be playful but knocked me to the side a little.

"That's not what I meant, and you know it," she said. "You've been with us since the beginning. You've had our backs, and we'll keep having yours. If you want him to back off but are too afraid to say the word because of what he means as far as finding a cure goes, tell me. Tell Sid. Tell any of us. We'll have your back and figure out a way to make things work where you're not the sacrificial lamb."

I was touched beyond measure by what she was saying.

"Being the focus of Molev's attention isn't a sacrifice, Roni, and I think you know that. He's kind, almost to a fault, and extremely attractive despite—and because of—his differences. Which aren't a problem for me, by the way.

"The problem is that we have no idea what's going to happen one day to the next. And like you've pointed out, relationships don't only distract the people involved but the people around them. None of us can afford distractions. So, I'm fine with Molev's affection but not ready to reciprocate. He knows how I feel and seems okay with it."

"I doubt he's actually okay with it," Roni said. "But since you have it handled, I'll tell the rest to stay out of it."

"Just the rest? What about you?"

"Hell no. Molev's morning wood after snuggling against your ass demands a cheering section. Speaking of, are there any erogenous zones you'd like me to tell him to pay particular interest to?"

Her banter didn't fool me. I knew what she was doing. We all had our ways to cope with things when they started to go sideways. And after weeks in a cush, safe house, leaving for the field sure felt like things were tilting the wrong way again.

"I have a better idea. That blonde tonight was giving you some long looks and wasn't wearing a ring. I'm pretty sure he'd be happy to let you swing his vine any way you wanted if you knocked on his door."

She made a contemplative sound before shaking her head.

"It wouldn't be fair to him. No matter what he's packing, it wouldn't measure up. I'd rather hold out and play bachelorette with Molev's friends. He mentioned one of them, and I'm intrigued."

We rounded the far side of the playground and started back.

"It might take weeks or months to get there," I commented.

"Yep. With all that build-up, I'll be climbing some lucky guy like a tree," she said with a grin. "He won't know what hit him."

She talked a big game, but her smile was just a hint too wide. I realized Roni was nervous. It wasn't a typical emotion for Roni, but I'd seen it once or twice before when a situation challenged her. She liked to be challenged, though, so I wasn't too worried. At least, not about her.

"How's Katie been?" I asked, changing the subject.

"She's crying at night in the bathroom when she thinks I'm sleeping. I think Ted's death really got to her."

"Yeah. I think so, too," I said. "Should she stay here tomorrow?"

Roni thought about it for a moment and shook her head. "No. She's been focused during training and didn't hesitate at the evac field when Molev freed us. I think she'll be fine."

Fine was such a relative term now, but I understood what Roni meant. Katie was hurting a lot, but she wasn't hurting so badly that she'd crack under pressure. And I agreed.

When we reached the house again, we stretched outside in silence and then went in. Everything was already cleaned up, and no one was lingering in the common spaces. Roni gave me a knowing smirk and shook her head at me.

"Baby," she mouthed before heading to her own room.

Knowing I had no valid reason to avoid my bed, especially when we were supposed to meet up before dawn, I made my way to the room I shared with Molev.

He wasn't there.

I took the opportunity to clean up and got into bed mere minutes before he returned. He turned off the light I'd left on for him, and I listened to him undress in the darkness.

I waited for him to settle in next to me before rolling toward him.

"You followed us, didn't you?" I asked.

He didn't answer.

"Will you tell me why?"

At first, I didn't think he would answer that either. When he did start speaking, his voice was a soft rumble.

"In the caves, I let my instincts guide me. In the beginning, before I learned to trust what I felt, I died many deaths. Once I started listening, I died less frequently until this life.

"I trust my instincts, though I don't always understand them. And they are telling me we are not safe from the infected here. That is why I want to leave tomorrow to see what is happening. The infected have been changing since the beginning. What changes have I missed while here?"

I considered what he was saying.

"Okay," I said. "Then we'll stick together from now on. Even on the base. All of us."

He grunted, and the weight of his arm settled on my waist.

I forced myself to close my eyes and relax.

It wasn't hard for me to shut down and sleep. But it was

hard to get out of bed when Molev shook my shoulder hours later. The relentless training was catching up to me, and the idleness of the prior day let it set in. Everything ached. Not so much that I couldn't move but enough that I groaned when I sat up.

"What's wrong?" Molev asked.

"Nothing. Just sore. It'll work itself out once I start moving around."

Easing to my feet, I shook out my protesting legs and started stretching. I wasn't focused on anything beyond loosening up the tight muscles so they wouldn't slow me down. The palm that skimmed my backside when I was bent over sent a jolt of surprise through me.

Face flushed and heart racing, I spun to face Molev. His eyes locked with mine.

"I know you worry about what the future holds, but don't. I already know. You and I will be together, Andie." He gripped my ass and pulled me to him. The moment my feet left the ground, I grabbed his shoulders.

"Like this," he said, moving one hand from my ass to my leg so he could hook it over his hip. The position settled his engorged length between my legs, and my eyes almost rolled back.

Before I could push those thoughts and urges aside, he cupped the back of my head and kissed me. It was just as hungry and demanding as the day before and swept me into a whirling storm of need that abruptly ended when he pulled back to look at me.

"Nothing will stop this. Not your leaders. Not the infected. Nothing. Do you understand? There is nothing for you to fear."

I blinked up at him for a moment while my thoughts reorganized themselves.

"Is that your instinct talking?" I asked.

"Yes."

"Why are you telling me this now? Do you think something is going to happen today?"

He set his forehead to mine.

"This has nothing to do with today. By denying yourself the possibility of a future, you are telling yourself you have no reason to live, and that's a lie."

"If you think I'm ready to die, Molev, I'm not."

"Aren't you? You told me that you never expected to live to see this mission through. That, by signing up, you acknowledged your own death. You did so willingly to save Zion, who is safe. What reasons do you have to keep fighting?"

"We still need a cure and to stop the hounds."

"The doctors and scientists will work on the cure, and my brothers and I will kill the hounds. What's your purpose now, Andie?"

I extracted myself from his hold.

"Right now, my purpose is to head out to the field and observe the infected with a man who is only sometimes smart. Stay focused, Molev."

His mossy green gaze swept over me. "I am very focused, Andie."

"No. You're distracted because of a kiss. Since you have seven immediate people counting on you, along with the rest of humanity, you don't have the luxury of enjoying some diversions, and neither do I. Focus on today and coming back alive so none of us end up infected."

Turning on my heel, I strode to the bathroom where I'd left my clothes the night before.

When I emerged, Roni was leaning against the wall. Her crossed arms and angry expression said everything, but she threw some words in there, too, for good measure while I put on my riot gear.

"You're not a baby; you're an idiot. When someone you care about worries about you, you don't throw it in their face. You say thank you and try to ease their worries."

I sighed.

"I apologize for being loud."

She shook her head at me.

"Fix this before we leave, or you stay behind. As things stand, you're a distraction and a risk."

My temper briefly flared, and she saw it.

"I think that's the first human reaction I've seen out of you," she said. "About time."

"Of course I'm upset. You're only seeing the situation through one lens. I don't think Molev is truly worried I'm going to die. I think he wants me to see him as my sole reason for living now."

"That's what you got out of your conversation? You are an idiot. He's been with us long enough to see you like we do. You're not emotionally connected to any of us in any significant way. You're going through the motions, but none of it is touching you. We can all see it. That detachment was exactly what was needed in the field, but not here where we're safe."

I shook my head slowly.

"That's exactly the problem, Roni. We're not safe yet. Not even here. This is just an illusion waiting to break. Our people are so focused on a cure that they're not seeing what we both know. A cure isn't the final solution. We won't be truly safe until every hound and infected is dead.

"If you see me as insensitive instead of focused, that's fine. Just make sure you're focused on what's going on out there as soon as we leave. If we don't have each other's backs, there won't be a future to worry about."

I started out of the room but paused when she straightened away from the wall.

"For the record, I'm not the only detached person in the group. We all have our ways of coping with what's happening. And detachment is exactly what's helping some of us survive."

She followed me out of the room where everyone else was waiting. Molev was absent.

"Anyone else have anything to add?" I asked, knowing they'd been listening.

"Nope," Brandon said. "I think you summed everything up well. Head in the game. Don't die."

"Live to fight another day," Sid said.

"Then let's stop treating my love life or lack thereof like a daytime drama and get to work. Molev wants to see how the infected have changed since we've been here. Keep sharp, watch everything, and stay alive."

I headed for the door, comforted by the familiar feel of my gear.

Molev waited outside by the jeeps, his expression stoic as he watched my approach.

"Are you focused?" I asked him.

He nodded once, and part of me wished I knew what was going through his head. Now and when he'd said all that stuff in the bedroom. Rather than focusing on it, though, I stayed in the moment.

"Which truck are we in?" I asked.

He motioned to the lead one. I got in and made enough room for him to sit beside me.

It was a quick drive to the meet-up point, where the rest of the platoon was already gathered. The jeeps stopped by a Stryker where Waurlyn waited with Patrick. He looked us over, his gaze lingering on me as I got out of the jeep after Molev.

"Patrick will accompany you and act as my eyes and ears to provide you with what you need while you're away," Waurlyn said to Molev. "Will that suit you?"

Molev nodded once, and she smiled.

"Patrick spoke highly of your resourcefulness when out in the field, but I still ask that you exercise caution and not take any unnecessary risks." She glanced at the rest of us. "I look forward to meeting with you all again in three days."

She left us with Patrick.

"Hope you're rested up," he said, moving to get into the Stryker. "We have a long drive ahead of us."

"Where are we going?" I asked.

"Gypsum, Colorado, just inside the secured zone," Patrick said.

"I thought we were doing a supply run." I took the seat beside him and glanced at Molev as he sat across from us.

"We are," Patrick said. "Everything between here and there has been evacuated through the mountains, and the supplies from the towns have already been cleared. We need to head outside of the barrier. Loveland's not far from Gypsum. There's a distribution center there that they want us to secure."

I thought back to what I'd heard weeks ago as the door closed.

"Wasn't the Denver-Fort Collins area bombed hard?" I asked.

"It was. But they focused the majority of it on the residential areas. There are pockets that are still standing. The highway near the distribution center is still intact. If we can reach the location, we'll secure it and contact the Gypsum FOB. They'll airlift the supplies out while there's daylight."

The Stryker's engine rumbled to life, and I settled in for the ride. It was long and boring. Conversation wasn't really easy because of the noise, and there wasn't a whole lot to say. So most everyone napped or stared off into space, lost in their own thoughts.

Molev watched me, ignoring everyone else until our first stop. Katie, Roni, and I used a ditch and stretched our legs during refueling. Molev was gone from his seat when we returned and didn't come back when the engine started.

"Thought for sure he'd rather stay in here with you," Patrick said when we got underway again.

"Why's that?" I asked.

"Does he ever stop watching you?" he asked.

"I'm not sure. Sometimes I sleep."

Patrick snorted. "Same Andie."

"Same world," I retorted.

We slowly made our way northeast through the mountains. I saw Molev at each stop. He wasn't watching me, though. He was studying the soldiers as they refueled or stood guard, or he watched the mountains around us.

That he was on edge was clear to me. However, no one else seemed to notice.

It was well after dark when we finally reached Gypsum.

"Sergeant Bromwell," a soldier said, saluting Patrick the minute he climbed out of the Stryker. "I'm here to escort you to the debriefing."

Patrick glanced at me. "Molev didn't eat. Make sure he does."

With that, he walked away, yelling, "Someone, show Alpha Team to the mess."

I scanned the area and easily spotted the FOB soldiers. They kept staring at Molev.

"Steve. See the one by the fueler? Get him to show us the way," I said.

Steve jogged toward the guy, and I focused on Molev.

"Why didn't you eat?" I asked.

"It was a meal bag with red sauce."

"Next time, ask for something else. Don't skip meals, especially when you're running all day."

Molev's gaze locked with mine, and before I knew what he meant to do, he threw me over his shoulder and ran.

CHAPTER TWENTY-ONE

Two breath-defying jumps later, we were standing on a metal roof.

I swallowed the bile in my throat and studied Molev's thunderous expression.

"If you don't like me showing concern, all you need to do is say so," I said calmly.

His gaze narrowed.

"You are intelligent, Andie, and know the difference between censure and concern."

"Okay. Fine. That was censure. I apologize."

More irritation flashed across his face.

"Just say what's on your mind, Molev."

"You frustrate me. Every time I think we advance a step, you retreat three."

"How did I retreat three?" I asked, truly confused.

He advanced on me, shoving his fingers into the hair at the back of my head and fisting the strands in a way that set my heart racing hard.

"Did you like when I kissed you?" he asked with soft anger.

"Yes. Is that what this is about? That I liked it and didn't immediately jump on you?"

The hold on my hair tightened as he pulled my head back.

"Do you truly not see?" he asked, leaning over me. His breath fanned my throat as he dipped his head, and my heart went wild. Unable to help myself, I gripped his arms. His biceps jumped under my touch, adding fuel to the fire slowly building inside of me.

"You control everything," he said, brushing his lips along the column of my throat. "My thoughts. My actions. Yes, I want you to live only for me, Andie. I already live only for you."

His teeth scraped my skin.

"Tell me you don't like knowing that," he said. "Tell me you want me to let you go."

I understood what he was saying. He wasn't talking about what he was doing right that second but forever.

"Why are you doing this?" I panted. "Why right now?"

He started to nip and suck my throat. I groaned.

"Because you're ready for me now but continue to fight it," he murmured before he found that sweet spot at the base of my neck.

"Molev, I need you to stop. Please."

His snarl vibrated through me even as he straightened us. He didn't release his grip on my hair, though, not that I minded.

"I can't focus when you're distracting me, and I want a real answer," I explained. "How did I take three steps back?"

"We kissed, Andie. You said you liked it but needed more time. Then you tried going to bed without me."

I didn't bother denying it and shouldn't have been surprised he'd caught on. Roni had, too, after all.

"How is completely avoiding me not taking three steps back?"

I considered him, noting the growing frustration in the depth of his gaze.

"What would you do if I said I was ready for sex?" I asked. "Right here. Right now."

His pupils expanded, rounding out in his irises, even as he narrowed his eyes.

"Is that why? You think I'm so mindless that I would forget everything, risk everything to have you?"

"You've already said I'm your only reason for living."

"You are. But I wouldn't jeopardize your safety to have you."

"So all of this is because I tried going to bed without you?"

"Do not downplay what is happening in here," he said, releasing my hair to tap my head.

I stared at him, feeling a healthy amount of frustration of my own. My first thoughts were that he was doing exactly what I'd told him had killed all my previous relationships. That he was trying to force me into some role. But he wasn't. Not really. The only thing he was asking me to do was to stop denying what I was starting to feel for him. Once I realized that, I took a calming breath.

"I'm afraid that if I don't try to retreat a little, we'll advance to a place I'm not yet ready to be."

"I've already told you. If I do something you don't like, tell me."

"That's the problem, Molev. I like everything you do," I said, letting my frustration show. "I freaking love it when you get forceful. I love the sting of my hair being pulled by you. The way you look when you're angry is both terrifying and a turn-on.

"If the world were in a different place, I'd already be naked

317

and on my back, enjoying everything you have to offer. But the world is what it is, and I need some damn breathing room so I can keep a clear head and live to see another fucking day. Why is that so hard to understand?"

I slapped both hands on his chest, venting the pent-up frustration I was feeling. "And don't ever toss me over your shoulder like that again. *That* I did not like. At all."

He captured my hands and brought them to his mouth, kissing their backs.

"If you promise to stop retreating, I will promise not to carry you over my shoulder."

I tried to tug my hands free, but he kept them trapped in his.

"You're asking me to be vulnerable. Take a good look around us, Molev. Is this really where you want me to be weak?"

"Caring about me won't make you weak, Andie. It will make us both stronger."

I closed my eyes and sighed. We were at an impasse, neither of us willing to see the other person's side.

"Fine, Molev. Tell me exactly where we stand so I know what I'm not supposed to retreat from."

He made another angry sound before his hand was back in my hair.

"I think I'll show you."

My eyes flew open just before his lips crashed down onto mine. He didn't give an inch as his mouth demanded everything I had to give. And I did give. There wasn't any other choice. The moment he felt me trying to withdraw, he pulled me closer, wrapping my legs around his waist. The next time I tried, he pressed his hand against my ass to grind his hard length against my core.

I got the hint after that. He would stop demanding more if I just surrendered to what I *was* willing to give.

Framing his face with my hands, I slowed the kiss instead of trying to stop it. He immediately eased up. That insane, hungry part of me wanted the aggression back. The reasonable side whispered that this wasn't the time or the place. I kissed him tenderly and tried to ignore the ache growing in my chest when he returned everything I gave.

When he finally pulled back, my lips felt swollen, and I could barely think straight.

His hungry gaze swept over my face, missing nothing.

"No more retreating," he said.

"Do I have a choice?"

The corner of his mouth twitched.

"No."

"Didn't think so," I muttered. "Now, can we go down? I'm hungry, and they're probably still waiting for us."

He leaned in and kissed my forehead, adding to that ache in my chest.

"No more retreating," he repeated.

"I'm not retreating. I'm asking you to carry me down— nicely this time—so we can eat."

His gaze held mine for a long moment, and I crossed my arms.

"You suddenly don't trust me?" I asked.

"I trust you with everything but listening to your own heart."

He swept me off my feet in one fluid move and looked down at me.

"When you retreat, it's in your heart and in your mind. You allow one to control the other and rarely allow the effects of either to show on the outside. So when I say no more retreating, I mean in your heart and in your mind. Not your body."

He jumped down from the roof before I could answer and jogged over to where we'd left the others. The soldier that I'd sent Steve to get was with them, his attention bouncing between me and Molev.

The rest of the group was a bit more subdued in their interest regarding what they'd witnessed. Roland wore a slight smirk. Katie looked shocked. And Roni just subtly shook her head at me as Molev put me down.

"Where's the mess hall?" I asked, looking pointedly at the soldier.

"This way," he said.

I started to take a step and felt Molev's hand close around the back of my neck. It was enough to make me realize I had already mentally distanced myself from what happened on the roof and the present moment.

Rather than try to deny it, I sighed and slipped my arm around his waist.

"This is crossing into ridiculous," I muttered.

His low chuckle wrapped around me.

"No, it isn't."

We walked like that, side-by-side, his hand on my neck and mine resting on his side, all the way to the mess hall.

"Are you going to make me get my tray with one hand?" I asked. The fingers resting on my skin tightened fractionally in silent warning.

I smirked, and he released me. But he didn't leave my side. We moved through the line together. The food looked decent, and there were plenty of protein options for Molev to pile on his tray, which he held in one hand so the other could rest on my neck again as I led the way to a table. He sat on my left while Roni quickly took her place on the right.

"So, that was interesting," she said.

"Don't start." I took a bite of food and caught Sid's jerky move across from Roni. She grunted and started eating as well.

"Sid, no kicking Roni outside of training," Molev said, not even looking up from his tray.

Steve snorted, and any awkwardness faded away...until Patrick showed up five minutes later.

"Miss Wells, could I have a few minutes of your time?"

I glanced at Molev, who was chewing thoughtfully as he considered Patrick.

"Sure," I said, starting to stand.

Molev caught my wrist, stopping me. "Why do you need her?"

"Even though there's very little I can do about it, I'd like to speak with her regarding her relationship with you and if it ever makes her feel threatened in any way. But I would like to have the conversation privately so I know she's answering honestly."

I had to hand it to Patrick. He had balls. And he'd also gotten smarter about speaking frankly to Molev.

"I'll be fine, Molev," I said.

He swallowed his bite as he looked at me. "Stay close."

I nodded and walked out of the mess with Patrick. We didn't go any farther than the door.

"Several personnel reported that Molev aggressively carried you to a roof and kissed you. You didn't appear willing. Is he interested in you sexually?"

"Do you think he named me specifically as part of his deal to help just because I was the first one to trust him?" I asked.

"You're the one who's good at reading people. You tell me."

"Yes, he's sexually interested in me, Patrick."

"And the female volunteers?"

"What about them?" I asked.

"Does he plan on using them for sex as well?"

"Hold up. First, Molev isn't using *me* for sex. Second, he didn't ask for female volunteers because he wants to collect a harem. He truly wants people who are open to living in a diverse community. He would prefer females since we're typically less aggressive or quick to anger. Age doesn't matter. Sexual orientation doesn't matter. Marital status doesn't matter. And not because he's going to disregard all of it. It doesn't matter to him. His first priority is to build better relations between our races. Which is why he would like to meet with the volunteers personally to gauge their reactions to him and ensure there's no fear too intense to overcome or any negative emotions. And, yes, he's going to want me there, too, to get my opinion."

"Was Waurlyn made aware of these additional stipulations?"

"No. At the time it was discussed, it was in front of a crowd she was trying to calm so they wouldn't storm the evac site. I didn't think adding conditions would achieve her goal just then."

"I see. Very well. Carry on, and report to me if anything changes."

I crossed my arms, not leaving despite the clear dismissal.

"What exactly do you mean? A change in what?"

"Anything."

"Patrick, I respected you for making some hard decisions when we were out in the field. That respect has been eroding with each prejudiced decision you've made since Molev showed up. You say that I'm the one who's good at reading people and have followed my suggestions numerous times, but rarely with Molev. Which means talking to you about anything dealing with Molev is pointless. You will hear what you want and do what you want."

I started to turn and paused.

"The sexual attraction is mutual, by the way. That's why he's interested in me. If I weren't interested, he wouldn't have taken me to the roof and kissed me like he did. And yes, it was a little aggressive, but I'd frustrated him just before that. And no, he didn't hurt me at all. That should have been the first question you asked if you truly wanted me to believe you cared about me as a person rather than as a means to control Molev."

The door to the mess opened, and I glanced back at Molev. He didn't leave the mess, just extended his hand to me.

"You need to eat," he said.

I nodded and went to him without looking back at Patrick. Everything that needed to be said had been said, and Patrick was still as unlikely to listen to reason as he'd been before we'd talked.

"Mutual attraction?" Molev murmured when I drew close. "I doubt what you feel for me is even close to what I feel for you, Andie."

I shook my head at him. "Nope. We're not going there. I've given as much as I'm willing to give today."

He chuckled and took my hand. Everyone was already finished by the time I returned to my seat.

"What was that about?" Steve asked.

"Patrick thinks I requested female volunteers for a harem," Molev answered, proving he'd been listening.

"Damn," Steve said. "From all the way across the room and through a closed door and background noise?"

"I was focused."

Knowing they were waiting for me, I ate quickly.

"What did Andie tell him?" Roland asked.

M.J. HAAG

"That I did not have a preference for age, sexual orientation, or marital status to prove that I was more interested in non-aggressive volunteers willing to live with my brothers and me." Molev focused on me. "You were wise to state that we want to interview them."

"Are you crazy?" Brandon asked. "That'll take forever. If you want to find out who's easygoing and who's going to avoid you, don't do interviews. Do what we did with our neighbors."

"A mixer," Roland said with a nod. "That could work. Food, drinks, and music. People will be more relaxed and themselves."

I nodded. "The ones who go out of their way to avoid you would probably be too afraid."

"And the ones who come up to kiss your ass will probably be government plants," Roni said.

Molev grunted. "These are good ideas, and you have my thanks. I will speak with Waurlyn about a mixer when we return."

Steve, Roland, and Brandon grinned. Sid and Katie seemed lost in their own worlds. It'd been a long day.

I shoved in my last bite and watched Molev carry my tray away as I finished chewing. He was good to watch. I liked the way he moved, a predatory prowl. The muscle show wasn't any hardship either. Yet, I rarely let myself enjoy it. The risk that I would fall that much deeper into what I felt had me wanting to look away. And that was exactly what he'd meant by retreating in my head. I was fine with the night cuddles and the long looks from him, but I wasn't fine with returning any of them because I was afraid. Afraid of being distracted. Afraid of making mistakes. Afraid of opening my heart just to be hurt again. All my fears resulted in sending him mixed signals for weeks.

I hated when I didn't see things objectively. And I hadn't been when it came to Molev, which made me think of Patrick's treatment of him. Was I really any better?

Even though I wasn't ready to give, could I manage to hold my ground just where I was without retreating?

I stood when he returned to me and held out my hand. He took it without hesitation.

"Ready to figure out where we're sleeping?" I asked.

He grunted, and I looked at Steve. "Did our escort give any hints about where to go next?"

He had, so we followed the directions to a barracks with a few empty bunks. The narrow beds looked as if they would barely fit Molev, never mind the both of us. I was just going to suggest we take the two bunks side by side when he shoved them together.

"Saw that coming," Roni said with a smirk. "Katie and I will go up top. Molev can get a taste of harem life." She sniggered at her own joke.

Katie didn't look amused. She looked tired.

"You okay?" I asked softly before she climbed into her bunk.

"Yeah. Fine. Long day."

I nodded and was watching her settle into her place beside Roni when I felt a tug on my shirt. I glanced over my shoulder at Molev, who nodded toward the lower bunks.

"Impatient?" I asked.

"Yes." He hooked an arm around my waist and towed me to the bed.

"All right. All right." As soon as I settled into place, he curled around me, the weight of his arm comforting on my waist.

Molev's patience and flexibility had limits. I'd seen that for myself in his interactions with Patrick and the general, and I should have been watching for the signs that he'd reached that place with me.

Unless I proved that I hadn't just received his message but would embrace it, he would be unrelenting in his stubbornness. Would he even be willing to give an inch if I showed I wasn't retreating, though?

Did I care if he did or didn't? My pulse started to race at the memory of that kiss and the way he'd kept insisting until I gave in. I knew initiating a kiss would show him I'd heard. But would he still stop if I said so?

I rolled over under his arm. He watched me, his gaze more wary than hungry, and I almost smirked. He knew something was up.

He didn't do anything when I stroked his cheek lightly with my fingers. But when I started tracing his scars, one by one, he closed his eyes and grabbed my hand.

"Go to sleep," he rumbled.

I stretched a little and kissed his chin.

"Goodnight."

He opened his eyes and considered me.

Tugging my hand free, I went back to tracing his scars. There were so many of them. Most faded to almost nothing. I found one that disappeared into his hairline, which distracted me. His hair was coarser than mine but still silky to the touch. I ran my fingers through it a few times and accidentally brushed his ear.

His pupils rounded, devouring the vivid green of his irises as his eyes narrowed on me.

I stretched again, and this time, he dipped his head to capture my lips. He kissed me tenderly despite the suspicion I'd seen in his gaze and didn't fight to maintain the kiss when I pulled back a few minutes later.

Without a word, I closed my eyes and snuggled against

him. His hand lightly stroked my back then stilled when his lips brushed my forehead.

That was it. No complaint. No pressure for more.

He'd accepted what I'd given him and had let me decide when it had been enough. It helped define the line between retreating and stopping.

Content, I drifted off to sleep. But it didn't feel like I'd slept long enough when Molev woke me with a hand on my shoulder.

"Patrick said we need to leave within the hour. Do you want more sleep or a chance to eat?"

"Eat," I said, already sitting up.

The bunks above us shifted, and I knew Roni and Katie had heard as well.

"We're coming too," Katie said.

Roland, Brandon, Steve, and Sid started moving as well.

It was still dark out when we headed toward the mess hall, but personnel were still moving around out there. Patrick was speaking to someone near our Stryker. He didn't stop us from going to the mess when he glanced our way, though. We ate quickly and returned to the yard just in time.

A platoon stood in neat lines in front of Patrick and the other man. Obviously trained soldiers, not like the original platoon sent to find Molev had been. However, it was half as many personnel we'd arrived with.

The other man began talking. "The Denver and Boulder watchtowers have reported increased activity in both locations. To avoid drawing the attention of the undead, the convoy will head east, picking up one-nineteen, seventy-two, and seven. Once we reach the watchtower at the outskirts of Loveland, it's a straight shot on thirty-four. By all reports from the watchtower there, the bombs left the road mostly intact. Undead activity is minimal. However, the sound of our engines will draw any in the area. We will need to keep the numbers low until we reach the distribution center and can establish a perimeter. Every vehicle in this convoy is carrying the personnel and supplies needed to complete this mission. We will not lose a single one. Am I clear?"

"Yes, sir!"

He dismissed them to their vehicles, and I looked at Molev.

"Ride with us until the watchtower, okay?"

He nodded and took my hand, leading us toward Patrick, who missed nothing.

"We'll reach the watchtower before midday. It should give us plenty of daylight to reach the distribution center and set up a fence and lights. If all goes well, you'll be back in your own beds by tomorrow night."

Patrick turned on his heel and got into the Stryker. I hurried after him.

"What's the activity in Loveland?" I asked, taking the seat beside him.

"Lieutenant Darbin never said."

"I know," I said, not falling for Patrick's play on words. "That's why I'm asking you."

CHAPTER TWENTY-TWO

MOLEV SAT ACROSS FROM US, TUCKING MY GEAR UNDER HIS SEAT as he waited for Patrick's answer.

"The last report was that there was no activity," Patrick said. His steady gaze and body language were all wrong. It felt like he was challenging me to disagree.

"When was the last report?" I asked.

He sighed and rubbed a hand over his shaved head as the engine rumbled to life.

"You really don't miss anything, do you, Andie? They were due to report two hours ago."

"That means they went dark between two and twenty-six hours ago," I said.

"How many other watchtowers have fallen?" Roni asked.

"Just the one. We'll reestablish before continuing on and remove any undead we find."

The vehicle rolled forward, and I looked at Molev as my mind raced. How many alternate routes were between the two locations? Would the infected be wandering the mountains, or would they stick to the roads? If we were four hours away by road, how long would it take any infected to reach Gypsum?

Was that why we'd left so many men behind at Gypsum? Because they anticipated the infected were already on the move? Most likely.

"We're using the FLIR, then?" I asked.

"We are."

Everyone was watching me as if waiting for my opinion on the matter, and I realized why. Molev was inside the vehicle where he would be the least effective if something came our way. And he was here because of me.

"What's the most likely scenario?" I asked Patrick.

"Each tower has a ten-man crew. If the tower fell, it would have involved either a single hound or a group of undead. If it had been a hound, we believe we would have heard it last night. Which means we have an unknown number of undead within the barrier."

"Not unknown," Katie said. "At least ten."

Roland shook his head. "The guards will be newly turned and slow. They'll linger around the watchtower until something catches their attention."

Patrick nodded. "Exactly. Which means an unknown number. The reports are that the undead are evolving. Their traps are growing more complex. We're not sure what we'll find or what to expect along the way. But it doesn't change our orders. We need supplies, and that distribution center was the most accessible location outside the barrier."

"There's nothing inside the barrier?" Steve asked.

"Everything known between the Sierra Nevada Mountain range and the Rockies has been cleared and moved to storage facilities in western California. Everything that is shipped to the sanctuaries or sent out with the FOBs is from there.

"Collection between the Rockies and the Appalachian Mountains was postponed until we better understood the threat."

"Fine," I said. "We're not sure what to expect, and that's why you want Molev outside. But is it smart to ask him to use his energy on four hours of running when we have no idea what we'll face at the watchtower or when we reach Loveland? It makes more sense to conserve and wait to use him until necessary."

"The roofs of these vehicles are sturdy and can hold me," Molev said. "I won't expend unnecessary energy while still watching and listening."

I glanced at him, taking in the multitude of scars he already wore, and felt a surge of annoyance at myself and him. We really couldn't have picked a worse time to try to start laying the groundwork for a relationship.

While holding my gaze, he very subtly shook his head. The warning told me he knew exactly where my head was going.

"You want to ride up top? Fine. Knock on the roof if you see something and need to deal with it. That way, the convoy knows to slow down and wait for you."

Roland made an unhappy sound. "Twice when you're leaving and want us to slow down and three times if you're leaving and want us to keep it steady." He glanced at me. "I don't want to slow down for traps if we don't need to."

I agreed, and Patrick moved to radio the change in plans. Molev took his seat.

"Don't start with me," I warned. "If you don't want me to pull away, make sure you don't wear yourself out before the fighting really begins. It's not easier for me to watch you be bitten than it is for you to watch me. Only I don't have the luxury of telling your opponent to stop biting so hard. Got it?"

Molev cupped the back of my head and pressed his forehead to mine.

"Thank you," he said.

331

"There was still plenty of censure mixed in with that concern, so I don't know why you're thanking me."

He chuckled and kissed my forehead. Five minutes later, he was on the roof. I closed my eyes and tried to rest, knowing there wouldn't be much opportunity for it once we finally reached the shitstorm we were heading into.

The drone of our vehicle's engine faded into the background as I drifted. When I tipped into Patrick because of an incline, I roused enough to check my watch and saw an hour had passed without incident. Then two. Then three. My ass went numb from the vibrations somewhere in there, and my lower back started to tweak. I leaned forward to stretch it. And that's when the first double-knock echoed from above.

Patrick radioed that Molev wanted us to slow down and asked if anyone had eyes on him.

"We see him on the FLIR," someone reported. "To the east. Four other people. Nope. Not anymore. I really hope they were undead. I've never seen anything move that fast. He's like a damn mountain goat."

The radio went silent for a moment.

"He's headed north. There's a group ahead." Another few moments of silence. "He cleared them too."

"Gunners ready," someone else said.

"Hold fire," another said. "Do not shoot the grey. I repeat. Do not shoot the grey."

I glanced at Patrick.

"They were warned," he said.

I hoped, for everyone's sake, there wouldn't be any accidental discharges in Molev's direction.

The terrain didn't make it easy to see where the infected were without the FLIR, and sometimes, due to the steep slopes, it was impossible. Yet, Molev seemed to know right where they were. Disappearing occasionally, only to return with news of what he'd found.

We continued like that, at a slower pace, until we reached the watchtower. Molev's kill tally totaled fifty by the time he opened the door. His shirt was a mess of red and brown bits as his gaze swept the others and locked onto me.

The engines quieted as everyone got out. I scanned his arms and face.

"Turn around," I said.

He did, and I saw his back was clean.

"And that's how it's done," Steve said.

"How what is done?" Molev asked, glancing at him.

"How a guy avoids having to sleep on the couch. It would have been a bitch to find one out here for you. Good job."

Roni snorted as she scanned our surroundings. I did the same, noting the craggy faces of the mountain on each side of the road. A tower crowned a steep incline to the north with stairs built alongside the rock. The barrier blocking the road ended at the rock face, but I saw a chainlink fence on the hill.

"Stay close," Molev warned.

"We need to get to that radio and let Gypsum know how many you killed," Patrick said. "They need to get something in the air to look for any you missed."

"Where is the radio?" Molev asked.

My attention returned to the intact barrier crossing the road ahead of us. The steel-enforced gate was firmly bolted from the inside. I scanned the hill where the fence changed to chainlink near the tower. Everything looked like it was intact there as well.

"It's up there," Patrick said, indicating the tower.

The men moved out around us. Some circled the vehicles to stand guard. Some took higher perches on top of them as lookouts. The rest came with us up the hill.

"Stay here," Molev said when we reached the tower's base. "I will check first."

Patrick didn't argue, and Molev disappeared from sight. A moment later, two headless bodies were tossed out from above us.

"I think that's the all clear," Roni said.

A few soldiers went ahead of us while the rest stayed below.

We found Molev near the radio, looking at its dark panel.

"They have a battery backup and only turn it on during their assigned time," Patrick said.

He flicked a switch, and we all listened to the static for a moment before Patrick started talking.

"Loveland's tower is recovered. Fifty were intercepted, off road, on their way south near thirty-four north of Estes Park. Need eyes in the air to ensure that's all of them. Over."

"Copy that," someone replied. "Airborne in ten. Over."

Patrick looked at the soldiers with us. "Ears on the radio; eyes on the horizon."

The men nodded, and Patrick's gaze swept up. "No time like the present."

As soon as we reappeared, the men around the vehicles started moving. A few climbed on top to either guard guns or provide fire for the ones without.

I knew Molev would be jogging alongside now and didn't like the idea of being stuck where I couldn't see what was happening.

"We stick together," I said to Molev as we approached the vehicles.

"You will be safer inside the vehicle."

"But will you if I'm in there? I stay with you. You deal with the infected, and I'll make sure there aren't any accidents."

"I will be safe, Andie."

I stopped walking. He did the same and looked down at me.

"You wanted me to care. This is me caring. If you try to put me in a box, this isn't going to work between us."

He frowned slightly.

"I already warned you that I didn't do well with roles being forced on me."

"I'm trying to protect you, not force you into a role."

"Aren't you? Sticking me inside is putting me in the weak, damsel-in-distress role. I might not be as strong as you are, Molev, but I'm not weak. And I've never been the damsel in distress who needed saving. I ride up top where I can keep an eye on you."

His fingers twitched at his sides, and I had a feeling those digits would already be buried in my hair if they weren't coated in infected blood and I wasn't wearing my helmet.

"No retreating," I said, holding his gaze. "This is who I am, an at-your-side kind of girl."

He looked at Sid and Roland, who'd already climbed up top. "Help her up."

"Bullshit," Roni grumbled under her breath as she went inside with Katie.

"No unnecessary risks," Patrick reminded Molev before joining them.

I climbed up top and glanced at the rest of the personnel riding above. They weren't focused on Molev but on the two men who were opening the gates. The metal groaned as they pulled them inward. Two ladders fell inside, clattering on the pavement.

"Guess we know how they got in," Sid said.

"Not good that the infected know how to use those," Roland added.

Unable to disagree, I glanced at Molev to see what he

M . J . HAAG

thought. His troubled expression as he considered the ladders wasn't a comfort.

The lead vehicle started forward, and Molev jogged beside us as we rolled out. Despite how easy it had been for the infected to overcome it, the barrier still held a sense of security I didn't like leaving. So I focused on the scenery as I scanned for signs of infected.

The flat face of the mountain bordering the road grew taller and crowded closer with each mile. And it wasn't quiet outside for a change. The sounds of our engines weren't quite enough to drown out the sounds of the river running beside the road. It was hard not to take in the breathtaking views and the peace of the mountains.

At least, until right after we crossed under the enormous pipe and the landscape opened up. We spotted our first infected near a store just down the road. It heard the engines and came running toward us. Molev killed it quickly, but everyone was more on edge after that.

When the land started closing around the road again, and we spotted a pile-up of cars ahead, I knew we were in for trouble.

Molev ran ahead, pounded twice on the lead vehicle's side, then sprinted toward the wreck. Infected called out as soon as he reached it, spilling from the cars and the backs of trucks.

The gunner with us swore when Molev disappeared under a wave of mauled bodies.

"Wait," I called. "Molev can handle this."

The vehicles slowed, and above the noise of the engines, I heard it–the roar that sent a shiver of fear through me every damn time.

The gunner swore under his breath.

A moment later, the first head flew out from the pile. Then another and another. I glimpsed Molev as the bodies were knocked outward. He moved like a blur, removing heads faster than I could count until the last infected fell. Then, without stopping, he ran back to the lead vehicle and jumped onto the top with the men there.

The convoy picked up enough speed to barrel through the cars, knocking them out of the way.

We picked up even more speed as we continued downhill. That didn't stop Molev from jumping down and running beside the convoy again, though. We passed a few buildings and old barns along the way, but no infected emerged. The stillness of everything was unnerving.

My gaze kept returning to the road ahead, waiting for the first signs that we were close to the outskirts of Loveland. Rather than spotting the city, I saw an RV pulled across the road. Molev once more pounded on the lead vehicle.

We slowed as he sprinted ahead.

No infected poured from the vehicle this time. They came running from the trees across a bridge to our right. Molev went to the nose of the RV and started pushing. It rolled back toward the bridge, running over infected or knocking them into the river below. After he cleared the vehicle from the road, he leapt over it and started beheading again. I watched him as we passed unmolested. His shirt was bloody from before but now had tears in it and, based on some glistening spots, new bites too.

"If you can move fast enough to kill them, then avoid their damn teeth," I said.

His bark of laughter rang out over the sound of the engines as he continued to end each undead attempting to get to the convoy. When he finished, he ran up alongside me. Blood spattered his face but didn't take away from his sexiness as our gazes locked.

"It's hard to avoid all of their bites when they pile up on me."

"Then don't let them pile up on you," I said.

His lips twitched. "If I don't let them think they have a chance, they would chase after you."

"Well, Sid's getting bored anyway and won't mind if he has to shoot a few."

"The gunfire will carry farther than the sound of the engines. This way is better."

"For us, not for you. It's going to be worse in town. Don't use everything up before we get there."

His smile widened. "Yes, Andie."

"Are they flirting?" Roland asked Sid. "It's hard to tell."

"Keep Andie safe, Roland," Molev said before jogging ahead again.

"Should have kept your mouth shut," Sid said. "One scraped knee, and he's going to have a problem with you."

Mentally rolling my eyes at them, I continued to scan our surroundings. Any humor I felt faded when I spotted the overgrown elementary school. We all grew somber as we passed the reminder of what we'd lost.

The homes were more frequent after that. We didn't see more traps, but we started accumulating a following of infected that were too slow to catch us when we passed. Molev purposely lagged behind a few times to thin their numbers. I didn't let myself think about how much effort he was exerting already. Instead, I kept watching for signs we'd reached Loveland.

The official outskirts crept up on us slowly with the majority of the houses hidden by trees and set back from the road in rural subdivisions. But once we hit the first set of lights, the city opened up, and I understood why the main road was still intact.

Loveland's sprawled layout had saved it. Farther back from the main road, I saw evidence of the bombings in a barren expanse of rubble glimpsed between still-standing buildings. I also saw movement. The charred remains of the few undead who'd survived the bombs faltered toward the sounds of our engines.

Molev continued to remove the heads of those that gathered. The nonstop work didn't appear to have depleted his energy in any way, and I recalled Roni's comment about Molev's stamina. His current level of effort was probably nothing to him. But I wasn't only thinking of that moment. I was thinking of the hours ahead of us too.

Patrick had said we should be in our own beds again by tomorrow night. That meant a night here, in the city. It would be nothing like the nights we spent in the field. It would be worse. Much worse.

While I watched Molev move, I thought of our last true night in the field. The night the hounds had attacked.

Molev caught my gaze and ran up to our vehicle. I knew what he was going to do a second before he vaulted on top and landed in a squat beside me. As covered in grossness as he was, he maintained a careful distance as he leaned toward me.

"What are your thoughts?" he asked.

"I'm wondering why you're letting me distract you."

His eyes narrowed slightly, and I huffed out a breath as I looked away to scan for infected.

"The last time we were out in the open, things didn't end well for you. And that was in the middle of nowhere. What do you think crept into my thoughts just now? I told you this wasn't a good idea. Distractions are—"

He growled.

At me.

We stared at each other for a long moment.

"I think this is something we should discuss when you're not covered in goo and can grab my hair the way you want to," I said.

The corner of his mouth quirked.

"You are smart, Andie. And keep caring about what happens to me. No one else will."

"Hey," Roland said. "We care."

Molev grunted and jumped off the top, sprinting toward the back of the line where the infected were gathering again.

"You might care," I said, "But we both know you're not ready to be Molev's little spoon."

Sid smirked, and Roland made a face as he went back to watching.

I spotted the lake ahead, and Sid saw a problem on the other side.

"Undamaged neighborhood coming up," he called.

Molev sprinted up from behind.

The number of infected that came running from the nearby undamaged neighborhood was more than I knew he could deal with alone. Yet, he hit the lead vehicle three times. It immediately sped up as he jumped over it to head off the infected.

Rather than focus on him, I watched the road ahead. With him distracted, we couldn't afford to run into anything else. The convoy dodged around abandoned cars, and I spotted the first section of damaged road where bombs had gone off too close.

More appeared beyond that with greater frequency, and I would have lost my seat a few times if not for my death grip on a bar bolted to the top. I glanced at Roland and Sid, who were hanging on like me and watching everything.

The intersection with a gas station on the corner was almost completely obliterated, and the drivers had no option but to slow to avoid the worst of the upheaved blacktop. The level of damage indicated how overrun the area would have been if not for the bombs.

The number of infected emerging from the rubble increased, and not all of them were burned. They ran after us in bursts. I looked back for Molev but didn't see him at first. When I did, my stomach dropped at the mass of infected I saw running behind him.

He sprinted through the group collecting behind us and jumped to land on the last vehicle. As soon as he was clear, they opened fire. The reports rang out as the infected fell like toppled dominos. Molev jumped from vehicle to vehicle until he reached ours and squatted beside me. The scent of rot and old blood filled my nose.

"The sound will draw more. If you need me, call for me." His gaze traced my face. "If anything happens to you, Andie—"

"You won't let anything happen. I trust you. Now trust us to do what we need to do to stay alive and stay focused."

He grunted and leapt down, racing ahead.

CHAPTER TWENTY-THREE

THE NEXT TWENTY MINUTES WERE FILLED WITH GAMES OF CHANCE. Whenever the road forced us to slow down, the number of infected would build up around us. We would use our firearms to thin their numbers until we could speed up again. We passed the second and third bodies of water that way before the city gave way to overgrown fields.

With a stretch of open road, we gained speed and increased the distance between the end of the convoy and the infected following us. When we took a left without slowing, I would have lost my balance if not for my low position and hold on the bar.

We raced down that road, passing a few scattered houses, until I saw a massive building and parking lot filled with semi-trailers ahead. All of it was encircled with a tall fence.

We took another left, arriving at the distribution center's entrance a few minutes later, where the fence ended. As soon as the convoy stopped, those who'd been riding inside poured out from the vehicles. Someone was shouting orders. Those of us on top provided cover while people scrambled to close the gaps in the facility's fencing. Another set of men had a ladder and were racing toward the building.

"Sid, go with them," I said with a nod. "Keep eyes on Molev."

He ran off to join them while Roland moved closer to me and Brandon took Sid's place on top of the Stryker.

Back-to-back, we watched all sides. Shots rang out as the infected slowly caught up to us. They made things easier for us by trying to cut the corner instead of following the road to the entrance. The existing fence stopped them. So did Molev.

He roared and started beheading.

"Got some to the west," Brandon called. "No fence. They're going to need help over there, too."

"Molev, stay where you're at," I said, pivoting to face the west with Brandon.

The soldiers setting up the temporary fencing ignored the oncoming infected and worked on stabilizing the fence as quickly as possible. I saw right away it wouldn't be enough. Not with the number of infected appearing in the distance.

Shots rang out behind us, and the infected rushing toward the soldiers started to drop. I glanced back at Sid and the other two men on the roof and then at Molev, who was in the thick of over one hundred infected. He couldn't help us.

We needed more firepower, or we needed that fence up now.

I looked at the trailers around us. Some of them were still connected to the trucks themselves.

"Patrick," I yelled. "Can we use those?" I pointed.

He called for a few men to go with him. They ran across the parking lot. An infected tumbled out of the first truck they opened. One of them shot it while the other tried to start the engine. It didn't even turn over. The second one did.

They pulled the trailer around, and I watched the soldiers

shoot out one side of its tires as another man released the trailer from the truck. The trailer tilted precariously.

Molev appeared out of nowhere and rammed a shoulder into the trailer, straining as he heaved upward. The groan of metal was echoed by an infected. The trailer started to tip, and then Molev was gone. It buckled a little as it crashed, but that didn't matter. Patrick was already yelling for another one as a pair of soldiers climbed onto the first one to provide cover fire.

Time seemed to slow no matter how fast everyone moved. The number of infected emerging outside the fence grew. Another trailer was backed against the tipped one. Someone else got another truck moving.

I scanned the parking lot, taking everything in.

"Steve," I called, "I need you as my eyes. Roland, get on the second trailer."

My feet had barely touched the ground when Molev appeared in front of me. His rage-filled gaze locked with mine.

"No sexy looks when you let one of them bite your cheek. I like that cheek. Keep it safe."

I tried stepping around him, and he caught my arm.

"Molev, they need you more than I do right now. Get those trailers tipped over. I'm going to clear some cars. Go."

I got more than a growl this time.

He snarled at me. An actual lip-curling, life-threatening snarl. Then he was gone.

"Pretty sure he's not happy with you," Steve said as he climbed inside the Stryker with me.

"Pretty sure you're right," I said, ignoring the way my heart was racing. Instead, I focused on what I needed to do.

Everyone got out of my way at the sound of my engine. I pushed the first three cars out of the way then turned around, running over a group of infected in the process. One pass at a time, I made room for the additional trailers and kept the infected relatively clear.

A shot pinged off the Stryker when I drove through someone's line of fire.

"We're fine," I yelled loudly.

"You think he heard that?" Steve asked, pointing to some more infected I could run over. I swung around to get them as I answered.

"Do I want to take that risk? If he heard the ping, then he heard me. Don't forget that he knocked Evan out for shooting when I was in the line of fire."

"Good point."

I pushed the last car outward, using it to run over a few more infected. However, one of them didn't go down. It jumped onto the car I was pushing and looked at me through our windshield. The moment burned itself into my mind, but before I could call out for Molev, the once-young man jumped off the car and ran away.

Turning hard, I ditched the car and returned to the trailer border.

"That was fucked up," Steve said.

It was more than fucked up. It was terrifying.

I parked, cut the engine, and was out the door a minute later. Steve watched me scramble to the roof and shield my eyes to stare in the direction the infected had run. In the distance, I saw a lone figure standing there. Two more joined it.

"Molev, I'm looking at three. One of them wasn't acting as undead as we're used to. His eyes weren't as white. I could almost see a hint of his pupil in them. And I swear he looked me right in the eyes like he was...I don't know. Memorizing what I looked like, maybe. And he moved differently, too. Faster. More in control of himself. Almost normal."

"I'm not liking what you're saying," Steve said.

"Neither am I."

As I stared, I saw Molev dart into the street behind them. He had the heads off the two before the one who'd looked at me even turned. He lost his head too. Instead of throwing it, Molev looked at it.

"That's a little morbid," Steve muttered.

"He's probably checking its eyes. Better him than us... unless you're volunteering."

"Hell no."

Molev tossed the head aside and started running back. With the last trailer in place, closing the gap in the fence, the remaining undead outside the fence were being picked off by the men on the roof. Molev ignored the stragglers and came to me.

"You're right. It was different. I want you to stay out here while I help clear the infected inside."

I glanced at the building. "I'm guessing the shots would have let whatever's in there know we're here."

"Yes. But they like to hide and wait for you to find them."

"That's not a game of hide-and-seek I'm interested in playing," I said. "Go have fun."

"Will you help Sid keep watch from the roof?"

"Don't think for a second that I don't understand what you're doing. Yes, you can put me safely out of reach on the roof. This time."

He grunted and looked down at himself.

"A little contact goo won't hurt me," I said.

He didn't look happy when he picked me up and was quick to jump to the roof. The second he landed, I was on my feet.

"Stay here."

He leapt off the edge but returned with Katie, followed by

a grumpy Roni and two other women I hadn't noticed. One stumbled away from him as soon as he released her, and the other thanked him.

Then he was gone.

"The roof is huge," one of the snipers said. "We can use the lookouts. Yell if you see anything."

We spread out on the roof and watched the infected gather around the perimeter fence as the sun slowly moved across the sky.

"We're secure," someone yelled.

I stayed where I was until someone else came to take over for me. When I made my way back to the ladders, Molev wasn't the one waiting for me when I descended. Patrick was.

"Where is he?" I asked.

"I was hoping you could tell me. He disappeared."

"What do you mean he disappeared?" I asked.

"Just what I said. According to Private Daniels, they were sweeping the building for undead, and Molev vanished."

"Were there any signs of infected where he was last seen?"

"No. Nothing that would explain his disappearance."

Hearing that helped settle the ball of worry that had started to form. We'd witnessed Molev take care of scores of infected alone. Unless there was a hound hiding in the building, which I doubted since only Molev was unaccounted for, Molev left on his own. Something he'd done countless times before.

"Then, we'll have to wait until he gets back for an explanation," I said.

"If he comes back," Patrick muttered.

"Patrick, when he does, I'll be sure to point out that you still don't trust him despite the injuries he sustained today during his herculean effort to keep us all safe. And when you include this in your report to Waurlyn, be sure to also mention

DEMON DEFEAT

this was the first time ever that we went into a city without losing a single person."

"What makes you so sure he'll come back?" Patrick asked.

"Like your opinion of him, his goals haven't changed. He wants to stop the spread of this plague as badly as we do and is very determined to find a way to live with us peaceably. Now, if that's all, I'd like to help unload and set up."

Patrick waved me away, and I went to help Roni locate a few tents and some rations. Rather than setting everything up on the ground level, we hauled what we could to the roof. If we had to be outside, higher was always better than on the ground. After we set up, we sat to eat a quick meal.

Below us, personnel backed the trucks to a pair of trailers already docked at the bay doors. The hum of motors running outside the building, in addition to those inside the building, wasn't enough to draw more infected, proving that the ones close by were already dead.

If we didn't shoot, we wouldn't draw any more.

Until the sun set.

Still eating, I moved to the edge of the building to watch where we were erecting the lights that would draw in the infected. It was better that they were on the ground from a visibility standpoint. If they were higher, they would be seen from a greater distance. However, they were more vulnerable on the ground too. Patrick seemed to have the same thought because he ordered several of the lights hauled to the roof as a precaution. Those were arranged around the tents.

Before they finished, Molev appeared with wet hair and wearing a different shirt.

I watched from above as he jogged over to Patrick, noting the new bites on his arms and face. I didn't like it. Each sign of his vulnerability made me want to close myself off like I'd done so easily in the past. But after the snarl, I knew any sign of retreat wouldn't go well. And now wasn't the time or place to further test Molev's patience with me.

So I embraced the worry and the situation as best as I could.

"Patrick was moody about you leaving," I said softly as he spoke to Patrick. "He thought you abandoned us. You should tell him you went to clean up and put on a tighter shirt so I'd be tempted to make out with you more."

Molev stopped talking and looked up at me.

"What? It looks good on you, and I'm a sucker for well-defined pecs."

"Are you dirty-talking him from here?" Roni asked from behind me.

I hadn't even heard her sneak up on me and startled a little on the inside. On the outside, I played it cool and didn't turn to look at her when I answered.

"No, I'm stating the facts. I like his muscles, and he went to clean up."

Molev crossed his arms as he continued to look at me. Patrick turned to look too.

Roni snorted. "You're going to get him into more trouble."

"No, I won't. Not if he admits to Patrick that I'm sassing him and that he can hear it from there. Those little nuggets of information will go a long way to reassuring Patrick that Molev's not trying to hide anything."

Molev glanced at Patrick again and said something. Patrick shook his head, and they both looked at me.

I shrugged at them.

"What are you going to do if Molev comes up here all hot and bothered?" Roni asked.

"Feed him. If he's nice, it will be a meal without the red sauce."

"Cruel," Roni said with a laugh.

Molev spoke again and came jogging over. However, instead of using the ladder, he picked up speed and scaled the side of the building in a jump and a half.

"Shit," Roni breathed next to me as he landed in front of us.

"Hungry?" I asked him.

His heated gaze swept over my face in response.

"Good," I said as if he'd answered. "Let's go find something to eat."

I turned to go back to the tent, but his arm hooked around my waist and anchored my back to his chest. His lips brushed the side of my head, and his exhale teased the shell of my ear.

"I did not like today," he said. "I learned that I did have a role in my heart for you. One you will not like."

Several scenarios ran through my mind, and I couldn't bring myself to hate any of them.

"And what role is that?" I asked as Roni moved away from us.

"You waiting for me somewhere safe while I deal with the things that might harm what I need more than anything else in this world."

I tried not to let his words get to me, but they did. They stoked the flames of my own need, which felt similar to his, based on what was pressing into my back.

"Good. Then you'll understand how I feel when you're out there, risking yourself."

His lips brushed that place behind my ear, and I shivered. He rumbled and kissed the side of my neck. My pulse picked up, and I fought not to lean back into his touch.

"There's a difference between retreating and discretion," I said, fighting not to sound breathless. "I'd like to postpone this level of affection until we're on our own."

He turned me in his arms. The feel of his fingers in my hair, paired with the hand on my ass, robbed me of a good portion of my higher reasoning.

"What does it matter if we are alone or not?" he asked. "Does it change how you feel for me or how I feel for you?"

"Nope. However, this type of affectionate display can make other people feel uncomfortable. Consider it a cultural thing."

"A cultural or an Andie thing?" He tipped my head back. "Roni looks like she's enjoying this very much. So do many others." He ducked his head and started kissing the column of my throat. "Are you enjoying this?"

"Molev, you need to think with your brain and stop letting desire rule your thoughts. When you—"

"You only wish to retreat," he said before nipping my skin. The jolt of desire fueled my need to make him listen to reason before I lost all sense of mine. I grabbed a handful of his hair and pulled, but not in the sexy way he did to me.

He grunted and eased back enough to frown at me.

"Listen for two seconds. If anyone is looking to control you, you're showing them how right now. You're painting a target on me when you do stuff like this in the open. If it's intentional, fine. If it's not, then stop."

His expression darkened as he leaned in.

"You are mine."

"Great. Fine. I'm yours. And they're going to know what to take away from you when you don't do what they want."

"You misunderstand. You're mine. No one will take you from me."

His lips crashed onto mine, and he kissed me savagely. I lost myself in it so thoroughly that when he pulled back, I realized I had my legs wrapped around his waist and was hanging onto his shoulders for dear life.

"I need to eat and rest before dark," he said, starting to walk...with me still clinging to him. "You will stay with me."

"You're already all set up in here," Roni said from behind me. "And don't worry. No red sauce in the MRE. Enjoy."

A second later, Molev walked into the field tent, and the flap closed behind us.

"Are you going to put me down?" I asked.

His answer was to kiss me until I forgot my own name. Dazed, I blinked up at him when he finally put me down. He brushed his fingers over my cheek as he studied me.

"This is what I wanted. What I hunger for. You looking at me like you want to touch me as badly as I want to touch you."

Not thinking clearly, I reached out and palmed his hard length through his pants. He hissed out a breath and captured that hand. Instead of pulling it away, he pressed harder.

"Take care, Andie. I understand kissing you in front of others does not upset you. But I know stripping you bare and feasting on your body while they listen outside these thin walls will not be acceptable to you."

"Are you sure?" I started to move my hand.

I was on my back a second later, his large body pressing me into one of the cots that had been set up.

"Tell me what you want, Andie," he said, holding my gaze.

I knew what answer he wanted me to give. That I only wanted him. And I opened my mouth to give it because, at that moment, it was true. But reason kicked in. He was giving me a choice because he knew this wasn't the right time. We were in the middle of a questionably fenced-in zone. Dark was approaching. And he needed rest now since, once the sun set, he wouldn't get any.

"You're right," I said. "I just scolded you for not thinking straight and then go and do the same thing." And that wasn't like me. Not at all. "I'm sorry."

He exhaled heavily, closed his eyes, and rested his forehead against mine.

"No, Andie. I am sorry for stopping you. I like when you tease and test me. And I like it more when you embrace what you feel." He lifted his head enough to kiss me gently. "Soon."

He lifted himself off me and sat on the neighboring cot where Roni had tossed the MRE. Taking a moment to ground myself, I stared up at the ceiling before sitting up as well. He watched me as he tore open the MRE.

"What are you thinking when you look at me like that?" I asked.

"I wish we were somewhere else. That the world was different so we could focus on each other instead of this." He glanced at the tent around us.

"And what would we be doing if the world was different?" I asked.

His gaze grew even more heated. "Andie, I only have so much restraint."

"I didn't mean that. I mean, what do you see our lives looking like? I'm assuming you working a nine-to-five isn't what you're seeing."

"Explain."

"Before the quakes, people had jobs. They would work for eight to twelve hours a day, three to five days a week. Commute for about an hour a day. Go home, spend a little bit of time with their families if they had them, then go to sleep and start it all again. It was a routine that people were comfortable with.

"Now, everything's different. The jobs are minimal, and the pay is simply something to do to contribute to the safety and food everyone needs. But what happens if we actually find the solution and somehow not only end the plague but kill every last undead and hound? What are you and your brothers going to do as the humans try to pick up the pieces of the world they know? Where are couples like us going to fit in?"

"In the communities we make," he said.

"Okay, but what are we going to be doing there? The fey and the humans?"

He nodded thoughtfully as he chewed.

"In the caves, we grew our food, hunted, and made things to make our tasks and lives easier. We had many jobs to fill our time. Do you think it will be any different for us here?"

I considered his question while he continued to eat. Would it be different? They'd obviously led simpler lives in those caves, but that didn't mean they couldn't live the same way when this was over.

"What was the community you made with the humans like when you left?" I asked.

"We would look for supplies like we are doing now. Only there would be more of my brothers and fewer humans willing to risk their lives. And we wouldn't stay out after the sun set. We always returned to the safety of our homes."

"What did the humans who stayed behind do while you were out getting supplies?" I asked.

He frowned slightly. "They visited each other."

"So, no tasks? No jobs?"

He grunted.

"It's a little ironic, really. Most humans grudgingly work and dream of a day when they don't need to work. But the reality is that most of us lose our sense of purpose and self when we stop working. Typically, that happens when we're older and retire, though. What was everyone's mood like?"

"Either fearful or angry," he said, sounding tired.

I reached across the space and set my hand on his forearm.

"That's nothing that can't be changed. We just need a better vision of what we want the future to look like."

His gaze held mine as he nodded.

"You're thinking about sex again, aren't you?"

His lips twitched, and he slowly shook his head as he set aside the remnants of his meal.

"Not simply sex, Andie, but having you in my life for the rest of my days."

He stood and picked up his cot. I tucked my legs out of the way, already knowing what he planned to do. Once his was beside mine, I lay down, facing him. His creaked under his weight.

"It'll break if you add me to it," I said.

He grunted and draped his arm over my waist.

"Sleep, Andie. It will be dark soon."

I gently traced a finger around the new bite mark on his cheek and closed my eyes, trying to imagine what a future with Molev would look like.

A faint howl woke me sometime later. My eyes flew open, and I was off the cot in a heartbeat. In the tent's dim light, I saw the cot beside mine was already empty. The rest were full, though.

I opened my mouth to wake them then decided against it. The howl had been faint, and we had plenty of people to guard the lights in shifts if they could sleep through the noise to come.

I strode through the tent's opening. Outside, I spotted people standing sentinel at the edge of the roof around the building. The lights glowed from below in addition to the ones on the roof.

"There's sleeping beauty," Steve said from nearby. "I was wondering if you'd sleep through that."

"No way in hell," I said. "Where's Molev?"

"He's been keeping the fence clear since dark," he said, joining me.

We walked toward the northern edge, and I saw where Molev had created a body pile of beheaded infected. Another one sat a few hundred yards from that one.

"Watch this," Steve said, pointing toward an infected shuffling our way at an awkward jog. The second it noticed the body pile, it slowed.

"What's it doing?" I asked.

"It's second-guessing its unlife choices, I think." The infected pivoted and started running away.

"We've got a runner to the northwest," a guard called out.

A few seconds later, Molev came sprinting into view.

CHAPTER TWENTY-FOUR

MOLEV CAUGHT THE RUNNER AND REMOVED ITS HEAD BEFORE tossing both onto the pile. Then he disappeared again.

"The piles make more sense now," Steve said. "Patrick's the one who suggested Molev start placing them closer together."

"That's interesting," I said softly.

"Yeah. So was that kiss Molev gave you. Patrick wanted to know how often that happened."

"And what did you tell him?"

"That I'm not into voyeurism, but if he was, I wouldn't hold it against him."

"How'd that go over?" I asked.

"Fine." Steve grinned. "Molev showed up before Patrick could lay into me."

I could imagine the situation clearly and wasn't sure if I was more amused or frustrated by it.

"Where's everyone else?" I asked.

"Sleeping in the tent or standing guard somewhere, which is what I was doing, by the way. Standing guard."

I side-glanced at Steve, who was grinning at me.

"Spit it out," I said.

"Molev asked me to watch over you so you wouldn't wake up and wonder where he was. He also told me to tell you he'd like you to stay on the roof and to call him if you need him."

Another distant howl rang out. I wasn't sure, but it didn't sound like the first one. That meant two hounds were out there.

"How long has that been going on?" I asked.

"About ten minutes."

"Where's Patrick?" I asked.

Steve nodded toward the far side of the roof, and I started that way. When he kept pace with me, I glanced at him again.

"Molev told you to stick with me all night, didn't he?" I asked.

"Yep, two seconds after Patrick gave me orders to guard the wall. Patrick wasn't happy, but I'd rather deal with an angry Patrick than an annoyed Molev, you know?"

I did know and agreed with Steve's choice. However, I didn't fully agree with Molev's. Asking Steve to babysit me was a waste of Steve's time. But if it allowed Molev to stay focused on what he was doing, so be it.

Patrick saw our approach and broke away from the soldier he'd been speaking with to meet us halfway. Frustration radiated from him.

"Andie, I'm glad you're here. We need Molev to go after those hounds before they discover us."

"And what did he say when you told him that?"

"He refused to leave, stating that he was needed here." Patrick rubbed a hand over his head. "I get that he's worried about you, Andie, but we need him to understand the bigger picture."

"And what's the bigger picture?" I asked.

"Yours isn't the only life that matters. There are fifty other immediate people counting on him and millions more beyond that. He has a responsibility."

"He's well aware of that, which is why he's staying close and not taking any unnecessary risks. Besides, those hounds aren't after the infected. They hunt us. And they always hunt in pairs or packs. If he leaves to try to track one down, what do you think the other one will do?"

"We have the lights," Patrick said.

"We still have the lights on because Molev is killing the infected. Look at the body piles. If he wouldn't be killing them, they would be trying to find their way in. We would be shooting, which would draw even more in. Then what?"

"You're acting like we've never been in a situation like this before? We've held—"

"Patrick, look around. The infected are changing. When we were in the field in the beginning, the infected moved slower and didn't care about light. As they got faster and smarter, we lost more lives. There are seven of us are left. Seven, Patrick. And that's because of Molev. Start trusting him before you're the one who costs us more lives."

"And when the hounds come?" Patrick asked angrily. "We both know he can't fight two at once."

"He won't need to. While he's fighting one, the other will be trying to find its way to us. All we need to do is keep the lights going and wait for Molev to finish them off one at a time."

"I hope you're right, Andie. For all of our sakes." Patrick strode away to the next guard stationed on the roof.

"Where's Sid?" I asked.

Steve pointed him out along the edge of the roof, and we jogged over.

"Did we bring anything that would slow a hound?" I asked.

"Yep. We have a few Mark 19s…if we can hit one," he said.

"If?" I asked. "We've done it before."

"I think that was half luck. The hounds don't exactly hold still. But the blast zone is bigger, so…" He shrugged slightly. "But the sound is going to carry. Are you sure we want that?"

"Molev was ripped up the last time we faced one. Part of that was our fault for not understanding what he was doing. Part of it was due to what he was fighting. We need to be his support. If we can slow them down and make them easier for him to kill, then he'll be able to handle whatever else we draw in. Hopefully."

My gaze slid to the ground below.

"If I'm wrong, Molev will let us know."

Sid nodded. "Take my spot. I'll find someone to assist. It's in the Stryker down by the trucks."

"Take a knife with you for Molev," I said. "He needed it last time."

Sid jogged off, leaving Steve and me to take over.

"We need to spread the word so there aren't mistakes like last time," I said. "One of us has to stay put."

Steve made a face. "Fine, but you get to explain why I'm not glued to your side."

"Baby," I said, already turning to jog away. Out of the two of us, he was the better shot, and I was better at making sure people understood what they needed to do.

I went to the next soldier and explained what Molev would likely do once the hounds showed up. Then the next. Katie showed up on the fifth explanation and listened to what I was saying.

"I'll start on the other side," she said.

Another howl punctuated her words. Then a second and a third from different directions. West, south, and east. They were surrounding us.

Katie's eyes went wide.

"Stay focused, Katie. Molev knows what he's doing. We need to make sure everyone here knows what to do, too."

She nodded and took off across the roof.

I managed to talk to half a dozen more before the first set of eyes was spotted. The call crackled over the radios. Another chorus of howls followed. The chilling wails rang in the night sky, bouncing off the sides of the building.

I borrowed the nearest radio. "Did Molev get his knife?"

"He has it," Sid responded.

A roar came from the south, followed by snarls.

"The roar is Molev," I said over the radio. "Do *not* shoot where he's fighting. Does anyone have eyes on the other two?"

"I have eyes to the northwest," a voice came over the radio.

An engine started below, indicating that Sid was moving into position. The intensity of snarls from the other side increased, and Molev roared again. Threads of fear wove their way through me as the image of his injuries from the last time resurfaced.

I sprinted across the shadowy roof and arrived at the edge just as Molev dragged the hound into the circle of light. Smoke spiraled up from the creature's heaving black sides. Its head thrashed side to side until it caught sight of us on the roof. It tensed and snarled low, no longer fighting the direction Molev was dragging it.

Molev noticed its sudden interest and glanced up at us. I took in the new scratches on Molev's torso and his shredded shirt as his gaze swept over me and the nearby soldiers, who already had their weapons trained on them.

"Molev has this one," I said. "Watch the dark for the other two. Last time, one came at him from behind."

Barrels shifted as most of them focused on the shadows just

beyond the pool of light where Molev and the hound struggled.

Blood glistened wetly as Molev heaved the hound up and slammed it into the ground. He pinned it with his weight and pulled the knife from the strap on his thigh.

The rapid bap-bap-bap of the fired grenades echoed from the other side, punctuating the plunge of Molev's knife into the hound's ribs. The savagery wasn't any easier to witness than it had been the last time as he carved and bashed his way to the beast's heart. It struggled even harder underneath him, raking its claws over his shoulder.

I flinched at the new wound.

He punched his fist into the hound's chest and pulled his hand free a moment later. I felt that sickening pull-push at my center as I stared at the blank lump of the creature's heart.

The rapid succession of explosions from the grenades barely registered. I watched the hound underneath Molev continue to thrash and howl as Molev squeezed his fist around the heart. The muscles in his forearm strained until the heart burst into black dust in his hand.

The beast stilled underneath Molev.

He slowly got to his feet and looked up at me.

"We have a medic with us," Patrick said from beside me. "We need to address those wounds before you go out again."

"I will be fine," Molev said before disappearing into the darkness.

Patrick looked at me. "He won't do any of us any good if he passes out from blood loss. Get him up here."

"Patrick's not wrong, Molev," I said loudly enough for my voice to carry. "Meet me by the tent, or I'm leaving this roof to drag you up here myself."

Molev was already shirtless and sitting by the tent when I arrived. His scowl said it all.

Ignoring it, I grabbed a jug of water and handed it to him as the medic cleaned the larger wound.

"Drink while you frown at me," I said.

"You will not leave this roof," he said before taking several large swallows.

"We have too many hours until dawn for you to be losing this much blood already. If you don't want me to leave this roof, then take care of yourself. Humans have sports where they fight, and in those sports, they have breaks between rounds to hydrate and take care of injuries. This is no different. After each round, you come up here and have the medic treat you. Deal?"

The medic cut the thread for the last stitch he placed and stepped back.

"I have some liquid skin to stop the bleeding on the smaller ones," the man said. "It will only take a minute."

He started digging through his kit as Patrick walked over, carrying a vest.

"This is the biggest one we have. I'd like you to wear it. It should minimize injuries to vital organs without restricting your movement."

Molev accepted it but didn't put it on until after the medic was done covering the rest of his injuries.

"We're seeing movement to the north," Sid said over the radio. "I think the explosions are bringing in more infected."

Molev fit the vest over his chest. He gave an experimental flex, which made a few seams pop, but the vest held together.

"Here's a radio," Patrick said, handing him a device. "Put it in the front pocket. If you need something from us, use it."

Molev gave Patrick a considering look before nodding and focusing on me.

"Stay on the roof, Andie," I said in a Molev-like tone,

which made him frown at me. "I already know what you want from me, Molev. Just be careful."

He grunted but continued to hold my gaze.

"We'll give you a moment," Patrick said, motioning for the medic to follow him.

"What did you see when I fought the hound?" Molev asked when we were alone, surprising me.

"Feral intelligence," I said. "It fought going into the light until it saw us. Then it hesitated."

"The hounds have always feared the light. If they stop fearing it, humans will not survive."

"Do you think that's what's happening?" I asked.

"I don't know. But we need to keep watching."

"I will."

A howl rang out to the north.

"Does anyone have eyes on the hounds?" Patrick asked over the radio.

"We lost sight of the one we fired at after the explosions," Sid said.

"Stay safe, Andie," Molev said.

I watched him jog to the nearest edge and jump off.

"Andie," Patrick called.

He waved me over to the northern side of the roof and handed me what looked like bulky binoculars.

"Take a look."

When I looked through them, I saw different colored shapes in a field of colors. The smaller ones were moving slightly, and there were a lot of them. Something was moving faster in front of them in a back-and-forth pattern.

I watched for several unsteady heartbeats, understanding that I was seeing a mass of infected behind a pacing hound.

"That's new," I said.

"It is," Patrick agreed. "Why would the hound be holding them back?"

"Eyes to the south," someone called over the radio.

Patrick's gaze held mine as he spoke into his radio. "Molev, there's a hound to the north, holding back at least a hundred infected. Are the hounds smart enough to set traps like the infected?"

Silence echoed for a long moment.

"Yes."

Molev's single-word reply had the nearest soldier swearing softly.

"Sid, stay where you're at," Patrick said. "We may need you to the north. Molev, can you handle the one to the south on your own?"

A roar followed by an outburst of snarling to the south answered Patrick's question.

I lifted the binoculars to look north again. The hound had paused its pacing, and the infected weren't moving at all.

"I am not a fan of that," I said, handing the binoculars to Patrick. "I'm going to keep an eye on Molev. Let us know if that changes."

I left him to his study and went to find Molev.

I didn't like how the infected were changing. It brought back all the questions that Molev had previously asked. When would the changes stop, and what would the infected be once they did stop? I wasn't sure I wanted to know because I was certain they weren't reverting into humans again.

Hurrying across the roof to the far edge, I watched the darkness with the others as the snarls continued.

"Eyes to the west," someone else said.

I frowned. Had the one to the north moved or was there another one?

"Sid, keep the one to the west distracted," Patrick said.

The rumble of the engine didn't drown out the sounds of Molev's struggles. I listened to the grenades fire and explode twice before Molev finally appeared with the hound. This one was bigger and had stubby black horns sticking from its head. They glistened in the light, as did Molev's arm and neck.

It fought Molev every inch of the way. Smoke billowed from its hide as Molev struggled to pin it to the ground, and blood dripped freely from his straining neck. He pulled his knife. The hound thrashed, and the knife slipped from Molev's hands.

The hound howled, a chilling sound that made the back of my neck prickle.

"The west hound is on the move," Sid said. "He's heading south."

"Slow him down," the soldier next to me said into his radio. "Molev needs more time."

Molev didn't try for the knife. Instead, he started punching the hound's exposed rib cage. Its claws raked his arms, face, and neck as it fought to free itself.

Bap-bap-bap rang out again.

The creature under Molev howled. Another echoed from nearby before a series of rapid explosions cut it short.

"He needs a knife," I yelled at the same time Sid said, "we got it," over the radio.

Three knives dropped to the pavement near Molev. One was close enough for him to grab. Black gunk flew as he hacked his way to the creature's heart and tore it free. The misshapen stone was almost larger than his hand. He snarled as he squeezed it with one hand and listed to the side when it turned to dust and the hound underneath him stilled.

He looked up at me as he opened his hand and let the black powder fall free.

Without looking away, he reached up to his radio. "Stay on the roof."

He tucked a spare knife into the back of his pants and strode into the darkness.

I wanted to be angry, but I understood. If the other hound was knocked out, it was better to try to kill it now than wait until it came to.

He reappeared a minute later, carrying a petrified heart in his hand. I could feel that same wrongness as before, pushing at me. Telling me to run.

A howl rang out from nearby.

"It's moving again," Sid said over the radio. "Heading north."

Molev paused and looked up at me.

"I see it," Patrick said over the radio. "It's reached the undead and the hound there."

The confirmation that there had been four nodding at Molev to hurry up. He'd said "packs," but four was more than we'd ever seen at once. Or maybe others had but hadn't survived the encounter. If Molev hadn't killed that first one so quickly...I shuddered at what might have happened and at what could still happen.

"They're advancing," Patrick said. "Sid, get ready. You'll need to thin their numbers—"

Molev started to squeeze the heart.

"—or we'll risk being overrun. Molev's in no condition to—"

The heart burst into black dust and poured from Molev's fingers.

"Wait," Patrick said as a howl rang out. "It stopped advancing."

The low keen went on and on until it cut off with a whine.

"Get up here," I said to Molev.

He leapt up and swayed a little on his landing. The vest had saved him from having his guts ripped out from the looks of it. But it hadn't prevented the gash along his neck or the puncture wound in his bicep.

"You look like hell," I said softly.

He frowned at me.

"Let's get you patched up while we can." I held out my hand, but he shook his head and walked off without me. I had to jog to catch up.

The medic was already waiting for him. He cut the vest free then handed Molev the jug of water. Molev dumped it over his head, rinsing away the caking blood. Once he was done, he sat.

I stood nearby and watched the medic reglue a few injuries, add stitches to Molev's neck, and disinfect the puncture.

"What's this from?" he asked. "Bullet?"

"A horn," Molev said.

"They have horns?" the medic asked.

"Some of the males do," Molev answered.

"Well, at least we don't have to fish a bullet out," the medic said. "That's good news."

He lightly clapped Molev on the shoulder and said he was done as Patrick joined us.

"Rest. Eat. Do whatever you need to do. The last hound left with the undead," he said.

"They left?" I asked.

Patrick rubbed a hand over the top of his head.

"Yeah. As soon as the second hound dropped, the first one howled then ran. The undead followed it."

I glanced at Molev to see what he thought of it. He was looking off to the north.

"Don't even think about it," I said.

His gaze met mine.

"We need to know," he said. He stepped close and pressed his forehead to mine without touching me anywhere else. "There are many hours until dawn. If it finds another..."

"No unnecessary risks, remember?"

"This is necessary, Andie. I am sorry."

He left before I could grip his arms. I dropped my hands to my sides and turned away from the empty space to face Patrick.

"You don't seem too upset about him taking off this time," I said.

"He's right. The last time he let an undead go, it came back with more."

"You said there are over one hundred infected and a hound. Molev is held together with more glue and stitches than skin right now. How do you think this is going to end? He's our hope for a cure, Patrick. Why can't you see that?"

Patrick exhaled heavily. "I am seeing that, Andie. I'm also seeing how much he cares about you. I don't think he'll do anything that would stop him from returning. He's smart. He's proven that time and again. Trust him."

I crossed my arms and studied Patrick.

"What changed?" I asked. "This wasn't your opinion a few hours ago."

"Because I finally understand why he's doing all of this," he said. "It's you, Andie. He's doing it for you."

"He's doing it for more than just me. He's doing it for all of us. Humans and his people."

"But he's willing to do it for the rest of us because of you, Andie. I can see that in the way he looks at you and talks to you. But there's a lot I still don't understand. If Molev's people know how to kill the hounds, why did they live with them in the caverns? Why not kill them all while they were trapped with them? Or since they were freed?

"Molev's people have been living much closer to ground zero than here. Why are we still seeing so many hounds? Why haven't they killed them all?"

"Based on my conversations with him, I think Molev and his people have only recently discovered how to kill the hounds. That's why the first two fey were running from them."

"If they truly wanted to keep us all safe, wouldn't they try hunting them now?"

"Molev said that's what the first two are doing now."

Patrick's expression turned thoughtful. "Only two? Makes me wonder how many fey there really are."

"Does it matter?" I asked.

"You know it does, Andie. Even if they aren't a threat to us now, will they become one once the hounds are dead?"

"The only threat to humanity will be the people who continue to think in terms of 'us' versus 'them.' We need to fully embrace working together to find a future, Patrick, or it will never happen."

"There's a handful of undead by the fence to the south," Brandon said over the radio.

"Prevent a buildup as quietly as possible," another voice ordered.

The sound of a silenced shot barely carried across the roof.

"When's the airlift due?" I asked.

"If the watchtower and this fence hold, the first one will fly out of Gypsum at first light."

After seeing the number of infected that had been waiting here, I wondered what else was out there. Maybe Molev was right to go after the infected and prevent them from tracing our steps…if they were smart enough to do that. The trail of bodies we'd left on the road wouldn't be that hard to follow.

"How many FOBs have gone quiet since we returned with Molev?" I asked.

"That's not information I have."

"After what we saw tonight, I think it's something you need to find out," I said. "We need a better understanding of what's changing, or Molev's going to want to leave more often to keep tabs for himself."

Patrick studied me for a moment.

"You don't like that he was hurt."

"No, I don't. And you should feel the same concern. How many injuries can he sustain until he fails? That's a question I never want to learn the answer to. If he fails, we fail."

Patrick nodded once.

"Agreed. I'll speak to Waurlyn." He shook his head. "This first-name basis shit is enough to prove the world is changing."

I almost laughed. "What would you have called her before all of this?"

"Madam Secretary," he said. "And there wouldn't have ever been a reason for us to speak directly."

"The world's changing," I said as another volley whispered across the roof.

"It is," Patrick agreed. "Let's hope we live long enough to see the outcome."

"I'd settle for living long enough to see dawn."

The quiet firepower kept the number of infected from becoming too much over the next several hours as we waited for Molev's return. I stayed near the tent and saw Steve and Brandon when they came in for their turn to sleep.

The medic and I heard a distant howl once, but after that, the night continued to pass quietly.

A few hours before dawn, Molev returned, dripping from another swim in the lake.

He had more cuts and bites and looked like he was ready to collapse as he sat for the medic.

"Bathing in lake water will probably lead to infection," the medic said as he started cleaning the new wounds.

"Unlikely," Molev said. "It never has before."

The medic made a doubtful face but didn't say anything. Patrick came jogging over.

"Are you all right?" he asked.

Molev glanced from Patrick to me. "A few infected escaped. But not enough to cause immediate trouble."

"He's asking about you, not the infected," I said.

"I will heal," Molev said. "I believe those were the only four hounds in the area. If there were more, we would have seen them by now."

"That's good news," Patrick said. "As soon as you're done here, get some sleep. We can maintain the perimeter without you for a few more hours."

Patrick started to turn away and paused.

"Good work tonight, Molev. Thank you."

He left, and Molev stared after him.

"Almost done here," the medic said. "Not sure how you managed it, but nothing needs stitches. Any more hounds and I might have run out of glue, though."

CHAPTER TWENTY-FIVE

MOLEV GRUNTED IN ACKNOWLEDGMENT AND EXTENDED HIS HAND to me as he stood.

His steps were slower as we made our way to the tent together, but I didn't comment on it. The cots that had been pushed together were still there. He lay down on his, and I hurried to join him.

"We need to find a better way to stop them," I said.

"We do," he agreed. He closed his eyes and exhaled heavily without putting his arm around me.

A moment later, his breathing evened out.

I studied his side in the dim light, and not seeing any injuries, I gingerly draped my arm over his waist before closing my own eyes.

The whomp-whomp-whomp of an approaching aircraft penetrated my dreamless sleep a while later, and I opened my eyes to the lighter interior of the tent. Molev still slept beside me, his expression peaceful.

Rather than moving and potentially waking him, I stayed as I was and studied the new marks on his face and neck. The bite on his cheek hadn't been that deep and was already scabbed over. The stitches on his neck were another story. The puffier skin didn't look good.

"Do I still look like hell to you?" he asked.

I glanced at his closed eyes.

"I'm not sure how to answer that," I said.

"Honestly," he said.

"The scars you've collected since I've known you concern me. You told me no more retreating but then disappeared for hours to fight things that have wiped out hundreds of people in minutes. I never held back from taking physical risks, but risking my heart is different. It's scary. So, looking at these new scars? Yes, you still look like hell to me because I'm scared."

He opened his eyes as he cupped the back of my head.

"Explain what you mean by look like hell."

"You look like you were beaten up and are suffering."

The corners of his mouth twitched.

"What did you think I meant?" I asked.

The tent flap opened, and Roni ducked in.

"Snuggle time is over unless you two plan on staying another night," Roni said.

Molev released me and sat up in one fluid motion.

"No, we are ready to leave."

We joined her outside.

"You missed some excitement," she said as we made our way to the ladder. "A bunch of us had to collect the remains of the hounds you killed. Just the ones inside the fence. I think one of the soldiers almost peed himself when we lifted it and the head flopped to the side."

She laughed and started down the ladder. Molev scooped me up and jumped down before I knew what he planned.

"Why did you collect the remains?" he asked Roni when she jumped down the last few feet.

"For the scientists. This is the first body they'll have the chance to study. They're hoping to find another, less-risky-to-you way to stop them."

I glanced over at the enormous twin-rotor helicopter waiting on the far side of the parking lot. Nearby, soldiers were loading a large shipping container with items from the distribution center. I'd witnessed a supply drop with smaller bundles and knew how those worked but hadn't ever witnessed something of this scale.

"Let's go," Patrick said. "Our team is on the first flight back to Gypsum."

"How long will the others remain?" Molev asked.

"They'll work all day to empty what they can and leave before dark. We don't want to attract any attention that will follow us home."

"We left a trail of bodies on the road leading to the gate," I said. "If we don't want to attract attention, that'll need to be cleaned up."

"Lieutenant Darbin and his people will take care of that on their way back," Patrick said.

Molev grunted as we followed Patrick. The rest of the team was already waiting for us inside the aircraft. Sid's head was back, and his eyes were closed when I took my seat. Katie looked almost as exhausted. None of us spoke as the aircraft lifted off the ground or as it hovered over the storage container.

Once the supplies were attached, we left.

We passed several others of the same type of aircraft along the way to Gypsum. All carried storage containers like ours.

After we unloaded the cargo at Gypsum and landed, we moved to a smaller helicopter that was waiting for us and the hounds. Flying with the corpses was unsettling even if a tarp hid them from immediate view. I could see the others were just s bothered by them. Not Molev. He stared at the tarp the whole way, and I wondered what he was thinking.

A team eagerly awaited the remains when we landed in win. So did Waurlyn. With a smile on her lips, she marched ɔ to Molev and extended her hand.

"We can't thank you enough for what you've done. With this, we might have a chance to find more than a cure."

She shook his hand firmly.

"I know you're likely exhausted and would like nothing more than your bed for a few days, but I'd like you to come with me to the testing facility. The doctors there would like to take a look at your injuries, and there are things I'd like to discuss along the way."

Molev took my hand without looking at me.

"Yes. We will speak with you."

Waurlyn didn't give away any of her thoughts as she nodded.

"It's not necessary for your whole team to join us if you think they would rather rest. But we do have the room if you'd like their company."

Molev and I glanced back at the others.

"Up to you," Sid said. "You lead; we follow."

"Rest," Molev said. "We will return to the house when we are finished."

His thumb smoothed over my hand in a comforting way, and I wondered what gave away my thoughts that separating wasn't a great idea. It didn't matter that Molev had won over Patrick. Patrick wasn't the leading body of what was left of the world.

"Don't take too long, or we'll come looking for you," Roni said with a nod.

While they headed for another vehicle that would take them to the house, we followed Waurlyn to hers. She sat in the front with the driver but turned in her seat to speak with us.

"Patrick managed to send a brief report about your efforts. You impressed him and me. Four hounds killed in a single night. Two recoverable. How are you really? The medic's report is that you sustained numerous injuries, many requiring stitches."

"I will heal," Molev said simply.

"I'm sure you will. But I'd still like the doctor to look you over and hear your version of the night's events."

"My version?" He shook his head slightly. "There is only one version. The infected are changing, and they seem to listen to the hounds now. A cure may no longer be enough."

By the time we reached the building, he'd filled us in about what happened while he'd been away from the distribution center. The infected had followed the hound. Those at the back of the group, Molev had picked off silently. The hound hadn't sensed Molev as long as he stayed several hundred yards away. However, once the hound herded the remaining infected into an abandoned building, Molev had seen enough. He'd killed the hound and then the infected. The infected hadn't tried to run. They'd just stood there and let him behead them all.

"That is disturbing news," Waurlyn agreed as she led us into the building.

"How many FOBs have gone dark since we arrived?" I asked.

"Over half," she said without hesitation. "We're consolidating the remaining personnel and reinforcing strategic locations. Such as those in remote areas that are easier to defend for refueling. I can show you a map if you'd like."

"I think we would," I said.

She opened the door to a room with a team of medical

people waiting inside. The doctor who'd taken Molev's blood several times already greeted Molev with less enthusiasm and more concern than Waurlyn had.

"How do you feel? Weak? Dizzy?" she asked.

"No," he said as she indicated the exam table.

"Wait. Do you have any injuries on your lower half? That's a lot of blood." She waved for one of the other people in the room, and they stepped forward with a hospital gown.

Molev glanced at me, and if not for the time we'd spent together, I would have never known the doctor was making him uncomfortable.

"She wants you to change so she can check you over," I said. "Make sure there wasn't anything that was missed."

"While you're changing, I'll make the calls necessary to get the map we spoke about," Waurlyn said, moving toward the door.

"We'll step out for a minute as well," the doctor said. "Just open the door when you're ready." She and the techs left the room.

Molev looked at the gown she'd handed him. His face showed his skepticism.

"If you don't want to change, you don't have to. You don't have to do any of this."

"Yes, I do," he said, handing me the gown. "Waurlyn has proven she will keep her word. Now I need to prove that she can trust me."

His pants were off, and he was standing in the buff a second later.

I tried not to look and stay focused on the conversation, but it wasn't easy. The man was a dream and fascinating to watch when clothed. Unclothed, he could easily cause my brain to short-circuit if I allowed it.

"Uh, what does letting the doctor examine you have to do

with Waurlyn trusting you?" I asked, maintaining eye contact as he took the gown from me.

"She needs to trust that I know my own limits. If that means having doctors look at me, then I will. How do I wear this?"

"Usually, the opening goes in the back," I said.

He frowned at it, shook his head, then slipped his arms into the short sleeves.

"Is there a closure?" he asked, turning to show me his beautifully sculpted backside.

"There is, but it's not going to do much."

After I tied the back, I let the doctor know he was ready.

She and her team drew blood and checked his vitals, his reflexes, his eyes, and his ears...she even looked up his nose. The dry look he shot my way had me covering my mouth and looking at the ceiling for a moment.

"By human standards, you're in excellent health. I wish I would have had a better baseline from when you weren't injured," the doctor said almost absently as she read the bloodwork results. "Or another one of you to compare yours to."

She sighed and looked up at him.

"What's your pain level right now on a scale of 1 to 10, with 1 being the lowest and 10 being the highest?"

Molev's gaze flicked to me again.

"I don't think he has the same scale we do," I said. "His is more of a can I still run or can't I."

That led to a test on the treadmill. When he didn't show any signs of exertion at the max speed after fifteen minutes, the doctor had him walk to cool down then lift things. The treadmill. The exam table. Me.

"Is this really a good idea with the stitches?" I asked, looking up at him.

The corner of his mouth twitched, but he put me down so she could check everything again.

"You are a true wonder, Molev. I recommend a day of rest tomorrow, even though you don't appear to need it. If you decide to return to the training grounds and would be willing to entertain more demonstrations, please let me or Waurlyn know. I would very much like to be present."

He grunted in his noncommittal way, and she left so he could get dressed again.

I stayed to untie the back and enjoy the view.

"You have to be starving," I said. "I know I am."

He glanced at me as he tied his pants and frowned.

"You should have told me you were hungry."

"No. What you were doing was more important. Besides, we're still waiting for Waurlyn and the map. It's taking a while, isn't it?"

He made another vague sound as he moved closer to me. His fingers caught mine, and he inhaled deeply while studying me.

"What are you thinking?" I asked.

"I think I would rather go home than wait for the map."

My insides melted a little at his implication, and I struggled to quiet the need to pull back emotionally and physically. And based on the way he was watching me, he knew it.

"Okay," I said. "Then let's go home."

We only managed a few steps in the direction of the door when it opened and Waurlyn walked in. I embraced the reprieve until I noticed her typical unruffled façade was missing some of its polish when she smiled at us.

"I apologize for the delay," she said. "If you'd like to follow me, I have the map waiting in a conference room."

"What happened?" I asked as we started following her.

She glanced at me, letting some of her distress show.

"The latest trial isn't going as well as the team had hoped. While they've isolated what makes Molev immune, they're having difficulties stabilizing it. Hopefully, studying the source of the outbreak will give them more insight regarding why the vaccine isn't working."

A horrible thought hit me. "They won't try using anything from the hounds to create a vaccine, will they?"

"It's not outside the realm of possibility," she answered, opening a door to a conference room.

My stomach churned as Molev and I followed her to the table.

"Waurlyn, you can't let them do that."

She looked up from the map already laid flat on the surface. "Why?"

"The hounds were created to bring suffering to my people," Molev said. "If you use them to create a vaccine, it will not end the way you hope."

She turned back to the map and gestured to the markers on it.

"The black ones are the ones that have already fallen. The yellow are in the process of evacuation. The white are the forward operating bases that we believe are defensible and necessary. As you can see from all the black markers, nothing is currently going the way we'd hoped, Molev. Your blood isn't working, and we're running out of options."

"Where is Whiteman?" he asked, studying the map.

She looked it over and pointed to a black marker in Missouri. I witnessed a shift in Molev. It was so subtle that, if I hadn't been watching him, I might not have noticed. But the news deeply impacted him.

I reached out, briefly touching his arm. "Whiteman went dark around the time we left Irwin. Going dark just means they stopped sending transmissions at their assigned time. If you were at Whiteman when we met, then that marker shouldn't mean anything because it was there before you left."

"When I left, there were many survivors," Molev said. "Matt Davis was in charge, but he is not part of your military. He told Mya that the previous leader ended his life after an attack."

"That makes sense then. Matt wouldn't have known when to send a transmission or on what channel," Waurlyn said. "There's no reason to believe anything has changed since you've left."

He studied all the other black dots. I wondered if he was as surprised as I was by the number of them. The ones in the Midwest, starting from Texas and going north to Illinois, were dark. Wisconsin and Minnesota still had a few yellow. Most of the markers near the east and west were yellow as well, but the ones behind the mountain ranges were white.

Were we putting too much faith in the mountains to keep us safe? The watchtower near Loveland had already fallen once. How long until it fell again?

"I would be foolish to think nothing has changed when over half the bases have fallen since I left," Molev said. "I have seen how the infected are evolving. They are growing smarter. If we do not want more black markers, we need to grow smarter too."

"What do you have in mind?" Waurlyn asked.

He gestured to the chairs, pulling out one for me. "There is much you do not know."

Waurlyn listened attentively for the next twenty minutes as he explained the caves, how the fey had been trapped there, and what had created the hounds. Disbelief flickered across her expression when he explained how they'd discovered that a hound's heart was the key to its death. When he finished, she sat in silence for a moment.

"That's a lot to take in," she said finally.

"Magic doesn't exist," I said. "We all know that. But we also knew that fey weren't any more real than dogs with glowing red eyes that can live even after their heart is removed, and look at where we are now."

Waurlyn nodded slightly, a wry smile on her lips. "Very true."

"Do you now understand why you cannot use the hounds?" Molev asked. "They are corrupted by the curse placed on us. It would be unwise to trust anything that comes from them."

"I understand," she said. "And I will do my best to convince everyone else. But we're desperate for answers."

"And desperate people do desperate things," I said.

"Unfortunately," she said in agreement.

"How are the vaccines failing?" Molev asked.

She considered us for a moment and motioned for us to follow her.

"It'll be easier to show you."

She led us to an elevator that went down to the basement level. When the door opened, I saw two soldiers stationed on the opposite side of the hall. Two more waited around the corner. No one stopped us, but they all stared at Molev.

Waurlyn used an ID card from her pocket to open another set of secured doors. People in lab coats sat or stood at workstations with equipment I had no names for. Beyond them, I spotted another set of doors and heavily armed guards.

Molev's appearance drew everyone's attention as we crossed the room. Work and conversation stopped as Waurlyn used her ID again to open the doors.

The doctor sat on a chair in the large, open space just inside the doors. A camera was set up nearby and aimed at one of the three "glass" enclosed rooms to the left.

Only one room was occupied, and I couldn't speak as I looked at the woman on the bed. She panted heavily, shaking and twitching in her bra and underwear. Patches of mottled grey covered the otherwise pale skin of her stomach and legs.

The doctor looked up at us at the sound of the door. When she saw Molev, she stood swiftly.

"Are you all right? Are you feeling—"

The way he abruptly raised his hand made her flinch.

"He's not threatening you," I said quickly, seeing how he was staring at the woman. "Tell us what's happening."

The doctor looked at the woman.

"This is Sara. We injected her with the latest trial serum thirty-six hours ago. The grey discoloration occurred during the previous trials, we're not sure why that's happening. What we injected shouldn't—"

The woman opened her eyes and started babbling, begging to make it stop between sobbed moans. She curled onto her side, holding her middle.

Molev set his hand on the glass. He radiated anger, unlike anything I'd previously witnessed. And I'd seen plenty.

"Open the door," he said.

"I'm sorry, Molev," the doctor said. "There's nothing we can do for her. She's already exhibiting signs of infection. Look at her eye."

I moved closer to the glass, partially stepping in front of Molev to get a better view. The woman immediately stilled. In a blink, she was standing in front of me with one slightly cloudy eye, staring at me.

"Remarkable," the doctor said. "We haven't had this type of response in previous trials."

The woman swayed slightly as she studied me.

"Death is nature," she said. "There is no escaping it."

She jerked violently and vomited blood all over the glass.

Her gaze tore from mine, and she started to cry again. Pink tears came from one of her eyes.

"Make it stop," she begged, looking at us again. "Kill me. Please."

I saw familiar flecks of sandy-yellow in her irises, and as I watched, her pupil elongated at the bottom. She cried out again, grabbing her head as a bloody tear trailed down her cheek.

"Open the door," Molev ordered.

"We can't risk spreading the infection, Molev," Waurlyn said.

Molev turned to her, showing all the anger he felt.

"Do not allow her to die alone."

She wasn't deaf to the threat in his words.

"Okay," Waurlyn said quickly. "The three of us will wait in the lab and unlock this door for you remotely. However, to protect everyone in the lab, we cannot open these doors again until the infection runs its course."

He didn't answer. Instead, he crouched with Sara as she slowly crumpled.

Waurlyn grabbed my arm and pulled me away from him. He didn't look up as we left or when the doctor closed the door behind us. She went to the panel and tapped a few more buttons. Then she went to a workstation and turned a monitor around so the rest of us could see Molev crouched in front of the woman.

When Sara's door light blinked green, he entered. She flew at him, biting his neck. He wrapped his arms around her like her bite had been a hug and held her as she vomited again. This time on him.

He sat on the bed, cradling her as she shook and twitched and occasionally tried to bite him. His anguish at her suffering was clearly visible to anyone with eyes.

When she finally stilled, he pressed his forehead to hers.

"Forgive me." His broken whisper tore through me, and I didn't know what I could do to help the raw hurt I saw on his face as he sat there with her.

"They don't come back," the doctor said softly. "When each one of the trials fails, the volunteers stay dead."

Molev carefully laid the woman on the bed and left the room. The doctor unlocked the doors so he could leave.

When he emerged with hands fisted and radiating rage, his gaze locked with the doctor.

"No more female volunteers," he said.

"This was the first and only," she said quickly. "We thought we might have better results with a woman since all the previous tests were done on men and failed."

He looked at Waurlyn. "I will be present for each trial, or I will leave."

She nodded. "I understand."

"Will you allow me to clean up that bite?" the doctor asked hesitantly.

He took a steady breath, his gaze finding mine. I could see how badly he wanted to leave.

"Change doesn't happen in seconds," Waurlyn said. "It takes steps. Learning from mistakes. We've made a mistake today, Molev, and we've learned from it. Please believe we're trying."

I could see some of the anger fade from his eyes as he nodded.

It took some time for him to clean up and for the doctor to check over all his previous injuries after she stitched his new bite. Once she cleared him, he turned to me, and I was up in his arms a second later.

"I can walk."

"That will take longer."

He was out of the exam room's door and jogging down the hall a second later. His impatience with the elevator startled a few people when he ran out, but everyone just moved out of his way, and no one made a big deal about it.

Outside, he ran faster. We reached the house before I finished counting the stitches in his neck.

"Hey, strangers," Steve said, opening the door at our approach. He stepped back to let us in, grinning at me in Molev's arms. "How'd everything go?"

Molev didn't stop to answer him. He strode to our room and kicked the door shut behind us.

The second I was on my feet, he started removing my gear. He moved so quickly I didn't understand what he was doing until I stood in my bra and underwear in front of him. He turned me twice then fell to his knees in front of me, wrapping his arms around my waist and pressing his forehead to my sternum.

His shaking finally penetrated my shock. I smoothed my hand over his still-damp hair and held him close.

"I'm okay," I said softly. "I promise."

"You've touched so much infected blood."

Someone knocked on the door.

"Um, everything okay in there?" Roni called. "You have a bunch of worried people out here."

Molev exhaled heavily and rubbed his face against my stomach. It made my heart do some crazy beats until he let go and got to his feet.

"I apologize," he said, handing me my shirt.

I shook my head and slipped on the covering. "There's nothing to be sorry for. What happened upset you. It upset me too. Do you want to talk about it?"

He shook his head slightly. "Not yet."

"Okay. Are you still hungry?"

Weeks of dealing with death and fear had conditioned me. I could watch an infected die and eat a sandwich within five minutes if necessary. However, what had happened to that woman was on a whole other level, and I wasn't sure if I'd be able to eat. But I knew we both needed to.

He took my hand and led me from the room. Roni was waiting outside the door.

"It's been a rough forty-eight hours," I said.

She snorted. "It's been a rough couple of months. We get it. Is everything okay?"

"As okay as it can be," I said. "Is there anything to eat?

In the kitchen, I let Molev tell them whatever he was comfortable sharing. He stuck to describing his exposing gown and the tests as we ate the burgers they'd kept warm for us. The others laughed, and I could see how their humor helped ease some of Molev's strain.

"Sorry I missed it," Roni said. "Bet there was a good breeze in that hospital gown. Now, did they make you run commando, or did you get dressed first? I mean, there had to be some serious swing factor if you were commando. Any thigh bruises?"

"Jesus," Steve said. "I *can't* with you anymore. I'm going outside."

"For a run?" Roni asked with a snigger.

He left without answering. Roni winked at me and hurried to follow him. Katie shook her head and retreated to her room.

"Glad you're okay, Molev," she called over her shoulder.

Roland, Brandon, and Sid went to have a beer on the back patio. I watched them and felt a tightening in my chest. Did we have any chance at all of surviving?

"Don't," Molev said when I looked down and tried to push away what I felt.

"Don't what?" I asked.

"Retreat from them. They care about you, Andie. Allow yourself to care about them in return."

"Why? Caring about them like they're my family is dangerous. If I care too much, there's a good chance I'll break when something happens to one of them."

"Retreating isn't living, Andie. It's waiting to die." He reached over and threaded his fingers into my hair, pulling my head back so he could lean over me.

"And I'm not done with you yet, Andie."

Thank you for reading Demon Defeat: Part 1. Keep reading for details regarding the next book, Demon Blind, *and Angel's long awaited baby!*

AUTHOR'S NOTE

So many things to say!

First, this isn't the end and I'm really sorry. I thought Molev's story would be easy to tell. However, he and Andie haven't cooperated with my efforts to wrap things up quickly. Which is why this book ends the way it does. This is the first part of, hopefully, the two-part finale. Many readers have already assured me that they wouldn't mind if I wrote a dozen more, but I truly don't want to drag it out any longer than necessary. So, the second part will be on its way soon!

Second, please forgive the misuse of military jargon or any unfavorable characteristics I gave those in the military. I created characters to keep the story interesting and the plot moving. And every story needs its antagonists. Unfortunately, due to the nature to what's happening in this fictional world, I couldn't have a botanist, a dairy farmer, or a chef as an antagonist. Someone in a higher position of power was needed. Any negative association conveyed toward those in power is solely for the purpose of this story. I truly thank and honor those who've served in any capacity.

And thirdly, I'm not a scientist. I do my research to the best of my ability and fudge what needs fudging within what I hope is reasonable believability to fit the narrative the story needs. So if I fudged too far on some of the scientific details, please forgive me.

If you're an avid reader of the series, you may have noticed/questioned a few things...

Such as, why are there only ten people in the tank scene in the beginning instead of what Cassie noted in Demon Deception. The answer is simple. Perception. Cassie was in the heat of the moment. Things were happening quickly, and she was focused on one thing: finding her baby. She didn't stop to take time to count. Her estimate was an inflated perception of the obstacle keeping her from her son. It's the same reason witnesses to crimes will always have a different version of what "actually" happened. Perception influences everything. (Note: If you've read both the male and female points of view stories to the Judgement of the Six series under my Melissa Haag pen name, you already know what a big believer I am of the whole "two sides to every story" adage.)

Or maybe you're wondering why Tommy stole the supplies Cassie and her group gathered. The answer was subtly woven into the story. Andie's group was charged with finding a solution to stop the plague. Patrick decided the best way to do so was make contact with the fey to gather information and assess. But not as military. He wanted the group to act like raiders. Tommy ran with that concept by stealing their truck. Poor Tommy...

Or perhaps you're wondering why in the hell I would give the good doctor a hellhound corpse. The answer to that will have to wait until Part 2. ☺

This first part was so fun to write, and I can't wait to share the world-changing conclusion. There's so much story to tell, and I'm truly hoping I can get it done in the 100,000-word maximum I've allotted.

A special thanks to my brother for answering a million military-type "what-if" questions and going with me to a military museum so I could see the vehicles I was writing about. And to my father for answering how to tip a semi-trailer. Turns out a tornado wasn't necessary.

And special thanks to my proofing group (aka The Proof Posse). Without the meticulous attention to detail of these extraordinary women, I wouldn't have the courage to keep publishing these stories. From the bottom of my heart, thank you for all that you do.

For those of you eagerly awaiting news of the feybies (a.k.a. Angel's ninja), you do not want to miss Demon Blind, a novella that takes place during Demon Kept. Also, be sure you check out the Resurrection World Timeline I've included at the beginning of this book if you're curious how all the events in these books are overlapping.

If you want to stay up to date on what I'm writing, please visit my website at mjhaag.melissahaag.com and check out where to follow me socially.

If you love what I write and want all the behind-the-scenes goodies that aren't on my website, be sure to check out my Patreon page at https://www.patreon.com/MelissaHaag.

Until next time, happy reading!

Melissa

THE
RESURRECTION CHRONICLES

Humor, romance, and sexy dark fey!

BOOK 1: DEMON EMBER

In a world going to hell, Mya must learn to accept help from her new-found demon protector in order to find her family as a zombie-like plague spreads.

BOOK 2: DEMON FLAMES

As hellhounds continue to roam and the zombie plague spreads, Drav leads Mya to the source of her troubles—Ernisi, an underground Atlantis and Drav's home. There Mya learns that the shadowy demons, who've helped devastate her world, are not what they seem.

BOOK 3: DEMON ASH

While in Ernisi, cites were been bombed and burned in an attempt to stop the plague. Now, Marauders, hellhounds, and the infected are doing their best to destroy what's left of the world. It's up to Mya and Drav to save it.

BOOK 4: DEMON ESCAPE

While running from zombies, hellhounds, and the people who kept her prisoner, Eden encounters a new creature. He claims he only wants to protect her. Eden must decide who the real devils are between man and demon, and choosing wrong could cost her life.

BOOK 5: DEMON DECEPTION

Grieving from the loss of her husband and youngest child, Cassie lives in fear of losing her remaining daughter. To gain protection, Cassie knows she needs to sleep with one of the dark fey and give him the one thing she isn't sure she can. Her heart.

THE
RESURRECTION
CHRONICLES

The apocalyptic adventure continues!

BOOK 6: DEMON NIGHT

Angel's growing weaker by the day and needs help. In exchange for food, she agrees to give Shax advice regarding how to win over Hannah. If Angel can help make that happen, just maybe she won't be kicked out when her fellow survivors find out she's pregnant.

BOOK 7: DEMON DAWN

In a post-apocalyptic world, Benna is faced with the choice of trading her body and heart to the dark fey in order to survive the infected.

BOOK 8: DEMON DISGRACE

Hannah is drinking away her life to stanch the bleeding pain from past trauma. Merdon, a dark fey with a violent history, relentlessly sets out to show her there's something worth living for.

BOOK 9: DEMON FALL

June never planned to fall in love. She had her eyes on the prize: a career and independence. Too bad the world ended and stole those options from her. Maybe falling in love had been the better choice after all.

THE BEASTLY TALES

Beauty and the Beast with seductively dark twists!

BOOK 1: DEPRAVITY

When impoverished, beautiful Benella is locked inside the dark and magical estate of the beast, she must bargain for her freedom if she wants to see her family again.

BOOK 2: DECEIT

Safely hidden within the estate's enchanted walls, Benella no longer has time to fear her tormentors. She's too preoccupied trying to determine what makes the beast so beastly. In order to gain her freedom, she must find a way to break the curse, but first, she must help him become a better man while protecting her heart.

BOOK 3: DEVASTATION

Abused and rejected, Benella strives to regain a purpose for her life, and finds herself returning to the last place she ever wanted to see. She must learn when it is right to forgive and when it is time to move on.

Be careful what you wish for...

PREQUEL: DISOWNED

In a world where the measure of a person rarely goes beneath the surface, Margaret Thoning refuses to play by its rules. She walks away from everything she's ever known to risk her heart and her life for the people who matter most.

BOOK 1: DEFIANT

When the sudden death of Eloise's mother points to forbidden magic, Eloise's life quickly goes from fairy tale to nightmare. Kaven, the prince's manservant, is Eloise's prime suspect. However, when dark magic is used, nothing is as simple as it seems.

BOOK 2: DISDAIN

Cursed to silence, Eloise is locked in the tattered remains of her once charming life. The smoldering spark of her anger burns for answers and revenge. However, games of magic can have dire consequences.

BOOK 3: DAMNATION

With the reason behind her mother's death revealed, Eloise must prevent her stepsisters from marrying the prince and exact her revenge. However, a secret of the royal court strikes a blow to her plans. Betrayed, Eloise will question how far she's willing to go for revenge.